W9-CBF-708

Middleton Public Library
7425 Hubbard Ave
Middleton, WI 53562

The

LEHMAN
TRILOGY

The

LEHMAN TRILOGY

A NOVEL

STEFANO MASSINI

Translated from the Italian by Richard Dixon

HarperVia

An Imprint of HarperCollinsPublishers

The Lehman Trilogy is a work of fiction. While many of the characters portrayed here have some counterparts in the life and times of Lehman Brothers, the characterizations and incidents presented are the products of the author's imagination. Accordingly, *The Lehman Trilogy* should be read solely as a work of fiction.

THE LEHMAN TRILOGY. Copyright © 2020 by Stefano Massini. All rights reserved. Printed in the United States of America. No part of this book may be used or reproduced in any manner whatsoever without written permission except in the case of brief quotations embodied in critical articles and reviews. For information, address HarperCollins Publishers, 195 Broadway, New York, NY 10007.

HarperCollins books may be purchased for educational, business, or sales promotional use. For information, please email the Special Markets Department at SPsales@harpercollins.com.

Originally published as *Qualcosa sui Lehman* in Italy in 2016 by Mondadori.

FIRST EDITION

Designed by Terry McGrath

Library of Congress Cataloging-in-Publication Data is available upon request.

ISBN 978-0-06-294044-5
ISBN 978-0-06-304891-1 (ANZ)

20 21 22 23 24 LSC 10 9 8 7 6 5 4 3 2 1

in memory of Luca Ronconi

CONTENTS

Book Three—Immortal

"We walk along the sheer ridge
where History becomes Legend
and News dwindles into Myth.
We don't look for truth in fairy tales,
nor do we look for it in dreams.
And while all human beings can one day say
they were born, they lived, they died,
not all can say they've become a metaphor.
Transformation is everything."

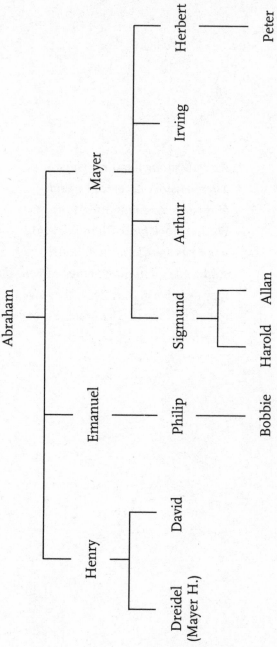

Family Tree

Book One

Three Brothers

1
Luftmensch

Son of a cattle dealer
circumcised Jew
with just one suitcase at his side
standing stock-still
like a telegraph pole
on jetty number four at New York harbor
Thank God for having arrived:
Baruch HaShem!
Thank God for having left:
Baruch HaShem!
Thank God for being here, now, at last,
in America:
Baruch HaShem!
Baruch HaShem!
Baruch HaShem!

Children shouting
porters weighed down with baggage
screeching of iron and squeaking pulleys
in the midst of it all
he
standing still
straight off the boat
wearing his best shoes
never yet worn
kept in store for the moment *"when I reach America."*

And now this is it.
The moment *"when I reach America"*
is writ large on a cast-iron clock
high up there
on the tower of New York harbor:
seven twenty-five in the morning.

He takes a pencil from his pocket
and on the edge of a scrap of paper
notes down the seven and the twenty-five
just long enough to see

his hand is shaking
maybe the excitement
or maybe the fact that
after a month and a half at sea
standing on dry land
—*"hah! Stop swaying!"*—
feels strange.

Eight kilos lost
in the month and a half at sea.
A thick beard
thicker than the rabbi's
grown, untrimmed
in forty-five days of up and down
between hammock berth deck
deck berth hammock.
He left Le Havre a teetotaler
landed at New York a skilled drinker
practiced in recognizing at the first taste
brandy from rum
gin from cognac
Italian wine and Irish beer.
He left Le Havre knowing nothing about cards
landed at New York champion of gaming and dice.
He left shy, reserved, pensive
landed convinced he knew the world:
French irony
Spanish joy
the nervous pride of Italian cabin boys.
He left with America fixed in his head
landed now with America in front of him
but not just in his thoughts: before his eyes.
Baruch HaShem!

Seen from close up
on this cold September morning
seen standing stock-still
like a telegraph pole
on jetty number four at New York harbor
America seemed more like a music box:
for each window that opened
there was one that closed;
for each handcart that turned a corner

there was one that appeared at the next;
for each customer that got up from a table
there was one that sat down
"even before it was all prepared," he thought
and for a moment
—inside that head that had been waiting for months to see it—
America
the real America
was no more nor less than a flea circus
not at all impressive
indeed, if anything, comic.
Amusing.

It was then
that someone tugged his arm.
A port official
dark uniform
gray whiskers, large hat.
He was writing in a register
names and numbers of those getting off
asking simple questions in basic English:
"Where do you come from?"
"Rimpar."
"Rimpar? Where is Rimpar?"
"Bayern, Germany."
"And your name?"
"Heyum Lehmann."
"I don't understand. Name?"
"Heyum . . ."
"What is Heyum?"
"My name is . . . Hey . . . Henry!"
"Henry, okay! And your surname?"
"Lehmann . . ."
"Lehman! Henry Lehman!"
"Henry Lehman."
"Okay, Henry Lehman:
welcome to America.
And good luck!"
And he stamped the date:
September 11, 1844
gave him a pat on the shoulder
and went off to stop someone else.

Henry Lehman looked about him:
the ship on which he had landed
looked like a sleeping giant.
But another ship was maneuvering into port
ready to berth at jetty number four
dozens more like him:
maybe Jews
maybe Germans
maybe wearing their best shoes
and just one suitcase at their side
they too surprised that they are shaking
partly with excitement
partly because of the dry land
partly because America
—the real America—
seen from up close
like a gigantic music box
has a certain effect.

He took a deep breath
gripped his suitcase
and with a firm step
—though still not knowing where to go—
he entered
he too
the music box
called America.

2
Gefilte fish

Rabbi Kassowitz
—so Henry had been told—
is not the best acquaintance
you might hope to make
after a forty-five-day crossing,
having just set foot
on the other side of the Atlantic.

Partly because he has
a decidedly irritating sneer
fixed on his face
glued to his lips
as if from a deep-down contempt
for anyone who came to speak to him.
And then there are his eyes:
how can you avoid feeling uneasy
when faced with a stubborn old man
swamped in his dark suit
whose only sign of life comes from that pair of squinting,
anarchic, crazed eyes
that are always glancing elsewhere
unpredictably
bouncing like billiard balls unpredictably
and, though never stopping to look at you,
they never miss a detail?

"Prepare yourself: go to Rab Kassowitz
it's always an experience.
You'll be sorry you've been,
but you cannot avoid it,
so summon your courage and knock on that door."
That's what Henry Lehman has been told
by German Jewish friends
who've been here in New York for a while,
for such a while that they know the streets
and talk an odd kind of language
where Yiddish is dressed up with English,
they say *frau darling* to girls
and the children ask for *der ice-cream.*

Henry Lehman
son of a cattle dealer
has not yet been three days in America
but pretends to understand everything
and even makes himself say *yes*
when German Jewish friends
grin and ask if he can smell
the stench of New York on his clothing:
"Remember, Henry: at first we all smell it.
Then one day you stop,
you no longer notice it,

and then you can really say
you've arrived in America,
and that you're really here."
Yes.
Henry nods.
Yes.
Henry smiles.
Yes, yes.
Henry, in fact, can smell the stench of New York
all over him:
a nauseating mix of fodder, smoke, and every kind of mold,
such that, to the nostrils at least,
this New York so much dreamed about
seems worse than his father's cattle shed,
over there in Germany, in Rimpar, Bavaria.
Yes.

But in his letter home
—the first from American soil—
Henry hasn't mentioned the stench.
He has written about German Jewish friends
of course
and how they had kindly given him a bed
for several days
offering him a splendid fish-ball soup
made with leftovers from their fish stall,
seeing that they too are in the trade
yes sir
but animals with fins, bones, and scales.
"And are you earning well?"
asked Henry, not mincing words,
just like that, to get some idea
to begin to understand
seeing that he's come to America for the money
and will have to start somewhere.
His German Jewish friends
laughed at him
since nobody in New York
goes without earning something
—not even beggars:
"With food there's always money to be made,
people are always hungry, Henry."

"And so? What makes good money?"
he asked them
amid the crates of cod and barrels of herrings,
where the stench of New York
is pretty difficult to beat.
"But what questions you ask.
Money is made from what you cannot avoid buying."

They're clever folk, his German friends:
money is made from what you cannot avoid buying . . .
that's pretty good advice after all.
For it's true that if you don't eat, you die.
But honestly, can a Lehman
who has left his father's cattle sheds
come all the way to America
to trade here, too, in animals,
whether fish, chickens, ducks, or cattle?
Change, Henry, change.
But choosing something that *you cannot avoid buying.*
This is the point.

There.
And while Henry is thinking what to do
his German friends give him a bed to sleep on
and fish-balls in broth for supper,
always fish
to make the greatest saving.

But Henry doesn't want to abuse their hospitality.
Just enough time to work things out.
Just enough time to get his legs back
his legs are sluggish
incredibly sluggish
for having been so long at sea
hammock berth deck
deck berth hammock
it's not so simple
to order your lower limbs
—the locomotive division—
to get back on the trot,
all the more if this music box called America
has ten thousand streets,

not like Rimpar where the only streets are those,
and you count them on the fingers of one hand.

That's right. Legs.
But the point is not just this.
If only.
To live in America, to live properly,
you need something else.
You need to turn a key in a lock,
you need to push open a door.
And all three—key, lock, and door—
are found not in New York
but inside your brain.

That's why—they told him amid the cod and the herrings—
whoever comes ashore
sometime or other
sooner or later
needs Rab Kassowitz:
he knows.
And we're not talking about Scriptures, or Prophets,
which for a rabbi is normal:
Rab Kassowitz
is famous for being an oracle
for those who have sailed *from there to here,*
for those who come from Europe
for transoceanic Jews
for the sons of cattle dealers
or, well
in other words
for immigrants.
"You see, Henry: anyone coming to America
is looking for something not even he knows.
We've all been there.
That old rabbi, for all his squinting eyes,
manages to look where you cannot see,
and to tell you where you'll be in this other life.
Take my word: go and find him."

And once again Henry said *yes.*
He arrived at eight in the morning,
clutching in his right hand a respectable example of a fish
a gift for the old man,

but having thought long about it
he concluded that to arrive holding a large fish
didn't give a particularly decent impression,
so he slipped the creature into a hedge
for the shameless joy of the New York cats
and after a deep breath he knocked on the door.
Yes.

It was a November day,
with an icy chill, like over there in Bavaria,
and a vague hint of snow.
As he waited, Henry brushed the first flakes from his hat.
He was wearing his best shoes,
those he had kept aside for the moment *when I reach America*:
he thought it was maybe a good idea to wear them again
for this strange visit
in which—he felt—
he'd really see America face-to-face,
for all it was, immense and boundless,
and would hold it in the palm of his hand.
He sincerely hoped so.
For until now he felt he was in a mist.

He was so wrapped in these thoughts
that he didn't hear the click of the door handle,
nor the voice coming almost from another world
that told him the door was already open.
The wait, in short,
lasted some while,
enough to irritate the old man,
causing him eventually to shout from inside
an eloquent *"I am waiting."*

And Henry went in.

Rab Kassowitz
was sitting at the far end of the room,
a dark figure on a dark wooden chair
all at one with its many angles,
as if he were almost a geographic sum of cheekbones, knees, elbows
and parched wrinkles.

The son of a cattle dealer
asked and did not obtain
express permission to step forward.
When he asked
—and with great deference—
he was simply told: *"Stop there: I want to look at you"*
followed by a whirl of eyes.

Yet Henry Lehman didn't flinch.
He stood stock-still like a telegraph pole
remained ten steps away,
holding his hat,
in an eternal silence
contemplating
how in that book-filled room
the stench of New York seemed concentrated
overpowering
and for a moment
inhaling fodder, smoke, and every kind of mold
he thought he might even faint.

Fortunately he didn't have time.
For stronger than the smell
was finding himself
suddenly
the subject of a cruel laugh,
which coming at the end of long observation
seemed most offensive
and more than that: an insult.
"You find me amusing, Rab?"

"I laugh because I see a little fish."

Henry Lehman
couldn't work out there and then
whether the phrase was a rabbinical metaphor
or whether the old man
really was insulting him
due to the aroma of sardines and bream that he was spreading in
    the air.
And he would certainly have opted for the second explanation
if the rabbi hadn't
fortunately

added to his opening words:
"I laugh because I see a little fish
that flaps its tail out of water:
it has flipped itself out
and claims it wants a taste of America."

And so
not without some relief
Henry could proudly reply:
"That little fish, I would say, has no lack of courage."

"Or has no lack of craziness."

"Should I go back home?"

"It depends what you mean by home."

"A fish lives in the sea."

"No. You're tiresome, how foolish you are: I could turn you out."

"I don't understand."

"You don't understand because you're thinking too much,
and by thinking you lose your way
you're foolish because you're sharp,
and sharpness is a curse.
You're behaving like someone who hasn't had food for three days,
but before eating
he asks what dishes, what spices, what sauces,
whether the tablecloths, cutlery, glasses are right
—in short
before having decided on everything
they find him lying dead with hunger."

"Help me."

"Quite simply: a fish lives in water,
and water is not just to be found in the sea."

"And so?"

"And so, out of water you die,
in water you live. And that's the end of it."

"And so, I'm not cut out for America?"

"It depends what you mean by America."

"America is dry land."

"And that's a fact."

"You say I'm a fish."

"And that's a second fact."

"The fish is not made for land, but for water."

"Third and last fact."

"And what do you expect me to do?"

"It's a good question,
so good that I offer it to you:
ask yourself."

"A fish doesn't ask questions, rabbi:
a fish knows only how to swim."

"And now we're beginning to think:
a fish knows only how to swim,
it cannot pretend it can walk.
Our fish might then be crazy
not for wanting a taste of America,
but for wanting to do it out of water! Baruch HaShem!
If the fish—which has reached New York from the immense sea—
then makes its way from that sea into a river,
and from the river into a canal,
and from the river into a lake,
and from the lake into a pond,
then I ask you:
wouldn't that fish in fact manage
to get around the length and breadth of America?
Nothing's stopping him: water flows everywhere.

The fish only has to remember he lives in water,
and if he leaves it, simply, he dies."

"Yes, Rab Kassowitz, but my water, what exactly would it be?"

"Didn't you say a fish doesn't ask questions?
Enough. You've exhausted all the attention you deserve.
Now leave me in peace:
I have little time left before I die
and you have taken a part of it free of charge."

"With respect, indeed: I'd like to leave you a few dollars,
for your Temple . . ."

"Fish don't have wallets,
with money they'd sink to the bottom. Out!"

"One last question, Rabbi, I beg you:
America is vast,
where do you suggest I go?"

"Where you can swim."
And with these words
Henry Lehman
found himself back on the street
confused and more pensive than before
with the only certainty that rabbis never speak clearly
learning from their Superior One
who instead of explaining himself
sets bushes on fire, *and it's for you to understand.*

Meanwhile
an exceptional storm had gathered over New York.
But in all honesty, could a Lehman
who had left the pines of Bavaria,
come all this way to America
to end up shoveling snow?
Change, Henry, change.

So this at least was clear:
wherever he went
—and he didn't know exactly where—
there would certainly have to be

plenty of warmth
plenty of light
plenty of sun.

And with this idea turning in his head,
cursing the American winter,
he buttoned his jacket to the neck:
after all, a man needs to keep himself covered,
just as much as he needs food.
Yes.

3
Chametz

The room is small.
A wooden floor.
Boards nailed one beside the other:
in all—he has counted them—sixty-four.
and they creak when walked over:
you feel it's empty below.

A single door
of glass and wood
with the *mezuzah* hanging at the side
as the *Shema* requires.
A single door
opening—directly—to the street
to the neighing of horses
and to the dust of the carts
to the creaking carriages
and to the city crowd.

The handle
of red brass
turns badly, sometimes sticks
and has to be lifted, by force, with a tug:
at that point, somehow, it opens.

A skylight in the ceiling
as large as the whole space
so that when it rains hard
the raindrops beat against it
and always seems as if it's about to crash down
but at least, throughout the day, there's light
even in winter
and it saves using the oil lamp
which doesn't burn forever
like *ner tamid* at the Temple.
And costs money.

The storeroom is behind the counter.
In the middle of the shelves there's a curtain
and there, behind it, is the storeroom
smaller than the shop
a back room
crammed with parcels and crates
boxes
rolls
remnants
broken buttons and threads:
nothing is thrown away
everything is sold; sooner or later, it's sold.

The shop, sure, you'd have to say, okay, it's small.
And seems even smaller
split as it is in half
by the heavy wooden counter
propped like a catafalque
or the *dukhan* in a synagogue
stretched lengthwise
between those four walls
all of them
covered
to the top
with shelves.

A stool to climb to halfway up the wall.
A ladder to reach higher—if need be—
where the hats are
caps
gloves

corsets
aprons
pinafores
and up at the top, the ties.
For here in Alabama no one ever buys
ties.
Whites only for the Feast of the Congregation.
Blacks on the day before Christmas.
Jews—those few that there are—
for the *Hanukkah* dinner.
And that's it: the ties stay at the top.

On the right, low down and below the counter
rolled fabrics
raw fabrics
wrapped fabrics
folded fabrics
textiles
cloths
swatches
wool
jute
hemp
cotton.
Cotton.
Especially cotton
here
in this sunny street in Montgomery, Alabama,
where everything—as we know—
relies
on cotton.
Cotton
cotton
of every kind and quality:
seersucker
chintz
flag cloth
beaverteen
doeskin that looks like deer
and finally
the so-called *denim*
that robust fustian
work cloth

—*"doesn't tear!"*—
which has arrived here in America from Italy
—*"doesn't tear!"*—
blue with white warp
used by the sailors of Genoa to wrap the sails
what they call *blu di Genova*
in French *bleu de Gênes*
which in English gets mangled into *blue-jeans*:
try it and see:
it doesn't tear.
Baruch HaShem! for the cotton *blue-jeans* of the Italians.

To the left of the room
not fabrics but clothes:
stacked in order on the shelves
jackets
shirts
skirts
trousers
work coats
and a couple of overcoats
though here in the South it's not like Bavaria
and the cold rarely comes knocking.
Colors all the same
gray
brown
and white
for here, in Montgomery, only poor folk are served:
in their wardrobes, one good set of clothes, just one
for the Sunday service
and on every other day, all to work
head down
no slacking
for people in Alabama don't work to live
if anything, surely, they live to work.

And he
Henry Lehman
twenty-six years old
German, from Rimpar, Bavaria,
knows that deep down
Montgomery is not so different:
here too there's the river, the Alabama River

like the River Main there.
And here too there's the great dusty white road
except that it doesn't go to Nuremberg or Munich
but to Mobile or to Tuscaloosa.

Henry Lehman
son of a cattle dealer
makes money to live
working like a mule
behind the counter.
Work, work, work.
Closing only for *Shabbat*
but staying open, for sure, on Sunday morning
when the blacks on the plantations
all go to church for two hours
and fill the streets of Montgomery:
old folk, children, and . . . women
women who—on their way to church—remember
their torn dress
the tablecloth to stitch
the master's curtains to embroider
and since Sunday is not *Shabbat*:
"Please, come in, Lehman's open on Sunday!"

Lehman.
It may be small.
But at least the shop is his.
Small, minimal, minuscule, but his own.
H. LEHMAN is written large on the glass door.
And one day there'll also be a fine sign, above the door
as big as the whole frontage:
H. LEHMAN FABRICS AND CLOTHING
Baruch HaShem!

Opened with mortgages, guarantees, bills of exchange
and tying up all the money he had:
everything.
Not even half a cent left over.
Everything.
And now, for who knows how long
work, work, work:
for folk buy fabric by the yard
stinting over every inch

and to make a hundred dollars takes three days.
Calculations to hand
which Henry Lehman does and redoes every day.
Calculations to hand:
at least three years to recover expenses
pay the debts
give back to those he owes.
Then, once everyone is paid
then yes
calculations to hand . . .
but here Henry Lehman stops:
meanwhile to work
as the Talmud says:
throw in *chametz*, the yeast
and then?
Then he will see.
Throw in *chametz*, the yeast
and then?
Then he will see.
Throw in *chametz*, the yeast
and then?
Then, he will see.

4
Schmuck!

To hold down the paperwork of his accounts
when the wind blows at Montgomery
Henry Lehman
son of a cattle dealer
has an inlaid stone and iron paperweight,
carved and painted
in the form of a globe.

It sits on the shop counter,
on a pile of expenses and receipts,
even if its purpose

its real purpose
—and Henry knows, he knows for sure—
is not to stop them blowing away:
the miniature globe
sits there
to remind him always
that it is night in Alabama when it is day at home.
At home, yes.
The real one.
For even though he's been here some time
still
"home is not where I am, home is where they are."
Globe in hand.
Staring at it.
"Me here." Turn the globe. *"Here them."*
"Night here." Turn the globe. *"Here day."*
Alabama, turn the globe: Bavaria.
Montgomery, turn the globe: Rimpar.
Incredibly far away.

All the more since
there's only one way of communicating
between a night and a day:
by letter.

One letter every three days.
My esteemed father.
Dear brothers.
One letter every three days
makes 120 letters in a year.

Unbelievably expensive.

Postage
not surprisingly
is part of the shop budget
receipts and expenses
but on this expenditure there is no stinting.
In the accounts book
in fact
this is the first heading,
it comes before all the others,
and is not called MAIL

but HOME,
quite separate from the ACCOMMODATION heading
which would then be where Henry sleeps.

Savings can be made on food.
On that, yes.
And Henry eats just bean soup.
But correspondence . . .
Savings can be made on clothing.
On that, for sure.
And Henry has a total of three shirts
two pairs of trousers
and a work coat.
But correspondence . . .
Savings can be made on the barber, which is a luxury: a razor is
    enough.
And, after all, isn't a horse also a luxury?
It is perfectly fine to walk.
Correspondence, however . . .
That is sacrosanct.
My dear mother.
Beloved sister.
And so forth.

It costs what it costs.

700 dollars a year.
A considerable expense.
But inevitable.

The problem is that communication
between Henry and the Bavarians
apart from being expensive
is not so simple.

For one thing because
each time
Henry has to remember
—to be careful, most careful—
that he is Henry only in Alabama,
while over there he is still Heyum,
and woe if he signed himself with the wrong name.

They wouldn't understand.
I must sign myself Heyum.
I must sign myself Heyum.

All the more because
over there in Rimpar
it is his father who commands,
and it is he
—him alone—
Abraham Lehmann
—with two n's—
cattle dealer,
and only he who is permitted to receive
and who is permitted to reply:
it is he who opens the envelopes
it is he who reads
it is he who writes.

And this is the second point:
what does he write?
Or rather: how much does he write?

If Henry sends long letters,
his father confines himself to notes.

Nothing strange.
Old Abraham Lehmann
has always been a man of few words.
He used to say
"if there were something to be said,
then goats and hounds would learn to speak"
and since he felt a mutual bond
with the animals he used to sell
he avoided making sounds
not strictly necessary.
He had always done so.

Now the old man makes no exception.

"DEAR SON,
WHERE THERE ARE TWO JEWS
THERE IS ALREADY A TEMPLE.
YOUR DEVOTED FATHER."

This is the rich content
of the last message
postmarked Rimpar,
that arrived in a sealed envelope
addressed to Herr Heyum Lehmann.
With two n's.

Henry had to expect it.
*"Where there are two Jews
there is already a Temple"*
was one of his father's
favorite sayings
after which he would often add
beneath his breath
"Schmuck!"
which means idiot.

For the cattle merchant
didn't like it
not at all
when certain Jews from out of town
drove more than an hour by cart
down to the valley
to sit stinking
next to him
"in our Temple."
Not at all.
Why were these farmers coming?
Why at all?
If there are two Jews
there's no need for a Temple.
Idiots.
Let them stay in the countryside. Idiots.
"Schmuck!"

Maybe
Abraham Lehmann
—stubbornly with two n's—
had only ever spoken in proclamations.
*"Where there are two Jews
there is already a Temple"*

was just one of a thousand.
He coined them in dozens.
A constant flow.
Surprising.
There was never a phrase
on his lips
that didn't sound like a verdict.
Implacable.
And what is worse,
is that Abraham Lehmann
cattle merchant
was madly attached to his pronouncements,
finding them a remarkable concentration of wisdom,
the only answer to the decay of creation,
and so
in purely altruistic spirit
he dispensed them to the world
expecting an instant acknowledgment.
If this were then absent,
there came an inevitable *"Schmuck!"*
dealt scathingly
through grinding gnashing teeth
like a cattle brand,
like the L of Lehmann
stamped with fire on sheep cows and bulls:
indelible and perennial.
"Schmuck!"

There.
What distinguished his beloved children
from the rest of Bavaria's human fauna
was not having deserved
ever
a single *"Schmuck!,"*
evidence of total excellence
of a most perfect lineage.

He ought to have known it, Henry.
He ought to have thought, therefore,
before running the risk
—a serious risk—
of being taken for an idiot
on the other side of the ocean.
And yet . . .

And yet he had dared
enthusiastically
to put the idea there, in a letter:
"WE ARE AT LEAST TEN FAMILIES,
DEAR FATHER,
HERE, IN ALABAMA, TO CELEBRATE PESACH:
APART FROM ME
DEAR FATHER,
THERE ARE THE SACHS, THE GOLDMANS,
    AND MANY OTHERS:
SOONER OR LATER
PERHAPS WE WILL BUILD A TEMPLE
AND WE WILL DO IT
DEAR FATHER,
IN GERMAN STYLE!"

No sir. No.
Absolutely not.
The cattle merchant
did not like it.

For one thing
because Alabama was not America,
only New York was America:
that was where his son had to go,
he had promised him.
Why had he headed South?
And then, what need was there for a Temple
even in German style
down there in that remote land
where his son will remain for only a few years,
long enough to make himself rich
and to then return?

To then return.
That was the pact.
To then return.

You don't go to America to stay,
you put only one foot in America,
and the other stays at home.
All the more if you promise to go to New York
and end up in Alabama.

So?
So what's this about a Temple?
So what purpose does it have?
Why build a Temple
and then leave it, for the Americans?

Struggling to catch his breath,
overcome by his own thoughts,
Abraham Lehmann
at this point
muttered a distinct *"Schmuck!"*

Through the whole of his life
this was the first time
he had directed it at a son.

5
Shammash

All the more since
his son Heyum
couldn't remain too long
in Alabama:
he still had a commitment.
And some commitment.

An engagement.

With Bertha Singer.
A girl of pallid complexion.
And not just her complexion: her voice as well.
And not just her voice: her manner too.
It could be said that Bertha Singer
was the female essence of pallor.
And of thinness.
And of timidity.
A young girl of ninety,

daughter of Mordechai and Mosella Singer,
both seemingly younger than her,
endowed with that minimum of life
that distinguishes a dying person from a corpse,
and of which the daughter was
severely
lacking.

Nonetheless
Heyum Lehmann
had chosen her,
asking her
respectfully
to allow him
to call her henceforth *süsser*,
meaning "sweetness."

A wise decision,
since the Singers were a most prominent family,
an aspect, this,
which much pleased
the cattle merchant
with two n's
who had blessed the union
with one of the more successful
of his pronouncements:
"Love cannot be seen,
but even a blind man
sniffs the scent of money."

So that
Heyum Lehmann
before leaving
had asked *süsser* for her hand.
Obtaining it.

It is even said
that *süsser* had shown a hint of a smile,
a memorable event
which her own mother strongly doubted.

So before Heyum became Henry
he had taken the step,

and the *kiddushin*
would be held on his return.
In a couple of years.
Maybe three.
Maybe four. Four at most.*
Enough time to make money.
To make money in America.
In New York.

But meanwhile
in the meantime
in Alabama
on the other side of the globe
no letter
was ever sent to the Singer house:
just as two people
engaged to be married
could not remain alone
out of their parents' sight,
so the son of the cattle dealer
out of respect
out of courtesy
out of decency
never wrote directly to the girl,
but sent his
most affectionate greetings
through his father,
who promptly passed them on.

Now
there's no doubt
that over time
Abraham Lehmann
the man himself
became aware
of a certain deterioration in this engagement,
dependent as it was
purely and simply
on the *most affectionate greetings*
conveyed in person
by an old man of very few words
to a young girl more dead than alive.

Well, time passed.
The months. The seasons.
And so?
Since the time for his return was imminent
and with it the *chuppah*,
why was his son Heyum
now thinking
down in Alabama
of building a Temple?
Why was there no mention
of returning?
Did it not occur to him
that Bertha Singer
—his *süsser*—
in the long wait
might be sad
and then fading toward death,
more than she was
already by nature
grievously
saddened faded and dead?

It was almost normal
now
at all hours
passing along the street
in front of the Singer house
to see the town's doctor
entering and leaving
baby-faced
curly-haired Doctor Schausser,
disconsolate, shaking his head,
and yet
what treatment can be devised
for a spouse
condemned
—still alone, and for how much longer?—
to wait.
"Bertha's candle
was already burning dimly,
but now it is almost out"
Mordechai Singer told
the elders of the Temple.

And since then
the whole of Rimpar is asking
why
Heyum Lehmann
son of the cattle dealer
has not decided
once and for all
to return.

It is a question that
Abraham Lehmann
also asks himself
and though a man of very few words
he knows when it is time to speak
which is why
he decides to send
across the ocean
on his own initiative
another note,
in a sealed envelope
addressed to *Herr Heyum Lehmann.*
With two n's.
"THE WORD OF A MAN,
DEAR SON, IS CARVED IN STONE;
THE WORD OF A FOOL
IS WRITTEN ON CLOTH.
AWAITING YOU,
YOUR ESTEEMED FATHER."

And nothing
about that note
passed unobserved.

Henry recognized
perfectly
the contempt with which he had written the word *cloth*,
and for a moment
like a true merchant
he felt a shudder
in defense of his cotton.
But most clear of all

was the meaning of that final AWAITING YOU,
which sounded like an order to his cattle
to return to their shed
or be whipped.
With no alternative.

He acted instinctively
and surprising
first of all himself
he crumpled up the note.

That night
if Henry had been in Rimpar
he would have known
that old Abraham
in his distress
hardly slept a wink,
and when he did
he dreamed of a great Temple
packed full of stinking farmers
who came from out of town
but spoke English,
and among them was his son,
as a *shammash*:
he laughed sadistically
looking up at the women's gallery
where a young girl was crying in a coffin
calling out his name: *"Heyum! Heyum!"*
but he was laughing loudly
without a care
and when he went up to open the Scripture rolls,
the Torah appeared like a single banner
of pure white cotton
on which was written
a gigantic
AUF WIEDERSEHEN.

6
Süsser

Word has spread
even beyond the river:
Henry Lehman's merchandise is *first choice*.
Baruch HaShem!

Doctor Everson
said so this morning:
he treats the slave children with measles,
and while he treats them
he hears what the people say
in the plantation huts.

Henry Lehman's merchandise is *first choice*.
That's what people say.
Baruch HaShem!
Henry Lehman's cotton is the best.
Best on the market.
This is what they say.
Baruch HaShem!
Even in the owners' drawing rooms
Doctor Everson has heard what they say
about the curtain fabrics
and tablecloths
and sheets.

And Henry has toasted his success.
Alone, behind the counter,
with a bottle of liquor
he had bought on arrival
three years ago,
kept in store
to celebrate
sooner or later.
Baruch HaShem!

There again
the account book
is clear enough:

the shop has made
almost a quarter more than last year,
and it is still only May.
Below the sign H. LEHMAN
the red brass door handle
sticks
each time customers turn it to come in,
and with simple business sense
the owner
doesn't intend to fix it:
it will bring luck,
leaving it as it is
will bring him luck,
as much luck as it has brought so far.
And more.

So that
nothing strange
if even now
for the umpteenth time
under the sign H. LEHMAN,
the red brass handle
sticks once again
under the timid hand
of an unfamiliar customer:
Henry at the counter carries on cutting the cloth,
doesn't even look up:
"You have to lift it, young lady:
give it a push as you turn,
and at that point, somehow, it opens . . ."

There.
It was at that moment
through who-knows-what mysteries of womankind
that the timid hand became impatient
and yanked the handle
with such unimaginable force
that
the door didn't just open
but came off its hinges
and crashed to the floor,
with shards of flying glass

that cut the cheek
of the unfamiliar customer.

And Henry Lehman
son of a cattle dealer?

Standing still
behind the counter,
he watches her bleed
not lifting a finger
not even when she asks him please
in resentful tone
for a handkerchief.

"Young lady, exactly which handkerchiefs do you wish to buy?
I have them at two dollars, two fifty, and four."

"I don't wish to buy them,
I want to wipe the blood from my face,
don't you realize I've cut myself?"

"Don't you realize you've broken my shop door?"

"The door of your shop had stuck."

"It had only to be lifted, gently:
if you had listened . . ."

"Look, for the last time:
would you be so kind as to give me a handkerchief?"

"And would you be so kind as to apologize
for the damage you have done?"

"But excuse me, which is more important: your door or my cheek?"

"The door is mine, the cheek is yours."

To this remark
the unfamiliar customer made no reply:
she could not,
finding herself before a true masterpiece
a rare masterpiece

of reasoning.
She admired him,
and the sense of admiration
as sometimes happens
was greater than the sense of suffering.

"The door is mine, the cheek is yours"
was indeed an extraordinary example
of how Henry Lehman interpreted reality.
"You're a Head"
his father
the cattle dealer
had said one day
down in Rimpar, yes sir, in Bavaria.

Henry Lehman: a Head.
Pure truth.
Rab Kassowitz was right when he said it, that day:
Henry after fasting
would rather die of hunger
than eat whatever there happened to be.
And it has to be said
Henry was proud
of this way of his,
considering himself endowed
with a deadly weapon
—his head—
before which everyone yielded.
Until that day.

For it just so happens
that the unfamiliar customer was not so pliant.

Hearing him say
"The door is mine, the cheek is yours"
had instantly cooled
though not defeated her.

And here
through who-knows-what mysteries of womankind
the bleeding creature came forward
to the counter
and in a flash

took hold of Henry's tie,
wiped it across her face
soaking it well
then staring at Mr. Head
spoke a few words
but words of *first choice*:
"The cheek is mine, the tie is yours"
and not waiting for a response
she left
trampling the glass with her heels.

There is always something tremendous
about the meeting between two Heads.

Had she not backed down to him?
He couldn't back down to her:
he pursued her,
demanded payment for the damage,
she refused,
he threatened her,
she carried on regardless,
he took hold of her,
she shook him off,
and with all this tussling
on the public street
under the southern sun
they began shouting at each other
to the amusement of the children
for quite some distance along the street
from Lehman's shop
to the gate of the Wolf house,
where she turned to him:
"If you don't mind, I have arrived,
thank you so much for your company,
thank you for your kindness, for your discourse,
for your compliments, and for the handkerchiefs: you are a gentleman."

At this provocation
Henry Lehman
there and then
made no reply:
he could not,
finding himself before a true masterpiece

a rare masterpiece
of rationality.
He admired her with all his being,
and the sense of admiration
as often happens
was greater than the sense of suffering.

Yet it lasted an instant,
for he felt
the strongest urge
to insult her,
and he did so pitilessly:
"Are you the housemaid to the Wolfs?"

"Only if you are the shop assistant to the Lehmans."

"For your information, I am Henry Lehman:
that shop has been mine for three years."

"For your information, I am Rosa Wolf,
and this house has been mine for three days.
So, if you don't mind,
don't make enemies of your customers."

This, a phrase of sure effect,
ably delivered by Miss Wolf
with that withering look
which on a woman's face
cuts down artless victims.

Moreover
she spoke these words just as she was closing the gate,
like a stage curtain,
much disappointing the curious passersby.

There is always something divine
about the meeting of two Heads.

And financially advantageous.

For from that moment
indeed
without realizing it

Henry Lehman
wrote home less frequently
reducing
considerably
the postage costs.
From one letter every three days
he moved to one every seven,
then every ten,
settling in the end on an average of two a month.

And only after seven months
was it suddenly clear to him
that Rosa Wolf
destroyer of glass doors
might detain him in Alabama
for well over three years.
Maybe five.
Maybe ten.
Maybe forever.

What a shame that nothing is more inconvenient
for a Head
than the thankless prospect of falling in love,
for it is well known
that
of all that goes on in the world
love
is the least cerebral.

Henry Lehman tried a way of his own,
that led him to love, yes,
but rationally.
And so:
no flowers,
no pretty umbrellas,
no fond looks,
no gentlemanly courtesy,
but instead
just
just simply
discounts on goods displayed
which for Mr. Lehman,
being much more than merchandise,
his justification for life, his pride and means of survival

were like offering
—to his way of thinking—
no more nor less than life itself.

Financial resources
therefore taken
from postal traffic
were reinvested
prudently
in a broad opening of credit
and generous commercial offers
"... WHICH I HAVE DEVISED JUST FOR YOU, MISS ROSA WOLF,
A FOND CUSTOMER OF MY BUSINESS."

To Henry Lehman
this note
could and should have been read
as a clear expression of courtship.

It was not.

On the contrary.

Miss Rosa Wolf went 'round
telling everyone
not just in Montgomery
but as far away as Tuscaloosa
that Lehman's shop
yes sir
was knocking down prices
yes sir
so that half of Alabama felt aggrieved
at not receiving the same treatment.

To calm the wave of protest,
he had fixed to the shop door
a large notice

REDUCED PRICES FOR FAVORED CUSTOMERS

and throughout the states of the South
it was perhaps the first time
that a shop devised such an enticement.

Did Henry Lehman think he would make a loss?
He came out with a profit, making double,
and so he congratulated himself
and thereafter
told himself and others
that he had indeed done it intentionally.

But more importantly
by reducing prices on a wide scale
he had to devise for Miss Wolf
a treatment different from the mass,
so that
where discounts were not enough
he had to move on to free gifts,
and so
for the destroyer of glass doors
the high life began:
if she ordered two packs of ribbons,
she magically received four,
if she paid for five spans of lace fabric
she had at least ten,
and if the price list showed cotton at so many cents a yard,
for her it was paid with a smile
so that in the end
Miss Wolf understood,
why—let it be spelled out clearly—
a head does not feel love,
but understands it.

And she was happy to have understood.

So she allowed
Mr. Lehman
from now on
to call her *süsser*.

There.
This in effect is where the problem began.
For from that moment
in theory
two *süssers*
were breathing
on planet Earth

arranged
geographically
one in Alabama
and one in Bavaria
covering the whole planisphere.

Henry said nothing to his American *süsser.*
And he said nothing either to his Bavarian *süsser,*
and curious indeed
was the fate
of the *most affectionate greetings*
that traveled
for four years
in every letter
across planet Earth
to *Fräulein* Bertha Singer:
for on account of his being a head
and therefore by nature a contorted soul,
Heyum Lehmann, now Henry,
suddenly embarked
on writing to Bertha herself,
and the more he wanted to tell her the truth,
the more he was struck with fear,
prompting him
—in writing—
to send loving kisses
and tender embraces
and sweet caresses
and promises
and fond wishes
and every tenderness
without revealing to his *süsser* that
to Rimpar
—he felt—
he would never return.
But how could he tell her?
Alone and abandoned
on the other side of the planet:
she might perhaps kill herself
if he refused her.

The cadaverous Bertha,
for her part,

reacted with surprise
on seeing herself inundated
with all that rapture.
At first she hesitated.
Then
through who-knows-what mysteries of womankind
she was unexpectedly overcome:
the American outpourings of her Heyum
were answered
with the Bavarian outpourings of *süsser* Singer,
and the whole Atlantic Ocean
was spread with
tons and tons
of treacle.

Fortunately Alabama and Germany
are so far apart
that if it is day here it is night there
and where the sun shines darkness falls.
Just as well.

For in this whole exchange
of loving ardor
Henry made no mention of his Rosa
but Bertha too
made no mention of her own secret:
how could she be blamed, after all,
if after four years of
most affectionate greetings
a local doctor
with the face of a child
had seized her at the gate of Valhalla?
How could she be blamed
if by dint of treating her body
sweet Schausser with the curly hair
had touched her soul?
She had fallen in love with the doctor.
Requited, moreover,
to such an extent
that the visits and consultations
exceeded
by far
the worst tuberculosis.

But how could she tell him
about that Heyum living far away
who was now sending her
all that affection?
Alone and abandoned
on the other side of the planet
he might perhaps kill himself,
if she rejected him.

So that
love letters
furrowed the ocean
back and forth
for more than a year.

It was the cattle dealer
who put things straight,
as soon as a doubt arose,
as soon as he noted that Bertha
certainly
for quite some time
was much much better
even though Doctor Schausser
was shaking his head just the same
increasing the frequency of bloodletting.

He thought therefore
that such a doubt
might urge his son
to return to the stable,
once and for all
and he wrote the fateful note:
"THOSE WHO LEAVE THE NEST TOO LONG
CANNOT THEN COMPLAIN . . . EVERY MATE GROWS COLD.
HOPING YOU TAKE HEED, YOUR FATHER."

Never was a paternal message
received
with such joy:
how splendid
marvelous
that a mate should grow cold

and should warm herself!
Let *süsser* Bertha tend her own nest!

And *süsser* Rosa?
She would have her American wedding!

On that day, a bright sun
shone over Montgomery,
a thousand miles away from the chill of Bavaria:
the shop flourished,
the cotton was *first choice*
the reduced prices drew customers
and
not far from Court Square
measurements were being taken
for plans
to build
a Temple.

7
Bulbe

Late morning of *Rosh haShanah*.
Paint bucket in the street
in front of the shop
in front of that door
with the handle that still sticks.
"Good morning, Roundhead! God bless you!"
"God bless you, Mr. Lehman! You're painting the new sign?"

Paint bucket in the street
while from the wagon
they unload
rolls of cotton three feet by one
25 rolls
7 hanks and 12 of raw
according to the list
that Henry Lehman is holding

standing at the door
and he ticks off the numbers and sizes one by one.
"Into the storeroom, Roundhead, take everything into the storeroom."

Paint bucket in the street,
Henry has given them the task:
"Finish the sign by this afternoon."
Eighteen feet by three high.
To finish painting it
while Henry receives the cotton
and checks the quality
he checks it, personally, better than anyone
he checks it by climbing on the wagon
before unloading
especially the raw cotton
that Henry buys
directly
from a plantation:
he has an arrangement with Roundhead Deggoo
a large negro over six feet tall
called Roundhead because in effect
he has a perfectly round skull
always inside a white straw hat.
Roundhead Deggoo is in charge
at the Smith & Gowcer plantation:
the whites have understood
that slaves work faster and better
if there's a black like them to give orders
they just need to find someone smart,
so that
Roundhead Deggoo, in effect, is a trusty:
halfway between the slaves and the whites.
Every Sunday, promptly
singing the psalm
white straw hat on head
dressed for church (where he plays the organ)
Roundhead Deggoo
travels the whole main street of Montgomery
bringing to Henry Lehman's shop
a wagon of raw cotton, hanks and rolls:
"Roundhead, you've brought me a stringy cotton!"
"Roundhead, this is not the best! Take it back!"

"Roundhead, I'll pay you less for this!
Take it inside but I'll give you a third."
"And what's this stuff, Roundhead?
It's not worth even the fodder for the horse!"

Paint bucket in the street.
For the new signboard
they've chosen the color yellow.
Family meeting at the Lehman house.
All together, the previous evening, at the shop.
Only Rosa was missing:
"You're pregnant, you cannot come, stay at home."

That's right.
Written in yellow on a black background.
It will catch the eye:
attract customers
said Henry.

The two
one after the other
dip in their brush and
dripping
carry on work:
precise
careful
keeping inside the marked edges;
those drawn by Henry—in pencil
since untidy lettering would look bad
said Henry
and would put off customers: he's right.
Henry's right.

The "L" of Lehman will be capital.
Of the two, it is Emanuel who paints it:
Emanuel Lehman
Or rather: Mendel, his real name.
But here in America, as we know, everything changes, even the name.

Emanuel, yes.
Five years younger than Henry,
with whom sparks fly,

so the terms are clear:
"If you come to America you have to stay below me!"

Agreement made.
Emanuel is a kid who has grown fast.
Hair blacker than pitch
mustache like a Prussian artilleryman
incendiary nature
one who flares up
and on flaring up he told his father
"I'm going across to America too,
Bavaria is a straitjacket."

And now, there he is,
Emanuel bent kneeling
on the ground
armed with a paintbrush
wearing an apron so as not to mark his clothing
for the shop remains open
and if someone arrives
a paint-splattered shopkeeper mustn't be seen
he would put off customers,
Henry said.
And he's right.

The "B" of Brothers will also be capital,
capital like the "H" of Henry had been until now.
It was his decision to have it removed, away, enough:
from today no longer Henry Lehman
but
LEHMAN BROTHERS.

The B of Brothers is painted
sweating
bending down
with the greatest care
by the third and last of the brothers
who arrived in America like a package barely a month ago
terrified by the journey, by the ocean, by the storms
even by the old rabbi to whom he was entrusted
who would take him to his brothers, down there, in Alabama.

Mayer Lehman
aged twenty or thereabouts
the image of his mother
cheeks always red
without even drinking wine
and a smooth smooth skin
on which there's still no sign of whiskers
as smooth as a freshly peeled potato,
and his brother Emanuel
doesn't miss the chance in front of everyone
to call him in Hebrew
whistling to him like a dog:
"Mayer Bulbe!"
Mayer "Potato."
And *Bulbe* was the name of a dog they had
over there in Europe
at their home, over there in Germany
in Rimpar, Bavaria,
where a cattle dealer
has lost his sleep
once and for all
and mutters *"Schmuck!"* from morning to evening.

Three kids, the Lehman brothers.
Henry.
Emanuel.
Mayer.
Of the three, Henry is the head
—his father told him, down there in Bavaria—
Emanuel is the arm.
And Mayer?
Mayer *Bulbe* is the one you need between the head and the arm
so that the arm doesn't smash the head
and the head doesn't shame the arm.
They had called him here to America for this as well:
to stand between the other two when necessary.
A head, a potato, and an arm:
all three of them will be there
on the new wooden signboard ready to be fixed
nice and large
to cover the whole frontage
LEHMAN BROTHERS FABRICS AND CLOTHING
written in yellow on a black background.

framed
carved into the wood by Henry and by Emanuel
outside working hours, at night
each day
once the shop door had closed
without losing time for customers
who otherwise, you bet, would not come back
as Henry says
and
"The customer, remember, is sacred
—Baruch HaShem!—
like our father's cattle!"
Here too
Henry is right.

Every morning
just like this morning
the three Lehman brothers
get up at five
while it's still dark
the lamps are lit
with whale oil.
In the three-room house
in Court Square
there's only a bucket of water for washing.
"It was better in Germany!"
Emanuel said
on his third day in America
but after the slap Henry delivered straight across his face
he never tried to say it again.
Each morning
just like this morning
the three Lehman brothers
while the city is still asleep
—and America no longer seems like a music box—
each morning
before going out
around the table
they recite prayers
all together
as in Germany
as they once did in Rimpar, over there in Bavaria.

Then they put their hats on
and leave
inside the music box that starts to move
they open the door of the shop
with the handle that always sticks
because it was put back exactly as it was
after Rosa Wolf
Mrs. Lehman
knocked it to the ground.

Another day.
Another day.
Another day.
Wool
hemp
and
cotton
cotton
cotton: *King Cotton*
for from today Henry—the head—
has had the idea:
seated on the ledge of the open window,
with his legs drawn together
and an arm up at the back of his neck
he has decided
that the Lehmans
from now on
will sell not just clothing and materials, no
clothing and materials are no longer enough:
"We'll sell everything required to cultivate King Cotton.*"*
Emanuel—the arm—has raised his eyes
and given him a harsh look:
"I've come to America to be a trader not a farmer."
"And that is what we're doing: trading.
We sell and we will continue to sell."
"I don't want to sell buckets and spades for slaves."
"You're here to do whatever I decide:
I was the one who opened this shop."
"And on the signboard it says: Brothers.*"*
"Because that's what I decided and what I wanted
but the shop is still mine."
"I'm not dirtying my hands with plantations:
I want to sell cloth."

"I've done my calculations:
plantation owners buy
seeds equipment wagons."
"Your calculations are not mine:
I want security!"
"You keep quiet, I'm the one who . . ."

At this point it is Mayer *Bulbe* who butts in
smooth odorless as a potato:
"Hey there, Roundhead Deggoo:
if we start selling seeds and equipment
would you buy them?"
"Seeds and equipment, Mr. Lehman?
God bless you! I'd buy them straightaway:
the nearest place that sells them is on the other side of Tennessee!"

Emanuel spits on the ground
bends down and starts painting the sign again
black and yellow that attracts customers
and from the street, Henry said, it will be seen best of all:
LEHMAN BROTHERS
has a good sound
has a very good sound.
This too is what Henry said.
And *Baruch HaShem!*
Henry Lehman is always right.

8
Hanukkah

Baruch atah adonai
eloheinu melech ha'olam
asher kid'shanu b'mitzvotav
v'tzivanu l'hadlik neir
*shel Hanukkah.**

---

* Blessing for the lighting of the candles (festival of Hanukkah): "Blessed are You,
  O Lord our God, King of the Universe, Who sanctified us with His commandments
  and commanded us to kindle the Hanukkah lights."

It's the evening of *Hanukkah*
just as Henry is lighting the seventh candle
standing behind the table
with all the family
Baruch HaShem!
It's the evening of *Hanukkah*
before the presents are opened
when at the door of the Lehman house
there's loud loud banging
that almost brings everything down.
Roundhead Deggoo has never been seen so agitated
with his straw hat on his head
he is shaking, crying, shouting:
"God bless you, Mr. Lehman: the fire!
At the plantations: the fire!"

And they go down to the street
Henry Emanuel and Mayer
leaving Rosa at the window
—*"You're pregnant again, you cannot come"*—
they go down to the street
Henry Emanuel and Mayer
in the darkness of the night which isn't dark but seems like day
in the air in the wind
they go down to the street
Henry Emanuel and Mayer
smoke everywhere
which stings the eyes
and wagons that hurtle, madly
along the streets, madly
people with buckets, men, boys
smoke in the air
in the throat in the nose
—Henry Emanuel and Mayer—
"Everything's burning, down there, in the fields!"
The dormitories of the slaves
the storehouses, the huts
the whole of Montgomery there in the street
the whole of Montgomery there, running
—Henry Emanuel and Mayer—
"Four five plantations are burning! In flames!"
Columns of smoke a hundred feet high
like the bell towers down there, in Bavaria

dense thick heavy smoke
like the smoke of the ships from Europe to Baltimore
which Mayer *Bulbe* still dreams about at night.
Even the night is stained red
painted like the sign
the walls of the houses, the street:
reflections
flashes
deafening explosions from down there
where they are running to help
and others running away
escaping
holding babies
half naked
men and women
whites blacks fleeing
falling to the ground
fainting
they cannot breathe
smoke in their throats
in their noses
in their eyes
"Everything's burning, everything, the cotton is lost!"
The horses are rearing
in the smoke
wagons overturned
carts scattered
broken wheels
"Run to the river! To the canals: water!"
The noise all around
is a gigantic
roar
echoes
rumbles
between the walls
between the windows
"Everything's burning, everything, the cotton is lost!"
Dust ashes
like rain from above
gray red black white
flames like swords in the sky
—Henry Emanuel and Mayer—
injured people carried on shoulders

soaked bandages
legs arms heads burned
the heat in the air the heat
"The wind is rising: the flames will spread!"
"To the river! To the river! Bring water!"
Roundhead Deggoo with his cart
the family safe
"God bless you! Help!"
Those who curse
those who pray
middle of the night but it is day
Montgomery awake
the plantations in flames.
There'll be nothing left.
There'll be nothing left.
There'll be nothing left.

Baruch atah adonai
eloheinu melech ha'olam
asher kid'shanu b'mitzvotav
v'tzivanu l'hadlik neir
shel Hanukkah.

It's the evening of *Hanukkah*
just as Henry is lighting the seventh candle
standing behind the table
with all the family
Baruch HaShem!
It's the evening of *Hanukkah*
when the news arrives:
cotton in flames
everything lost.
But at the same time
Baruch HaShem!
everything new to repurchase:
seeds equipment wagons;
everything to redo
to start again:
seeds equipment wagons.
"Please gentlemen: Lehman Brothers is open!
Lehman Brothers has everything you need!"

"So tell me, Roundhead Deggoo:
at Smith & Gowcer
what do you need?"
"God bless you, Mr. Lehman:
everything, from the start!"
"And if the fire has ruined you
how will you pay?"
"The masters will make a pledge
with a written agreement."
Emanuel—the arm—
raises his eyes and gives Henry a malicious look.
"I've come to America for the money
not for bits of written paper."
"If there's no money, how do you want them to pay?"
"If there's no money, we sell them nothing."
"You're here to do what I decide!"
"But on the sign it says Brothers."
"Keep your voice down and don't start threatening me!"
"I told you it was better to sell cloth."
"We are selling for sure, these are buying everything we have."
"They're buying but not paying!"
"You keep quiet, I'm the one who . . ."
It is at this point that Mayer Bulbe intervenes
slipping in
as smooth odorless as a potato:
"Listen here, Roundhead Deggoo:
if you sow now, how long until the harvest?"
"A season, Mr. Lehman
but then, before selling the raw cotton . . ."
"And you pay us with raw cotton:
a third of the harvest, fixed, as from now.
You give it to us and we resell it."
"God bless you, Mr. Lehman!"

It's the evening of Hanukkah
just as Henry is lighting the seventh candle
standing behind the table
with Emanuel and Mayer
Baruch HaShem!
It's the evening of Hanukkah
when something changes everyone's life:
they used to sell cloth and garments
the Lehman Brothers.

But from now on
the fire has decided:
buying and selling of raw cotton.
Alabama gold.
Marvels of a potato.

9
Shpan dem loshek!

But as this is no simple step,
it will be best to move wisely.

When they meet
to decide something important
the three Lehman brothers
don't sit down at a table.

Emanuel wanders about the room.

Mayer prefers his round stool,
placed halfway
between the head and the arm.

Henry however
each time
walks into the room confidently
and goes to sit
on the ledge of the open window,
with his legs drawn together
and an arm up at the back of his neck.

There.
This is always their position.
Even today, as they decide
whether to dispose, sell off, handkerchiefs, bedsheets, and tablecloths
to turn to commerce
—real commerce—
still in cotton, but raw cotton.

Mayer in favor.
Emanuel votes against.
And since there are three of them, Henry has the deciding vote.

"So then, Henry? How do you vote? For or against?"

Henry takes his time.
It is one of the privileges of being a head.

He remains still, seated
on the ledge of the open window,
with his legs drawn together
and an arm up at the back of his neck.
Then says nothing.
Just nods.
And the change is done.

Of course: raw cotton is not like banknotes.
Ever since Roundhead Deggoo
for the Smith & Gowcer plantation
and likewise also Mr. Saltzer, Mr. Bridges
Mr. Halloway at the plantation beyond the river
and even Mr. Pellington from Tennessee;
ever since they all no longer pay Lehman in banknotes
but in raw cotton,
since then the small storeroom
—that back room behind the curtain—
is not enough, no, is no longer enough.
They have taken a bigger one
three blocks away
behind the Baptist church
where Roundhead Deggoo plays the organ every Sunday.

It works like this:
the Lehmans give the plantations seeds equipment
and all they need,
the plantations give the Lehmans raw cotton
the Lehmans fill the storehouse with cotton
and resell it to manufacturers
at a higher price:
"A little more!"
says Henry;

"Double!" thinks Emanuel;
"One-third: midway!" thinks Mayer *Bulbe.*

You give me the cotton, I resell it.
You pay me today with cotton
I get paid tomorrow in banknotes.

Business?
Business.
And it hardly matters that others too are trying to do the same:
the Lehmans do it better.
Better than everyone.
Better even than that certain
Jew like them
German like them
who arrived in America from the Rimpar area;
they, yes:
the family of Marcus Goldman
and that of Joseph Sachs as well.
All in Alabama.
So that a cattle trader
deprived of his sleep
hasn't missed the opportunity for sarcasm
and has written a note:
"DEAR SONS, IN THAT CITY OF YOURS
YOU COULD PUT UP A SIGN
WITH 'RIMPAR' WRITTEN ON IT,
EXCEPT THAT IN AMERICA THEY ARE ALL ILLITERATE."

And so it is: the cotton market
works wondrously,
for the trick—the real trick—
is to sell *what people cannot avoid buying.*
This is what Henry Lehman has said
to those who asked his advice,
to the Marcus Goldmans, to the Joseph Sachses,
to all those German Jews
who disembarked wearing their best shoes,
lost and rather confused
like fish that had jumped onto the shore
to be told to return to the sea.
"After which, let's be clear, business is war,

so that you for yours, we for ours,
and we'll make no allowances just because you're Bavarian."

Henry clearly makes no mention
about the real secret of the Lehman Brothers.
After all, how could he
explain the recipe that puts head and arm in potato sauce?
And yet he is sure: that's where all the difference lies,
written moreover in yet another note
that arrived only yesterday from far away:
"DEAR SONS, MAKING MONEY IS NOT A BUSINESS,
IT'S A SCIENCE. BE CUNNING, BUT ALSO WISE
WITH DEVOTION, YOUR FATHER."

Cunning and wise.
Two portentous words. And necessary.
Of which fortunately there is no shortage here,
having a tuber that acts as a watershed
between a wise head and a cunning arm.
The balance is certainly delicate,
and so as not to upset it
Henry Lehman is never away from the shop
never on any occasion
not even when Rosa gives birth to their first son:
he has sent Mayer *Bulbe* back home
instead
in haste, this yes,
armed with a bunch of camellias,
telling him to kiss his wife and child on his behalf, and to whisper in
     her ear
"Your husband sends me to tell you he is happy,
but unfortunately he is rather busy.
All the same, congratulations:
is he a fine little boy, can we rejoice? Mazel tov!"

There again there's much to do,
and in three they can hardly manage.
The small room
on the main street of Montgomery
with LEHMAN BROTHERS writ large
has become a stopping place for all kinds of folk.
The straw hats of the plantations now enter

but also the lighted cigars of industrialists;
the boots and work coats of the plantations
but also the leggings and linen suits of industrialists;
blacks like Roundhead Deggoo
and white traders from the North:
like Teddy Wilkinson
a barrel wearing a tie
white beard, always sweating
immediately renamed by Mayer *Bulbe*
"Perfecthands"
because he always boasts:
"My hands have no calluses, they're perfect:
I've never touched a spade
I just count money."
For some folk Lehman sells seeds and equipment
for others Lehman deals in cotton.

Cotton, they buy it at the weight of gold.
They come to Alabama from beyond the Mississippi
and from factories in the North
those that take raw materials from the South
and turn them, as they say, into "products."
That's what Teddy Perfecthands Wilkinson calls them: *"products."*
"You give me eight wagons of raw cotton
I'll pay you at the full rate
then it's up to me to make money on the products
that's my affair, my business.
If it's okay with you, we'll sign."
And they signed. Yes.
Lehman Brothers on one side
Perfecthands on the other.
Agreement made.
Baruch HaShem!
Suppliers of raw cotton from the South to the North.

With success like this,
can you take a break from work
just because a son of yours is born?
Come on.
All it needs after all is a minimum of common sense.
By calculating times, for example
on the basis of shop hours.
When Rosa for example

felt the first pains
of her second son,
she sent for Henry immediately
but the storehouse inventory was in full progress,
so that Mayer *Bulbe* was instructed to play the substitute,
armed with a bunch of camellias
whispering in her ear:
"Your husband hopes you will not suffer too much.
He'll be busy until late this evening
and asks whether you could delay the birth
so maybe he can be present."

But only on the fourth happy event
did Mrs. Lehman
achieve the perfect result
of optimizing the times of her labor
with the superior demands of the business.

Meanwhile
from the time they signed the first agreement,
Teddy Wilkinson
is seen increasingly often in Montgomery:
his carriage with silver-colored spokes
stops outside the door
and Perfecthands appears at the threshold
like a barrel wearing a tie,
demanding eight wagons of raw cotton.
"But if you have any more, I'll take them!"
He says it each time, throwing onto the counter
his two bundles of banknotes.
Then mops the sweat, lights his cigar:
"One of you Lehmans must come sometime
to see my factory."

And Emanuel Lehman
on one occasion
accepted the invitation. Yes.
He decided.
And went up North
to see the factory
of Teddy Perfecthands Wilkinson
four days on the road there and three back
when the cotton wagons are now empty

and travel light.
Emanuel, he went to see for himself
to find out what happened up North
to the raw cotton of the plantations.
"There's work to do here
and you're going off for ten days?"
Henry had told him sternly
a moment before Mayer *Bulbe* intervened:
"We've already agreed:
I'll do his work for ten days."
And so Emanuel left
with the excuse of personally accompanying
the eight wagons of raw cotton paid at full rate.

It's a vast factory with the sign
WILKINSON COTTON
he told them on his return
full of people who work for Perfecthands
people paid: salaried, not slaves
"my workforce" he calls them.
A barrack-like building sixty feet high
with a gigantic tube that appears from the roof
smoking
nonstop, night and day
just like Perfecthands' cigar, and more,
as he wanders the building dressed in white
checking
in the middle of an infernal noise
around those dozens of steam looms
with mechanical rakes
twenty feet long twelve high
that comb and wind the cotton
continuously
back and forth
comb and wind
back and forth
comb and wind
back and forth
comb and wind
then gather and push
onto long long metal channels
filled with water
where women all sitting in a line along the edge untangle threads

which Perfecthands checks as he passes
while a drum orders
thousands of threads
onto the winders
and from there to the weavers in another hall
and from there to another and yet another
to produce the textile
"Doesn't tear!"
done
finished
"Doesn't tear!"
brand-new
"Here's the product!"
Perfecthands would say
mopping the sweat
since there inside
amid the puffing of steam
you sweat double.
"And the more raw cotton you find for me, the better:
I'll buy it
all of it, all of it . . ."
Everything.
At that point Emanuel—or at least so he recalls—
turned to look at the steam machines
that swallowed up raw cotton
—those eight wagons brought from Alabama at full rate—
hurling it down, whole wagonloads
greedy, insatiable
but so much of it that Emanuel Lehman, spellbound
couldn't help thinking
that if he had
another 100, 200, 1000 wagonloads
they would all be swallowed up
nonstop
to the joy of Perfecthands and his workforce
people who are paid: salaried, not slaves.
Baruch HaShem!

When Emanuel finishes his story
Henry behind the counter pretends not to understand.
Simply because he is the head and his brother is the arm:
not the other way 'round
and no arm starts giving ideas to the head.

Mayer *Bulbe*, however
—who was and still is a potato—
can put one and one together
with the innocent straightforwardness of a vegetable:
"Okay, fine:
if it's like you say, we'll find more cotton."

Neither of the other Lehman brothers
utters any sound of a response.

Simply because no head and no arm
accepts advice from any tuber.

Mayer *Bulbe*, however
—precisely through being a vegetable—
can put two and two together:
"And if the raw cotton they give us is not enough
we'll buy it: then resell just the same to Perfecthands
and the profit is guaranteed."
Neither of the other Lehman brothers
seems to have heard a word.
They look at each other, yes
one behind the counter
the other leaning against the wall
like a head and an arm
that study each other
with the intrusion of some kind of potato
that even talks:
"Let's see:
if Roundhead's plantation sells us the cotton
for fifteen dollars a wagon
we could ask Perfecthands for twenty-five.
And we'd be left with ten.
Multiplied by a hundred wagons
makes a thousand dollars.
More than double what we're making up till now.
What did our father used to say?
Spur the horse.
And spur it far away
as far as New Orleans!"

Spur the horse.
"Shpan dem loshek!"

And it's with this phrase
that an insignificant twenty-one-year-old potato
succeeds in getting an answer from two human beings.
Or rather
to be exact
the head replies in a pure cerebral style:
"*On the sign outside*
it doesn't say
'Buying and selling.'"
and the arm in pure manual style:
"*I'll write it tomorrow morning.*
If you wish."

That last
"*if you wish*"
certainly smooths the argument
between Henry Lehman and Emanuel Lehman
and next morning
straightaway
Shpan dem loshek!
a bucket of paint
appears once again on the street
on the ground, beside the dismantled signboard:
LEHMAN BROTHERS COTTON TRADING
all in capital letters
as the head and the arm
have decided
by common agreement.

Painting the sign
bent down
on the ground
yet someone swears
they have seen
not an arm
but
a potato.

10
Shiva

The air here is dry.

Sitting on two wooden benches
backs to the wall
the two Lehman brothers
wait
greet
thank.

The door closes
then reopens: another comes in.

Long beards, both of them,
unshaven ever since the mourning period began.

Ever since
yellow fever
suddenly
without knocking at the door
took one of them away
in the space of three days.

"It's Yellow Jack, if I'm right."
That's what Doctor Everson said,
the doctor who treats slave children with measles.
He said it shaking his head, the day before yesterday
when he entered the room
and raising the oil lamp
looked him in the face:
that coloring
yellower
than the yellow of the Lehman Brothers sign.

"It's Yellow Jack, if I'm right . . ."
And if, God forbid, I'm right . . ."
Doctor Everson didn't finish the sentence
the day before yesterday.

He stayed silent
like the two brothers now
sitting on two small wooden benches
backs to the wall
as the door closes
then reopens
and someone else comes in.

They observe all the rules, they have decided:
Shiva and *sheloshim*
as they did over there in Germany
all the rules as though we were in Rimpar, Bavaria.
Not to go out for a week.
Not to prepare food: to ask neighbors for it, receive it and that is all.
They've torn a garment, as prescribed
they tore it to pieces as soon as they came back
from the burial
at the old cemetery
tired thirsty sweating
for the air here is dry.

They have also recited the *Qaddish*
each day
morning and evening
the two Lehman brothers
from when the mourning period began.
Now
with a voice barely audible
tired eyes
sitting on two small wooden benches
backs to the wall
they wait
greet
thank.

The door closes
then reopens: another.

They closed the corpse in a dark wooden coffin
Roundhead Deggoo nailed it up
he wanted to do it
came here

with the best nails
and with the best wood, the best of all, the most expensive
bought by the brothers.

Today the shop stays closed.
Like yesterday and the day before.
Today and for another week.
It has been there ten years
and for ten years it has never closed,
for such a long time,
the Lehman Brothers' shop
on the main street of Montgomery, Alabama.
Curtains drawn.
Door closed.
Double locked.
No notice, no announcement:
everyone knows
that one of the three
one of the Lehmans
has died
like that, so suddenly
of yellow fever.
"Yellow Jack"
Doctor Everson said.

Sitting on two small wooden benches
backs to the wall
the two Lehman brothers
now
wait
greet
thank.

The door closes
then reopens: another.

The first Lehman to die here in America.
He will have a stone plaque
carved in English, in German, and in Hebrew.
It will cost, but who cares.
Four? Five wagons of raw cotton?
"Even if it were fifty!"
says one of the two.

"Even if it were fifty!"
the other repeats.
Dressed in black.
Hats on heads.
"Even if it were fifty!"
"Even if it were fifty!"
The door closes
then reopens: another.
"Even if it were fifty!"
"Even if it were fifty!"

11
Kish Kish

Chloe can count to five.
To five, yes.
For now that Mr. Tennyson's plantation has been added
there are five in Alabama
that sell raw cotton to the Lehman Brothers.

She can count to five, Chloe.
She cannot count all the years of her age,
since Chloe is fourteen,
and the two Lehman brothers have bought her for 900 dollars:
their first slave.
1, 2, 3, 4, 5! Well done Chloe!

Until recently
before the yellow fever took one of them
there were four suppliers:
the Smith & Gowcer plantation
where Roundhead Deggoo works,
Oliver Carlington's small plantation
just outside Montgomery,
Bexter & Sally's with two hundred Caribbean slaves
and the so-called Mexican plantation
because the owner is old Reginald Robbinson
aged eighty-one

who never goes down to the plantation
and gets his three trusty Mexicans to do it all,
from choosing the slaves to selling the cotton.

Five plantations.
Just under four hundred wagons of raw cotton
to buy and resell.
Two hundred wagons are taken
by Teddy Perfecthands Wilkinson
and the rest go to two factories in Atlanta
and on the coast, at Charleston:
found
by Rab Kassowitz's nephew from New York.

Fixed profit for the Lehman Brothers
is twelve dollars a wagon.

It seemed a lot at first.
In fact, all in all, it's very little.

Because transporting raw cotton
from Alabama to the North
costs.
The horses cost, the wagons cost
the porters and unloaders cost
even if Roundhead Deggoo, by arrangement
sometimes gets help from the slaves
at the Smith & Gowcer plantation.
But even with the slaves
twelve dollars per wagon is a pittance
a trifle
and the costs are high
too high
it's not worth it
for twelve dollars
it's not worth it
calculations at the ready
for twelve dollars
might as well give up now.

To make a profit you'd need at least twenty dollars a wagon.
At least.
And a minimum of four, five hundred wagons of raw cotton.

A minimum.
Which means twice the number of plantations.
Twice.
And so: if all ten of the largest plantations in Alabama
were persuaded to sell cotton now and then to the Lehmans
business
yes
it would begin
—for sure—
to be worthwhile.

Of the two remaining brothers
Emanuel Lehman is more certain.
He, Emanuel, wants to go ahead
like every self-respecting arm
figures on paper aren't enough, he wants action.
After all, sure, isn't it easy enough?
Just go to the cotton owners
and explain that the game is worth it for them too:
for as soon as the harvest is ready
they'll get their money in less than a day
by selling all their raw cotton to the Lehman Brothers
who from then on
are there just for them
ready straightaway to buy it
the cotton
from them
and to pay them for it
yes sirs
everything
—a reasonable price—
but in cash.
All here.
What more do you want?
He, Emanuel, wants to go ahead:
and in fact it is he
—with his beard still long with mourning—
who went knocking on the doors of all the owners
sat on their drawing room sofas
joined them for dinner on the veranda
listened to their little girls who play the piano;
he who can't stand music, or the piano
"How beautiful, Miss!

Your daughter is wonderful!
Do play some more!"
But these words
through clenched teeth
with gray face
and trying not to doze off during recitals
are the maximum diplomacy that he can manage:
Emanuel Lehman is no fine weaver of words
is no politician
is no smiler
his father always used to say
there, in Rimpar, Bavaria:
"you're no Kish Kish"
which means "kiss kiss."
And it's true.
Without a doubt.
No arm is a *Kish Kish*.
Least of all Emanuel.
Who gets easily annoyed, angry
goes red in the face
terribly red
each time the masters of the house
plantation owners
fail to understand his offer
or tell him:
"I'll think about it . . ."
"We'll see . . ."
or even worse:
"Why exactly should I be giving cotton to you?"
and on saying this they call for their daughter
to play the piano.

All good American families in the South
have a little girl pianist.
All of them get her to play for guests,
even for those who come to talk about cotton.

The impossible ideal
utopia
mirage
would be a businessman who teaches piano.
Baruch HaShem!

The idea of trying out
the other surviving Lehman brother
isn't even considered.

Partly because no potato understands diplomacy.
Partly because Mayer *Bulbe*
for some time
has had other things on his mind
since the festival of *Purim*
when at the table of fritters
he kissed Barbara Newgass
known as "Babette"
on the forehead
whispering in her ear—it is said—
"Babette, beautiful as the moon . . ."
which is an uncommon feat
for a vegetable of poetical bent.

Age nineteen, Babette.
A small red birthmark on her right cheek, Babette.
With luminous eyes, Babette.
Her plaits held in a cork grip, Babette.
Hair darker than the wooden counter of the shop, Babette:
the counter where Mayer
for some time
gets even his additions and subtractions wrong
—Babette—
and leaves the storehouse door open
—Babette—
and
—through distraction and for no other reason—
breaks his fast
tasting Roundhead Deggoo's soup.
Yes: Babette, always Babette.

The parents of Babette Newgass
well know
who the Lehman brothers are.
And their nine children too.
They pass along
the main street of Montgomery
in front of the black and yellow LEHMAN BROTHERS signboard.

And yet Babette's father
begins precisely from there
seated in an armchair
surrounded by all eight sons
in a circle behind him
—since Babette is the only daughter: *mazel tov!*—
like a firing squad
lined up
facing Mayer *Bulbe*
wearing his best suit already seen at the funeral
but with hair combed
a bunch of flowers, cold sweat
and his beard, alas, still long with mourning.

His brother Emanuel three steps behind
motionless, silent
there by force:
the family representative.

"Since you wish to introduce yourself
I'd like to know
young man
exactly what you do in that shop of yours."
"At one time we sold fabrics
Mr. Newgass
now no longer."
Babette and her mother
in the next room with the colored servant women
are posted
with an ear to the door and an eye to the keyhole.

"If you are no longer selling, what is the purpose of a shop?"
"Because
we do sell, we are still selling
Mr. Newgass."
"Selling what?"
"We sell cotton
Mr. Newgass."
"And cotton is not fabric?"
"No not yet . . . not when we sell it
Mr. Newgass."
"And if it's not fabric then who buys it?"
"Those who will turn it into fabric

Mr. Newgass.
We're in the middle, in fact.
We're right in the middle
Mr. Newgass."
"What sort of job is that
being in the middle?"
"It's an occupation that doesn't yet exist
Mr. Newgass:
we're the ones who are starting it."
"Baruch HaShem!
No one lives from an occupation that doesn't exist!"
"We do, Lehman Brothers do.
Our occupation is . . ."
"Come on: what is it?"
"It's a word invented:
we're . . . middlemen, there, yes."
"Ah! And why should I give my daughter to a
'middleman'?"
"Because we're making money
Mr. Newgass!
Or rather: we will be making money
I swear: trust me."

And on this "trust me"
Mayer *Bulbe* gives
such a wondrous smile
so certain
so sure
so credible
that Mr. Newgass and his eight sons
in fact
relent
indeed more:
they *trust*
and, through trusting,
they entrust to a potato
their only daughter and only sister
who bursts merrily through the door.

But most surprised at this triumph
is Emanuel Lehman.

The truth is that since the time when Henry
no longer sits
on the ledge of the open window,
with his legs drawn together
and an arm up at the back of his neck.
Emanuel has always felt—up to now—
as though he were alone, entirely alone,
and not with a brother
but with a vegetable.

For this reason
he now stares in surprise
with true admiration
he watches him
pay his respects to the lady of the house
he hears him laugh, relax, joke
and even
most courteously
kiss—*Kish Kish Kish Kish . . .*—
in a way that for him, a good arm, there is no way:
he doesn't know how.

Next morning
First day of official engagement
—720 days left to the wedding—
Mayer Lehman
—once called *Bulbe,* now *Kish Kish*—
is formally recruited:
on behalf of the Lehman brothers
he will be responsible
for business dealings and relationships
knocking on the doors of all owners
with his fine funeral suit
going to all plantations
sitting on drawing room sofas
eating dinners on the veranda
listening to little girls who play the piano . . .
which won't be too hard, since Babette
—*süsser* Babette—
plays the piano too
and teaches the piano
like no one else.

In March 1857
94th day of official engagement
—627 left to the wedding—
thanks to Mayer *Kish Kish*
to Babette and to Chopin
the plantations that sell cotton to Lehman
increase from five to seven.

September 1857
274th day of official engagement
—447 left to the wedding—
thanks to Mayer *Kish Kish*
to Babette and to Schubert
the plantations that sell cotton to Lehman
increase from seven to ten.

January 1858
394th day of official engagement
—327 left to the wedding—
thanks to Mayer *Kish Kish*
to Babette and to Beethoven
the plantations that sell cotton to Lehman
increase from ten to fifteen.

June 1858
544th day of official engagement
—177 left to the wedding—
thanks to Mayer *Kish Kish*
to Babette and to Mozart
the plantations that sell cotton to Lehman
increase from fifteen to eighteen.

December 1858
720th day of official engagement
—one day left to the wedding—
thanks to Mayer *Kish Kish*
to Babette and to Johann Sebastian Bach
the plantations that sell cotton to Lehman
increase from eighteen to twenty-four.

"Mazel tov!"
Twenty-four suppliers of raw cotton.
From Alabama to the edge of Florida.

From Alabama to South Carolina.
From Alabama to New Orleans.
Plantations, plantations, plantations:
on which slaves work night and day
whose raw cotton
sooner or later
is purchased by the Lehman brothers
2500 wagons of raw cotton a year.
earning 50,000 dollars
which pass through a small room in Montgomery
with a handle that in remembrance of Henry will always stick.
Buy and resell.
Buy and resell.
Buy and resell.
Buy and resell.
Between the two things
right in the middle
as *"middlemen"*
are the Lehman Brothers.

CLOSED TODAY FOR WEDDING
is written on the card fixed to the door.
And Emanuel Lehman
as a wedding present
has a beautiful
grand piano
delivered
from New Orleans.

12
Sugarland

א as in Avraham
ב as in Bein haMetzarim
ג as in Ghever
ד as in Daniyel
ה as in Yeled
ו as in V'haya

ז as in Zekharya
ח as in Hanukkah
ט as in Tu BiShvat
י as in Isaia
כ as in Kippur
ל as in Lag baOmer
מ as in Moshe
נ as in Nisan
ס as in Sukkot
ע as in Asarah BeTevet
פ as in Pesach
צ as in Tzom Gedalya
ק as in Katan
ר as in Rosh haShanah
ש as in Shabbat
ת as in Tishri

Who knows what Henry would have said
if he had seen
this creature of his
recite the alphabet from memory
along with the months, prophets, and Jewish festivals.

This little David
is really bright.
Perhaps a little too bright.

It's no coincidence
that when Uncle Mayer and Uncle Emanuel travel
they prefer to take
his brother:
today as well, when they are expected in Louisiana.

There are still three hours to go.
Even if they seem near on the map
it's not so short a ride
from Montgomery to Baton Rouge.
And when you think that the slaves
do this whole road
on foot,
as Roundhead Deggoo
told them,
who once

before cotton
worked sugar in Louisiana.

Sugar.
Meaning sugarcane, of course
and not the white one
of sugar beet
which Aunt Rosa
—Henry's widow, that's what they call her now—
keeps in small lumps
in a glass bowl
and when her children drive her 'round the bend
"Bertha! Harriett! Leave the cat alone!"
just to enjoy a moment's peace
"David! Will you stop shouting?"
she gets them to play a game:
"All right children: a sugar lump
for each of you:
now put it on your tongue
mouths shut
and the one who keeps it longest wins!"

This is the only trick
to get some silence
in the house made all of wood
that Henry built beam by beam,
he who over there in Rimpar, Bavaria,
had built a whole shed
in wood
for his father's cattle.

But of all four children that Henry has left behind
there is one
who had never much liked
sugar lumps on the tongue,
for the simple reason
that no games are needed
to keep him silent:
the little boy is silent
by character
naturally
totally silent

a worthy descendant of his granddad Abraham,
in fact his nickname "Dreidel"
was given to him
at the time
when he was a baby
at the age of *da-da-da*
when he amazed everyone
on an evening of festivity
when he took a spinning top
between his tiny hands and said without hesitation,
when he said word by word,
in almost perfect Yiddish
"Dem iz a dreidel!"*
to the enthusiastic approval of his relatives who
with hugs and kisses
greeted the precocious phonetic debut
of a natural future orator.

They were wrong.
Entirely.

For Dreidel
—who would in fact take the name of his Uncle Mayer,
in honor of the fact that he alone was present at the birth—
stopped talking very early:
that eruption
marked the beginning and the end
of his eloquence.
From then on
for several years
the child confined himself
to a bizarre counting of other people's words:
he listened as they talked, with sharp gaze,
suddenly bursting out
with phrases such as
"Uncle Emanuel, that's 27 times you've used the word HORSE,
42 times you've used the verb TRADE
25 times you've said UNFORTUNATELY
14 times you've said AGAINST MY BETTER JUDGMENT
and 9 times you've used CONSTRUCTIVE.
What exactly does CONSTRUCTIVE mean?"

---

* Literally *"This is a spinning top!"*

This was the little boy's obsession:
unable to make a conversation of his own,
Dreidel kept count of what others said
with mathematical precision
and was able to say how many times
in the last week
his mother had called
his brother, David,
an ass, a devil, or a pest.

Then even this slowly vanished,
so that he fell
into such a strange silence
that
the Lehman house
felt a growing conviction
that Dreidel
in his silence
was turning his back on the human race.

A matter of no small significance
for a young kid in short trousers.

Aunt Rosa, it has to be said,
for her part did not reproach him.
Indeed
the other three made so much noise
that a quiet child
seemed heaven-sent,
and might
—Aunt Rosa thought—
even be an offering from that father
so prematurely departed
who
being a good head as he was
had had the forethought to include a silent child
in a litigious family
of arms and potatoes
left suddenly
orphaned of its brain.
And for this she accepted him,
heartily thanking her dear departed Henry.

Every so often
however
certain questions arose
in Emanuel's and Mayer's minds.
About the future more than anything else.
About the future of the business.

For it was clear
—and old Abraham, in Rimpar, had even written them about it—
that one day Lehman Brothers
king of cotton
would slide
naturally
without realizing it
onto the gentle slope of lineal descent,
and then
from three sons of a cattle merchant
to the grandchildren of that Lehman with two n's.
And then? To whom?

Emanuel Lehmann,
stubborn arm
and as such
animated with muscular fervor more than loving tenderness,
seemed far distant
not just from being a father
but even from choosing a wife,
his brother being convinced
that the ribs chest and spinal column
of any poor woman
would snap to pieces
at the first embrace.

Mayer *Bulbe* on the other hand
already had a pregnant wife,
feeling in this expectancy
not merely the birth of a son
but a future for the family business
so that
not a day passed without him repeating to his Babette
"I know you can do nothing about it,
but if there is something,
then concentrate on it not being a girl."

In the meantime,
while putting their trust
in order of importance
on the Eternal One, on fortune, on Babette's confinement, and on
      Mother Nature,
the two Lehman brothers
carefully
watched
Aunt Rosa's young boys,
and though they still had their milk teeth
for them they were already in line for power.

Exactly.
This made them tremble.

How was it possible that a head such as Henry
so thoughtful to a fault
had produced as offspring
two males who had not even the minimal hope
of professional achievement?

Since,
while Dreidel didn't speak,
his brother, David, would have been worthy
without a doubt
of the same nickname
as his brother but in a very different sense:
in his case
he himself was the spinning top
incapable of staying still
frantic and restless
who had gone as far as telling his mother:
"I don't want to sleep because it's a waste of time."
but was then incapable of using his time
for anything other than acrobatics
so that
he seemed destined
evidently
for something quite different from a role in commerce
and instead
—his uncles said as they watched him—
for a promising career, yes,
in a circus.

The fact is that
Dreidel & Dreidel
grandsons of a cattle dealer
were incapable of playing hide-and-seek
or with a skipping rope
or on a seesaw
without seeing Uncle Mayer and Uncle Emanuel
hovering around
like two large flies
visibly worried
so worried
that when David snatched a lollipop from a younger sister,
Emanuel went immediately to Aunt Rosa
shouting furiously
"No one in our family business
has ever appropriated the resources of another!
and Mayer added
darkly
that three days before,
when he tested
his young nephew,
the boy had mistaken
ordinary hemp for *first choice* cotton.
Unforgivable.

Having therefore ruled out
hot-headed David,
seriously destined
for an athletic, military, or equestrian career,
the two brothers' hopes
could only be placed
on the silent scion
whose nevertheless razor-sharp gaze
—as he slowly grew up—
instilled in more or less everyone
the uncertain thought
that Dreidel was an extreme
though undependable
concentration of wisdom,
worthy heir—for sure—to the paternal head,
and that in this condition of perfect cerebralism
he understood the workings of the world so well
that he had no words to express his contempt.

He remained silent, yes,
but deliberately so.

Aunt Rosa
did not mind such a picture.
And indeed she allowed
the family to give this three-year-old
the label
which inspired awe in more or less everyone
of something halfway
between philosopher and rabbi
who therefore
—it went without saying—
would assume
a future role in the company.

For which reason
it was decided that Dreidel
should accompany
Mayer and Emanuel
year after year
on occasional business trips
like this one
along the slave road
as far as Baton Rouge in Louisiana.

Did sugar
have an irresistible attraction
on the Lehmans too?
Well yes.

Sugar.
The one who mentioned it first
was Benjamin Newgass
one of Babette's brothers who lives in New Orleans,
where sugarcane is lord and master:
"You have your cotton, of course,
fortunately, you have already found your line of business,
but I swear to you that sugar in Louisiana
seems like a gold mine.
If you're interested, just to find out, come and see for yourselves!"

And Emanuel is interested for sure.
For when all is said and done
to an arm, cotton sleeves feel tight
and I haven't come here to America
to shut myself up in Montgomery
just as if I were over there in Bavaria.

Mayer, however, no.
He disapproves.
And he has told him so,
straight out:
"There's work to do here, and you want to go off to Louisiana?"
but since a potato doesn't know how to talk straight
and an arm is still an arm, even at the age of forty
three days later they were in the coach
accompanied
by a silent spinning top
on their way to *Sugarland*
where hundreds of thousands of slaves
lined up in rows
cut, trim, and stack
whole fields of crop
as far as the eye can see.

After which
greeted warmly
arm potato and spinning top
sit down
in the shade of a white veranda
sipping fresh lemon juice
with this man with full beard
dressed in a white white suit
the color of sugar
which is said in these parts to be King:
"You have asked to meet me?
To be honest, I don't understand why.
Of course, Messrs. Lehman, your fame
has reached as far as Louisiana:
it is said you've done wonders
on the cotton market . . . But I don't deal in cloth."

Of the three
arm potato and spinning top

unfortunately
it is Emanuel, an instinctive limb
who replies
aggravated here by the exhaustion of the journey:
"Have you taken us for two cloth dealers?"

"I have taken you for who you are:
excellent cotton traders,
and I admire you, but it's not my line of business.
Would you mind if my niece now plays the piano for you?"

Terror-struck by the sudden reemergence
of the unassuaged specter of the ivory-basher
Emanuel Lehman explodes into a kind of roar:
"I haven't come to America
to shut myself up in a single line of business!"

"What do you mean, Mr. Lehman?
Are you proposing to abandon cotton?
Only a madman would do that in your situation.
Serenella, play us some Chopin."

"Keep the child on a leash:
I'm not abandoning cotton or anything else,
I just wish to know: how much does your sugar cost?"

"I don't discuss my sugar prices
with someone who doesn't even know what it is."

"For you know nothing at all of business,
you know less than this young boy of ours."

At which point
his brother intervenes
smooth odorless as a potato,
stitching onto his face the picture of a smile,
taking Serenella's hand
and sitting with her at the piano,
where they start a wonderfully lively duet,
over which Mayer can easily add a few choice words:
"My brother means to say, sir,
that the cotton trade is so very hard:
every three days it brings us trouble,

and therefore—if we choose—
might we not be entitled to sugar it as we please,
just to sweeten the palate a little?
Don't lose the rhythm, Serenella: you have some talent!
We, sir, have plenty of customers: businesspeople.
I think we could do good business, we and you.
I have a feeling about it. Trust me."

The sugar king
though cheered by the duet
looks at Mayer Lehman
with a certain vexation,
though not because he feels annoyed:
he wonders how
that *Kish Kish* way
fits with the rudeness of the man sitting next to him.
To sweeten the situation
he has a Bohemian glass bowl
brought to the table
filled with sugar as though it were gold:
"Before speaking, try my sugar,
the best in Baton Rouge: choice nectar.
If you like it, Mr. Mayer Lehman, we can talk."
and he holds out three silver teaspoons,
for the tasting.

It is curious how at times
children
take only a moment
—only one—
to step from childhood to maturity.
In the case of Dreidel
(whom everyone considered already mature
indeed more than ever
verging almost on the wisdom of an old man)
it was to be a step backward,
and he took it
in an instant
dropping down
from the upper level of silent genius
to that humiliating position of stupid brat
just as
everyone on that white veranda

was extolling the pleasure of *King Sugar,*
he broke the silence
with the phrase
"I hate it"
repeated moreover several times
"I hate it."
Insisting
"I hate it."
with a voice no longer that of child but of a tenor
"I hate it."
which was not enough
to stop
the looks of the servants
nor the smiling excuses of Uncle Mayer
nor the angry fit of the bearded sugar merchant
nor the hysterical cry of Serenella at the piano
nor even
the slap delivered directly across the face
which an uncle-arm
couldn't help but administer
to teach the young boy
that in life it is better to keep silent
than to venture
into the perilous realms of speech.

They left
homeward
in silence:
the Lehman foray
into the land of sugar
had been worse than bitter
disastrously bitter
and now that Dreidel
had embarked on sabotage
a further shadow fell
over the future
of the family business.

All lay in the hands
—or rather: in the womb—
of tender Babette
whose last four months of pregnancy
were spent

as an accused man
might wait for
reprieve
or sentence of death.
The birth of a baby girl
would have been disastrous,
so that
no Lehman
prayed so much
as Mayer and Emanuel
in the anxiety
of those passing months.

It was a rainy afternoon
when Babette
all of a sudden
playing cards
during a particularly fortunate hand
fixed her eyes on Aunt Rosa
as if she were about to discard a joker
and had just enough time to say *"What a strange sensation . . ."*
before bending over in pain
and throwing her cards on the table.

Hurriedly
they sent Roundhead to call
hurriedly
her husband and brother-in-law
hurriedly
because the wait had certainly ended
and the labor had begun.

Someone related how
as soon as the two brothers
in great agitation
entered the house,
their faces turned pale
on seeing a terrible omen:
on the table
Babette's cards
left there as a sign
were
a full set of queens.

It was a night of anguish
of torment and of sweat.
In the bedroom, Babette suffered.
But in the drawing room
they suffered just as much—if not more.
Emanuel pacing 'round the room,
Mayer on his round stool,
and a vague feeling in the air
that there was also someone else
on the ledge of the open window
with his legs drawn together
and an arm up at the back of his neck.

Then toward dawn
Aunt Rosa appeared at the doorway
smiled to Mayer
and said only
"You may come in."

She hadn't finished the phrase
before they were already inside.

13
Libe in New York

When Mayer sets foot there for the first time
he almost can't believe it.
The door handle here doesn't stick
and the room is certainly bigger:
perhaps double
the one Henry Lehman opened fifteen years ago
in Alabama.

Mayer gets out of the carriage
just there
where his brother has told him to go:
119 Liberty Street
no longer Montgomery:

New York,
where you breathe a strange odor
of fodder, smoke, and every type of mold.

They are putting up the signboard at that moment:
black and yellow freshly painted by three kids
with a paint bucket in the street.
Mayer Lehman gets out of the carriage
and it feels strange to him
to stop
at 119 Liberty Street
and see this sign
LEHMAN BROTHERS COTTON
FROM MONTGOMERY ALABAMA
that the three kids are hauling up with ropes
over the window of this branch office in New York
for now everyone knows
that all the trade in raw cotton
King Cotton
happens here
no longer in the South.
Now in New York
where no one has ever seen a cotton field.
LEHMAN BROTHERS COTTON
FROM MONTGOMERY ALABAMA
is magically
turned into
banknotes.

Down in Montgomery
there is still the small room on the main street
with the handle that no longer sticks
since Roundhead Deggoo has fixed it
and behind the counter
—where Mayer and Emanuel no longer have the time
or inclination to be—
two account clerks hired a month ago:
Peter Morrys with two rabbit teeth
and Isaac Kassowitz
bookkeeper with *tefillim*
nephew of a certain rabbi
whom Henry once knew in New York.

No one is going to close it
the small room in Montgomery.
Of course not.
That is still the office of Lehman Brothers
to all intents and purposes:
LEHMAN BROTHERS COTTON
FROM MONTGOMERY ALABAMA
as the black and yellow sign says
since the plantations
are in Alabama, of course
not in New York,
where no one has ever seen a cotton field.
But Montgomery
compared to New York
is like the Germany of Rimpar, over there in Bavaria:
it's fine for Roundhead Deggoo
who plays the organ on Sunday morning,
it's fine for Doctor Everson
who treats slave children for measles,
it's fine for the families of owners
with a piano on the veranda.
But business
agreements
contracts
money
money, yes
money
real money
money
it's here that money is made:
Emanuel Lehman is sure of this.
Once again
he has followed the advice of Teddy Perfecthands Wilkinson
and one fine morning
has left for New York
to see
the Cotton Fair
where the real buyers go
the northern manufacturers who say *"product"*
those with factories full of workers
people paid: salaried, not slaves.

"The fair in New York?
What has New York got to do with cotton?
In New York they've never seen
a cotton field!"
this is what his brother Mayer told him straight out.
But since a potato doesn't know how to talk straight out
and an arm is always an arm
even at the age of forty
three hours later he was in the coach.

Emanuel had never been to New York.
A rabbit warren, he thought from the windows of the coach
while crowds of every kind
carts pulled by horses or by hand
weaved around him
New York
sellers
crates and boxes
children and old folk
New York
orthodox Jews and colonies of blacks
Catholic priests, sailors, Chinese, and Italians
New York
the gray of stone-faced buildings
statues and gardens, fountains, markets
New York
preachers and policemen
and more animals, dogs on leads and strays
New York
aristocratic little girls with open parasols
dying beggars
witches, fortune-tellers
New York
drummers
English gentlemen
aspiring poets, soldiers
New York
uniforms and tunics
hats and cassocks
New York
walking sticks and bayonets, flags, banners
everything and the opposite of everything

all at the same time
with not the least dignity, blatant, and yet
grand, magnificent, sublime
New York
Baruch HaShem!

The Cotton Fair
it could be said
occupied more or less a whole district.
Sellers and buyers
swarmed everywhere:
bargaining tables, tariff boards
rolls of cloth
and raw, processed, semiprocessed cotton
blackboards with all the prices
written down and immediately changed
zeros
zeros
zeros
zeros
clouds of chalk
different accents
of traders from every part:
top hats and lighted cigars
from New Orleans, from Charleston, from Virginia
colorfully striped clothes of landowners
from the South with buxom wives
and vice versa the austere white, gray suits
of northern industrialists
from Boston and from Cleveland and from Washington
who come down here to bargain
and to sign and to pay:
jangling coins
bundles of banknotes
a hundred times more than Teddy Perfecthands Wilkinson
jangling coins
bundles of banknotes
and, in the background, beyond the glass and iron dome
the ships at the port of Manhattan
that take cotton from America
all over the world.

Emanuel walks among the people
with chin high
boldly, despite being no one
for he knows
—knows very well—
that behind his surname
behind Lehman Brothers
down there, in Alabama
2,500 wagons of raw cotton a year
are ready waiting
lined up in a row.

"I'm looking for cotton, for sure
but the quality I want
comes only from Alabama."
These words reach
Emanuel Lehman
from a table to the right
where a dozen Jews in ties are negotiating
swathed in cigar smoke:
they reach his ear
crystal clear
despite the crowd and the deafening noise.
"If you're interested, I'm selling raw cotton from Alabama."
A tall distinguished man
with snow-white hair
and rabbi's beard looks him up and down:
"Are you? You have a plantation, do you?"
"I have no plantation
but I sell cotton
from twenty-four plantations."
The other old men laugh heartily.
"I resell the cotton from twenty-four plantations:
they sell it to me, I resell it to you."
The other old men laugh heartily.
"And what sort of job is that?"
"Lehman Brothers: brokers."
The other old men laugh even more heartily.
"At what price?"
"At one suitable both to you and to me."
No one is laughing any more.
"Well, kid: let's meet.

I imagine you have an office here in New York."
"Not now, sir.
But from next week for sure."
"You look then for Louis Sondheim, in Manhattan."

And having said this
taking his gold-topped walking stick
the tall man motions
to someone in the crowd: it is late, he wants to go.
Emerging from the swarm
in a white dress and straw hat
is a girl as slender as the branches of certain newly planted trees
over there in Germany: in Rimpar, Bavaria.
The girl looks at Emanuel
for a fraction of a second
bothered
amused
vexed
intrigued
by that man who stares at her.
"This is my daughter Pauline"
the white-haired rabbi has time to say
before taking his daughter's arm
and disappearing, into the crowd.

Three days later
Emanuel
tells his brother Mayer
only that
at 119 Liberty Street
there were empty premises ready to become an office.
"Because, Mayer, it's at New York
only at New York
that cotton
is turned into banknotes."

He said nothing
of course
he couldn't
he said nothing
about Pauline Sondheim.
About her straw hat.
About her white dress.

He said nothing.
Except that he had to go back to New York
straightaway
immediately
in the greatest hurry
with no time to lose
he had to pack his bags immediately
or no
or yes
or rather, tomorrow morning.

And the other Lehman
didn't understand a word.
Or rather
he understood very well
that an arm
can
sometimes
lose his head.

14
Kiddushin

Mayer lives in Montgomery.
Emanuel in New York.
Two of them, the Lehman brothers
miles and miles apart
but as though they were a single thing
joined all as one by cotton.

A commercial marriage
between Montgomery and New York.

Mayer lives in Montgomery
which for cotton is home.
Emanuel lives in New York
where cotton is turned into banknotes.
Mayer lives in Montgomery

among the plantations of the South.
When he goes by carriage along the main street
the blacks remove their hats out of respect.
Emanuel lives in New York
and when he goes by carriage through Manhattan
no one removes their hat
for in New York there are hundreds like him.
All the same, Emanuel feels unique
the greatest.
And nothing is more dangerous than an arm
that feels great
because a head in the worst of cases *thinks big*
but—alas—an arm acts.

Proof of it came that day
when Emanuel Lehman arrived
officially
in Manhattan
with a bunch of flowers
there, at the door of Louis Sondheim's mansion
looking not for the father
but for his daughter Pauline:
"Good morning, young lady.
You don't know me:
my name is Emanuel Lehman
I will become someone important
and ask you to marry me."
The girl
this time in a blue dress
and without a straw hat
looked at him much longer than a moment
bothered
amused
vexed
intrigued
before laughing at him:
"I'm already engaged!"
"Ah, yes? But not with Emanuel Lehman!
Whoever he is, he's not worth your while.
Not as much as me."
"And who says so?"
"I do. You cannot make a better marriage
nor a more profitable one:

I sell cotton from twenty-four plantations."
"Congratulations, but what does that have to do with me?"
"It has much to do
once we are married
you and me."
"Me and you?"
"I leave it to your father
to decide on the date and the ketubah."
"And what do you leave to me?"
"Why? You want something?"

When the door of the Sondheim house
slammed
violently
in his face
Emanuel Lehman did not lose heart:
he resolved to return
there
within a week
and he put the bunch of flowers in a vase
so as not to have to buy some more.

Over the next six days
he met cotton sellers and buyers
throughout New York
signed contracts with businessmen from Wilmington
Nashville and Memphis;
sold a hundred tons of cotton to the West,
where the new railroad now arrived
and therefore saved
handsomely
on wagons.
The office at 119 Liberty Street
under the black and yellow sign
LEHMAN BROTHERS COTTON
FROM MONTGOMERY ALABAMA
saw visits from the Rothschilds and the Sachs
the Singers and the Blumenthals
and also
one evening
by special invitation
from a tall man with snow-white hair and a rabbi's beard
and gold-topped walking stick:

Louis Sondheim
who was looking for cotton, but only from Alabama
and found it at Lehman Brothers
for sure
in enormous quantities
and
—not insignificant—
at a price, in his case, more than reasonable
most reasonable
because an arm
if he's a good arm
knows how to act
in real terms
for sure!

"Good morning, young lady.
I came seven days ago:
my name is Emanuel Lehman
I'm your father's main supplier
and I ask you to marry me."

Pauline Sondheim
this time in a lilac dress
looked at him much longer than a moment
bothered
amused
vexed
intrigued
before laughing at him once again:
"Haven't I already given you my answer?"
"Yes, but not as I had wished."
"And so?"
"So I leave it to your father
to decide on the date and the ketubah.*"*

When for the second time
the door of the Sondheim house
slammed
violently
in his face
Emanuel Lehman did not lose heart:
he resolved to return

there
promptly
within a week
and put the bunch of flowers in a vase
so as not to have to buy some more.

Over the next six days
he shook the hands of over a hundred industrialists
from America and Europe
from Liverpool
from Marseille
from Rotterdam
lit cigars, poured whisky
collected bundles of banknotes
and personally saw
for the first time
freight cars with the word: COTTON.
He signed contracts with businessmen from Norfolk
Richmond
Portland
heard the discussions of several pessimists
on Abraham Lincoln who was threatening war.
The office at 119 Liberty Street
under the black and yellow sign
LEHMAN BROTHERS COTTON
FROM MONTGOMERY ALABAMA
was visited by all the greatest
and all the best:
the Palace of King Cotton
the Court of New York
for Jews especially
or rather
—not insignificant—
all the relatives
all the friends
of Louis Sondheim
because an arm
if he's a good arm
knows how to act
in real terms
for sure!

"Good morning, young lady.
I came seven days ago
and seven days before that:
my name is Emanuel Lehman
I'm one of the richest Jews in New York
and I ask you to marry me."

Pauline Sondheim
this time in a turquoise dress
looked at him much longer than a moment
bothered
amused
vexed
intrigued
and was about to laugh at him once again
when he
anticipated her move
and
in real terms
like a good arm:
"I understand, young lady:
I'll see you in seven days."

And after seven days he returned.
And after another seven.
After another seven.
After another seven.

On the third month
twelfth return
Pauline Sondheim
this time in a summer dress
let him find the door already open
and a maid
waiting at the entrance.

"Is Miss Pauline Sondheim not at home today?"
"She's waiting in the drawing room, Mr. Lehman,
with her father.
Please give me your hat."
And in just two hours
everything was decided:

the date of the wedding
the paper for the *ketubah*
the canopy for the *chuppah*
and even the tablecloths for the reception.

On the day of the wedding
his brother Mayer came
to New York
with Babette Newgass
and their little firstborn son, Sigmund
who without knowing it
just by being born
had already secured the family's future lot.

Aunt Rosa came
with her four children
including the two spinning tops
of whom one in ascetic silence.

Roundhead Deggoo sent a turkey from Alabama:
it was given to the servants
who didn't touch it
since it came from the South
and don't you just know they'll have poisoned it?

Also invited
was a large bearded man
who in Louisiana was King of Sugar
and came with great pleasure:
how, after all, could he not be there,
since a *Kish Kish*,
without spinning tops in train,
had patiently
persuaded him
to sugar the cotton a little
for their mutual benefit.

And lastly
industrialists came from throughout the North
and the owners of twenty-four plantations in the South
but had to be separated in the very middle of the reception,
as they began throwing insults at each other

and dishes
when Oliver Carlington
on lighting a cigar
dared to say that George Washington
—yes, he himself, and so?—
owned several slaves.

That evening
Emanuel Lehman
stretched out on his bed
looking at the ceiling
thought that now indeed everything
was going truly well.
He had a wife.
An office in Montgomery.
An office in New York.
Bundles of banknotes in the safe.
Twenty-four suppliers of cotton in the South
fifty-one buyers in the North
and sugared icing over everything.
Lulled by these thoughts
he was about to sleep
peacefully
when a chill breeze
twitched an ear
for a fraction of a second:
there was only one thing in the world
that could perhaps destroy everything
and that was a war
between North and South
But it was just an ugly thought
one of those that twitches an ear before sleep.
He put it out of his mind
and
calmly
dozed off.

15
Schmaltz

Mayer lives in Montgomery.
Emanuel in New York.
Two of them, the Lehman brothers
miles and miles apart
but as though they were a single thing
joined all as one by cotton.

Sure
compared to one time
Mayer Lehman
is no longer the same:
he finds it hard to recognize himself
even in that portrait
hanging over the fireplace.

Mayer has grown fat
yes
exceedingly fat
and what is this except the consequence of business?
For here in the South
business is done
only
at the table,
at luncheons that go on for six hours,
amid the aromas of roast meat
and the flow of liquor.

So
choosing a good cook
is crucial.
It becomes a financial question.
A company's cook
is now more valuable than its bookkeeper.
And Mayer Lehman
has even
—to some displeasure—
stated publicly:

"A good cook?
I'd be prepared even to pay him."

Fortunately
there was no need.

Babette and Aunt Rosa
in their search for culinary talent
have tried out
all their slaves
eighteen in all
men and women
without distinction
of whatever age
without distinction
"Let us see what you're worth!"
"Stuff a quail!"
"Season a broth!"
"Candy a dessert."
Loretta, Tea, Reddy, and Jamal
almost set the kitchen on fire: rejected.
That blockhead Robbie
confused sugar with salt: rejected.
That idiot Nanou
couldn't tell the difference between a thigh and a wing: rejected.
Roundhead was busy with the cotton, which was better.
Mama Clara and her six daughters
had dared to ask
why in the Lehman house
shin of pork was forbidden: rejected.

And when each of the remaining few
was tested on how to do salted capon
it was old Holmer who won the title.

From that day
the kitchen at the Lehman house
is a military machine.
Holmer commands it as though it were a barracks.
Tilde his wife looks after the pantry.
Ellis, Dora, Sissi, and Brigitta
chosen from among the most presentable
clean tidy

with cap on head
will serve at table
and seeing that the silverware is of finest quality
may Heaven be sure
they are up to it.

Brand-new tablecloths
and jugs
and carafes
and swan-shaped platters:
investment
in the dining room
financed
with company funds
since
Lehman Brothers
has doubled its earnings
not surprisingly
since the new cook
—on the recommendation of a potato—
invented
in strictly *kosher* tradition
turkey pie with pomegranate
    "Would you like a taste?"
and then the green tomato sauce
    "Mr. Tennyson, another portion?"
and the chicken fricassee
    "My wife goes crazy over it!"
and beetroot puree
    "Mr. Robbinson, can I tempt you?"
and duck stew
    "Another plate, it's so delicious."
and pheasant soup
    "Unforgettable!"
but especially
above all
in pride of place
the dessert
heavily sweetened
"Do you like it? It's Lehman sugar, from Louisiana!"
namely
"spiced aniseed cake"
which Aunt Rosa brings

personally
to the table
at the moment of the signatures,
when the master stroke is required.
And it works.
All the more if the cake is soaked
with a glass of rare liqueur,
kept aside
for special occasions.
"An extraordinary flavor!"
"Goodness how appetizing!"
"You want to spoil us!"
"Another slice?"
"And how well it goes with the wine!"
"Is there any more?"
"Where do we sign?"

Mayer Lehman
had to have
his whole wardrobe
retailored:
his trousers were too tight,
waistcoat buttons were popping off,
ties pulling around his neck
but it's the price of business
and his office
is now
in the dining room
seated at the head of the table
with napkin to his neck
and fork in hand:
"Where do we sign?"

On the other hand
the stakes
are high, very high:
mistakes cannot be made.

For his brother Emanuel
up there in New York
—where cotton is turned into banknotes—
is no doubt very good at shaking the hands of industrialists
but it is here

here in Montgomery
in the wretched splendid deep South
that the earth sundered by the sun
throws out
tons and tons and tons
of magnificent cotton
and Mayer Lehman's purpose
now
is no longer
not just
to have it sold at the best price
from twenty-four plantations
but
—intuition of a tuber—
to have it guaranteed
—ambition of a tuber—
for much more than a single harvest
—yearning of a tuber—
which means
promising
in writing from henceforth
to supply exclusively to Lehman Brothers
for how long?
for five years?
　　"May I have the pleasure of your company at lunch?"
for ten years?
　　"We'll talk about it over dessert!"
and if we make it fifteen years renewable for the same period?
　　"The spiced aniseed cake is on the table!"
or twenty years and we'll say no more.
　　"A liqueur for the digestion?"

Megalomania of a tuber:
to cut out competition.

Yes, for this is the point.
Competition.
Mayer Lehman
has said enough
to sleepless nights:
he has lost his peace of mind
since that wretched evening
when Oliver Carlington

from the small plantation outside town
came to tell him
"Please don't take it as an insult,
I'm more than a friend to you, Mr. Lehman.
But this year . . .
they've made me another offer.
I wish you the best, and my respects to your wife."

Respects to your wife?
Another offer?
I wish you the best?

What darned better was possible
for him, for Mayer Lehman,
if any upstart had the courage
—the arrogance!—
to steal his customers from him?
In his potato mind
it had never
ever
for one moment
occurred to him
that twenty-four plantations
instead of rising to twenty-five, twenty-seven, or thirty
might drop
like now
to twenty-three . . . and perhaps twenty-two, or even lower than
        twenty.
In short
was there therefore
some real possibility
of Lehman Brothers
taking a step back?

Sudden identity crisis
for a tuber:
the new prospect
was unthinkable.

He wrote his brother Emanuel nothing about it
was always cheerful with Babette.
said nothing to Aunt Rosa.
And as often happens

to someone who keeps something to himself
Mayer Lehman
lost sleep.
As soon as he closed his eyes
he dreamed
immediately
—who knows why—
about his father's cattle shed
over in Germany, in Rimpar:
a wonderful timber cattle shed
—put it up by Henry, beam by beam—
chock-full
of goats heifers and bulls
on each of which
strangely
the family brand did not appear
but instead
—folly of dreams—
the words *first choice*.
And if that were not enough
the animals found
neither hay nor oats nor forage
in the mangers
since their food
was bales of white cotton.
In these very curious stalls
Mayer paces
step by step
until he distinctly hears
his father
crying.
He runs to him
kneels to comfort him,
but old Abraham Lehmann
—with two n's even in the dream—
grabs him by the arm
and pushes him away
shouting
"Look what you've done, Bulbe*:*
you've left the door of my cattle shed open!
Look, you villain: they're stealing my cattle!"
And there indeed
with a thunderous din

all the animals
goats heifers and bulls
were rushing out
in a matter of a moment.
And the stall is more than empty: deserted.

Nightmares of a tuber.

And so Mayer decided to act.
Eliminating
the slightest risk
of leaving the cattle shed doors open.

For one thing
he had to secure his customers:
there were twenty-four plantations
and twenty-four they would remain,
including that of Oliver Carlington
who—he was sure—would return with head bent.

And if his brother Henry
had once hung up
outside the shop
the sign "REDUCED PRICES FOR FAVORED CUSTOMERS"
Mayer Lehman
hung up no sign
but did more and better:
he revised the price list
inventing conditions
unprecedented
unrefusable
and
so as not to lose his sleep altogether,
planned
to invite to dinner
one by one
all his customers
explaining
one by one
that the offer
—unique and unrefusable—
was valid only
on condition that

they signed
a long-term
and binding commitment
to the Lehman Brothers
excluding competitors.

And so the dances begin:
the turkey pie with pomegranate
     "Would you like a taste?"
and then the green tomato sauce
     "Mr. Tennyson, another helping?"
and the chicken fricassee
     "My wife goes crazy over it!"
and the beetroot puree
     "Mr. Robbinson, can I tempt you?"
and the duck stew
     "Another dish, it's delicious."
and the pheasant soup
     "Unforgettable!"
and then of course
spiced aniseed cake
with a sip of rare liqueur.

All this gastronomic
contractual ceremony
multiplied
for each of the twenty-four old suppliers,
each of which
on average
takes around three luncheons
to understand
and another two at least
to capitulate
from which he reckons
that overall
the business operation
so as not to lose his sleep altogether
is equivalent
to around a hundred and twenty luncheons
namely
a hundredweight of turkey with pomegranate
     "Would you like a taste?"
two barrels of tomato sauce

"Mr. Tennyson, another portion?"
a whole chicken coop in fricassee
   "My wife goes crazy over it!"
three casks of beetroot puree
   "Mr. Robbinson, can I tempt you?"
a massacre of pond ducks
   "Another dish, it's delicious."
the extinction of all pheasants in Alabama
   "Unforgettable!"
but especially
above all
in pride of place
industrial quantities
of spiced aniseed cake
soaked in rare liqueur
so rare
as to flow more plentifully than the Mississippi.

Fatness of a tuber.

But since
persistence always pays off,
Mayer Lehman
brings home the result:
Oliver Carlington returns to the fold
and twenty-four cotton suppliers
are transformed
into twenty-four exclusive contracts
of varying length
generally around twenty years,
which means
literally
a guarantee
that whatever happens
whatever might occur
Lehman Brothers
will remain
masters of the market
cotton king
beyond doubt
beyond dispute
and if anyone seriously wants to question it
an invitation to lunch is enough

and in this respect
Lehman wins:
there is no competition.

The shed doors
are now
shut and bolted.

The twenty-four contracts
are framed
and hung in the dining room,
on the walls,
over the fireplace
around that portrait
of a much thinner Mayer.

Meanwhile that evening
having hung up
the last frame
with the twenty-fourth contract
Mayer Lehman
stretched out on his bed
staring at the ceiling
thought that now after all
things were going truly well.
He had a family.
An office in Montgomery.
An office in New York.
Bundles of banknotes in the safe.
Twenty-four cotton suppliers in the South
and fifty-one buyers in the North,
all sweetened by sugar.
And lulled by these thoughts
he was about to fall
peacefully asleep
when a chill breeze
for a fraction of a second
twitched an ear:
there was only one thing in the world that could ruin everything
namely a war
between North and South.
But it was just an ugly thought,
one of those that twitch an ear before sleep.

He put it out of his mind
and
at last
calmly
dozed off.

16
A glaz biker

The first gunshot of the War of Secession
wakens Mayer Lehman
before dawn
three days after Montgomery is proclaimed
capital of the states of the South.
Yesterday
a man as calm even as Doctor Everson,
who until a year ago in New Orleans
was treating slave children for measles,
was shouting
"Cotton salutes North America!"
in the street
and waving the new flag.

Drafted into the army
off for the front:
exempt only
those who can pay 300 dollars
among whom the Lehman brothers.

The first gunshot of the War of Secession
wakens Mayer Lehman in Montgomery
his thoughts fixed on the cotton warehouses.
He throws open the windows:
Montgomery has gone crazy
banners and flags
folk in the street celebrate the war
posters everywhere with Jefferson Davis:
the rebellion has begun

the Cotton States are leaving the Union
the plantation states
of the slaves
of the trusties
of the owners of farms and estates
the states of the South
of the Lehman brothers:
off, out, away from America.
Independence!
"Cotton salutes North America!"

The first gunshot of the War of Secession
wakens Emanuel Lehman in New York
with his thoughts fixed on the company buyers:
if North and South
suddenly split
how can the Lehmans remain in between?
Just like that
a wall is raised
between Roundhead Deggoo
and Perfecthands
how will cotton be turned into banknotes?
He throws open the windows:
New York is going crazy
a music box out of tune
banners and flags
folk in the street celebrate the war
posters everywhere with Abraham Lincoln:
the hour of reckoning is nigh
the Industrial States want justice
away with slavery, away with privileges
everybody equal: Constitution and Rights!
And those who won't accept it
will pay with blood
for America is one
and with a single president!

A race to join the army
in Montgomery as in New York:
officers enlist with tailored uniforms
and ordinary folk with uniforms approved by the regiment.
Caps, bayonets, guns
cannon, artillery, muskets

North against South
South against North
marching compact
responding united
Abraham Lincoln for the Union
Jefferson Davis for the Confederacy
in the middle
between the two
squeezed
trapped
like a glass
a vast
mountain
of cotton.

Emanuel Lehman's father-in-law
in New York
Louis Sondheim
tall, white-haired, rabbi's beard
eagerly supports
Abraham Lincoln:
"If the South wins
the factories will close, and then
dear Emanuel
you won't sell another pound of cotton!"

Mayer Lehman's father-in-law
in Montgomery
Isaac Newgass
sitting in his armchair
surrounded by eight sons:
"If the North wins
they'll close the plantations, and then
dear Mayer
you won't have a single pound of cotton!"

In the middle
between the two
squeezed
trapped
like a glass
the Lehman brothers.

In Liberty Street
the young children of a New York arm
learn by memory
the Northerners' hymn,
and know how to recite it
with their hands on their hearts.

On the main street of Montgomery
Aunt Rosa watches the parade:
with her hand on her heart
there are also two spinning tops
aged ten or not much less,
one who sings the hymn at the top of his voice
the other murmurs it on his lips,
and it hardly matters that even in this case
Dreidel nicknamed "the silent one"
has broken his law of silence
when it was least appropriate to do so
and having jumped on the stage in the square
and had shouted that he hated the flag
causing general embarrassment.

In New York
in the carriage
before a fund-raising dinner
for the Northern army
Pauline Sondheim
Mrs. Lehman
would not hear mention of certain scum:
"*I warn you, Emanuel: I forbid you*
to tell anyone
even inadvertently
that we have an office still open
down there in that despicable place
where they keep blacks chained up
and your sister-in-law probably even whips them."

In Montgomery
in the carriage
before a piano recital
to equip the Southern army with boots
Babette Newgass
Mrs. Lehman

makes it clear which side she supports:
"I want you, Mayer, to fix a banner
on the shop and on the front of our house,
and flags wherever possible,
against that Abraham Lincoln."

In the middle
between children and wives
squeezed
trapped
like a glass
are the Lehman brothers.

In the third month of war
Teddy Perfecthands Wilkinson
has closed his factory:
the workforce
—paid folk: salaried, not slaves—
are all drafted
—conscripted—
since he doesn't have
300 dollars a head to pay.
Everyone to war, for the North!
Railroad lines blown up, stations on fire
contracts cancelled:
there's no need for cotton in wartime!
Roundhead Deggoo
and all the slaves at Smith & Gowcer
are forced to fill cartridges:
munitions, fuses, and gunpowder;
plantation closed, set on fire
battlefield:
soldiers sleep
where raw cotton had once been.
Everyone to war, for the South!
Contracts annulled:
there's no need for cotton in wartime!
In the middle
between the two
squeezed
trapped
like a glass
the Lehman brothers.

Of twenty-four plantations that sell them cotton
eight are set on fire
nine bankrupt
seven survive, through determination and force of arms.

Of their fifty-one buyers
thirty have closed
ten are at war
eleven survive, through determination and force of arms.

The South no longer sells cotton to the North.
The North no longer buys cotton from the South.
The Lehman office in Montgomery
closes its shutters:
draws its curtains, double locks.
The Lehman office at 119 Liberty Street
broken windows
sign set on fire
during the New York riots:
barricades
against the war
against the crisis
against the North
against the South
against Union and Confederacy
against those who don't pay
against those who don't sell.
In the middle
between the two
squeezed
trapped
like a glass
the Lehman brothers.

Emanuel Lehman
in New York
he who is an arm
does not give in: he wants to act.
He cares about money
he cares about business
only cotton
only cotton
to save what can be saved:

amid the gunfire
(while 120,000 die at Chattanooga)
a Lehman
desperately
(while 70,000 die at Atlanta)
loads
(while 40,000 die at Savannah)
700 tons of cotton
onto a ship for Europe
where there's no war
where there's no Union or Confederacy
no Northerners or Southerners
but above all
where
cotton
is still sold!

Mayer Lehman
at the same time
in Montgomery
he who is *Kish Kish* and *Bulbe*
a sentimental potato
wholeheartedly
defends
Alabama where he lives
and amid the gunfire
(while 50,000 die in Georgia)
a Lehman
heroically
(while 70,000 die at New Orleans)
proclaims
(while 20,000 die in Virginia)
"I, Mayer Lehman, defender of the South!"
and with Lehman money
frees prisoners
with Lehman money
funds armaments
with Lehman money
supports widows, orphans, wounded
but above all
he runs to the defense
of what is left of cotton!

And it is here that
without knowing it
amid the gunfire
Lehman Brothers
manages
miraculously
to stay on its feet
since
while half of America falls to pieces
in this or that direction
—North
—South
—Union
—Confederacy
—Abraham Lincoln
—Jefferson Davis
the two brothers
Emanuel and Mayer
keep their flag high
and at the end of the mayhem
in a sea of debris
just
one
glass
remains standing.

17
Yom Kippur

Everything has stopped.
Nothing is moving.
Could the world have come to an end?

The ticking pendulum
reflects
a yellow glow
across
the wallpaper.

The silence is devastating.
Not even the birds
have a voice any longer
there, outside,
they have lost it
at the sight of fire and flames
as far as the eye can see
in every direction.

The fine cotton curtains
sewn
by Aunt Rosa
are drawn
behind the open
but motionless
windows:
there is not a stirring of wind.

Everything has stopped.
Nothing moves.
Could the world have come to an end?
This surreal peace
sticks like glue
to the ornaments
and to the rugs
and to the stucco plasterwork
of the grand house on the main street in Montgomery
besieged
first by soldiers
now by silence.

All is still
on this afternoon
of the day of *Yom Kippur*
when sins are solemnly confessed
and the *shofar* sounds in the Temple.
Not today.
It will not sound today.
Silence has taken control,
and will not let itself be stained.

Emanuel Lehman
standing

by the piano.
Black suit.
Since the war began
he had not been seen
here in Alabama.
He fills his pipe with tobacco.
Presses it with his finger.
Lights it.
Puffs. Inhales.
Lets a spiral of smoke
out through his nose
that swirls up
toward the chandelier.

Mayer Lehman
sitting on the sofa
several yards away
counts the planks of the floor
under the chairs
under the table
along the walls
carefully
concentrating
without losing count
without losing attention.

Sooner or later
one of the two
will have to begin
on this afternoon
of the day of *Yom Kippur*
when sins are solemnly confessed
and, if the Almighty so wishes,
you may be forgiven.
But between an arm and a potato
it's not easy
to decide who begins,
above all if the arm has a touch of arthritis
and the garden around the potato has been bombed.

And yet.
And yet
once upon a time

in Rimpar, over there, in Bavaria
there was a cattle dealer
who in very few words
used to say
"if the sky wishes to rain,
it matters not
which cloud begins."

So
in the Lehman house
the storm of *Yom Kippur*
began
by chance
when the arm
noticed some music on the piano
on which was written "MISS EVELINE DURR"
and this
apart from reminding him of ivory-bashing little girls
was enough
to give a pulse to the arm:
"Are you still doing business
with that scoundrel John Durr?"

"I think we had agreed:
you're in charge in New York, I in Alabama."

"I asked if you're in league
with John Durr, whom I dislike."

"John Durr is in the cotton trade."

"John Durr is in the trade of whatever suits him."

"John Durr is involved in business like us."

"John Durr is not one bit like us:
involvement in business is not enough to be like the Lehmans."

"Why then, who are the Lehmans?"

"The Lehmans are not traders, they are dealers."

"And John Durr deals in cotton."

"John Durr doesn't deal, John Durr just sells cheap."

"You don't like John Durr because he's not Jewish."

"There, in fact, you're right: he's not Jewish."

*"And your industrialists in the North,
aren't they all Protestants?"*

*"But they buy, they give us their money:
we're not giving our money to them.
You, however, are using Lehman money to make money with a non-Jew."*

"Jew or non-Jew, what does that have to do with it?"

"It is crucial. Or are you forgetting who we are?"

*"If you want to do business only with Jews,
then I'm no longer interested. Money is something else,
money doesn't look at who is circumcised and who isn't.
John Durr moves money,
Lehman needs him: long live John Durr."*

"All right, we remove the family surname."

"What do you want to remove it for?"

"Our father's name can't be put wherever you want."

*"But hold on, haven't you been using our money
to finance the army in the North?"*

"And haven't you been using it for the army in the South?"

*"I financed uniforms, you financed weapons: there's a difference.
The soldiers of the South had bayonets,
those of the North had machine guns:
the money to buy them came from New York,
and therefore also from us, also from you."*

*"I couldn't do otherwise.
And anyway, I know for sure that you obtained explosives
for the Southerners."*

*"So in other words we've been funding both
at the same time, no?"*

*"Our father sold cattle:
did you ever hear him asking a customer
what side he was on?"*

*"Now you're contradicting yourself.
Well done, you're right: our father
he would have done business with John Durr."*

And here
Emanuel turned pale,
as it was right that he should,
finding himself cornered
by an enterprising potato
with no mean gift
for argument
whose pride
urged him even one step further:
*"I at least sell cotton with John Durr,
and you, to what kinds of dealings do you want to stoop to?"*

The nature of an arm
however
is irrepressible
even when it finds itself in a minority.
And though *Yom Kippur*
is a day for the acknowledgment of sins,
Emanuel Lehman
could not stop himself
from exclaiming:
*"Hell! What kind of potato are you?
There's been a war, Mayer
everything has changed:
that damn cotton is finished,
it's finished! It's finished!
It's all different now!"*

"Oh yes? What's different?"

*"I don't know. But whatever it is
it's worth finding out first."*

And he felt pleased with himself.
For, as sometimes happens,
an arm
can for one moment
lose its usual meanness of articulation
and obtain
a wondrous sense
that its muscles
are not just formed through toil and burden,
but can even whirl about
—unless proved otherwise—
like the creative arms
of an acrobat and a dancer.

This is what happened
in that drawing room at *Yom Kippur*
to a New York arm
called Emanuel Lehman
who
could suddenly surprise himself
with a light
about-face
worthy of a head,
such as that of his brother Henry.

What a shame though
that on the other side
there was a tuber
exhausted moreover by a war
that had made the surrounding landscape barren:
"So let me understand:
I should stop doing business with John Durr
and go off in search of something you don't know?"

"Tell me Mayer: who invented cotton?"

"What sort of question is that? Cotton has always been there."

"Actually, no. Someone whom we don't know
at some point
woke up one morning
and thought of using that plant
—that very plant!—

to make something to wear out of it!
You understand?"

"Understand what?"

"I want to invent another cotton,
before everyone else, before the others.
That's how money is made, Mayer,
not with the cotton of John Durr,
which everyone now has.
I want to go somewhere else!"

"Where?"

"I've no idea."

"Exactly."

And here it was obvious to both
that they wouldn't get out of it easily
for the simple fact that there were two of them,
and with two votes,
if there's no agreement
there's no majority.
They gazed instinctively
toward the ledge of the open window,
but where no one was sitting
with his legs drawn together
and an arm up at the back of his neck.

Emanuel had the distinct feeling that the matter would not be
    resolved.
And Mayer without saying it
had the same impression.
For the first time
they were on opposite banks of the same river.

And just so it couldn't be said that he hadn't tried everything,
Emanuel had a go with this card:
"Money sits in people's wallets, Mayer:
if you want them to give it to us,
we have to be ready,
ready to give in exchange . . ."

"Give what?"

"Who knows.
What they're looking for. What they need.
Mayer: anything whatsoever."

"And this is exactly what I don't like."

"You don't understand anything: you're a dead weight."

"And you're a threat."

These were
the last words
spoken before
a very long silence.

If, on the other hand,
rather than sitting in a drawing room
they had been in the fine Temple
at the end of the street
now smoke-blackened by the war
the *shofar* would already have sounded.
Each person's sins
would have been righted,
and another *Yom Kippur* would have come to an end
with its twenty-five hours of penance.

If they had been living
in normal times
they would have ended their fast
with a blissful lunch.

But the cook had died in the war.
And the servants were no longer slaves.

So that potato and arm went without dinner.
And they pondered
separately
over the first real crisis
in the history of Lehman Brothers.

18
Hasele

For several years now
Emanuel and Mayer
have avoided talking to each other.

Emanuel in New York.
Mayer in Alabama
so nothing has changed
even though everything has changed.
Everything.

Meanwhile, ever since the Northerners won the war
Montgomery
is no longer the same.
The Lehman Brothers office with its black and yellow sign
is still there
of course
with the handle that is suddenly sticking again.
That hasn't changed.
Nor has Mayer Lehman's veranda changed
in that grand house on the main street of Montgomery
where his wife, Babette,
gives piano lessons to her children:
Sigmund, Hattie, Settie, Benjamin . . .
"You're the children of Mr. Lehman Cotton"
Roundhead Deggoo once used to tell them
when he still went about
with his straw hat on his head
at one time
a few years ago
yet it seems like a thousand years
when there were still plantations in Alabama
and there were still slaves.

Ever since the Northerners won the war
ever since Abraham Lincoln
by signing his name on a sheet of paper
in a second
had freed

in a second
all slaves
ever since then
Montgomery is no longer the same.
Doctor Everson
who treated slave children in New Orleans for measles
shakes his head
as he once did for the yellow fever:
"Freedom suffocates
when swallowed all at once, Mr. Lehman:
like a chunk of turkey that's too big
it gets stuck in the throat. And if, God forbid that I'm right . . ."

Roundhead Deggoo
is no longer a slave:
thanks to the North, to the war, and to Abraham Lincoln
he's a free man, now.
No longer forced to live in a slave hut.
No more food kitchen
no chains for the hotheads
no labor under the sun
and whippings on the back for speaking out of place.
And yet.
And yet Roundhead is no longer seen about.
He has disappeared, Roundhead, vanished.
Even at the Baptist chapel
on Sunday morning
he's no longer seen playing the organ
with those hands too large
that play two keys instead of just one.

And on Mayer Lehman's large veranda,
where his wife, Babette,
gives piano lessons to her children,
one evening the two youngest
tugged her by the sleeve
to ask if
by chance
Roundhead
was dead.
Babette didn't stop playing.
She smiled at them
let them sit beside her,

and as she played
—who knows why—
she told them a story:
"Once upon a time there was a rabbi
who knew all the teachings of the Torah by heart
knew every single one
even the most boring and the most terrible.
But that rabbi's tongue was so fast
that he gabbled and was very funny
so that everyone searched him out for company
they called him "Reb Lashon"
which meant "Rabbi Tongue"
and they laughed like mad as soon as he began.
Each evening at the Temple the rabbi prayed:
Riboyne shel oylem
help me, so that my tongue might not speak so fast.
And one day after many years his prayer was heard.
From that day the rabbi spoke normally
and the people could understand his teachings
which were so boring and terrible
that gradually
one by one
they all left him alone
and in the evening at the Temple he raised his eyes and said:
Riboyne shel oylem
you were wrong to make my tongue normal
for when I spoke badly I spoke to everyone
whereas now . . .
I don't even have a dog to talk to!"

But the children
didn't understand a word
and they looked at each other
rather doubtfully.

This would have been no great problem
if it were not that
the one who seemed most puzzled
was sweet Sigmund,
the eldest and favorite child,
who couldn't really understand
whether Roundhead was actually dead
or had become some kind of rabbi.

Now, this tender uncertainty in his eyes
—he of all of them!—
could hardly leave his parents unmoved
knowing that the boy was not like the others
in the well-studied plan for positions of command.

He had been cautiously forgiven
for the innocence of his younger years
and his childish love of games,
but this concession had been granted only
in the impatient anticipation that he would move on
as soon as possible
to the cynicism of adulthood
and of an adulthood in commerce.
Besides, there cannot be light alone
in the eye of anyone who does business:
there must always be an area of shadow,
to ensure he won't let himself be tricked.
Yet this shadow was very late appearing
in the oh so tender eye
of Sigmund Lehman, darling of Alabama:
a bright sparkling light
radiated from his face
without the slightest hint of spite,
his was such an amiable tenderness
that the adults in the family grew anxious.
Noticeably anxious.
Sigmund, in short, was expected
as time passed
to display some kind of distinction
some intuition,
some degree of excellence—whatever it might be—
not to say some small scrap of commercial acumen.
He grew up, yes, as a paragon
but of generosity.
An eager philanthropist
a model of self-sacrifice
and would have willingly held himself up as an example
except that his future was not in asylums or in hospices
but in the cutthroat arena of commerce.
Instead,
even in the most ordinary games
Sigmund showed himself to be pitifully helpless

so pure in that babyish smile
and unfortunately
so easily tricked in any form of barter.
He even handed over ten puppets in exchange for two donuts
and, worse still, was publicly proud of it
so that his father punished him by locking him
in a poky cupboard under the staircase.
It was a cruel decision,
but Mayer didn't regret it for one moment,
partly because of the harm it would cause to the company image
and partly because he hoped wholeheartedly
that the injustice inflicted might make Sigmund feel some resentment.

It was useless.
From the dark grotto where he had been incarcerated
Sigmund sang
merrily
the whole time
making up songs about little rabbits
and when Aunt Rosa
went down to free the prisoner
he pleaded to her:
"Please: can I stay in punishment a little longer?"

And from then on
it was clear to everyone
that
with this little rabbit
they had a problem.

19
Shvarts zup

Ever since the Northerners won the war
there is no market for sugar.
No slaves
no work
no goods

no profits:
with sweetness ended
bitterness has begun.

And sugar indeed is no longer sold,
but there's investment in coffee.
More profitable.

The problem is that, like cotton, you could see sugar.
But not coffee. It grows in Mexico, in Nicaragua.
As well as lower down, in Brazil.
In those places, maybe there are still people
with backs to break
while here—with slaves now free—
everyone expects to be paid.

So coffee is worth it.
There are those who buy it, load it on ships
and send it wherever,
ready to be sold
by those who can raise the price
can save on transport
can keep suppliers happy.
In short, by those in trade
who have a taste for bargaining.

"Lehman Brothers is a leader in cotton.
You've been successful with sugar.
With coffee, who is stopping you from trying?"
These are the words
with which Miguel Muñoz
a Mexican bear with more gold on him than a Madonna in procession
tries to convince a New York arm
by pouring out in front of him a whole sack
of fragrant dark beans
". . . My coffee is first choice:
if you don't trust me, come and see."

And Emanuel Lehman
has gone to see:
he has traveled down to Mexico
since *I haven't come to America*
to let myself be caged up.

Beneath a torrential rain
accompanied by a Mexican bear covered with gold
Emanuel Lehman walks through coffee fields
among tall trees laden with dark red dots:
hundreds and hundreds of women and children
watched by guards with dogs
fill whole wagons to be taken to market
shaking trunks and branches
pulling horses
whipping donkeys
and if a fight breaks out
there are gunshots.
The glinting figure of Miguel Muñoz
surveys his troops
like a general
and complains only about the mud
when it splatters his white suit:
"So you like the landscape, Mr. Lehman?
Just think how beautiful the coffee plant is:
it grows only around the Equator . . .
So if the whole world wants to drink cups of it
it has to buy it either from us or in Africa . . .
In Ethiopia, they say, prices are ridiculous:
the natives there spit blood
for a bowl of soup and a hut.
Here it's not so good.
But since the journey from Mexico is shorter,
no Ethiopian can compete with me,
at least in the American market:
I'll sell you the sacks, at the price I want,
after which the market, if you wish, is all yours:
from Florida to Canada, God knows how much coffee it will take,
and Lehman Brothers can swim in it!"

Who knows whether Miguel Muñoz
has also sold the coffee
that Mayer Lehman is now drinking
in Alabama
at this precise instant
never imagining
for one moment
that his brother Emanuel

is under the pouring rain
doing business in Mexico.

Perhaps Mayer Lehman
in the meantime
from morning to evening
is running here and there
around Montgomery
and beyond: around the whole of Alabama
as far as the Mississippi and beyond: to Baton Rouge
trying to convince himself
that the war is not lost
and that the South—with its blessed cotton—
is after all
still on its feet
not yet dead.

"How much cotton are you giving me with the next harvest
Mr. Tennyson?
Let's sign the agreement
just as before, like it used to be."
"But what are you saying Mr. Lehman?
What cotton? What harvest?"
"I'll buy all of it
at the usual price."
"There's been a war in the meantime
hadn't you noticed?"
"Yes but it's gone, it's finished:
your plantation is still there
I'll buy . . ."
"Open your eyes, Lehman: look around!
What hasn't been ruined
is ruined all the same!
Here we have to start all over again:
start from scratch, rebuild everything!"

In the carriage
returning to Montgomery
his horse tired
Mayer Lehman this evening
for the first time
looks at the landscape:

plantations closed
with a FOR SALE sign
storehouses burned down
huts where the slaves once used to live: empty
fences broken
land forgotten
carcasses of carts
and above all
everywhere
silence
like a great vast cemetery
as large as the whole of Alabama
—maybe the whole of the South—
derelict
lost
dead.
In the carriage
returning to Montgomery
his horse tired
Mayer Lehman this evening
thinks
that maybe
it is like that time
fifteen years ago
—Henry was still here—
when the fire broke out
and it was they
the Lehman Brothers
who brought Montgomery back to life.

Next day
in a dark suit
beneath two flags
Mayer Lehman
is standing
smiling
—he, *Kish Kish*, knows how to do it—
before the table of the governor
who, wearing spectacles on his nose in the French style
stares at him puzzled
as though looking at a madman:
*"Reformulate your proposal
Mr. Lehman:*

I don't think I've understood."
"Of course, Excellency.
We will reconstruct.
From the start
all over again
everything
as it was before . . ."
"Excuse me, wait!
You will rebuild with money from the state?"
"Yes sir: you give us the capital.
And Lehman Brothers will rebuild Alabama from new, plus . . ."
"Wait, stop:
so far as I know
Lehman Brothers
sells cotton."
"We are leaders in the raw cotton trade
Excellency
it is therefore for us . . ."
"Not so fast, please:
you're talking in such a hurry that I cannot follow.
I, governor of Alabama
would have to provide the capital to rebuild . . .
to a cloth company?"
"We are not tailors, Excellency:
we are businessmen."
"But experts in cotton."
"Yes, sir, that's right:
we started out with cotton.
Like you, after all:
isn't it true that you once had a plantation?
If a governor can start out from cotton
then cannot a bank be created from cotton?
Trust me."

And on this "trust me"
Mayer Lehman produces
such a wondrous smile
so certain
so sure
so credible
that the governor of Alabama
in fact
submits

indeed more: he *trusts*
and by trusting he entrusts
to an ex-potato
millions of dollars of capital.

On just one condition:
that over the door
with the handle that sticks
the signboard be changed
once again
to:
LEHMAN BROTHERS
and
next to it
BANK FOR ALABAMA.

Written in brown.
The color of the coffee that comes from Mexico.

20
Der boykhreder

A is for Atlanta
B is for Boston
C is for Chicago
D is for Detroit
E is for El Paso
F is for Fort Worth
G is for Greensboro
H is for Halifax
I is for Indianapolis
J is for Jacksonville
K is for Kansas City
L is for Los Angeles
M is for Memphis
N is for New Orleans
O is for Oakland
P is for Pittsburgh

Q is for Quincy in Illinois
R is for Raleigh
S is for Saint Louis
T is for Toronto
U is for Uniontown
V is for Virginia B.
W is for Washington
X is for Xenia in Ohio
Y is for Youngstown
Z is for Zenith in West Virginia

Philip
has learned the alphabet
on the cities with which his father trades.

The list
which he recites from memory
without the slightest hesitation
obviously doesn't include New York
for the simple reason
that New York is home
not a place for business.

To tell the truth
in Philip's alphabet
there isn't Montgomery either,
since his mother
doesn't think it so important
to let everyone know
that we come from there.

Especially now,
with the current atmosphere of excitement.
Ever since the Northerners won the war
New York
seems even more beautiful.
119 Liberty Street
with its brand-new
black and yellow sign
has never seen so many visitors
of every kind
since
Emanuel Lehman

son of a cattle dealer
became one of the founders
of the New York Cotton Exchange.
Arriving here in New York
where no one has ever seen a cotton field
there's all the cotton in America
all the cotton on the market
all the cotton it is possible to sell:
since the war has brought an end
in one fell swoop
to the arrogance of the South
and the disgrace of slavery:
enough, finished
all free, all equal
Abraham Lincoln has won
Washington has won
but especially
especially New York
where everything
everything
everything
not just cotton:
everything
is turned into banknotes so much so
that King Cotton
—the gold of the South—
as Emanuel says:
"Makes money, of course
but doesn't make you rich."

Ever since the Northerners won the war
New York
is no longer the same:
one spectacle after another
one surprise after another
always more
always more
always better
and Emanuel Lehman
can feel it
he can sense it
in the air
as he

and his wife, Pauline,
take their children
Milton, Philip, Harriett, and Eveline
to the Hebrew school.
Perfectly dressed
neatly groomed
sitting upright
well-mannered
they will be in class with the children of the Sachses
of the Singers
of the Goldmans
of the Blumenthals:
like them they will have their *Bar Mitzvah* at the Temple
like them they will learn to ride horses
like them they will try out that new sport
brought to New York by Miss Mary Outerbridge
called tennis.
And like them they will, of course, play the violin
because every New York family
has a child who plays the violin:
the violin is delightful
"it enhances the profile"
it is played standing up
in front of everyone
and is a modern instrument,
for tomorrow, slender
not a colossal bulk
like pianos on the verandas of the South.

Philip Lehman
is not yet six
and already plays perfectly.
He is the best in class
the best at the Hebrew school
the best at choir practices
can already read and write
in Hebrew in German and in English
he can count up to a hundred
in Hebrew in German and in English
and at parties
to everyone's surprise
his mother tells him to point out on an atlas
that tiny dot

called Rimpar, Bavaria.
Philip could also point out
Montgomery, Alabama,
but that—according to his mother—
would be of less interest to guests.
"Now, Philip,
let everyone hear
how clever you are in economics:
what are the family's two treasures?"
"Cotton!"
"Cotton?
What do you mean, Philip?
Listen carefully!
What does your father always say?
Lehman Brothers is built
on two pillars
and these are . . ."
"Coffee and industry!"
"Very good, Philip!
Now go off and play."

Coffee and industry.
Since the Northerners won the war
New York
has gone literally
crazy
over a dark liquid called *coffee*
and over a dark place called *factory.*

Next to the Cotton Exchange
they have opened the Coffee Exchange.
Emanuel Lehman is part of it
as are the Goldmans
the Blumenthals
the Sachses
the Singers:
Baruch HaShem for King Coffee!
A wondrous replacement for cotton:
coffee starts off from New York
negotiated
signed
paid for
loaded

shipped, away, 'round half the world.
There's demand for it in Europe
in Canada, all over the world.
Lehman Brothers had twenty-four cotton plantations
now it has twenty-seven coffee suppliers.
But coffee too
as Emanuel Lehman says:
"Earns money, of course
but doesn't make you rich."

What makes you rich
really rich
Emanuel knows
and his father-in-law confirms
is the great rush of industry,
all to be financed:
the whole of America has to be filled
all of it
with warehouses and factories
for textiles
machinery
chemicals
pharmaceuticals
from North to South
from East to West
distilleries iron and steelworks
from Washington as far as Los Angeles and Sacramento
from the Atlantic right across to the Pacific.
Even Teddy Perfecthands Wilkinson
has changed his business:
to hell with cotton
he now manufactures iron nuts and bolts,
and brings in twice as much money as before.

"One moment, Mr. Lehman:
so far as I know
Lehman Brothers sells cotton"
the Chief Inspector of the Union of Manufacturers says
when Emanuel Lehman
offers to act as intermediary, broker:
I supply raw materials, you process them,
and if you wish I could also build your factories:
"Yes, but why on earth, excuse me,

should we give capital for building factories . . .
to a cloth company?"
"I will not permit you to insult me!"
Emanuel shouted
furiously.
Though almost fifty
he is still an arm.
"I don't know, Lehman:
I want to think about it."
"Of course sir:
I'll come back in a week."

And Emanuel returned
exactly six days later
with the same offer:
"I don't know, Lehman:
I need to give it further thought."

And so on
every six days
unperturbed
with the strategy of an arm
tireless
but all the same
in this case
desperately
pointless
until
one evening
stretched out on his bed
before falling asleep
Emanuel Lehman
felt a breeze
twitch his ear
like the best of solutions
and it was a breeze
that blew from Montgomery
with a vague aroma of potato *Kish Kish*
so strong and clear
that he set off immediately
the next morning
at dawn

for that small room in the South
with the handle that once again sticks.

"Listen carefully, Mayer
this is not a social call.
I've decided something
and it concerns you:
you can't remain here any longer
you're needed in New York."

"Me in New York?
We agreed that I would stay here:
me in Montgomery
you up there
in Liberty Street."

"Hell! What kind of potato are you?
There's been a war, Mayer
everything has changed:
that damn cotton is finished
it's all different now!"
There's the whole of America to industrialize!
And anyway, I've decided:
you have to come, I need you and that's it."

"I'm rebuilding Alabama
with money from the state."

"You can do that just as well from New York!
In fact: you'll do it better from there.
Everything now happens in New York.
Listen, I'm your elder brother,
I know what's right for you."

And at that moment
in the rectangle of the door
appears the ever-silent face of Dreidel
a little over fifteen years old
with legs as skinny as two dry twigs.

It is curious how sometimes
words

melt like snow
before a single ray of sunlight:
something of the kind
happened in that room.

And not because Dreidel
did anything particular
at first.
Nor did he break his rigid silence.

Quite simply
that young boy at the door
did no more than stare, long, at his Uncle Emanuel
in a most unusual way
and stared equally long at his Uncle Mayer
before then walking confidently in
and sitting down
not at the table
nor on the sofa
nor in any of the armchairs
but
on the ledge of the open window,
with his legs drawn together
and an arm up at the back of his neck.

Mayer stares at his brother,
just in time to read in his eyes
the same identical thought,
the mathematical
absurd
certainty
that this young boy is a puppet
moved
who knows how
by a victim of yellow fever.

Equidistant between a head and an arm,
in a silence that seems like glue
Mayer *Bulbe* begins to speak
forcing his mouth and lips to obey him:
"We're talking about going to New York,
and going there not as a business
but as a bank.

Emanuel wants to do it, I'm not convinced.
But Henry, there are three of us: you make the majority.
What's your vote? Are you in favor or against?

Henry takes his time.
It is one of the privileges of being a head.

He remains still, seated
on the ledge of the open window,
with his legs drawn together
and an arm up at the back of his neck.

Then says nothing.

Just nods.

And the change is made.

Book Two
Fathers and Sons

1
The Black Hole

Yehuda ben Tema
in the *Ethics of the Fathers*
says:
fifty years to be prudent
sixty to be wise.

Emanuel Lehman
who is halfway between fifty and sixty
feels
without a doubt
both prudent and wise.
And he hasn't the slightest doubt.
Since wisdom for him means action.
And prudence for him also means action.
Which is why
if those are the ingredients
then he
by his actions
keeps a tight hold on them.
And nothing more.

There again, how can anyone not be active
if he lives in the heart of New York?
Everything here is movement,
everything here is action
everything here is energy
and therefore an arm
always feels at home here.

All the more since now
the watchword
has become one, and only one: fuel.

Marvel of the modern age:
how have we managed so many years without thinking about it?
There's only one distinction between man and the gods
and it's the fact that man toils away.
The gods don't labor

they never get out of breath
and this is because higher up
evidently
they have some constant form of energy.
Perfect.
Let this inspire us.
Let's copy their example.
In other words, let's give ourselves, give all humans,
a divine fuel!
Humanity will have no more limits
if we can power motors.

*"This perhaps, who knows,
could be a good investment . . ."*
Emanuel Lehman thought
when Mr. Wilcock, King of Coal,
invited him up North, to the mines,
if only just to see.

"I have to think it over"
Emanuel said to himself,
discovering that an arm
between the age of fifty and sixty
can even give himself time to think.

What a pity that this time
it hasn't lasted long.

Just long enough to see
that even David, the hotheaded son of Aunt Rosa,
though still only in his twenties
runs out of energy after a while
and even manages to doze off,
bringing his antics to a halt
for a few hours.

Incredible to say:
David is like a startled horse
roaming around New York
from Manhattan to the suburbs
and from the suburbs to Queens,
David is in a constant whirl

and has such a burning fire inside
that makes him talk in a strange way:
"Heyyah! Uncle! Hi!
Heyyah! What d'you say? Will it rain?
You're off out? No? Eh?
Staying in? Yes? Me? Well!
Dinner? My mother? Heyyah?
The horse? Where?
I'm off! Back this evening!
Heyyah! Okay! Bye!"

After which
if David is sitting down he's always shifting his legs
and he gets up
and down again
and gets up
and down again
jerking the muscles of his neck
in a kind of intermittent spasm
looks up
looks down
looks up
looks down
and yet, despite all this,
through some law of Nature
even David Lehman
a mechanical agglomerate in the form of a nephew
wonder of late nineteenth-century industry
comes to a halt
at regular intervals
due to an irrepressible need to recharge.
And this stops him! Renders him inactive!
In other words, is bad for him,
as David himself—one fateful evening—told him:
"Uncle sir! Heyyah! May I?
Tired? D'you mind? No?
I've done some figures! Interested? Maybe yes!
Well! How old am I? 24!
And how much do I sleep? 6 hours! A day!
So? D'you follow? Every 4 days one whole day is lost! No? It's a fact!
Every 4 days! One whole day I spend zzzzzzzzzzzzzzzz! Eh?
And in a year? Wait for it! 91! Days! Eh?

Get my point? Sleep! 91 days zzzzzzzzzzzzzzzz!
And in 24 years? You're not going to believe this! 2,190 hours! Or? 6 years!
    Whole years!
And you? More than double! Uncle? You're with me? 15 years! Or almost!
Eh? Crazy! Huh! For 15 years you zzzzzzzzzzzzzzzz!
Okay: just wanted to tell you! Keep well!
I'm off! Bye!"

At times you could throttle even someone dear to you.

There are moments in life
when you realize that from now on
there will be a before and an after:
Emanuel Lehman immediately felt
in the pit of his stomach
that this was the moment.

Not even news of his father's death
over there in Germany at Rimpar
had had such a powerful impact,
and not because it had arrived in a note, written in a few terse words.
Listening to his nephew
during the fifty-seven seconds of that unusually long discourse
marked an unforgettable step
in his existential journey.

It was all true.
Dramatically true.

Or rather: it was even worse,
seeing that the boy's relentless calculation
was based on six hours of sleep:
how could Emanuel admit that he slept for eight?

Left alone in the office
for a decisive face-to-face with his own wretchedness
Emanuel recognized
in effect
that from the time he had landed in America
in effect
he had zzzzzzzzzzzzzzzz for almost ten years.
And the thousand things he could have done
for himself

for Lehman Brothers
for his family
for his country
for its history and its glory
instead of zzzzzzzzzzzzzzzzz
passed before him
so that
he yielded to the insane feeling
of having cheated himself,
and for what?
For a dependence—contemptible and inborn—
on the excessively slow mechanism of rest?

After the abyss he glimpsed the light.

So he got up from his armchair
with the real urge
for a real mission:
if it was not the task of Lehman Brothers to reconfigure man,
then man could—must—be consoled
with a continuous
nonstop
production system
fed by divine fuels
with no more stopping
with no more pauses
with no more zzzzzzzzzzzzzzzzz.
And who in the world could do it if not an arm
urged on by his nephew in a war on sleep?

Here at last was the basis
for saving the whole of humanity,
bidding good-bye to worthy King Cotton,
all the more since at that very moment
his flight of thought led him to realize
that everything in bedrooms was made of cloth:
cloth sheets
cloth cushions pillowslips bedspreads
and so he felt at least responsible
for having covered millions of beds (including his own)
and
this was perhaps the first time
that one of the Lehman brothers

could not hold back a feeling of disgust
at the thought of being
a cotton trader.

Enough.
End of stupor.
End of lullabies.
The only comfort Emanuel could afford himself
was the thought
that at least one part of the Lehman business
was in coffee, the sleeper's foe.
And for this he felt thankful.

But now? What action?

A week later,
a New York arm
faithful to his plan of operation,
left the city
on an urgent business trip
which his brother Mayer preferred to forgo,
evidence of how a southern potato
is not cured by being transplanted north
and prefers
the tender embrace of sleep.

Never mind. Ever onward.
Emanuel left.
Accompanied this time
—since intuition must always be honored—
by an adrenaline-charged kid in his twenties
grandson of a cattle dealer
whose future potential was perhaps underestimated.
Though there was time to put things right.

They traveled two days by coach,
in which David Lehman
overcame the torment of idleness
doing and undoing
four times
the seat covers
and accompanying it all
with a nonstop flow

of *"heyyah," "hey!,"* and *"huh!"*
and other more or less syncopated sounds
of his own very particular creation.

The last *"heyyah"* was just before they descended
down a crag, all mud and rocks,
in front of an eviscerated mountain
that looked like a trepanned corpse
on a surgeon's table.
"Heyyah! Uncle! You've seen? Huh!"
Railroad track and hoists appeared one after the other
the noise was infernal, the smell nauseating,
but most striking of all was the throng
of people from every part of the planet
Chinese, Redskins, Africans, Hispanics
and even numerous whites—*heyyah!*—
the color of whose skin
however
was more or less irrelevant
since each—*heyyah!*—
without distinction—*heyyah!*—
had their faces covered by a layer of soot
black as pitch
thick as a glove
and their white eyes alone stood out. *Huh.*

"In the cotton plantations they were all black . . ."
Emanuel thought
". . . in the coal mines then it makes no difference."
And this might have given rise
to an interesting reflection on race
except that the purpose of their mission
was not philanthropic
but set on the business of coal.

Here is the owner, Mr. Wilcock,
fast in spite of the crutches
he has depended on for ten years
since his leg was blown off in a coal explosion:
the price of modernity,
or perhaps an offering to the mountain.
Not even invalids could stop still
in the great rush of the late nineteenth century.

Mr. Wilcock talked of nothing but coal.
Just the mention of it
brought a thrill
to that triangular pointed face
with its white drooping mustache
on lightly smoked skin:
"*Welcome to Black Hole, the biggest anthracite mine*
in the whole of North America.
If you want to go down and take a look,
you'll have to wear a helmet, like all the miners."
And he led the way,
leaping swiftly over rocks
despite his handicap.

Their experience in the mine was memorable.

And not because two rich white Jews
turned dark-skinned for an hour
stirring an unexpected fondness
for Roundhead Deggoo
a remembrance of Alabama.

There wasn't just this.
The fact is that Emanuel Lehman
was thrilled at the thought
that to provide bread for the great banquet of industry
all those people
from all parts
were scraping the bowels of the earth
and plundering energy itself.
Pure energy.

Holding on with his nephew
to the rusty edge
of a clattering wagon
plummeting fast
Emanuel Lehman
felt not the slightest fear:
but rather a stronger—splendid!—sensation
that from the lowest faces of the earth
miners were extracting not coal
but avalanches of gold ingots, and banknotes,

on which Lehman Brothers would surely lay their hands.
Just to imagine the possibilities
was for Mr. Arm
a kind of panacea
that repaid him
if only in part
for his fifteen years of deep sleep.

His nephew David, on the other hand,
couldn't stop laughing and jumping about:
he felt totally at home
among those tumultuous squads,
he envied them, how they hurled their pickaxes
and crawled along the ground,
and climbed down, and back up,
and hollering inside the mountain
unleashing the fury of an extraordinary echo.
He would have liked to imitate them,
though he didn't
—for respect of the family name—
but just as they were leaving
couldn't resist the urge
and received from Mr. Wilcock
the ultimate honor:
escorted by three Chinese to the end of a gully
he set off two charges of dynamite.
And the pleasure he obtained
was beyond words:
pure energy.

That evening, in fact, he couldn't sleep.

Nor, in the adjoining room, could his uncle.
Far from it.
Awake, with eyes wide open
to make up for the excess of lost time
he read and reread
at least five times
his first contract for coal.

2
Der bankir bruder

Yehuda ben Tema
in the *Ethics of the Fathers*
says:
fifty years to be prudent
sixty to be wise.

Mayer Lehman
is fifty
and doesn't know what prudence is
but if it happens to mean: *"stopping still and watching"*
then perhaps he is prudent.

His father
a cattle merchant
a thousand years ago
—over there in Germany, in Rimpar, Bavaria—
used to say that the prudent man is like those branches
that defy the wind
and refuse to bend.
"If that is so," Mayer thinks
"I'm all right."

Yes.
Because while everyone
is now
going crazy
about doing doing doing
building building building
inventing inventing inventing
Mayer Lehman
stays still.

Right now for example:
over the entrance to the New York office
they've just finished the sign
with the words:
LEHMAN BROTHERS BANK.

They've worked quickly.
Very quickly.

Because the old sign, after all
was just a long narrow rectangle
—as long as the whole frontage—
made of three planks in a line:
LEHMAN the first
BROTHERS the second
and lastly COTTON.

And so.
New York solution:
without too much ado
they just took down the last part on the right.
The last board: COTTON.
It's down there, on the ground
already old
on the street.
In its place they've hauled up a new board
with four letters: BANK.
Looks pretty darned good.
They've pulled it up with ropes
and they've lined it up to the inch
precise, perfect
beside LEHMAN BROTHERS.
The carpenters are now joining the boards
joining them together
joining them with nails
and it's all one:
LEHMAN BROTHERS BANK.

Mayer is sitting there, on a seat, watching them.

What does it mean to be a bank?
For us, what will actually change?

A potato generally reasons calmly:
the long period spent underground
considerably
curtails
its capering on the surface.

And here too
indeed
Mayer *Bulbe*
manages to grasp two simple concepts.

First: when we were in business
people gave us money
and we gave something in exchange.
Now that we're a bank
people give us money just the same
but we give nothing in exchange.
At least not for the moment. Then we'll see.

Second point: when we were in business
if your son asked what you did
you'd show him a roll of cloth
a wagon of sugar
a barrel of coffee
and the boy would generally understand.
Now that we're a bank
whatever words you try to use
your son doesn't understand, he gives up and goes off to play.
Yes. To play.

"After all"
Mayer Lehman thinks
"there must be some reason
why children play at pretending
to be teachers or doctors or painters
but never
ever
come out with 'let's play bankers'
for the simple reason that
the one who plays the part of the banker
has to take money from his friends,
and they have nothing left for buying candy:
so what sort of game is that?"
You try explaining it to children,
that the money in the bank serves for industry.
Try explaining that the system
needs to have a savings fund.
Mayer Lehman
has come to the conclusion

in short
that he'll feel a deep fondness
for this new side of the job
only when he sees with his own eyes
a banker
explain to children
how the banking game works.
And can get them to appreciate it.

Mayer *Bulbe*
ponders much upon it
as he gazes at the surname
on the sign
fixed next to the word *bank*.

His son Arthur
aged two
is sitting on his knee:
he's half a century younger than him
and pulls his beard up and down with his hand.
Mayer doesn't react:
he lets him provoke him.
Perhaps it's because Arthur was born in New York:
in his blood
there's not even a drop
of Germany
or of Alabama.
Arthur, new.
Arthur, brand-new.
Arthur, son of New York.

So that
to see them together
—he and his father—
they are rather like that old sign
LEHMAN BROTHERS
with that new word BANK beside it.
Is that why people laugh as they pass?
They laugh, yes.
And not because Mayer is strangely dressed
as a rich Southerner
with those striped leggings
that here in New York

no one
no one
would wear
ever
not even by accident.

No: what people notice is not his clothing.
It's the fact that Mayer is sitting
stock-still, smiling
there
doing what?
Nothing.
Having his beard pulled.
A strange sight.
Strange and funny that here, in the heart of the business area:
119 Liberty Street
where every minute is a shiny dollar
119 Liberty Street
where everything has a price
119 Liberty Street
where even the flies have a value
here
at 119 Liberty Street
there's a fifty-year-old Jewish millionaire
who is doing absolutely nothing:
sitting like that
in the street like that
with a child on his knees like that
watching an old sign being trodden underfoot
that bears the word: COTTON.
"What do we do with this board?
Shall we throw the old sign away, Mr. Lehman?"
Mayer doesn't answer.
"If you like, we'll cut it up
and you can burn it in the stove:
the wood is old but it's not rotten."
Mayer doesn't answer
he smiles, doesn't say what he thinks:
certainly they wouldn't understand.
"Okay, in that case we'll ask your brother."

Mayer smiles, nods.
Better that way.

Emanuel is an arm, he won't have any objection
and certain notions he doesn't really get:
they don't actually reach him.
Indeed the first thing he did this morning
he—the arm—
was to send out to buy
four buckets of paint
because as soon as the sign is ready
he wants a fresh coat of paint
to be given
straightaway
—but without delay—
straightaway
a fresh coat of paint
straightaway
immediately
since otherwise the new BANK
will be too obvious beside the old LEHMAN BROTHERS
and
"... we will look like a grandmother
with a little girl's bonnet."
The words of Emanuel Lehman
who has no intention
of looking like an old fool.
"If we turn the page, dear Mayer, we turn it for good!"
Perfect.

So?
So fresh paint: new colors
no more of that faded yellow of a cloth store:
"I want big letters now
the color of gold
on a black background.
And you know why, Mayer?
There's a reason, for sure!
I don't do anything by chance:
gold comes out of black
I mean, from the black of coffee
from the black of coal
and then ... from the smoke of locomotives!"

Locomotives.
Each time Emanuel mentions them

—and he mentions them often—
his lips twist into a strange grimace,
as though the hint of a smile
has turned into a cringe of embarrassment.
Maybe Emanuel is aware of it,
for he promptly exclaims:
"Railroad, Mayer! Railroad, for sure!
The train is not a sum of zero-points:
the railroad will bring us great capital!"

Mayer stares at his brother.
For some time
now
Emanuel
has been obsessed
about this *"zero-points"* stuff.

And he repeats it
like a refrain
—*"zero-points"*
—*"zero-points"*
—*"zero-points"*
ad infinitum
like once
over there in Germany, in Rimpar, Bavaria,
a thousand years ago
when as children
they heard a Jewish tune
sung by Uncle Itzaekel
and for months
they couldn't stop singing it.

But now
here
in New York
119 Liberty Street
the question is
from what kind of Uncle Itzaekel
has Emanuel learned
this rhyme about zero-points
and above all
the rhyme about the railroad
which would bring capital

seeing that Emanuel has been talking about it for years
but has never invested even a cent.

The railroad . . .
Emanuel has also put up
—in the doorway at Liberty Street—
a Northern Railway poster
with a locomotive puffing steam.
But then?
Then Lehman Brothers keeps going
on the market for coal
for coffee
for timber
not to mention what is left of cotton.

In short
everything apart from trains.

A mystery.

Meanwhile the days go by,
and the only railroad
to be heard in Liberty Street
is a wooden
canary-colored train set.
A gift from Uncle Emanuel to his nephews
to the youngest
Arthur Herbert and Irving:
"But one day, I swear, I'll give you a real one."

It's always fun to play with trains.

3
Henry's Boys

Henry Lehman was too intelligent
to leave his business
without an heir worthy of that name.

How could they
—Emanuel and that potato of his brother Mayer—
imagine that a head like Henry
would really stop giving them help
even if it were split between the brains of two sons?

In short, turbulent David
and his mute brother, Dreidel,
shared between them
—in different proportions through biological deficit—
the great cerebral heritage
of a founding father
of a pioneer
of a trailblazer.

This assumption
had to be borne in mind.

Henry Lehman was, after all, an inspiration.
During his life he dealt with everything.
And whatever path he took
proved to have some practical sense
except for
that wretched time
when he fell prey to yellow fever
and the cotton market
lost a leading figure.
And there again,
the name on the signboard
was still his own
while Emanuel and Mayer
were running over the meadows
in a mythical place called Rimpar.

This they couldn't forget.

All the more now
all the more at this stage
now that
Aunt Rosa's children
were in their teens, no longer babes:
both David and Dreidel
were wearing long trousers

with the first promises of a beard
on their faces.

They had to be included.
Sooner or later.

Exactly: sooner or later.

For the idea of handing over command
of having someone else beside them
didn't go down too well
with the arm or with the potato.

So they took their time.
All the more because—let's not forget—
Aunt Rosa's family
had never stopped receiving its share:
a third of the profits, promptly.
About this they could not complain.
So there was no great haste.

Or at least so it seemed.
All the more since gradually
day by day
something was changing
inside Lehman Brothers.

Was it perhaps the New York air?
Or simply the fact
that Mayer and his brother were aging?

In short, questions
about the future
arose from time to time.
And Henry's sons
were entitled to be a part of it.

First of all, David.

Agitated
in his constant jittering
incapable
of sitting still at a table

infused
from his ankles to his jaws
from his big toe to the tips of his ears
with a formidable electric tension
David Lehman
had just deserved
in his uncle's view
a heroic promotion:
the coal deal was due to him,
and even more
he was owed the highest recognition
for having jolted the family
out of its slumber.
What was this if not genius?
What was this if not business?
What was this if not the sign
of a Henry Lehman
so sorely missed?

And so
while Mayer remained doubtful,
Emanuel
prompted instead
by a "thank you" never adequately expressed,
wondered about involving him
indeed
in the management of the bank. *Heyyah!*

And the more he thought about it
the fewer difficulties he saw,
bearing in mind moreover
that David
in that explosive excess
was showing appreciable gifts
not so much of intelligence
as of physical resistance to stress
a factor by no means secondary
in the great rodeo of the New York market.
On more than one occasion
at parties and dinners
his unshakable good humor
—a commodity much in demand—
    "Heyyah! A joke? You like it? Shall I?"

together with a German tolerance of alcohol
    "More! Pour it out! Bottoms up! Another round?"
had given the Lehman Brothers
a seal of solid business trust
so much so that
compared to his uncles almost three times his age
he abundantly exceeded
the critical threshold of four uninterrupted hours of public relations.
So that if Mayer
on quite a different battleground
had deserved the status of *Kish Kish*
his nephew David
outclassed him pitilessly
as happens with new machinery
in comparison to the cogs and wheels of a century ago.
For his repertoire was far wider:
Mayer in the end had
a fine smile and an ear for music
but David
topped this with
numerical acrobatics
conjuring tricks
a store of Yiddish tales
German songs
a perfect knowledge of the English language
together with a brazen impudence
far beyond the limits of a healthy education
yet whose excesses
were instantly forgiven
by everyone
for
their profoundly American spirit,
a Buffalo Bill
in Jewish and metropolitan vein
with an inner ray of Alabama sunshine.
Moreover
young Lehman
turned out to be a figure much admired
by customers of the fair sex
mothers as well as daughters,
where the former admired the élan of the twenty-year-old
and the latter—en masse—
his wild antics

as they danced at a *Rosh haShanah*
until the first light of dawn. And would have started all over again.

In industrial circles
people asked
with serious interest
whether David
was a machine fueled by coal, diesel, or kerosene.

Emanuel Lehman
therefore felt
that having his very own Achilles
was an ace up his sleeve
and in his own mind
had already counted him
among his band of Atreides.

Yet there was a problem.

And it was the fact that between David and Dreidel
the position in the bank
was not really intended for the buccaneer of the polka
but was rightfully due to the silent prince.

Now, it should be said
that both Mayer and Emanuel
due to a kind of sacred respect
had never spoken to anyone
in the whole family
not even to Aunt Rosa
about that strange moment
when Dreidel
to all intents and purposes
had transformed himself
into the brother they needed for a majority vote:
in fact it was thanks to him
that Lehman Brothers
had now taken off in New York
as a bank.

The uncles
by tacit agreement
not wishing to unduly burden the boy

had kept the memory well to themselves,
promising each other
to award him a share of the company
once he had come of age,
since after all
though he never spoke
the episode of the window ledge was more than enough
to put an end to any question.

So they prepared for the day
when Henry's voice
would once again be heard
to all intents and purposes
inside Lehman Brothers . . .
assuming that
this voice would be heard
seeing that Dreidel
not only gave no hint of making any sound
but the few times he had done so
could not be considered a success.

Even the typewriter
had served no purpose:
a gift from Uncle Mayer
who had hoped at least
he might put down in writing
what he was hiding from the world in terms of speech.
To no avail: the sheets of paper remained blank.

No use either
trying to appeal
to the boy's pride
making him understand
in a roundabout way
that *maybe one day*
he would be the one
to take his father's place
at the very heart of the bank.
Nothing. The silence continued.

All hope was thus enclosed
in the seemingly broad lapse of time

that separated Henry's mute heir
from the official threshold of twenty-one years.

But time, we know, is a strange factor.
Man imagines he has it in his grasp
but its workings often operate in reverse
and what seems far away
is here in a flash.

Which is what happened
more or less
in the Lehman household
and the fateful birthday of a spinning top
however far away it seemed,
began all of a sudden
to be imminent.
And critical.

Why, alas
does the passage of time
catch us
nine times out of ten
unprepared?

Everyone
had now developed
the clear notion
that the boy's silence
had extended over time
into a semblance of ill will
like a repudiation of humanity in its widest sense.
There again, there was no doubt
that the intermittent moments of speech
to which he had so far accustomed them
had always amounted to
subtle variations on the theme of repugnance,
for which he gave no advance warnings.

But there was something more.

On watching his behavior
there was a clear impression

that Dreidel himself was becoming
like those insects
which, when attacked, yield to the first instinct of reacting
with all their strength
and in their reaction are ready even to die.

In short, a hornet
disguised as a spinning top
whose sting
was designed to strike just once in its life
violently
then all would be over.

But if this were the general impression,
why was it never expressed?

And yet there was no doubt:
year after year
everyone
starting with Aunt Rosa
felt more and more
first the doubt
then the certainty
that Dreidel was developing
the proud inner conviction that he had a deadly weapon
whose charge
he would fire
suddenly
sooner or later
on who-knows-who and for who-knows-why
in exactly the same way
that he had insulted the King of Sugar
on a veranda in Louisiana
or the southern flag
on that stage in Alabama.
While in the first instance
Dreidel was saved
by the margin of waywardness
that is granted to children,
on the second occasion
the situation was far more serious,
and it was only the town's remembrance of his father
that muffled the outcry

of those who hurled imprecations of
plague cholera and worse upon them.

In both cases
however
—and now it was clear—
Dreidel had offered
no more than a taste
—a preview, for those who chose to understand—
of just how much poison a hornet possessed.

They might underestimate.
They might minimize.
But meanwhile he was sharpening his sting.
They would see.

Sugar!
Did anyone really think
that Dreidel Lehman would stop at this?

The flag!
Did anyone in the family
think so little of him
as to believe that a real hornet
would stop at the risk of being lynched
for spitting on the standard at the start of a war?

Of course not.
He was capable of much more.

And if those had been
annoyances of an insect,
they were nothing
compared to the real sting
which at the critical moment
would be, yes, fatal.
And unforgettable.
The prospect was this.
Not exactly a pretty one.

The boy was preparing himself
like a volcano
to allow all his anger to explode

and he didn't care
whether in doing so
he would be banished
not only from the bank
but from every human frontier.

It would happen.
But for now he was perfectly quiet.

Silent.
Somber.
Dreidel Lehman
was waiting
coolly and calmly
for his moment.

4
Oklahoma

  1 like me: a little Arthur Lehman
  2 like *papa* Mayer and *mamele* Babette
  3 like me with *papa* and *mamele*
  4 like me with my three brothers Sigmund, Herbert, and Irving
  5 like us brothers with Aunt Rosa
  6 like us brothers with Uncle Emanuel and Aunt Pauline
  7 like us brothers with our sisters
  8 like us brothers with our Alabama cousins
  9 like all of us brothers and sisters with *papa* and *mame*
 10 like all of us brothers and sisters with cousins Philip, Dreidel,
    and David
 11 I don't know because there aren't any pictures with 11 people

Arthur Lehman
has found his very own way
of learning how to count to 10:
he uses family photographs
framed in the drawing room.

So valuable
since not many people have them.
And even more valuable
as they seem to be made especially
for learning arithmetic.

Arthur
sitting on the floor
with his exercise book
looks up
looks at his sepia-colored relatives
and goes back to writing his list:
1, 2, 3, 4 . . .

To go beyond ten
you'd need a photograph with everyone.
We did at one time have one
till Uncle Emanuel chose to send it
to a place across the sea
very far away
so far that to get there
will take
days and days more
than to get to Oklahoma.
And even Oklahoma is not so close.

Yes
Oklahoma.
For while Arthur Lehman
is doing his evening arithmetic exercises
it just so happens
that an arm and a potato
miles and miles apart
are watching the flames
rise toward the sky,
thanking *HaShem* for his infinite mercy:
if nothing else
he had seen to it
that such a disturbing scene as this
should take place a thousand miles from New York
in this arid wasteland of dry ground
less than half an hour
from the border with Arkansas.

Why the Lehmans should find themselves there
is easily explained
and has something to do
with that tiny
imperceptible
particle of carbon
that distinguishes steel from cast iron
and alters its resistance
by more than 26 percent.

Despite this,
the trip really had nothing
in the slightest
to do with iron.

Yet the point is
that in his fervent passion for industry
Emanuel Lehman
had for some time
taken to expressing himself
deliberately
with bold metallurgical metaphors
a result of his daily study
of machinery, equipment, processes
and of the most unlikely aspects
of technological progress
whose language—so he believed—
had to be the language of a modern bank.

And so
indoctrinated by the new language
Emanuel enjoyed
letting oxidations, carbon-coke, fusion temperatures
slip from his tongue
and used this metalworker's talk
all the more proudly
to comment on the soup being too hot
or the color of the wallpaper
and even
the cut of his hair at the barber's.

His brother Mayer listened with alarm
for he much feared

what might happen to an arm in flesh and blood
that reinvented itself
as a mechanical arm moved by ironware.

And so he made no comment
when his brother
with much self-satisfaction
expounded this philosophy of his
whose implication seemed devastating:
"You see, my dear Mayer, iron itself is a stupid element,
it seems strong but just a little oxygen can put it in trouble, believe me.
Whereas, if we add carbon to the iron,
the metal obtained becomes workable and perfect.
And yet in this amazing process
the percentage of carbon must not exceed 2 percent
and the mystery of steel, Mayer,
lies in this tiny figure alone
which separates steel alloy from common cast iron:
both are iron, but you should see the difference.
So the greatest care is required.
Get the quantity of carbon wrong by half a gram
and even the strength of a metal changes in its nature.
I'm sure you've understood the crucial aspect
of my reasoning
And so tomorrow morning we leave together
for an appointment."

Mayer obviously understood nothing
except that his brother
was running the real risk
of becoming all one with iron
experiencing his old age
as a process of oxidization
and the bank as a blacksmith's forge.

He shuddered
and against his better judgment
prepared to follow him
wondering what devil in the world
that rusty old madman
had arranged to meet.

In reality the key
lay not so much in iron
as in the carbon that makes the difference:
Emanuel meant that the power of the bank
—as resistant and strong as pure iron—
had been moved by him into the carbon sector
—and carbon for him seemed a perfect metaphor—
to make money in the industrial market.
But beyond what degree could they go too far with carbon?
Wasn't there a risk of becoming fragile
overexposing themselves if the sector collapsed?
His idea was this: not to go beyond a certain limit
investing in carbon, yes,
but with moderation and good sense.
Therefore
so as to vary the investment
Emanuel
had arranged a meeting with Mr. Spencer
in Oklahoma,
where a black gold spurts up from the drills
like the jets of a fountain
and this black gold sells at a price per barrel
a hundred times more
than the coal of Jeremy Wilcock.

If the trip to Black Hole
had been the opportunity
to put turbulent David to the test
perhaps the next day's mission
—to explore the prospects of crude oil—
could and should be
the right moment
to renew discussions
with stiff-faced Dreidel
so many years after
his disgraceful sugar sabotage.

The long journey south
served meanwhile as a prelude.
Questioned by his uncles on the fact that now, at the age of twenty
he could ignore
that absurd nickname of spinning top

Dreidel's reaction was disturbing:
he puffed and snorted through his nose and mouth,
turning suddenly purple
and swelling the veins of his neck.
But he said nothing
and like a toad
having puffed himself up
he shrank inside his excessively dark suit
which if anything
for one his age
seemed more fitting for a waiter than a future banker.
This too was pointed out to him.
And his reaction
differed not much from the previous one:
that they should let him seem a waiter.
And so it was.

Evening fell
as they reached their destination.

The avenue that led to
Mr. Calvin Spencer's
large pink villa
was surrounded on all sides
by tall structures of wood and iron
at the top of which
black blood
spurted portentously heavenward
celebrating
the future omnipotence of oil.
Barrels stacked in rows
separated the roadway
from the work sites
where busy teams of mechanics
leapt about
turning valves and levers
on a lattice of tubes.
The pump pistons
at full capacity
marked time
up and down
high and low
up and down

like pendulum clocks
and it was all too clear
that time was paid far more
in weight of gold
than a coal mine.

The omens, in short, were perfect.
The prospects for making money excellent.
There was a blue sky, a warm southern sunset:
encouraging horizons
opened up for Lehman Brothers
in the Eldorado of oil.

They were offered a seat outside,
around a white marble fountain
where instead of water
black liquid gushed
in constant circulation
spurting from the open mouth of a dolphin.
Impressive.
As impressive as the gold candelabra
shaped in the form of an S
like the symbol stamped everywhere
of SPENCER OIL.

Less pleasing, for sure,
was the first contact with the man who awaited them.
The oil king
turned out, from the very start,
to be irritating
unctuous and slimy
of indeterminate age between 14 and 80
parceled up in a finely tailored yellow suit
which perfectly matched the blond toupee
that squarely framed his face.
His eyes of irksome blue
throughout the interview
fixed
languidly
on that small
obviously stupid
white dog
that growled at Dreidel Lehman

not taking kindly
—like the uncles—
to him dressed up like a fake manservant.

Mayer trembled.
And not for his nephew.

Because there was only one thing in the world
that displeased his brother
more than little girls who adored Chopin
and that was capricious dogs
especially those with an intolerable
yelping bark
far worse than the mechanical orchestra of the drills.

Mr. Spencer's voice
though very deep
therefore reached the Lehmans
only against the background of canine hysteria.

They surmised—from his lip movement more than anything else—
that oil was *first choice,*
and for this very reason
His Majesty the Oil King
wasn't so sure about looking for contracts,
all the more since—so he understood—
they were already in the coal sector.

He was answered
courteously
by Mayer *Bulbe*:
Lehman Brothers was now a bank.
And he hoped Mr. Spencer wouldn't ask him
what exactly this meant.

He didn't.
Or at least so it seemed:
instead they had the impression
that behind the *yap!-yap!-yap!* of the little creature
the blond man was replying: *"A bank, sure!*
But a bank . . . which all the same is in the coal business."
so that Mayer *Bulbe* instinctively
found himself expounding

an interesting theory
(which surprised him too):
"A bank is not in any area of business, Mr. Spencer:
if anything, it's the businesses that are located in a bank."

It was a clear and simple concept,
and Emanuel Lehman felt reassured just to hear it
for he could see he had been right
to move his brother into a bank
taking him from the clutches of cotton.

Their host's reaction
was not so measured.
Oil magnates were a strange race
with their very own brand of excellence
that didn't take too kindly
to lessons on finance
especially from a potato:
"Look around: do you know where you are?
        yap!-yap!-yap!-yap!
You're inside the visiting card to the future:
        yap!-yap!-yap!-yap!
all that will take place tomorrow
        yap!-yap!-yap!-yap!
will be thirsty not for water but oil
        yap!-yap!-yap!-yap!
which is why it's not me who needs you
        yap!-yap!-yap!-yap!
but it is you who need me!
        yap!-yap!-yap!-yap!
And that's the difference between oil
        yap!-yap!-yap!-yap!
and every other business on planet Earth.
        yap!-yap!-yap!-yap!
If you're happy with this, fine,
        yap!-yap!-yap!-yap!
otherwise you've traveled a long way for nothing."

There.
And it was then
as the story goes
that the little dog
made its first attempt

to sink its teeth
into young Dreidel Lehman's black shoe.

He drew back, aiming a kick
which luckily didn't reach its target
but the King nevertheless noticed:
*"Messrs. Lehman, would you mind telling your manservant
not to try hitting my animals ever again?"*

At which the uncles
held their breath
fearing—and at the same time hoping for—
some verbal reaction
which was not forthcoming even here:
the spinning top muttered between his teeth
and the dog started barking again, even louder.

Mayer *Bulbe*
as always a *Kish Kish*
tried as best he could:
*"Your estate is splendid, Mr. Spencer,
just as much as your delightful dog.
Returning to oil, it is a market
that we are interested in exploring."*

*"You are naturally interested!
        yap!-yap!-yap!-yap!
You are looking for a bone to pick clean,
        yap!-yap!-yap!-yap!
but I'll gladly leave you with Wilcock
        yap!-yap!-yap!-yap!
and his filthy coal-covered face!"*

At this statement
though spoken with a regal smile
Emanuel could not remain indifferent:
the iron that fused within him rebelled
and on finding—from who knows where—carbon superior to
        2 percent
amalgamated with steel and cast iron:
"My friend, you have taken us for two miners?"

"Mr. Lehman, I have taken you for what you are:
       yap!-yap!-yap!-yap!
a competitor that sells coal
       yap!-yap!-yap!-yap!
but would like to get his hands on oil."

It was here
as the story goes
that the dog launched a second attack
at the silent Lehman,
who jumped to his feet
and taking hold of the candelabra brandished it
against the animal
like a circus tamer against jaguars.
"Messrs. Lehman, would you mind telling your manservant
not to sully my ornaments?
Instead, he can light the candles: it's turning dark."

At which
once again
the uncles feared (and hoped for)
some verbal reaction
which didn't come even then:
Dreidel obeyed muttering who-knows-what
and lit the candles one by one.

Indeed
at the sight of fire
the dog went quiet for a moment
in a celestial silence
broken only by the harmonic backdrop of pumping
and
Emanuel Lehman
took immediate advantage of this oasis:
"A few words, Mr. Spencer: figures and returns!
If our bank were to finance your
excavation, drilling, and transport of barrels?"

It was an extravagant proposal
which the oil king
(convinced that he had two amateurs before him)
sought to investigate with a smile:
"And for how long?"

"A period of three years renewable!"
the arm exclaimed impetuously.

"Your offer would be this?"

"That is what a bank is for!"
Emmanuel enjoyed the sound of such words.
Mayer, for his part, felt it was risky,
but didn't have time to restrain his brother
on the downward slope of his enthusiasm,
for the oil king
didn't let the offer slip:
"And why are you telling me only now?
If you'd like to stay, we can talk about it after dinner . . ."

But there was no dinner.

For here the critical event occurred:
the dog
having regained its strength
in that peculiar interlude of silence
relaunched the attack
but this time against a different leg:
it headed straight for Emanuel
who, taken unprepared,
didn't gauge his response
and having grabbed the enemy by its neck
hurled it into the monarch's lap
who in turn
rose up
in defense of the little prince:
"You filthy Jew!
He only wanted to show you how he does a somersault!"

"Oh yes? I haven't journeyed for days
to watch an animal with its paws in the air!"

"He does the best somersaults in Oklahoma!
That's why we call him Topsy
the Spinning Top."

Hardly a second elapsed
between the last syllable of the last word

and the flash that illuminated the villa:
Dreidel Lehman
having exhausted all patience
on hearing that his nickname had been given to the dog
grabbed the lighted candelabra
and threw it into the fountain of black gold.

Instantly
the flames leapt twenty feet high
so that Emanuel at first
was stirred by a shiver of delight
imagining iron melting in the blast furnace.

But it was only a momentary pleasure,
surpassed by the awareness
that Lehman Brothers
newly founded bank
was setting fire to the villas of oil magnates.

There was great pandemonium
among sovereigns, pages, vassals and chamberlains:
the whole court of oil
rushed with buckets to put out the blaze
while the pumps worked nonstop
since oil leaps high
night and day
never rests
gushes ceaselessly.

Ah! The burning bush!
Ah! *Ner tamid* that never dies down!

At last
they put out the flames
and by the time they were out
no Lehman was anywhere to be seen.

In religious silence
they were back on the road.
The uncles silent.
The spinning top mute.

Yet a hint of pleasure
could be detected on the boy's face
like a boxer who had just proved his worth.

No one knew about it
apart from them.

Maybe because in just a few months
Dreidel would be twenty-one.

In short
in all respects
the hornet was waiting for his moment.

5
Familie-Lehmann

The children, it must be said,
can see nothing from down here.
They have to lean out
or jump to the tips of their toes.
From the twenty-first row there is no view.
Though there again, the seats are allocated
and they can at least say they have them.

Yes.
In the Great Temple of New York
the Lehman family has its seats:
engraved on the twenty-first pew.

Of course: it's not the first row.
But we are not the Lewisohns
and until just now
half of us
were still in Alabama.
We have to be content, therefore. To be content.
Twenty-first pew.

That's fine.
Twenty-first pew.

On which is written
FAMILIE—LEHMANN
with two n's
and dear Sigmund feels ashamed of the mistake:
like a rabbit
that finds its burrow has been blocked
he stares at his brothers:
"They could have been more careful
and why did they do it to us?
They haven't written Lewisohn with three n's."

Yes. The Lewisohns.
They sit in the front row
since they control
none other
than the gold market.
We can't expect to equal them:
no one can compete
with anyone who is measurable in karats.

Gold, after all, we know,
is what makes the difference.
And it's no surprise that the first three rows
are always in hot competition:
the Lewisohns in first place
the Goldmans in the second pew
the Hirschbaums permanently in the third.
There they are.
Lined up, the keepers of the gold.

As for the Lehmans
at today's service no one is absent.

Mayer standing with Emanuel beside him.

Mayer with eyes closed: a mystical potato.

Emanuel in concentration
high concentration

because an arm is an arm
even in ascetic form.

Clinging to their trousers
are the boys under ten years old
bored and yawning
like their fathers had once been
in that synagogue in Rimpar.

Next to Mayer is Sigmund
still pink-cheeked,
a schoolboy overweight through munching donuts
a rabbit in spite of his years
with pockets full of candies
(and not to eat them: to offer them).
Sigmund: always ready to alter the parting in his hair
straight on the right, combed: as is now the fashion.
And so as not to ruffle it
he never wears a hat.

Standing next to Sigmund, on the other hand, tall, disheveled
the turbulent David
with unruly curls
as though a charge of dynamite
has exploded on his head each morning,
including days when there's a service at the Temple:
"Heyyah! But is it today? Really? It's a holiday? Huh!"

Lastly Dreidel silent introspective
who has grown a thick beard
as far as the cheeks up to his eyes
letting them almost merge with his dark brows.
He looks like an orthodox Jew
and that's not to say he is not, deep down,
judging at least
from that right side of his mouth
where he makes mumbled grunts of contempt
at anyone who gets an accent wrong as he reads.
But what
is an orthodox Jew doing
in
this American Reform Temple

where there's no women's gallery
and even English might sometimes get spoken?

In the twenty-first pew
where the family name is engraved
only Philip, Emanuel's firstborn son, is missing:
a perfect adolescent in a gray double-breasted coat
he sits at the front, not with the others:
in the first row
since Rabbi Strauss has made him his chosen favorite
and keeps him next to him
to hold his arm.

Among his youngest cousins
Herbert
has said without mincing words
that *he positively disagrees*
with this idea that Philip, he alone,
should sit twenty rows ahead.
For Herbert, after all,
the problem lies deep down
and is therefore a political question:
why should the excellence of one single person
be translated
into a right denied to others?
And so
while Herbert
sucking his finger
theorizes about social equality
his young brother Arthur
holding his teddy bear
feels authorized
to run down, to the first row
sitting himself down
and not just him:
sitting his teddy bear down beside him
since the Temple is for everyone
and woe betide anyone who says otherwise.

Philip has tried
to send him away with a frown.
In vain,

since Arthur
with all his six years
is a hard nut to crack.

And in fact when Rabbi Strauss says:
*"This place on the pew is not for you, my child,
this is for the Lewisohns, don't you see their name?"*
Arthur
takes his teddy bear
and sits with it
on the floor
for until proved otherwise
Mr. Rabbi
there are no names written on the floor.

In short
to dissuade him
—and using police tactics—
his mother, Pauline, has had to come down
from the twenty-first pew:
elegantly dressed
in a cloud of fur
swathed
in verbena perfume
that wafts through the Temple,
outside which Aunt Babette
is running beneath the porticoes
after her little girls
dressed in bows and ribbons.

Fortunately there's Harriett
who of all the little girls
is the one that most resembles her father, Emanuel,
and doesn't think twice about smacking her sisters.
Sigmund adores the way she hits them
he finds it really amusing:
*"If I marry you one day, Harriett,
would you give me a smacking too?"*
But there's no way Harriett will marry her cousin:
*"Stop eating donuts, Sigmund,
or you'll never find a wife
not even if you pay her your weight in gold."*

Harriett has a natural gift
for rapid-fire comments.
In this, she has taken the place of her Aunt Rosa,
who was also wonderful at clipping children around the ear.

But Aunt Rosa is not to be seen at the Great Temple:
the New York fashions
didn't suit her gray hair
and in the end she has gone back to Alabama
where she once destroyed a glass door
and trampled over the pieces.

She certainly tried, she tried it out in New York,
she made the effort, you might say.
But is it her fault
if she never really liked it?
She has returned South, and there she wants to stay.

After all, times have changed,
and "You see, Aunt Rosa, it won't be long
before we'll have an apparatus in our homes
with which—you there and us here—
we'll be able to hear each other!"

Aunt Rosa laughs heartily.
And that's no surprise: whoever would believe it?

The point is that in New York
it is possible to believe the impossible.

Aunt Rosa hasn't heard for example
that the other day
at the Universal Exhibition
in front of a New York crowd
a certain Mr. Bell of Scottish origin
proudly
displayed
a box made of metal and wood
with a wire and a receiver
and when he asked for a volunteer,
dear Sigmund Lehman
came forward smiling
like a rabbit

saying *"Will I be okay, Mr. Inventor?*
If you want someone better, I won't be offended,"
this last phrase which was not properly understood
due to the kick in the backside
with which his cousin David
propelled him into the Scotsman's arms.
After which
in the general enthusiasm
Sigmund
bright red
sweating heavily with excitement
confirmed
that he had heard loudly and clearly in the earpiece
without the slightest disturbance
the voice of his lordship Mr. Mayor from the upper floor.
Well done Sigmund: he was even entitled to a medal
for being the first customer of the telephone era.
They pinned it on his chest
and took photos for the *New York Times*
to which he declared: *"It was a magnificent experience!*
I believe that Mr. Bell could do no better
and I swear that I heard the mayor in the earpiece
as though he were seated right beside me!"

Oh, the tenderness of bunnies.
Well done Sigmund.

Luckily no one noticed
when at the end of the ceremony
with a sympathetic smile
and a tinge of regret
the rabbit
called the inventor to one side
to tell him quietly:
"Sir, if I may offer some advice:
I suggest you check the apparatus,
for to tell the truth
the voice of the mayor, I couldn't hear it:
there was just a constant uninterrupted whistle,
I didn't say so, for it seemed unkind.
Well done all the same:
even that whistle in the earpiece

was the best whistle
that I have ever heard."

And as a token of his respect
he offered him a candy.

But this is just a detail
a personal matter of little importance
between a rabbit and an inventor from Edinburgh.

What interests
investors
and bankers such as Lehman
however
is that Aunt Rosa
can talk to her children from Alabama
and can ask them one day
whether at that very moment it is snowing in New York.
This is what interests us.
As well, of course, as the fact
that to bring telephones from Maine as far as Texas
would require millions of wooden poles
and an amazing network of wires:
a fine business, involving quite a lot of money.
Lehman Brothers has signed up to it.

"It's just a shame that inventors are so slow,"
Emanuel immediately thought
"if rather than sleeping for eight hours a day
they had applied themselves first to an apparatus like this
then I might perhaps have heard the voice of my father
directly from his cattle stall."

And this was a further reason for backing
—as they say in New York—
the locomotive of progress.

Yes. The locomotive.

Is it possible that we are the only ones
not to be making money with trains?
Is it possible that this railroad

is a kind of mystery for Lehman?
"We have to find a way, Mayer:
give it some thought:
the market that counts is running on tracks,
I don't want to stay with the zero-points."

These zero-points again?

It was clear: his brother Emanuel
had some adviser
hidden among the shadows.
The only thing known about him
for the moment
was that he had a nickname:
"zero-point."

6
Der terbyalant David

Lehman Brothers has invested in oil.
Wells and drills in Tennessee, in Ontario, in California.
Everywhere apart from Oklahoma
and it's a mystery why in New York it has no response.

Having gone all the way
into coal and petroleum
into the sacred temple of combustibles
Lehman Brothers has energy to sell:
boilers at full capacity in engine rooms
and such is the force of our fuels
that we can even
give ourselves the luxury of sleep.

Yet the one who doesn't sleep
literally
is David Lehman.
Especially ever since
in his professional life

he has specialized in the emotional-sentimental branch
or rather in locating
on a large scale
that extraordinary combustible
which draws a male investor
toward a supplier of female labor.

In other words:
the basic law of the industry
by which supply adapts to demand
and the customer
chooses his future commercial partner
on the free market.
No more no less.

Henry's son
in this respect
is most careful:
before proceeding with a purchase
the quality of the goods
must at least be certified
and subjected
to the only real empirical proof
that prevents the purchaser
from receiving
adulterated damaged
or second-rate consignments.
In that case
—as we know—
it is always possible to send them back
without further obligation:
a cordial yours sincerely
and the deal is safely closed.

The wonders of commerce.

On the other hand
what did Uncle Mayer and Uncle Emanuel do
when they were cotton dealing
down in Alabama?
If the raw cotton was stringy
or the skein poor quality
did they feel entitled

to interrupt the contract
without anyone being offended
And with coffee? And with coal?
And lastly with oil?
"We invest only if the investment yields."
Too true.
And the yield, we know,
is measured on clear criteria.

Exactly.
Hurrah for clarity, thinks David:
it's essential in buying and selling.
His father would have said the same.

Even his granddad Abraham
—who sold cows and chickens in Bavaria—
had once written a note
that David has even framed:
"REAL BUSINESS, MY SONS,
IS DONE, NOT WITH FINE TALK,
BUT WITH THE EYES, THE HANDS, THE NOSE."

Ah, the wisdom of the old.

David Lehman holds the same view:
forget about intuition,
the only rule is to CHECK IT OUT.

And personal involvement
is what distinguishes
a true member of Lehman Brothers
from a hack-businessman.

Of course: it means sacrifice.
But if it costs effort, all the better,
since a good purchase is guaranteed
only through effort.

Having said this
the kid is nevertheless
indefatigable:
a tireless worker
a stern inspector

one who before giving his approval
insists on proof
and doesn't sign until he's sure.

So far so good.

The problem is that such *proof*
without doubt
is for David Lehman
the bodily union
between the seller and buyer.

The boy has reached
this essential stage
naturally—one might say—
developing an experience in the field
which in just a few years
has made him
an almost unrivaled authority.

A force of nature.

Which might be useful.

His Uncle Emanuel
has played a crucial role in this.

For chance would have it
that after the excellent success
built up around the coal business,
Emanuel Lehman
was increasingly convinced
that he could use
his nephew's natural talent
to carry Lehman Brothers
into the realm of transport.

Not just railroads.
But also boats.
And merchant shipping.
And—why not?—roads and bridges
which America surely so much needed
seeing that industry depends

yes sir
on infrastructure
and on transport links.

Then, yes, we could break through
at last
the suffocating barrier
of the *zero-points*!

And if for the moment
the railroad
was still a tough nut
for Lehman Brothers,
let's start at least
with the ports, with shipping
and with the road network!
But let's do it straightaway
undaunted and without falling asleep
for in all these years
we have slept too much.

Perfect.
From here the turning point.

From a careful investigation by Emanuel
the transport business
turned out still to be concentrated in a few hands:
twelve financiers in all
prominent New York families
equally distributed
between Jews and Protestants:
the cream of the bourgeoisie
top level
and perhaps even more than top: the very top.

Emanuel Lehman
being a good arm
applied himself with maximum dedication
in studying each of the twelve
and obtaining all useful information
—even the most insignificant—
about their habits, tastes,
practices, and preferences.

In the end
there was nothing about them
that he did not know,
including where they took their vacations
what they ate
and even details about their respective dogs.
So that the mosaic fitted perfectly.

Emanuel noted their names.
Or rather: they were so powerful
that he dared not even write them down
but
opted for a coded language
where each financier
was nicknamed
taking as his surname
the city or area where he was building
and as his first name
—after what took place in Oklahoma—
that, of course, of his dog.

And so
the leading figures in American transport
turned out like this:

    1. Mr. Buddy Massachusetts
    2. Mr. Milky Chicago
    3. Mr. Foxy Philadelphia
    4. Mr. Jump-Jump Washington
    5. Mr. Banana Colorado
    6. Mr. Princess Cincinnati
    7. Mr. Speedy Pennsylvania
    8. Mr. Honey New Orleans
    9. Mr. Lemonsoda San Francisco
   10. Mr. Paperina California
   11. Mr. Cherry Missouri
   12. Mr. Warrior Sacramento

These were the twelve
who had a share of the great cake
and to taste of it
—and I don't mean a slice—
the only alternative

was to be invited to their table.
But how?

Assistance came from Brooklyn.

For
one day in March
while sitting at the water's edge
watching
the construction of the new bridge
all of a sudden he felt a breeze
brush his ear
as with the best of solutions:
why hadn't he thought of it?
A bridge was needed
over twelve rivers
between Lehman Brothers
and the opposite shore.
And he had an engineer
ready to build these bridges,
exactly the same as Brooklyn.

It just so happened
indeed
that each of the twelve had—in addition to a dog—
at least one daughter
of an age—so to speak—sensitive
to the impetuous pedigree of his nephew.

Who was therefore summoned
privately
away from everyone's gaze
and particularly that of Uncle Mayer
since vegetables, as it is well known, are asexual:
he would not have understood.
And it was not so easy to explain.

After a long and stirring introduction
about the advantages of having an arm as an uncle
about the current and future merits of coal
about the family's business sense
and the enormous sacrifices his father had made,

David Lehman
was informed
of the immense undertaking to be placed upon him,
the task of opening
—no less—
a breach in the enemy walls
—no less—
with his masculine charm
as the sole bombardier.

All this of course
explained to him
using a technical-industrial language,
citing
the various properties of iron, nickel, copper
and many other sundry materials.

It was a question
however
of using the greatest caution,
and always moving in the shadows
to gain the fond trust
of princesses of the wealthiest realm,
so that each one
—believing herself to be the only one—
would grant her new suitor
the assurance
—absolute and certain—
of letting one of the Lehman brothers
sit at her parents' table.

Once indoctrinated by the daughters
the fathers
would comply
without resistance.

This at least
was what Uncle Emanuel
was convinced he had told his accomplice.

David Lehman
however
interpreted the assignment

in a slightly different way
and considered himself
officially
AUTHORIZED
to achieve the given objective
using *whatever way, method, and instrument*
proved necessary.

They shook hands.
And at that point
with a thousand cautions
the uncle handed his nephew
the fateful list
of the twelve magnates.

Though free to choose where to begin,
the turbulent David
gave a promising example of exactitude:
following strict alphabetical order,
he pointed his bayonet
at the famous Sissy nicknamed "Freckles"
beloved eldest daughter
of Mr. Paperina California.

And had immediate luck.

For it just so happened that the young girl
owed her celebrity
not so much to the freckles that entirely covered her face
as to a story
that had sadly marred
her childhood:
an Irish boy, who had made a passionate declaration
asking her—at the age of six—to marry him,
had broken his neck when he fell on the front door steps
a moment after Sissy
—having consulted her doll—
had asked him for time to think.
From that fortuitous coincidence
Miss California
had developed a kind of terror of refusing
and so as not to see another suitor drop dead

she accepted
her petitioner's embrace
without too much ado.

David Lehman
therefore
celebrated his debut in the best of ways:
the first eloquent gaze was enough
and he found the large girl
already hanging 'round his neck
ready to promise him much more
than Lehman's arrival
into the Eden of transportation.
Heyyah! What a girl!
Not even a hug
and he could already call her *süsser*.

It was much more difficult
to storm the fortress
of a splendid four-eyed mare
daughter of Mr. Milky Chicago:
in this case it was the not insignificant obstacle
of an official engagement
which obliged
David Lehman
to choose a less direct approach,
relying
on the foolproof remedy
of anonymous notes
and anonymous floral gifts
until the filly
anonymously impassioned
left the stable door
open.

And it was a crucial triumph.

For it instilled in David
that added value
engendered
by direct experience
in every profession:

the boy congratulated himself
and this self-congratulation
encouraged him further.

So that
the daughter of Mr. Cincinnati
and that of Banana Colorado
capitulated in the space of six days,
while Mr. Buddy Massachusetts
wondered why
his daughter Polly
allergic to every kind of pollen
suddenly enjoyed
long walks in the park.
He spoke about it to Mr. Missouri
who, in turn, asked his opinion
on the fact that his Christie
knew so much—all of a sudden—about coal . . .
"Coal?"
"Coal."

Impenetrable mysteries
of the female soul!

How do you explain certain changes
bordering on conversion?

Young Minnie
who taught at the Protestant school
and had always been harsh
toward the *"Jewish assassins of Christ"*
was seen walking near to the Temple
asking the carriage drivers if by chance
they had seen her beloved Isaac
(for David was well practiced in the choice of false names).

And if there were those who stopped sleeping
    "for did you know, dear father,
    how many years we waste through sleep?"
it is said that Yvette
daughter of Mr. Lemonsoda San Francisco
—owner of a whole naval fleet—
was congratulated by her father

when she started cooking him
a wonderful recipe
for an aniseed cake
they make in Alabama.

There was no doubt about it:
a strange fever had spread
among the daughters of respectable families.

A change of nature
was noted even in the dogs,
if it is true that Foxy
—the dachshund belonging to the mail-coach king—
began to lose its way back home
forcing
its young mistress
to disappear for whole afternoons
before then finding it
each evening
at the dogcatcher's.

And Mr. Pennsylvania's greyhound?
From the wonder it used to be
all of a sudden it grew tired
and took
three hours' more than usual
to walk around the block.
Poor Speedy, now so tired.

Emanuel Lehman
for his part
was already preparing
to become the thirteenth transport magnate.

In short
everything would have gone
splendidly well
had
his nephew
not gone too far:
having obtained the promise of intercession
he failed to loosen his grip
promising each young girl

simultaneously
that he would marry them
and even make them mothers
of three, four, ten children.

The physical prowess
of which he felt endowed
consoled him further in the task,
deceiving him
in less lucid moments
into actually believing he could
hold out
at the same time
in twelve parallel beds
of twelve goslings.

Or rather: eleven.
Because the twelfth liaison
was based
—at least for the moment—
on a relationship that was passionate, yes, but only epistolary.

She was
in fact
a plump
deeply religious
blond
whose public appearances
alas
were strictly limited
to Temple services.

Furthermore her father
Mr. Jump-Jump Washington
was the head of a strict family
of orthodox Jews
who attended services held
not at the Reform Temple of the Lehman clan
but
in a synagogue with a women's gallery.

David Lehman
found himself against a brick wall:

any contact with the girl
was in fact impossible
except through cousins of the same sex.

And here he made his mistake.

He wrote a first passionate letter
and placed it in the mercenary hands of a young girl
handsomely remunerated
with combs, hoops, and colored ribbons.
He then awaited her reply.
And when it came
it was only the start of a long exchange
all the more passionate
since it was in ink alone.

But the correspondence was intercepted
through espionage in the women's gallery.
The little girl had changed alliance
either due to a guilty conscience
or in exchange for a more equitable payment.

The fact is
that David's love letters
became public news
and within three days
they were the talk
of every New York drawing room
like extraordinary serialized novels.

Oh! Sodom and Gomorrah!
Oh! The Plagues of Egypt!
Oh! The Temple in ruin!

For the twelve girls
amid sobs and tears
immediately
recognized
the style, the metaphors,
the wording and vocabulary
including above all
that unmistakable repertory
of spice aniseed, coal mines,

dead fathers in Alabama,
whole years spent asleep
and last
—but no means secondary—
the request to persuade the parent
to allow Lehman Brothers
into the control room.

"Papa, it's him! It's my Isaac!"
"But this is Mordechai!"
"Tell me it's not Ezekiel!"
"How could you, Solomon?"
"Oh my Jacob master of the heyyahs!"
"He called me his süsser!"

There are catastrophes
even in the history of a bank.

This was equal to the disaster a year before,
when Jay Gould caused
the gold market to collapse
and New York held its breath.
For the Lehmans
in comparison
that was nothing.

They all
tried
to keep a distance:
"David? For us he has always been a wild horse."
"When he was a boy we used to say: he'll end up in a circus."
"None of us had ever thought him much of a genius."

It was no use.
The damage had been done.
Reputation lost.

But since every time you fall
you find yourself with a choice
between pulling out your hair
and stopping to think about why
and what had made you fall,
so

this time too
there were those in Lehman Brothers
who put all the facts together
and from the facts arrived at a question
and from the question to a constructive thought:
finance is to do with money
and money—we know—is often a filthy business
and yet
the first thing you ask of a bank
is that the person who looks after your money
keeps his fingernails clean.
This is what Uncle Mayer thought.

As for David,
he was punished in exemplary fashion.

Not even his mother defended him.
Indeed Aunt Rosa told him to his face
that his father, Henry,
would never but never in his life
have called two girls *süsser*
at the same time.
Shame on him.
Shame on him.

Gathered in plenary session
the sacred family tribunal
judged him
unanimously
(with one abstention: from Emanuel, it is said)
GUILTY
of all charges
sentencing him
with no right of appeal
to banishment for life
to be served from tomorrow
in the penal colony of cotton:
he would return to Alabama
and the future of the bank
would be left to his brother.

David Lehman
was therefore the first victim

sacrificed on the altar
of a new morality in banking.

And though the Lehmans
were not Puritans
nor Baptists, nor Mormons, nor Quakers
it was clear to all
that from now on
the sex life of the bank
would be
more or less
chaste.

7
Studebaker

After the embarrassing events
above,
the Lehman family
was demoted:
from the twenty-first row
they have fallen back to the twenty-fifth.

"Do we have to go so far back?"
Irving asks, holding his mother's hand.

Yes: so far back.

Philip Lehman
sitting next to the rabbi on the first row
is almost ashamed
to catch sight, down at the back,
of the gray and white hair of his uncle and his father.

His cousin Arthur
who has taught himself to count
and no one can explain how he's done it

refuses to accept the idea
of having to sit so close to the exit.

Even his brother Herbert
has said in front of everyone
that he doesn't agree.
For Herbert the problem lies deep down
and becomes a political question:
why must the error of a single person
be answered with a punishment for all?
Here once again
the difference between him and his brother
is that while Herbert just says it
Arthur changes the argument
always
into open attacks
acts of urban warfare
and concrete sabotage.

Since the age of two
if the soup was not to their liking
Herbert would turn his nose up
and moan and whimper
(for even then the problem was deep down,
and became a political question)
whereas Arthur
more than once
hurled his plate
violently at the cupboard.

Between the two young boys
there was therefore a vast difference,
one that distinguished drawing room politics
from militant struggle.

Today at the Temple
for example
Arthur is sitting on a low wall
outside the entrance
with no intention of going inside:
"You go to row twenty-five,
I'm sitting here on the forty-eighth

so far away that I'll sit in the street
to make sure there's no chance
of going any farther back."
And there they were out front
trying to make him see sense
when a sudden silence fell
and they saw the Lewisohns arrive
like out of an illustrated magazine
no longer in a carriage
but on a wondrous machine
all lamps and horns
a mechanical carriage
which no doubt has horses all the same
—and how could it not have them?—
but they're stuck inside the metal, poor beasts,
closed up in a box
so they aren't distracted
and don't get wet in the rain.

"A Studebaker! Then they really exist!"
whispered Sigmund
with a broad rabbit grin
before actually applauding them
and giving a candy to the chauffeur.

"I can well understand why they sit in the first row, look:
for the cost of a Studebaker
they could buy the whole Temple"
said Harriett who had a natural talent
for the well-turned phrase.
And Herbert:
"The problem lies deep down:
the Lewisohns travel in an autocarriage,
they sit in the front row,
and what's more they have their name spelled correctly,
not like us who they've written with two n's
as if one extra was a luxury.
Can someone tell me why
I have to walk here
and sit almost in the forecourt?"

Fortunately
before Herbert Lehman

—in the prime of his young years—
could arrive at a doctrine not far from Marxism
he was saved
by his brother Arthur.
It was he who diverted attention
with one of his usual spectacular gestures:
he ran behind the Lewisohns' automobile
and as soon as a young girl
climbed out of the vehicle
he literally threw himself at her
shouting like a lunatic
"In my house
they say everything you touch
turns immediately to gold:
I want to see if you'll turn me too!"

The little girl
(who answered to the name of Adele)
clearly wasn't accustomed
to fending off protesters
nor to dealing with public discontent.
Her only interest
seemed in fact aimed
at the irreparable damage
to a large bright blue bow
—absolutely disproportionate—
that adorned her head
with an effect frankly somewhat bizarre.
So she burst into floods of tears
while Babette Lehman
tried fruitlessly
to calm her son who in his fury
had trampled the aforesaid bow
into the mud.

How curious
the workings of the human memory.

For the family conserved
two quite different memories of that day.

Some remembered it as
that time when a Lehman

damaged Lewisohn property,
and it mattered little that the damage was a six-dollar bow.

For someone else
however
it was simply
that time when we envied
their Studebaker.

Yes. Because
for the adults it was a harsh blow.

The Lewisohns in an automobile.

There they are.
Who could ever imagine it.

Emanuel on seeing them
feels an instinctive disdain
and only later is he excited about the future unfolding:
automobiles are already on the street
and are we, instead of investing in them,
to carry on sleeping as if nothing had happened?

Mayer on the other hand is horrified:
if these monsters take over New York,
his brother would return to the attack
with his zero-points.
And that, in effect, is what happened.

The only one
who made no comment
on seeing the Studebaker
was Dreidel.
But this proves nothing.

Two hours later
once the service was over
Emanuel Lehman
took his brother by the shoulder
pulling him to one side
red-faced as if he had a fever:

"There are those who travel in an autocarriage.
There are those who go by train.
And Lehman Brothers what does it do, damnation?
It travels by foot or at most by horse.
We are behind, Mayer: we're behind."

"In the twenty-fifth row."

"Worse: in the eightieth, in the ninetieth.
There: do you hear how that engine roars?"

"In all honesty, Emanuel, do you actually trust these machines?
Would you take your family in one?"

"Of course! What are you saying?
I'm already in the twentieth century,
but you, you're old, you're out of date!
The truth is you still have cotton on the brain!"

"Let me remind you
we are Lehman Brothers
we owe it all to cotton!"

"But read the newspapers, Mayer, for goodness' sake!
In Egypt they want to dig a canal. Did you know that?"

"What the Egyptians do is irrelevant to Lehman Brothers."

"And that's where you're wrong, yes sir:
they want to dig the canal, they'll dig it, and they'll come out at Suez."

"I'm not following you."

"There will be a small port on the Indian Ocean, you understand?
A service port, opening onto the Mediterranean:
at that point Indian cotton, Mayer,
will take just a moment to invade Europe.
And you know what? Indian cotton costs less!
Which is why I'm already elsewhere."

"Where are you?"

"Engines, trains: everything that moves!"

A genuine mystery of science
is the aging process of an arm.
Instead of remaining more stationary
it is desperate to move about like a lunatic.
Emanuel has an obsession about movement.

Another mystery
for Pauline
is why Emanuel
    —now that cotton is obsolete
     since the Egyptians will do goodness knows what—
has gone down to Alabama
with his brother
saying he has a pending shipment of cloth.

It's an excuse that few believe.

The truth is that there was no choice.

It was worth making a long journey
to talk to Aunt Rosa
in person
about Henry's share
in the running of the bank.

They tell her they've given it much thought.
And have decided that at least for now
it is better not to go ahead
with any new appointment:
Aunt Rosa and her children
will of course keep their slice of earnings
—a third of the proceeds, as it has always been—
but as for allowing Dreidel
into the room with the word *Management* written on it . . .
In short, let us not be hasty:
under the age of thirty
    you understand, Aunt Rosa
a young man is not ready
and under thirty
    you understand, Aunt Rosa

he's only interested in girls
and then a bank
    you understand, Aunt Rosa
it's not the right business for twenty-year-olds.

Aunt Rosa makes no objections,
she listens in silence
putting slices of spiced aniseed cake
onto tea plates.

Finally, though,
before her brother-in-laws' forks
have reached their mouths for the first taste,
Rosa Wolf—who demolished a glass door—
bangs her fist on the table
as though it were a Bronx tavern:
"Let me and the two of you get something clear, face-to-face.
You've come down here now, at the last opportunity,
rather than talking about it before:
let's pretend it has happened by chance,
since I don't wish to think badly of you.
Having said this, I repeat: I want to get something clear.
When my husband founded Lehman Brothers
he was twenty-six, and there's no mistake about that.
Emanuel, I saw you arrive in Alabama
when you were still a kid and you used to pull cats' tails,
and your brother told me
"I have to be a father to him or he'll land me in trouble."
As for you, Mayer: you came crying to me
because you missed your mom, or don't you remember?
I do, I remember it. And remember it pretty well.
So please, enough of this nonsense:
have you come to tell me that below the age of thirty
you're not ready to work in a company?
Fine, then: let's not fall out over it.
But any agreement—if that's what you want, my dears—
has to be written down in black and white:
my children are entitled to have a say,
not just to have the money you earn for them.
You must therefore take one of mine.
It wasn't you who set up that business:
over it all is my dear Henry, the head,

and you come later, as a result.
So, if all is agreed then there'll be no trouble:
for the present everything remains as always,
but as soon as our firstborn sons
all reach their majority,
then the day after—you have to promise—
you hand everything over to them.
You were three brothers:
they will be three cousins.
You were equal: one-third per head,
and the same for them, without distinction.
For you, Emanuel, there will be Philip who's the oldest.
For you, if I'm not wrong, it will be Sigmund,
and for me you'll give a place to Dreidel:
he has a right to it, and I don't want to hear otherwise.
You have no alternative, this is the way ahead.
And listen: I'm not saying this for me, I'm saying it because it's right.
Is that clear? That's all I have to say.
Finish off the cake, which is as good as always.
After which,
go back home: mission complete,
greetings to your wives, a kiss to the nephews and nieces
and as for you
be careful
for Henry sees everything
and once a month
he comes to me in a dream."

She said no more
as there was nothing else to be said.

As for the two brothers
they ate the cake.
What could they do? It wasn't right to leave it.

They finished it, in fact,
as proof of the alliance.
Not a slice was left.

And it remained heavy on their stomachs.

8
Tsu fil rash!

Mayer Lehman would like to invest in gas.
He likes gas, very much, since it's transparent.
It's noiseless. It's invisible.
It doesn't dirty your hands, takes up little room.
Coal and oil
which his brother loves so much
disgust him
since black is a violent color.
How can you compare it with gas, which is there yet isn't?

Emanuel is not naturally opposed:
on the signboard it says LEHMAN BROTHERS,
and until the cousins invade
the two of them will decide
without interference.

But in all honesty
can an authentic arm
find any attraction in putting money
on gas which can't be touched, has no weight, can't be held?
No comparison with iron!

Fortunately New York
is the capital of commerce.
Mayer *Bulbe*
has signed a contract for gas
on the very same afternoon
when Emanuel was buying more iron.

Gas and iron: two steps ahead.
And in fact—as chance would have it—
the family pew
has been moved two rows forward, in the Temple.
Twenty-third row:
the children can see rather better
since there's more light:
we are under the window.

Maybe this is why
after Mayer Lehman's gas
they would like to try with glass
Transparent like gas.
Doesn't dirty your hands.
It's there yet isn't.

"Glass? But what are you talking about?
With glass you get zero-points, not capital!
Do you want to become a banker of zero-points?"
he asked his brother sternly.

And Mayer gives no reply.
He often doesn't answer: instead he smiles.

Like now: he nods and smiles.
Asking himself once again
who
could have put into his brother's head
this sing-song about the zero-points.

Meanwhile he nods and smiles.
Dressed in striped leggings
that no one here
—including his brother—
would ever wear.
Even yesterday, at the Temple
when Mayer went up to read on the podium
everyone was looking at him.
Laughing.
A potato with leggings.
Never seen such a thing in New York.
"Why is everyone looking at your shoes?"
his son Irving asked him
as calmly as he could
—Irving is an imperturbable child—
after they had found him, by luck
sitting on a Temple step
(for Irving is constantly getting lost,
and not because he runs away,
but for the simple reason
that everyone forgets about him).

"Why is everyone looking at your shoes?"
he asked his father,
who was delighted not to have lost him.

Mayer looked at him
smiled
but made no reply.

He could have told him that when he arrived from Germany
—Rimpar, Bavaria—
everyone used to look at his shoes
and so
if they look at your shoes
it's a sign that you come from far away
but from too too too far away.
He could.
But he didn't tell him.

There again
it's been quite some time now
that Mayer talks less.
He, who at one time
was worthy
of the title—and what a title!—*Kish Kish*
now bites his tongue
keeps his lips closed.
He smiles. He nods.

He has given up.
And for some time now.

Strange how at a certain point in life
you find yourself
without realizing it
thinking and saying things
just like your old father:
it's been nearly ten years
since the last note
arrived in Alabama
addressed always to both "DEAR SONS"
and signed "YOUR FATHER."
And yet it's as if that Lehmann with two n's
in his dying moment

had somehow been moved onto American soil
putting much of himself
into the bodies of his sons.

Mayer Lehman for example
often talks by way of pronouncements.
He avoids discussion, prefers sayings.
Was it a tiredness with life?
Or had he perhaps, by force of economizing,
applied his resource-cutting
even to his desire to speak?

Mayer often thinks about it.
And thinks it is no coincidence
that it all began several years ago
in Alabama, in his Montgomery,
when suddenly
even there
everyone was struck down with a "talking disease":
the idea
—his idea!—
about rebuilding the South after the war
had been transformed
into torrents of words
currents of air, tumults of discourse
and instead of building walls and fences
people made projects.
Sheets of paper.
Pamphlets.
Books.
Work plans
described in detail
promises over ten, twenty, thirty, forty years.
"How can I sign
if in forty years I'll already be dead?"
"Every good investment, Mr. Lehman,
is now long term."
"Yes, but how can I sign
if I'll never see what I've paid for?"
"With respect, Mr. Lehman,
all this is irrelevant for business purposes."
"But it is for me."
"You as a bank, Mr. Lehman,
are making a commitment: giving your word."

"What word can I give if in forty years' time
the bank might even collapse?"
"This too is irrelevant for business purposes."
"So what is relevant?"
"That you give your word."
"What word?"
"The word yes."

Words, that's right.

Then
it grew even worse
when he and Babette
arrived here in New York
where everyone speaks and there is never any silence.
Even in the Temple
during services
continual whispering
no respite, words everywhere
fixed to the walls, on the posters: words
in the street, in bars: words
in the commercial banks: words
all a nightmare of sound
questions-answers
answers-questions
questions-answers
answers-questions
words and more words
words words
words and more words
a whole ocean of discourse
greater than the ocean seen from Brooklyn
so much that here—Mayer thinks—the people are drugged
with words
and in New York
indeed
even at night
everyone
talks in their sleep.

And what is more:
better not to even think
what they'll do with the telephone.

9
Stock Exchange

The tightrope walker
is not much more than a kid.
His name is Solomon Paprinski
his brother is the *shammes* at the Temple.
Solomon stops
in front of the large building
and chooses two lampposts
fifty yards apart.
There: these two.
Just a few feet
from the main door.
Solomon opens his suitcase
pulls out his steel wire
fixes it
straight
taut
by climbing
up the lampposts.
The street is ready:
the wire is fixed.
What else does he need?
Courage.
Solomon Paprinski
pulls out a bottle
swallows a good mouthful of cognac
then
climbs up.
Solomon Paprinski
gets into position
and starts walking.
Perfect.
Overhead.
Light as a feather.
Solomon Paprinski
never takes a step wrong:
he's the best tightrope walker
New York has ever seen.
And today
he has decided:

he'll be here
every day
morning and evening
to do his exercise.
Wire taut
straight between the lampposts
there
a few feet
from the new doorway.

For
now
in this city condemned to talk
they have even opened
an entirely new
gigantic
place in Wall Street
and it's called
"STOCK EXCHANGE."

Literally it means
that goods are exchanged.

But inside
there are no goods!
At most, you'll see their name
written everywhere
as if, over the door of a shop,
were the words BREAD EXCHANGE
but no bread inside,
or FRUIT EXCHANGE
but not even an apple core inside.

What really matters
of course
is the value, not the object.

"A clever idea!" Emanuel said;
"a New York idea" Mayer thought.

The point is that rather than bargaining over
iron at the Iron Exchange
cloth at the Cloth Exchange
coal at the Coal Exchange

oil at the Petroleum Exchange
they have made a single
immense
enormous
New York Exchange
a synagogue
with ceilings higher than a synagogue
where hundreds, crowds, armies
from morning to evening
talk
speak
bargain
yell
nonstop;
from morning to evening
talk
speak
bargain
yell
nonstop;
from morning to evening
nonstop
since the incredible thing
—at least so it seems to Mayer—
is that there inside, in Wall Street
there's no iron
there's no cloth
there's no oil
there's no coal
there's nothing
and yet
there's everything
hurled about
between mountains
torrents
of words:
mouths open
which blow blow blow air
and talk
and speak
and bargain
and yell
from morning to evening nonstop and
there outside

in front of this temple of words
every day
from today
Solomon Paprinski
will do his tightrope exercise.

Who knows whether the air
blown out from all those mouths
will ever end up causing a blizzard
that will dash him
to the ground.

It's the only thought
that Mayer *Bulbe*
manages to formulate
as he walks
with his striped leggings
along the sidewalk in Wall Street
toward the main door.
The entrance door.

In fact:
it's not true
that this is his only thought.

His other thought
is that
Philip
his nephew
will certainly like Wall Street, for sure:
he will, yes.

And Mayer is right.
For Philip
—Emanuel's son
born in New York:
not even a drop
of Germany or of Alabama
in his blood—
is a talking machine.
Remarkable.
Philip, in his uncle's eyes, is another mystery.
He is the son of an arm
but doesn't lift a finger:

his talent is all in his lips.
At the age of twenty
Philip manages words
tackles arguments like no one else
he raises questions and provides—on his own—the answers:
"Dear Rabbi Strauss,
I have a question to put to you, if it's not indiscreet.
Our family, as you know, owns a bank.
And this, dear Rabbi, makes us rather special
where the term 'special' has a whole range of values,
values about which I have no wish nor need to trouble you.
There remains, dear Rabbi Strauss, among all these motives for
    excellence,
the incontrovertible fact, Rabbi, that a family of bankers
enjoys that facility for monetary investment
that few others can boast,
and I use this verb because I know I must not impute to myself
the tiniest amount, not of ostentation, Rabbi Strauss,
but nor even of that general degree of vanity
that one forgives in families where wealth has been acquired, inherited, or
    such like.
Now, dear Rabbi, our prosperity—if I may put it that way—as a bank
is without doubt translated into a preeminent role
even within a small community:
we indeed support the Hebrew school, Rabbi Strauss,
and then the hospital and the orphan asylum,
without this support ever once being the subject of any form of negotiation.
Perfect.
I have had an exchange of views with my relatives.
And therefore I come to request your verdict:
do you not think, in your wisdom,
that it is imprudent to harbor the thought
that anyone who invests money in good works should feel ashamed
rather than demonstrating pride, Rabbi Strauss, about what they
    have done?
What would you say, in all honesty, to someone who hides himself
almost in revulsion
instead of inviting others to do the same and support the Temple?
Would you consider it fit behavior
to look away as if to say that alms giving is some kind of crime?
I see you nod in agreement, and this fills me with delight:
I agree with you, Rabbi Strauss, fully,
that giving money to the Temple

must be a matter of pride, not of embarrassment,
and—like you—I believe it so much, Rabbi Strauss,
that without doubting your approval I will tell the shammes to move
    our family
from the twenty-third row to at least the fifteenth.
With which, begging your pardon, having other matters to attend to,
I offer you my respects, dear Rabbi, and take my leave.
Good-bye."

There.
Perhaps because he plays tennis
—always has done—
and in tennis the ball must always remain in play
must never go out of court:
always up, Philip
always aiming high, Philip
always in the air, Philip
and that's what he does, very well;
he plays tennis with his conversations
with his words
never letting the ball drop.
That's how he talks about economics, Philip
talks about politics, Philip
talks about finance, Philip
and about Judaism
and about culture
and about music
and about fashion
and about horses
and about painters
and about cooking
and about landscapes
and about girls
and about values
and about friendship
and about New York, above all.
Philip was born here:
"I don't believe there's a better city in the world
dear Uncle, sir: New York
offers to my eyes the best of America and the reflection of Europe
I don't know what you think
but if you ask my opinion on the matter
I would say that New York is to planet Earth

what Olympus was to ancient Greece:
a place that is divine and at the same time human, dear Uncle, sir;
or, if you prefer me to speak in Hebrew vein
I will say that it is like the ner tamid
that burns without holy oil:
a creation of man and at the same time a miracle;
so that to those who dislike this city one can only say
that it is like denying the light of the Sun, dear Uncle, sir;
and if you are of this view then I implore you not to tell me so:
you would lose much of the esteem that I hold for you
so that
while curious to ask you
I prefer in the end not to know
and spare you the embarrassment of telling me
with which
begging your pardon
having other matters to attend to
I offer you my respects
dear Uncle, sir
and take my leave."

Astonishing.

New, Philip.
Completely new, Philip.
Son of New York, Philip.
Yes
there is no doubt
he will like Wall Street.

10
Shavuot

It is strange sometimes how human beings
get so caught up in their own business
that they achieve a result
they then regret.

Emanuel Lehman
who had set off to wage war against sleep
would now give anything for a peaceful night.

And not because he works too hard.

The point is that people sometimes dream at night.
And Emanuel Lehman always dreams the same story.

It starts like a game.
There's a cowshed, with cattle.
For we are certainly over there in Germany
in Rimpar, Bavaria.

In the cowshed
there are two young boys, he and Mayer.
They are playing their favorite game:
the money tower.
Very simple.
Just put a coin on the ground.
Then put another on top
then another—Emanuel's turn—
then another—Mayer's turn—
then another—Emanuel's turn—
then another—Mayer's turn—
then another—Emanuel's turn—
then another—Mayer's turn—
then another—Emanuel's turn—
then another—Mayer's turn—
and the pile of coins
balancing one on another
grows
grows
grows
grows
grows
grows
in his dream the column is high, very high
so high
that Emanuel begins to climb it
to scale it:
he clambers up
up
up

up
higher
Emanuel
farther
up
up
up
higher
Emanuel
farther
until
up there at the top
almost touching the wind
the sky opens up
suddenly
wide open
like at *Shavuot*
and with a rumble
a deafening roar
a locomotive
comes out
racing
madly
whistling
at great speed
straight toward Emanuel
—*"the train!"*—
straight toward Emanuel
—*"the train!"*—
straight toward Emanuel
—*"the train!"*—
straight toward Emanuel
—*"the train!"*—

Ever since his wife, Pauline,
was laid to rest under a marble slab
there is no longer anyone
to hold his hand
as Emanuel falls
plummets
down
from the column
knocked down

torn to pieces
by the cursed train.

The dream returns each night.

And Emanuel waits for it
but in his armchair:
he sleeps, sitting there.
For lying in bed
he feels suffocated
by the smoke from the tracks.

But this is a secret.

Because ever since his wife, Pauline,
was laid to rest under a marble slab
there is no one in the world
who knows about that train
always on time:
the night service.

It takes some understanding:
how could an arm
go 'round Wall Street saying
that he owns a bank
but won't invest in railroads
because every night
he is terrified of the train?

Emanuel can't say it.

He can't say
that for the first time
—and yet it's true—
he is frightened.

And it's a big problem.

Because everyone in New York
is talking about railroads
and above all
they're talking about it in Wall Street.
There

through that dark doorway
outside which Solomon Paprinski
every morning
fixes his wire
swallows his mouthful of cognac
and walks his tightrope.

The words in the air
are now a torment:
*"You'll certainly have entered the railroad market
Mr. Lehman?"*
"In what exactly have you invested?
Pacific Railway?
Or Chicago United?
Trans-Atlantic?"
"We've put a stake on North Western"
"May I recommend Middle-Southern?"

There must be
some strange force in the air
in Wall Street
that makes even fish
want to talk,
to talk about railroads.

There's no other explanation.

For even
Irving
his brother Mayer's youngest child
is already showing an interest in railroads:
when they found him
luckily
sitting on a step at the New York station,
unperturbed he said:
"Uncle Emanuel! I've seen
two trains transporting goods and three of passengers.
And the wooden locomotive you gave me
—okay it's not real—
but isn't there some way of getting smoke to come out of it?"

The only consolation
—the way out—

for Emanuel
is his age.

For now he understands
—Emanuel had no choice but to understand—
that an arm
when it grows old
is still an arm
but the elbow wins over the wrist
and the hand
—which does the action—
is always farther away . . .
And so
it is possible
—for sure—
that an elderly arm
is no longer asked to do:
but to get others to do.

Excellent.
No longer to act
but to get others to act.
That obsession of his throughout his life
to move, to do, to try
can now be: *"you move, you do, you try."*

For him it's enough that the bank
doesn't stand still, yes.
He doesn't want a single opportunity to be lost
now that industry is going well
and factories are growing by the hundreds
everywhere
—doing doing doing
building building building
inventing inventing inventing—
even if
the New York way of talking
has worked its way in so far
that even the workers
want to open their mouths
and are starting something called a *union.*

All the same.
Union or no union
Emanuel doesn't want to miss a thing
now that Wall Street has opened a block away
and all markets pass through there.
Emanuel quivers.
Can hardly contain himself.
More than ever?
More than ever.
He feels as though the whole world
has suddenly shrunk
into a button
and that New York is the buttonhole:
just a small, tiny gesture
and the world will be in the palm of our hand.
To do, therefore.
To be, therefore.
To dare.
To dare.
To dare.
But since an elbow can do less than a wrist
Emanuel doesn't drive the carriage himself:
he gives instructions to his new coachman
who follows them:
"As you have requested, dear Father, sir
I have brought Lehman Brothers even farther into the heart
of the coal market;
as a result, from today we control the revenue
of the whole fuel market for the next year
calculated on Wall Street tariffs.
I feel obliged however to inform you dear Father, sir
that I have concluded the negotiation only and entirely
because you have requested it, since I am wholly convinced
(nor am I the only one)
that our investment solely in the coal market
is entirely devoid of sense
it being destined to be overtaken within a few years, dear Father sir
by the domination of the railroad business
whose merits I can enumerate
should you wish indeed
to look at the capital."

"Why, Philip, do you have this railroad obsession too?
We already have capital, my son:
we have control of iron coal and coffee throughout New York."

"I could describe them
—if I may use an expression of my own invention—
as the market of the zero-points
more zero-points more zero-points."

"Which yet gives us millions in the end."

"After 30 pages of sums."

"If you had my experience, Philip . . ."

"I don't have gray hair, dear Father sir
but precisely because it's still black
I'll tell you that if I have to put the life in front of me to good use
I would like to do so with a string of numbers before the point, not after it.
If you agree with me, we should quit this coffee shambles
for the railroad.
If however you prefer to count beans instead of millions
let me spare you the embarrassment of saying so,
with which, begging your pardon, having other matters to attend to
I offer you my respects
dear Father sir
and take my leave."

And if the young coachman of the zero-points
he himself
were to defy
the locomotive of *Shavuot*?
Philip's zero-points
are becoming an obsession.
And if he really listened to him?
Perhaps Emanuel
could go back to sleeping peacefully . . .
If the young coachman
were to climb up
balancing
on the column of coins
right to the top

where the trains shoot past
then
perhaps he would stop
waking up sweating
like a baker?

Maybe
if we lay our bet on Philip . . .

After all, he's the son of an arm.

He resembles a wrist with the gift of speech.

And also
he has that zero-point
of New York cunning,
sometimes even sadistic.
Not to say cruel.

Definitely:
Philip is perhaps the last card to play.

11
Bar Mitzvah

Yehuda ben Tema
in the *Ethics of the Fathers*
says:
five years is the right age for studying the Scriptures
ten years for studying the *Mishnah*
at thirteen begin to respect the *mitzvot*
fifteen years and you shall study the *Gemara*.

Well
now that the century is almost at an end
the Lehman family of New York
offers a fine range

of assorted ages.
For there's no shortage of children:
eleven in all
four for Emanuel
seven for Mayer
and as for their ages
there's plenty of choice.

Luckily none of them
has to stand on tiptoe in the Temple,
partly because they're getting taller as they grow
and partly because the family pew
has moved up to the tenth row.

Now
when the Lehmans enter the Temple
they walk the whole side aisle
not deigning a glance
at the rather sulky Russians
the Kowalskis
who sit at the back
in the twenty-first row:
"Skazhi mne, papa: kto eti ran'she?"
"Oni yavlyayutsya znamenityy Lehman."*

But Herbert Lehman
doesn't think it's right
to sit in front.
And he protests.

Herbert is eleven
and goes to the Hebrew school.
Soon
—like his brothers—
in the exams
he'll have to tell about the rise of King David;
and the story of the Maccabees;
and every detail on the life of Joseph;
Esau with the plate of lentils;
Jonah in the stomach of the great fish
and how Cain killed his brother.

---

* In Russian: "Papa, who are those in front?" "They're the famous Lehmans."

This last story
indeed
is
of particular interest
to Herbert
since his brother Arthur
(always a hard nut, but people can get worse as they grow up)
has the habit of asking for money
"Just a loan, Herby!"
cleaning out his pocket money every week.
Yet Arthur is five years older,
and heck, shouldn't it be the other way 'round?
In the natural order of things
it ought to be
younger brothers
who receive preferential forms of bank loan
offered at knock-down rates
through family links.

No.
Here no.
Here it's the other way 'round.
Arthur Lehman takes money from Herbert
and isn't worried if the other complains.
"Arthur you owe me a whole load of money!
May I know when I'm going to get it back?"

"Shame on you, Herby: you've no heart."

"I have a right to get my money back!"

"No, and anyway, be careful not to offend our Constitution!"

"Our Constitution, what's that got to do with it?"

"You dolt! The American Constitution says that everyone
—me included—
has the right to be happy!
I am happy with your money,
so if you claim it back you'll make me unhappy,
and I can even report you. Take it easy, Herbert."

At his tender age
Herbert Lehman
couldn't manage even to say *"I disagree"*:
with just the stump of a nose
it was several days
before he got the scent of being taken for a ride
and
determined not to give in
he vowed to put things right.

In the first place
he learned the whole Constitution by heart.
And how much it served him in life!

And so
reassured
about his constitutional rights
he decided to turn to the adult members of the family,
not so much as moral authorities
but as experts in banking practice:
*"Father sir, if a debtor doesn't give me back my capital,
what steps can I take to recover it?"*

His father, Mayer, looks at him.

The banking disease
infects even children.

Since the boy won't give up,
Mayer explains the whole situation
of additional charges
and penalties that gradually take effect.

Herbert doesn't agree:
shouldn't he ask for more money
apart from the amount
that Arthur already refuses to pay?
The problem lies deep down:
when someone has a debt, don't we increase the debt?

Fortunately there's Uncle Emanuel, who is much more practical
and suggests

—following appropriate formal notice—
the seizing of material goods.

So Herbert
after the umpteenth ultimatum
begins to confiscate things
from his brother's bedroom
during the night
and so takes possession of:
—2 leather balls
—3 geographical maps
—1 cloth hot-air balloon
—7 illustrated books
—1 mouth-organ
—2 pens with inkwell
—3 cream shirts
—1 straw hat belonging to one unknown Roundhead

And now that Arthur
has only his bed
Herbert has returned to his uncle for advice:
"Can I take that too?"

Unfortunately
though
it seems that even finance
must have a minimum of heart
and not even a powerful bank
can turn a brother into a tramp.

But for Herbert that's not enough
and he decides to at least play the intimidation card:
in the middle of the night he creeps into his brother's room
and as theatrically as possible
suddenly pulls back the blankets
announcing through a megaphone:
"This bed won't be yours for much longer:
if you want to sleep soundly,
Arthur, pay up!"
And without waiting for a reaction
he would have hurried out
except that his brother
—aggrieved by the sudden awakening—

leapt at him with his hands to his neck
and of all the insults that a money-grubber might have spat out
he opted instead
for a wondrous mathematical axiom:
"The probability of my letting you take it
is proportional to what you have to be paid!
And now get out, or come back here with a formal warrant."

In short
Herbert has much to worry about.
For now
he is sitting at the far end of the schoolroom
always rather distracted
and even forgets to stand up
when Rabbi Strauss
—who has more teeth in his mouth than hairs on his head—
comes down once a month to the class
and questions the children:
"Today I would like to consider
here with you
the meaning of the word punishment.
Punishment is a form of compensation.
It is never unjust.
Punishment gives the world its equilibrium.
If you by your conduct take something away
the scourge of HaShem will set the account straight.
And this is why HaShem punished the people of Egypt.
For keeping the Chosen People in slavery.
Now, when I call out your names
you will recite in perfect order
all the plagues of Egypt:
starting with you, Master Rothschild."

"HaShem *turned the River Nile into blood, Rab Strauss."*

"That's right, Rothschild. The second plague, Wolf."

"HaShem *invaded Egypt with frogs, Rab Strauss."*

"That's correct, Wolf. The third and fourth plague, Libermann."

"HaShem *sent gnats, Rab Strauss, and then flies."*

"The fifth plague is yours, Master Strauss."

"HaShem killed the livestock of Egypt."

"Excellent, Strauss. And now your brother will tell me the sixth."

"Boils on men and animals, Rab Strauss."

"Well done, both of you. The seventh, Master Altschul?"

"Hailstones came down."

"Very many came down, Altschul. The eighth plague, Borowitz?"

"Invasion of locusts."

"Locusts, yes sir. The penultimate plague, Cohen?"

"Darkness fell, Rabbi."

"And the last plague I want from you, Herbert Lehman."

"HaShem had the children of Egypt killed."

"Wrong, Lehman:
HaShem *didn't do this at all."*

"But I don't agree."

"As always: you want to give your own interpretation, rather than
    learning.
The Scripture says:
"At midnight the Lord struck down
every firstborn child in the land of Egypt."
And to say firstborn is not to say children, Lehman!"

"But I don't agree with the decision of HaShem, Rabbi."

"Lehman!"

"In fact I don't agree with any of the plagues."

"What I have to listen to!"

"Actually I disagree entirely
with the position of HaShem.
The problem lies deep down, Rabbi,
and becomes a political question:
why slaughter the people of Egypt
who were not to blame?

"This is intolerable!"

"In my view HaShem
—rather than wasting time on plagues—
should have killed the Pharaoh directly
and then the Israelites would have been free straightaway, and . . ."

"HaShem does not take advice from Herbert Lehman!"

"But Herbert Lehman is one of the Chosen People."

"You must be quiet, little boy! Right now!"

"I'll shut up, Rabbi, if you wish, provided it's clear
that I don't agree!"

Although he's ten years old
there are few things
about which Herbert Lehman
does agree.

He doesn't agree
about the fact that at *Hanukkah*
only the head of the family can light the candles.
He doesn't agree
that at *Purim*
the fritters are eaten only on that day.
He doesn't agree
—not at all—
about all those peach branches
cut from trees in blossom
to decorate *Tu BiShvat*.
And above all
he can't work out
why his brothers
have their *Bar Mitzvah*

with the full works
while his sisters—not them—
they get the
Bat Mitzvah
without going up to the podium
without commenting on the Torah
just answering a few questions on the house.

They've tried explaining to him
it's a tradition
and that traditions, dear Herbert
are not to be dumped
like old clothes
and a Jewish woman is not like a man
even if
the New York way of talking
has worked its way so far in
that even women
want to open their mouths
and make such a lot of rumpus
with something called *suffragettes*.
And now we want to change tradition?
Herbert shakes his head:
he doesn't agree
that a brother counts more
than a sister.

Their family is now large
and there are so many
brothers and sisters.

His brother Irving
for example
is now thirteen.
Thirteen years and a day.

He's forever being forgotten about
since he has the extraordinary ability
of passing unnoticed.
Today however no.
Today he'll be the center of attention.
For today
is his *Bar Mitzvah*.

Everyone at the Temple.
The whole family there
brothers, sisters, everyone
those born in Alabama
as well as those children of New York.
An important day.
Irving comes of age:
from today Irving is an adult
Irving becomes personally responsible
for keeping the *halakha*.

He will read a passage from the Torah
from the podium
for the first time.
And will discuss the Scripture
with others.

There, exactly:
he will discuss.

This is the awkward point.
Unfortunately for Irving Lehman
someone else
has his *Bar Mitzvah*
today
—on the same day—
and that someone
is none other
than the curly-haired
heir of Mr. Goldman.

The Goldmans do everything splendidly
and are proud of it.
They handle money
—just like the Lehmans—
sign contracts
—just like the Lehmans—
forge business relationships
—just like the Lehmans—
in short
there is nothing
the Lehmans do
that is not

exactly identical
to Goldman Sachs.
Even their beginnings are identical:
both
German families.
And both
have their vacation home
at Elberon:
neighbors
as chance would have it.

The only difference
—since the truth should always be told—
lies in the fact that the Goldmans
deal in that particular metal
called gold
and are so proud of it
that they flaunt it in their surname.

For this, and only for this,
they're in the second row
of the Temple.

There's an ancient hatred
between Lehman and Goldman.

That furious rivalry
which often divides
similar families.

They live on opposite banks of a river
Lehman Brothers and Goldman Sachs:
between them flows water
gold-colored water.
Both go fishing
in the same water
and they watch each other
stare at each other
ready to pounce
we here
you there
—since the river is the same
and so are the fish—

there, in Wall Street
which now also has its own newspaper
The *Wall Street Journal*
yelled out by paperboys on the sidewalks
while Solomon Paprinski
every morning
gulps his mouthful of cognac
and away:
walks along the wire
without ever falling.

There they are, lined up today.

Both.
At the Temple.
For the *Bar Mitzvah* of the thirteen-year-olds.
Both smartly dressed.
Both perfect.
We're Lehman Brothers.
We're Goldman Sachs.
We to the right.
You to the left.
We're Lehman Brothers.
We're Goldman Sachs.
We with ours.
You with yours.
We're Lehman Brothers.
We're Goldman Sachs.

Smiles between the ladies.
Handshakes between the men.

But the real war
is between the two mothers
on opposite sides of the Temple
as they straighten their boys' ties:
*"Go on, my boy, up to the platform, it's your turn, you're a Goldman:
do it for your father."*

*"Go on, my boy, up to the platform, it's your turn, you're a Lehman:
do it for your father."*

"You have to read perfectly, my son: no mistakes."

"You don't want to make us seem any less than their Irving, do you?"

"You carry a great name, my boy, don't forget it."

*"And don't ever forget that those Goldmans
arrived in America after us."*

*"Always keep in mind that those Lehmans
have southern blood: they're not like us."*

"And if that boy says anything, you stand up to him."

"If that boy with the curly hair starts making faces, just ignore him."

*"Now listen to me: if he tells you they have shares in coal, just laugh in his
     face."*

*"Before you go: if he tells you they sell coffee
shrug your shoulders and say: 'old hat.'"*

*"But above all, son: I want you to promise me:
You have to swear
not for any reason in the world
never to mention the business of tobacco."*

Yes.
Tobacco.
It's the latest invention devised by the Lehman brothers
perhaps because they have been truly astonished
by the sight
of that vast expanse
of backs bent down laboring
so resembling the plantations in Alabama.

And the memory of the past bewitches
even those arms more resistant to tears.

And not just that.
There's something else.

Tobacco has to be picked,
tobacco has to be processed
tobacco has to be rolled

or flaked
or boxed up.
In short, tobacco is toil and labor.

And the two Lehmans have it in their blood
working head bent
unstintingly
no pauses
no breaks.

Even rather too much.
For Philip Lehman
is not so keen
about all this hard work of theirs.
"Dear father sir
there's no reason for you to tire yourself so much:
let's leave the real labor to the employees
you sit much higher here:
don't forget you're a founder
your task is just to coordinate
to move the pieces on the chessboard."

Maybe he's right.
And now Emanuel does in fact coordinate:
he moves people about like pawns
he no longer leaves his office
he delegates to others
oversees the work
and work is flourishing:
there is not a day
compared with the day before
that doesn't have a plus sign
there
in those account books
where Mayer has now stopped
making entries
not because his eyes are weak
but it was impossible to do everything alone
and it is done now
in an office
of six people
whom Lehman pays
ten hours a day

to do only that.
"Dear Uncle sir
there's no reason for you to do
the work of a clerk:
let us leave the bookkeeping to the staff
you sit much higher here:
don't forget you are a founder
all you have to do is sign."

Maybe he's right.
And indeed Mayer now signs:
each day
with his brother
in the late evening
the accounts with the + sign.
the + sign: signed Mayer / Emanuel Lehman.
the + sign: signed Mayer / Emanuel Lehman.
the + sign: signed Mayer / Emanuel Lehman.
For years.
Always a + sign
because America
is a horse galloping madly
on the New York racetrack
and Lehman Brothers
is the jockey.
the + sign: signed Mayer / Emanuel Lehman.
the + sign: signed Mayer / Emanuel Lehman.
the + sign: signed Mayer / Emanuel Lehman.

"Dear Uncle sir
dear Father sir
there's no reason for you to do the auditing:
let us leave the signing of the accounts to the managers
you sit much higher here:
don't forget that you are the founders
it is for you to choose
on whom and what to invest
Not by yourselves, of course."

That's right: not by themselves.

12
United Railways

It's just a shame
that as Mayer Lehman gets older
he is more aware of being a vegetable.

Planted in the ground:
grown among clods of soil, with sunshine, with water.
And this is why
in recent times
he is interested
particularly
in tobacco.
In only that.
He has become fond of it over time.
Tobacco is dark brown:
like the earth in which the potato grows.
And then, tobacco is weighed, put into sacks:
like the cotton of once upon a time
which has now even been removed from the sign.
Tobacco is substance
and the figures it produces are not air
that will become real in forty years' time.
Mayer notes down figures in the account books
minuscule, exact
so small
that he has damaged his eyes over those scribblings
and wears two lenses fixed to his nose.
A potato with lenses.

"You have ruined your eyes
dear brother
and it's the fault of your darned tobacco!"

"What does tobacco have to do with my eyes?"

"Zero-point plus zero-point plus zero-point."

"What are you talking about?"

"*The figures for tobacco are small, Mayer*
and they all go after the decimal point.
Do you want to count cigars instead of counting millions?
I'll not be satisfied with adding up zero-points: I want to make capital."

"*We already have capital, Emanuel:*
we have control of the market in iron
coal, coffee, oil, tobacco . . ."

"*Zero-point plus zero-point plus zero-point!*"

"*Which gives a million.*"

"*After thirty pages of sums, yes of course, and with two eyes less.*"

"*Everyone carries the scars of their occupation.*"

"*But what are you talking about, Mayer?*"

"*I'm talking like a Lehman:*
our father caught cattle disease
Henry caught yellow fever from the plantations
I can lose my sight with tobacco."

"*Listen to me:*
my hair has gone gray, Mayer,
and if I have to ruin the last scrap of my life
I want to do it with a string of numbers before the point, not after it.
And this is why we'll invest in railroads."

"*Arthur was sucking his thumb the first time you told me this,*
and now he's at school."

"*The railroad is salvation.*"

"*The railroad is only talk.*"

"*I haven't founded a bank*
for the zero-points!"

"*And I haven't founded a bank*
just for talk!"

It was at that moment
that Emanuel suddenly understood.
For the first time he grasped the meaning
of his recurring nightmare
as well as what his brother meant
by *"the railroad is just talk."*

Like a ray of light shining into the room
everything became clear:
they were frightened, both of them, of the railroad
because in reality they had never seen it.
It was an idea, not a fact.

But everything would change
if they touched it with their hands
the crazy excitement
of actually seeing it—the railroad—being built!

To put an end to the nightmares
they had to go and see the tracks being laid
the stations being built
the nuts tightened
the screws turned
the bolts fixed
and then to hear the splitting of the coal
the whining of the sawmills cutting
thousands millions billions
of wooden planks
to lay in lines between the rails!

Mayer was still a man of the South at heart,
his thoughts remained in Alabama.
Mayer hadn't traveled to the North
thirty years before
to see Teddy Wilkinson's factories
where the machines were already puffing steam!
That's it, yes: steam!
Marvel of industries and now of trains!
How could Mayer have faith in the railroad
without Emanuel taking him
to see it being built
wondrous, surprising
but above all *mechanical*

real, so real
concrete, so concrete
all made of iron and steel
fire, bronze
sparks, clamps, cutters?

He decided.
He had to act.
He had to illuminate his brother's vegetable mind
just as his visit to Teddy Wilkinson
had illuminated his, thirty years before.

He spread the word.
and it was like lighting a fuse
because, from New York, words fly:
everyone everywhere knew that the two Lehman brothers
—owners of Lehman Brothers Bank—
were interested
at last
in the railroad market:
they wanted
to touch with their hands
the railroad being built
to touch with their hands
the beginning of the future;
they would take nothing on trust:
the Lehmans wanted to see.

A meeting was arranged
for the end of November.
Baltimore Railroad.
Under construction.
Emanuel's enthusiasm?
Uncontainable.
Throughout the journey
he didn't stop
enthusing to Mayer
—not for one moment—
about what awaited them: laborers at work
100 times
1000 times more than in the plantations
as far as the eye could see
for America is vast

and has to be covered with tracks and stations
from side to side.
"An enormous task, Mayer
like the pharaohs of Egypt
who are a true part of history;
not like your darned tobacco
that goes up into your nose and slips away!
And not like the darned coffee
that your Mexican friend produces!"

Though here Mayer had to remind him
that old Miguel Muñoz
was not a friend of his at all:
not only had they never met
but it was Emanuel who had gone to Mexico
straight after the war
to work out some way
of escaping from cotton.

Emanuel insisted: it wasn't true
no sir
it was Mayer who had dug his heels in
ten or more years ago
just to buy coffee from the Mexicans
and to add zero-points by the dozen.

Mayer felt aggrieved: enough.
He couldn't let his brother
always take the credit
and promptly
unload the blame on him.

Emanuel shouted: *"Listen here, Mayer!*
Lehman Brothers is like a sponge,
it must absorb the business that goes on around,
we can't allow ourselves to stand around watching!
We have to absorb!"

And Emanuel
came out with many other metaphors
some more successful than others
like he had never done before;
because an arm is an arm

and has no half measures
when it comes to action
or persuading others to act.

In that instance he drew a remarkable picture
of American railroad industries:
its labor force at work, raw materials
streams of molten iron
and then the screeching of steel
and then the infernal noise
and then
and then
and then . . .

. . . and then when they arrived
they were surprised
by the silence.

Total silence.

Three or four men were waiting.
From United Railways.
Well dressed? More.
Excellently dressed.
Newly tailored suits.
And immense smiles.

One of them came forward.
More than a person
one might say a smile
with a person around it;
"I am Archibald Davidson, at your service!"
Proudly
he raised his arm
to point out the spectacle.

Mayer strained his eyes.
He thought the coffee numbers
—those after the decimal points—
had completely ruined his eyesight
because the spectacle of the railroad under construction
seemed to him
absolutely

—how could one put it?—
nothing.

There was nothing there.

Nothing built.

Nothing being built.

Nothing to be built.

Nothing.

The absence of everything.

A valley.
A river.
Bushes.
Flies.

*"The railroad will run there through the middle:
the route is already down in black and white.
Here: on this plan you can see it
drawn out."*

"And the construction site? When will it open?"

"When you give us the funds."

"On paper?"

"On paper, Mr. Lehman."

"And when will the railroad be ready?"

*"Pursuant to the terms of the agreement.
Even though for you—for business purposes—it's irrelevant."*

"Ten years?"

"Or twenty, thirty, forty: it's irrelevant."

"Then what is relevant?"

"That you give us the go-ahead."

That enormous smile
called Archibald Davidson
had much more to add
and pulled out at least six or seven sheets of paper
as large as bedsheets,
where the railroad was perfectly drawn out.
In black and white.

The Lehmans nodded, of course.

As they were nodding
Mayer thought the ink
had the same dark color of coffee
and that so much of it had flowed across those sheets of paper
that maybe
—rather than trains!—
it would be a good idea
if anything
to investigate the market for ink.

Emanuel Lehman
however
mute, immobile, speechless
kept his eyes fixed
—in exceptional surprise—
on the tailored suits
of these men from United Railways:
suits of *first choice*
of finest
quality cloth:
cotton
a splendid
most expensive
cotton.
And while a part of him
kept at bay the temptation to mourn the past
a voice behind him
rang out
loudly
clearly

like that of coachmen
reminiscing over a horse:

"Dear Mr. Archibald Davidson,
your pieces of paper filled with drawings would fascinate a child
but we haven't come from New York
to look at pictures and to say 'well done':
the children at the Jewish school are very clever with pastels
they draw houses and bridges, yet no one would finance them as builders.
My father, Emanuel, and my Uncle Mayer, dear Mr. Davidson,
are expecting much more from you: figures, numbers, substance.
How much do you need from our bank?
How much are you prepared to pay in interest?
And over what repayment period for our capital?
You are talking to the Lehman brothers, in case you are not aware:
my father, Emanuel, and my Uncle Mayer—for I speak in their name—
are prepared to invest in railroads
solely and exclusively
if the Bank's earnings come to seven zeros.
Millions, dear Mr. Davidson, you have no doubt understood.
If this is the unit of measurement for you too
then the railroad can carry the name Lehman
and we can say: 'build it.'
If however you prefer to stick to your drawings
then we spare you the embarrassment of telling us,
with which begging your pardon
having other investments to attend to
we offer you our respects
dear Mr. Davidson
and take our leave."

"One moment, please. You are?"

"Philip Lehman."

"Mr. Lehman, you are talking to us about financing the railroads:
do you mean bonds issued by you to give us capital?"

"Dear Mr. Davidson, have you by chance mistaken us for cloth traders?
Or even worse for sellers of wholesale coffee?
Who do you think you have before you? Coal merchants? Or gasmen?
My father, Emanuel, and my Uncle Mayer here before you

mean
of course
bonds that we will draw:
those who subscribe will give us the money
we will return it to them with a small interest.
In the meantime you have the capital that you will repay with a
    considerable interest.
The profit lies in this difference.
For us, of course.
But for you too."

"The proposal of United Railways is a five million return."

"Dear Mr. Davidson, neither my father, Emanuel, nor my Uncle Mayer
    here before you
have come all this way to be insulted.
In their eyes I already note an air of disdain.
In case you are not already aware, our company title is BANK,
not BENEVOLENT SOCIETY.
And banks think in seven zeros, as I have indicated.
Which means, in other words, ten million: double."

"I'm in a position to offer seven."

"My father, Emanuel, and my Uncle Mayer here present will not go down
    to nine."

"United Railways cannot exceed eight."

"Dear Mr. Davidson, let me avoid the disagreeable business of bargaining.
I am quite sure that you of all people
would not stoop so low.
Lehman Brothers has a great history behind it:
we have no wish to appear to you
as though we were vendors in a fruit market.
The only possible point of agreement is ten million and not a cent less.
After which,
if United Railways considers the figure unreasonable,
I exonerate you from the indignity of saying so,
since neither my father, Emanuel, nor my Uncle Mayer here present
wish to be humiliated as though they were cotton traders.
So that, if you accept ten million
let us shake hands as a sign of agreement,

but if you do not accept
let us shakes hands and say good-bye forever."

And here.

They shook hands.

To tell the truth
without either Mayer or Emanuel
understanding exactly
whether it was a handshake of agreement or of good-bye.
No matter: they shook hands.
A long handshake.
Though not understanding why they were shaking hands.

But the fact that Philip smiled
certainly cheered them
making them feel sure
that something important had just happened
and this smile of satisfaction
the smile of historic moments
was painted on every face.

From that night
Emanuel Lehman
no longer slept in the armchair
but stretched out in his bed.
He was not frightened of any train.
For his coachman
had suddenly become
a station master.

And more.
Lehman Brothers
felt like a convoy
drawn along by locomotive power
and there was
at this point
no journey
to which the bank could not turn its thoughts.

The first
in order of time

departed from the tenth pew of the Temple
and took them to fifth position.
Emanuel and Mayer leaned out from the windows
celebrating like two children
and such was the enjoyment
that no one had the courage to warn them:
next day, Philip Lehman would come of age
and the pact with Aunt Rosa came into full force.

In short
on the locomotive named LEHMAN BROTHERS
three new railroaders
were about to climb aboard.

The first was a mute spinning top.

The second had the features of a rabbit.

The third was Philip Lehman. Full stop.

13
Wall Street

Say what you like,
but a trio of cousins
between twenty and thirty
can hardly be considered
qualified to run a company.

These more or less
are the thoughts
of an arm and a potato
as they wake each morning.

We have steered
the family bank
safe and sound
out of a war

and from Alabama to the Big City.
Why do we have to step back?
Because Aunt Rosa has the last word?

High finance
is not stuff
for any beginner.

Proof of which
came on that day
when a rabbit
bright red and sweating with excitement
entered
the Wall Street Stock Exchange
for the first time,
where financiers
—even the calmest and most moderate—
scowl
and throw daggers.

At ten in the morning
below the wire
on which Solomon Paprinski walks
in perfect equilibrium
four figures appear:
Emanuel Lehman
with his son, Philip,
and Mayer Lehman
with his son Sigmund.

The first three dressed in black,
the fourth in a white suit
with no hat
so as not to ruffle the parting in his hair
which he constantly combs.

The first three with a stern look
(which is almost a rule on Wall Street),
the fourth with the typical expression
—a mixture of joy and trepidation—
of a little boy
on his first day at school.

The first three with a pugnacious air,
the fourth with a ready smile
that he offers everyone like candies
making no distinction
between enemies, allies, or even traitors.

The first three tight-lipped,
the fourth with sugar on his chin
a morning remnant
of a first helping of donuts.

The first three conscious of where we are.
The fourth entirely out of place
like a cat
at the entrance to a kennel.

And yet
on the way there
Sigmund has been instructed
in every detail
about what kind of conduct
is expected
of those who enter that door.

As his Uncle Emanuel says,
the Stock Exchange is like a doctor's surgery,
where each day
a full examination is made
of all the banks
and quoted companies.
"Of course, Uncle sir: I understand."
But while a doctor
listens to your chest
to check
your state of health,
in Wall Street
it's not your health that's being checked
but instead
the level of confidence
that each of them earns on the market.
"Dear Sigmund, in business
talking about confidence
means talking about power

for no one in the world
is going to put their money
into a drawer
with a broken lock.
The procedure is exactly the same
there's no difference:
the financial system
is deciding all the time
in which drawer
its money will be safest
and to do so
it examines the locks
the strength of the wood
the shape of the key
and above all
it asks questions
relentlessly
about the cabinet's reputation
in the past."

"Of course, Uncle sir: I understand.
It's all very clear and I'm much obliged to you."

"Sigmund, I stress:
confidence is power
so that confidence has to be protected at all costs."

"At all costs, Uncle sir: of course."

Yes. At all costs.
This is the reason,
Mayer added,
why Wall Street
seems like a fish market:
everyone shouts about the advantages of their bank
everyone shouts themselves hoarse to sell their tunny fish
everyone praises the quality of their mullet
everyone speaks badly about the other seller's bream
and all it needs is a crate of anchovies
for sale at half the price
to suddenly
inexplicably

change the commercial fate
of herring and bass.

*"I have the picture perfectly in mind, Father sir:
I'm ready to do my duty."*

"Your duty is to fend off the daggers"
his cousin Philip concluded
as they were about to turn the corner.
*"To sum up:
there's only one rule
for surviving on Wall Street
and it's not to give in
by which I mean
there mustn't be a single instant
in which the financier loses his grip:
if he stops he is lost
if he takes a pause he is dead
if he relaxes he is trodden underfoot
if he stops to think he may bitterly regret it
and so prepare yourself, dear Sigmund:
every banker is a warrior
and this is the battlefield.
I'm sure you'll be equal to the challenge.
But if not, always remember:
hysterical laughter
is always preferable to tears
and it's better to talk too much than to hesitate.
Generally speaking
exaggeration is never a mistake.
If something goes wrong,
don't say that you're a Lehman.
On the other hand
if all goes well,
then say it loud and clear.
If you happen to lose control altogether
it's a good idea
to have a false name at the ready
appropriate for the purpose,
I'd suggest one like Libermann or Kaufmann
for us it's all the same:
they're both enemies, so take your pick.
Ah! And if you have a sudden attack of anxiety*

avoid any humiliating situation:
don't look for any help as you won't get it
so take preventative action
and hide yourself in the men's room,
locking the door if you can.
That's all, cousin, there's nothing else:
don't go looking for me if you need anything.
Wall Street awaits you
so enjoy yourself."

As soon as he set foot
inside the temple of Wall Street
Sigmund Lehman
felt his stomach sink.

From windows
amazingly high
an unexpected
milk-white light
flooded down
over everything
so that
it would have been impossible
hovering up there
not to have been struck
at every moment
by the details
of those faces all the same and all different
multiplied ad infinitum
like the shares, the securities, and the prices
they were jotting down
in their notebooks.

Never but never
would Sigmund have believed
that such a place existed
on planet Earth
in which mathematics
became religion
and its rituals
sung aloud
were no more than numerical litanies.

The first conversation he heard
between two bearded brutes
went in fact like this:
"Hello, Charles."
"Good morning, Golfaden."
"Are you asking 12 and 70?"
"14 and 10!"
"Net?"
"With three-and-a-half expenses."
"11 and 10 multiplied by how much?"
"91 or 94 at most."
"You've upped it 2 percent."
"After which I dropped 4."
"But for you I'll ask 12.45."
"If it gives you a return."
"There's no discussion with you."
"So good day then."

Distracted by this abacus
Sigmund was already alone:
the other Lehmans were lost among the crowd
and the numbers leapt everywhere:
iron that day was selling at 13
coal at 5 and 30
petroleum had dropped to 24 and 6
> *at least until*
> *a skeletal forty-year-old*
> *came back to life on an armchair*
> *springing to his feet to shout "Up! Up! Up!"*
> *and on a board the figure next to OIL*
> *rose from 24.6 to 24.62.*
Coffee was stationary at 2 and 12
gas had soared to 11 and 70
the railroad sector swung 3 points.
As for tobacco, it was on the down.

In that whirl of figures
Up and Down
seemed
the only permissible words,
as if everything in the world
could only
rise or fall
rise or fall

rise or fall
Up! Up! Up!
Down! Down! Down!
Up! Up! Up!
Down! Down! Down!

Sigmund Lehman
could only wonder
whether he himself
    as an individual
    as a biological organism
    as a sentient creature
was in an UP or DOWN
and opted for the second
without a doubt.

For it is known that the human being
—to which certain breeds of rabbit belong—
sometimes sets his own trap
like those painters
who on having to paint a portrait
become fascinated
by a wisp of hair
by a pointed nose
by the curve of a chin
and
concentrate so much
on that detail
that nothing else exists
and lose themselves there.
This is what happened to Sigmund Lehman,
who after only ten minutes
began to see
around him
nothing but jaws and teeth:
gaping mouths
ready to tear him apart
as though he were a rabbit
that had fallen by mistake
into a tank of alligators.
And at meal time too.

Yes.
For even though all those

who spoke of Wall Street
had told him about wild animals,
Sigmund
so to speak
hadn't properly grasped the significance
imagining
not a forest
but a zoological garden
where there were wild animals, of course
but safely locked in cages.

Here, instead, they were free.

And he was in the midst of them.

His neurons touched
and fired:
he began to run.
Numbers were sticking to him like glue:
a 13.18 unhitched itself from his shoulder
while two pairs of 99s tackled him at the knees
his right arm was victim of multiples of 7
his fingers a 11,111
and he barely had time to take his eyes off the 8s
before his chest
was churning inside
and under his shirt
he felt an exploding 48,795,672. 452
so that
he declared a truce with the troops of Pythagoras
and panting
bright red sweating with terror
he hid behind an urn filled with flowers
some in bloom others wilting
or rather
some *up* and others *down*.

Heaven at times blesses its offspring.
Or at least so it seems.

For chance would have it
that his cousin Philip
should stop exactly there in front

with a fellow all eyes
a financier from New Mexico:
Philip signaled with two fingers to ask him
for a light for his cigar
and the fellow was pleased to be of service.
At which he struck up a conversation.

Sigmund leaned forward
becoming all one with the marble urn:
his white suit helped to disguise him.
And unseen he listened.

Philip was a true master.
He listed one by one
all the reasons why Lehman Brothers was among the best:
top in industry
success in commerce
network of alliances
flood of contracts
and so on
with trains, oil, coal
stirring the greatest interest of the other
and when he was asked in confidence
whether he knew—by chance—
about a certain turbulent David
who had been engaged to marry
twelve times at once
Philip wasn't ruffled in the slightest:
*"Yes, of course. A dreadful business:
there are some despicable characters in high finance.
But I'll tell you all about it . . ."*

And to Sigmund's amazement
he began to tell him
about the amorous odyssey
of a certain David Libermann
*"Or no: perhaps it was the son of the Kaufmanns,
though it really doesn't matter."*

His cousin's lesson
eavesdropped through petals and stamens
was a real education
for Sigmund Lehman.

And this cheered him.
And what was more:
he suddenly felt ready
and hoisted the Up sign on his inner engine.

He straightened his tie
combed the parting in his hair
smoothed his crumpled sleeves as best he could
abandoned the florist's stall
and adopted a financial nonchalance.

Heaven at times blesses its offspring.
Or at least so it seems.

In one corner he spotted
an elderly well-dressed man
wearing a top hat over a span high.
He could have been from Michigan.
Or maybe Jersey.
In any event,
he decided that
wherever he came from
he would soon be returning.
Sigmund approached him.

With two fingers he gestured to the old man
asking whether he could light his cigar
and the other willingly agreed
proffering a lighted flame.

What a shame that Sigmund didn't smoke
and there was no sign of cigars in his pockets.

The embarrassment however was only temporary:
with a wondrous leap from Down to Up
the rabbit reacted brilliantly:
he feigned thoughtlessness
and in an entirely credible tone
cursed himself
for having left his cigar case
at the negotiating table.
The old man nodded:
he was certainly an expert

when it came to tricks of the mind,
so they both laughed heartily
and the doors of paradise opened.

Sigmund played all his cards.
Like an enterprising young man
he began to list the glories of the bank:
top in industry
success in business
network of alliances
flood of contracts
and so on with trains, oil, coal
in a crescendo of enthusiasm
so much so
that a small crowd gathered 'round
drawn to the strange spectacle
of a rabbit
singing the praises of its carrots.

As for the old man
he stared at him, not saying a word,
enchanted by such high spirits.

On seeing that he was surrounded
young Lehman
put more lubrication into the works:
bright red and sweating with excitement
he didn't even notice he was shouting
as he enthused to the old man
in a somewhat excessive tone
"... the name of a financial giant
which is already inscribed in the coming centuries
and Lehman Brothers, illustrious colleague,
will one day end up on the American flag
for there is not a citizen in the world
who would not go to any lengths, illustrious colleague,
just to have half a dollar
in the vaults of our bank
the securest of the whole Capitol.
But now tell me, illustrious colleague:
in what realm of finance do you operate?
And if we are discussing figures
how much can we talk about investing?"

And as he anticipated the answer
imagining the old man to be
the head of Studebaker
or mogul of the Vehicle Company
he felt a hand
take hold of his jacket,
pulling him away from his triumph in battle.

It was Philip and Emanuel:
"What on earth do you think you're doing?"

"I was about to make a financial alliance!
And what are you doing interrupting me?"

But his question went unanswered:
uncle and cousin
instead of praising him
were hurrying, away, toward the exit
through the crowds
all of whom in fits of laughter.

Mayer, his father,
had the thankless task of informing him:
"That was the usher, Sigmund.
And, if that's not enough for you, he's deaf as well."

14
Der kartyozhnik

Yehuda ben Tema
in the *Ethics of the Fathers*
says:
at eighteen years you will think of marriage
twenty years for running
thirty for growing strong
forty for growing shrewd.

Philip Lehman
has ticked all the boxes

hasn't left a single one empty.
For Philip Lehman
doesn't miss out on anything.
From the age of sixteen
he has kept a diary
always open on his desk
where he writes down in block capitals
all his problems
and day by day
has to write down in block capitals
the answer too.

THE SOLUTION IS ALREADY THERE, JUST FIND IT
these are the words
that Philip Lehman has written down
in block capitals
on the first page
of every diary.
That's what he decided to write
that day when
in Liberty Street
a dwarf in a top hat
dressed all in yellow
appeared on the street corner
and played the three-card trick
on a fruit crate.
Philip remained there for hours
standing
stock-still
watching him:
almost no one managed to win
the winning card was always hidden.
And yet it was there:
among the three
it was there
covered
but it was there.
Within reach.
So simple.
Just turn the right card.
So simple.
What's the problem?
To turn the right card

just don't get distracted.
Philip concentrated hard, that day:
kept his eyes glued to the dwarf's deft fingers
fixed his gaze on those hands
—*"no distraction, Philip!"*—
relentlessly
—*"no distraction, Philip!"*—
on the cards
—*"no distraction, Philip!"*—
following the movement
—*"no distraction, Philip!"*—
"The winning card is this!"

And he won.

He knew it wasn't luck.
It was technique.

Philip hadn't tried to win:
he had *decided* to win.

Since then
from that day
Philip Lehman is never distracted.
He concentrates, steadfast
allowing no exception:
he knows that if he can keep control
the winning card will not escape him.
Follow the movement.
Watch the dwarf's hands
don't lose track of the cards
keep control
keep control
control
control
control
like playing tennis
being sure the ball
always stays inside the lines
checked
followed
controlled.

And Philip Lehman has plenty of control.
You bet he has it!
Always:
For his life
is never written in italics:
always in block capitals.

At the age of twenty
—which for Yehuda ben Tema is the age for running—
Philip Lehman has run
—you bet he has run!—
he has raced
behind trains under construction,
He has written in his diary
in block capitals:
RAILROAD = CAPITAL, CAPITAL = LEHMAN
and
—not losing sight of the dwarf's fingers—
he has chosen
among all railroads
those that go from East to West
not those that go from North to South
for
—not losing sight of the dwarf's fingers—
Philip Lehman has understood
that the new frontier is the East-West axis:
what use does the South have now?
The South is a memory, nothing more.
And then thousands of crazy folk
are now going West
all looking for gold
so what better than to give them a train?
A logical argument.
A ready solution.
"The winning card is this!"

And he has won again.

Luck?
No.
Technique.

At the age of thirty
—which for Yehuda ben Tema is the age of strength—
Philip Lehman has grown stronger
—you bet he has—
with oil wells in distant lands.
He has written in his diary
in block capitals:
INDUSTRY = ENERGY, ENERGY = OIL
and of all the oilfields to be financed
he hasn't chosen those that everyone has rushed to
which will soon run dry:
he
—not losing sight of the dwarf's fingers—
has found new ones in Alaska, in Canada
among the glaciers:
for
—not losing sight of the dwarf's fingers—
Philip Lehman has understood
that it's best to get there first
where no one has yet gone
and to raise the flag there.
A logical argument.
A ready solution.
"The winning card is this!"

And once again he has won.

Luck?
No.
Technique.

At the age of forty
then
—which for Yehuda ben Tema is the age of shrewdness—
Philip Lehman has been shrewd
—and this is his masterstroke—
writing
in his diary
in block capitals:
NINETEEN HUNDRED = NEUROSIS, NEUROSIS =
    ENTERTAINMENT
and of all the entertainments to finance,
he hasn't chosen the one that most have gone for

namely alcohol
distilleries
—all Jewish—
no: too simple.
Philip
—not losing sight of the dwarf's fingers—
has laid a stake on National Cigarettes
which is, yes sir, a good bet
since cigarettes are small, they're for everyone
they'll become like bread
and if you want to make money
you have to go for simple things
before they become simple:
"the winning card is this!"

And once again he has won.

"It's not luck, darling:
it's simply technique, you know.
Simply technique!"

This is what Philip says
each time
to his wife.

They've been married for many years.
Because when he reached eighteen
the morning after his birthday
Philip Lehman
wrote in his diary:

SOLVE MARRIAGE PROBLEM
↓
CHOOSE ~~GOOD~~ <u>RIGHT</u> WIFE

After careful consideration
Philip Lehman
—not losing sight of the dwarf's fingers—
decided that the essential requirements were these:
she should be mild-natured
she should come from a family of equal status
she should not have a tendency to spend
she should not be a suffragette

she should prefer tea to coffee
she should appreciate art
and so forth
a well-thought-out list
with around forty headings
—both spiritual and domestic—
all written in block capitals
each with a score from 1 to 5
with a possible total
of 200 points
that would make
the PERFECT WIFE.

Search.
Search.
Search.

Not satisfied
Philip Lehman planned
a careful strategy
to investigate
a short list of twelve candidates
that he himself had picked
taking names
from the list of Temple benefactors.

The number twelve
was no coincidence
since Philip had determined
to devote one month
to the careful study of each of them:
so that in twelve months
therefore a year
—not losing sight of the dwarf's fingers—
he could regard
the question of MARRIAGE
as resolved
and could therefore move on
more profitably
to other business.

Thus began
the marriage year

whose operations
were noted down
scrupulously
—according to a fixed layout—
in block capitals
in his diary:

MONTH: SHEVAT.
CANDIDATE: ADELE BLUMENTHAL
APPEARANCE: SHABBY
NATURE: TEDIOUS
LEARNING: CONVENTIONAL
SUMMARY: OLD BEFORE HER TIME
SCORE: 60 OUT OF 200.

MONTH: ADAR
CANDIDATE: REBECCA GINZBERG
APPEARANCE: PUGNACIOUS
NATURE: PRICKLY
LEARNING: ABRASIVE
SUMMARY: TOUGH WORK
SCORE: 101 OUT OF 200.

MONTH: NISSAN
CANDIDATE: ADA LUTMAN-DISRAELI
APPEARANCE: AUSTERE
NATURE: STERN
LEARNING: HIGHEST
SUMMARY: A RABBI
SCORE: 120 OUT OF 200.

MONTH: IYAR
CANDIDATE: SARAH NACHMAN
APPEARANCE: CHILDISH
NATURE: IMMATURE
LEARNING: SCANT
SUMMARY: NOT READY
SCORE: 50 OUT OF 200.

MONTH: SIVAN
CANDIDATE: PAULETTE WEISZMANN
APPEARANCE: MOODY
NATURE: CANTANKEROUS

LEARNING: UNFATHOMABLE
SUMMARY: A RISK
SCORE: 30 OUT OF 200.

MONTH: TAMUZ
CANDIDATE: ELGA ROSENBERG
APPEARANCE: SHOWY
NATURE: STIFF
LEARNING: BASIC
SUMMARY: CHINA DOLL
SCORE: 71 OUT OF 200.

MONTH: AV
CANDIDATE: DEBORAH SINGER
APPEARANCE: ALL EYES
NATURE: INTELLECTUAL
LEARNING: ADVANCED
SUMMARY: ACADEMIC
SCORE: 132 OUT OF 200.

MONTH: ELUL
CANDIDATE: CARRIE LAUER
APPEARANCE: SOBER
NATURE: LUKEWARM
LEARNING: AVERAGE
SUMMARY: HOMELY
SCORE: 160 OUT OF 200.

MONTH: TISHRI
CANDIDATE: LEA HELLER HERZL
APPEARANCE: SLOPPY
NATURE: GLOOMY
LEARNING: BACKGROUND
SUMMARY: EASILY TEARFUL
SCORE: 70 OUT OF 200.

MONTH: CHESHVAN
CANDIDATE: MIRA HOLBERG
APPEARANCE: LANGUID
NATURE: KINDLY
LEARNING: MODEST
SUMMARY: SIMPERING
SCORE: 140 OUT OF 200.

MONTH: KISLEV
CANDIDATE: LAURA ROTH
APPEARANCE: COLORFUL
NATURE: LIGHTHEARTED
LEARNING: HERE AND THERE
SUMMARY: LAUGHS TOO MUCH
SCORE: 130 OUT OF 200.

MONTH: TEVET
CANDIDATE: TESSA GUTZBERG
APPEARANCE: GIRLISH
NATURE: PLEASANT
LEARNING: MORE THAN GOOD
SUMMARY: PERFECT
NOTE: SHE CAN'T HAVE CHILDREN
SCORE: USELESS.

SUMMARY 160 OUT OF 200
↓
<u>CARRIE LAUER</u>
↓
ASK FOR APPOINTMENT TOMORROW MORNING
MR. BERNARD LAUER

"My dear Mr. Lauer
thank you, first of all, for receiving me.
I imagine you already know the reason why I'm here
for Carrie
an adorable girl
is your only unmarried daughter.
You may say we are still young
but I tell you that if I have to commit to marriage for life
then I'd prefer to do so
with many years ahead of me
rather than behind.
You may also say there hasn't been time
for a real affection to grow between us
in which case I will give you the example of the internal combustion
    engine
for it just so happens that I
—yes I—
once convinced

my father and my uncle
to invest in the automobile market
unaware they were patenting
a new internal combustion engine
that would bring us much profit;
from which it follows
my dear Mr. Lauer
that the cause doesn't always precede the effect
so that marriage can precede and sentiment follow
without sentiment having to come before marriage.
If you agree with me
we can make arrangements for a respectable marriage.
On the other hand, if you prefer to wait for I-don't-know-what
I will save you the embarrassment of having to tell me
with which
begging your pardon
having other business
I offer you my respects
my dear Mr. Lauer
and take my leave."

The wedding
took place
—after an appropriate engagement—
in the times and ways
set out in block capitals
in Philip Lehman's diary.
He wrote down everything
lost control over nothing
from the color of the *chuppah*
to the quantity of tableware at the reception
including the waiters' names.

Carrie Lauer
for her part
from the very start
proved to be the right wife
right mother
right hostess
right mother-in-law
right benefactress.
No more.
No less.

Right.
Like a tennis ball
that never crosses the line:
no less
no more.

And once again
Philip Lehman
had to recognize
that he had called
the right card.

"It's not luck, my darling:
it's only technique, you know.
Only control."

15
Der stille Pakt

Each morning
Sigmund Lehman
walks smiling
into the gray and white building
from which Lehman controls America.

Each morning
he cordially greets the clerks at their desks
gives a three-dollar tip to the shoe shiner
and
having climbed the staircase to his office
hands his coat
to Miss Vivian Blumenthal
his secretary.

Miss Blumenthal's tasks
include
making sure
there's a cup of coffee

waiting on his desk:
she doesn't always remember
and Sigmund reminds her with a smile.

Dreidel Lehman also
walks into the office
at 119 Liberty Street
each morning
silently.
He sits in his office
behind a solid mahogany desk
and lights the first cigar of the day.

Before evening
he will smoke four.

The first covers the morning hours
namely the accounts check.
The second cigar
coincides with lunch
namely external relations
during which Dreidel remains silent
not wasting a word
swathed in his cloud of smoke.
The third cigar is for the afternoon
and is savored slowly
while he reads the newspapers
circling with a red pencil
possible areas for future expansion.
Finally, Dreidel smokes his fourth cigar
in complete solitude
when the last employee leaves,
usually holding
a paperweight
in the shape of a globe
used by his father, Henry,
half a century ago
to hold down his cotton accounts.

Now that his uncles Mayer and Emanuel
have passed the bank
to their sons' control,
Dreidel Lehman

is the oldest partner.
A funny thing to say
since he still has black hair.
And it's also funny
to hear him called
president
in those long meetings
during which the three cousins
sit
side by side
at the head of the table
though in the end
only Philip speaks to their advisers.
Sigmund says nothing because it's better he doesn't.
Dreidel says nothing because he won't or can't.

According to those in the know
however
Henry's silent son
makes his voice heard, for sure.
It's just that he uses a language of his own,
an alternative to using his lips,
and in doing so
he saves on breath.
An entirely new form of economy.

It is thanks to Dreidel
for example
that Lehman Brothers
has invested in mail-order catalogs.

A classic Dreidel idea.
For it's obvious
that on entering an emporium
you have to speak at least
five or six words
    the first of which will be HELLO
    the last GOOD-BYE
    and in between I NEED THIS
yet it requires
not the slightest oral activity
to leaf through a Sears catalog
and send a mail order

for the saucepans on page 78:
a silent transaction
ideal for hermits
and keenly supported
by the mute Dreidel:
presented to his cousins
in a folder three inches thick
of newspaper cuttings:
the voice of America
(since luckily it speaks)
is demanding at last to move
toward shopping on a larger scale
simplified as much as possible
maybe taking into account
that there are thousands of families
in remote ranches and huts
in deserts and on mountains
a thousand miles
from the top traditional store:
do we want them never to buy?
Do we want to exclude them
from the great whirligig of commerce?
Besides
now that factories
have given everyone a job
a salary to spend,
what could be better
than buying all and everything
from the pages of a mail-order catalog?

Well done Dreidel.
Lehman Brothers
will invest its capital
in an army
not of soldiers
but of mailmen and warehousemen.

The two old Lehmans
are not displeased by this new venture.
Not only because
it has brought them forward
from the fifth to the fourth row of the Temple
where they enjoy an excellent view

over the custodians of gold
the Hirschbaums in the third row, fat as ingots,
the Goldmans right in front, jangling about like coins,
and lastly the Lewisohns, glistening in the first row.

None of these three
will certainly ever
buy saucepans
from the mail-order catalog.

But Mayer, yes:
he'll insist on doing so.
For this at least
is a true STOCK EXCHANGE
where goods are actually traded!
And investment in this sector
is a pleasure to be seen.

Not like those *bonds*
that Philip is so fond of:
risky bits of paper
with so many numbers on them
bits of paper that Lehman staff
hand out in large quantities
to
finance the trains of tomorrow
the buildings of tomorrow
the industries of tomorrow
and a load of other things
all
always
of tomorrow
of tomorrow
of tomorrow
as the posters say
those that Philip has had printed
and stuck on the walls
of New York and beyond:
throughout America, if need be.

Bonds?
Modern inventions.

Money, of course, comes into the bank.
It floods in, according to Philip.
More than those three old COs:
COtton—COffee—COke
which are now the stuff of prehistory.

Mayer smiles. He nods.
Emanuel does the same.

But in fact
neither of them
knows *what*
exactly
is going on
inside that room
which once belonged to Mayer.
On the door there's a nameplate: PHILIP LEHMAN
while the two old men
have two desks on the floor above
in the same office.

Only one thing
was clear to both
when Charles Dow
the young journalist
who has started up a newspaper
in Wall Street
came
to the office at 119 Liberty Street.

Charles Dow
turned up
to interview
the *presidents emeritus.*
Philip sat
at the far end of the room
and listened not batting an eye.
But when the question was:
*"If the bank were a bakery
what would be the flour?"*
Emanuel said:
"Trains!"
Mayer:

"Tobacco!"
Then Emanuel again:
"Coal!"
And Mayer:
"At one time, cotton!"

Philip
then
raised his voice
and commented on the Scripture
like a young boy at his *Bar Mitzvah*
about to be received among the adults of the Temple:
"Dear Mr. Dow
the flour that you ask about
would be
neither commerce
nor coffee
nor coal
nor the iron of railroad tracks:
neither my father nor my uncle here present
have any fear of telling you that we are traders
in money.
Normal people, you see,
use money just for buying.
But those—like us—who have a bank
use money
to buy money
to sell money
to loan money
to exchange money
and—believe me—it is this
we use to make our bread."

Mayer smiles.
Emanuel does the same.

Like two bakers
who have lost their way
to the oven.

Enveloped in the haze of his afternoon cigar
Dreidel Lehman
has watched the whole scene,

but his expression
reveals nothing:
his cousin speaks for him,
he is glad to let him talk.

Besides
the transfer of loans
is a sector in which Lehman Brothers excels:
Philip deals with it
in person
with his own signature and guarantee
before the other parties.

The mechanism is simple:
a bank that has a debtor
sells that loan to another party
who buys it at a lower price.
"In other words"
Philip explained to his father
"if you owe me ten dollars
and I'm worried you won't pay up
I can pass the whole transaction on to someone else
who obviously won't pay me ten dollars but eight:
for me it's a good deal because out of ten I'll get eight,
for him it's a doubly good deal
because it's true he has spent eight straightaway,
but when you pay up you'll give him ten
therefore he'll earn two by doing nothing.
Multiply this, Father sir, by a hundred debtors:
that's 200 dollars which the bank pockets.
We would even venture to suggest
that the system of high finance
has only to hope that people don't pay their debts:
a loan that goes smoothly is certainly a good deal,
but a debt passed on to a third party
is an exceptional opportunity.
Do you like my invention?"

How complicated
it has become
to bake bread.
This is Mayer's only thought.

Emanuel agrees.
But he adds that touch
of paternal pride
since Philip is after all his son.

What Philip
in fact
has failed to mention
is that the idea isn't really his.
Indeed: if the truth be told, he has copied it.
And not from who-knows-which economist.
But from his young cousin
argumentative Arthur,
now aged twenty
who still, continually,
owes money to his brother Herbert.
One day Arthur turned up at the bank
and on asking to see Philip
made him a proposal:
"You pay my brother,
then you can take the money from my salary
when—sooner or later—I come
to work in this joint."

Philip tried to get rid of him
for at least three reasons:
first because brothers shouldn't steal from each other
then because a cousin ought not to take the risk
and third because a bank isn't—no sir—a joint.

But with Arthur Lehman
discussion is not so easy:
"For pity's sake, Philip, you're a filthy miser.
And if that weren't enough, let me just say:
you don't understand a thing about business
the bank wins out, damn it, don't you realize that?"

"Calm down, Arthur."

"No one tells me to calm down,
least of all a stuck-up cousin."

"Just think, Arthur."

"You say that to me? I'm the one who has to think? Me?
With my brother who's been threatening
to confiscate my bed for the past fifteen years?"

"Keep your voice down, Arthur."

"No I won't, I'll shout as much as I want!"

"Not in my bank!"

"It has my name on it too."

"Quite right: so ask your brother Sigmund."

"I can't: I owe him more money than anyone
though I've managed to hold him off with donuts.
Heck, Philip: I'm giving you a real opportunity.
Herbert would accept even a quarter less
just to get the money
and I'll be paying you 100 percent.
But why am I telling you? You don't get the idea.
Next time I'll go to Merrill Lynch:
they might be our competitors
but at least they'll know about business!"

Cousins can come in useful sometimes.
And not just that: the social impetus of twenty-year-olds.

Philip Lehman
suddenly grasped the implications:
he leapt up from his armchair
pushed the door shut and
as well as accepting the proposal
agreed with Arthur
a generous lump-sum payment
to acquire from him
—with no whys and wherefores—
ownership of the idea
of *debt transfer*
or whatever you want to call it.

They put it down in writing
and signed the agreement.

And from that moment Philip Lehman
has convinced even himself
that he has created a wondrous mechanism.

Arthur, for his part,
has gained a triple benefit.
Not only has he resolved an embarrassing situation with his brother.
Not only has he secured ownership of his bed.
But above all
thanks to Philip
he has realized from a momentary glimpse
that he has a special gift
for financial algebra:
boundless prairies of pure equations
have suddenly opened up before him
ready only to be applied.

Life sometimes offers
these sudden moments of inspiration.
So it was for Arthur.

Dreidel Lehman
however
is content to look on in silence:
if his cousin excels in handing over loans
he is expert in handing over all the rest
including half his bed.

For Dreidel
has managed
—to everyone's great surprise—
to get married
to a certain Helda Fisher
a young woman from a very good family
whom he met at Elberon
on the Atlantic coast
where the first ten rows of the Temple go
on annual vacation.

There are stories
—unsubstantiated—
about how there might have been
some minimum of courtship:

simply by exchange of glances?
Simply in writing?
Through intermediaries?
Was it perhaps a physical affair?
Or all a vaporous coalescence?

Uncle Mayer
produced a generally agreed-on version
advancing the metaphor of gas
which Lehman Brothers also dealt in:
it's not seen, it's not heard,
and yet, for sure, it catches fire.
Why then could his nephew
—despite being a fairly cold gas—
not burn with love?
He certainly could.

In fact.
Dreidel like helium.
Dreidel like methane.
An evocative idea.

But most astonishing of all
if anything
was how could a hornet
—with its poisonous sting
always about to strike—
ever manage to marry.

Everyone thought this.
Yet no one put it into words.
It might have been a question for Aunt Rosa
except that now it was too late.

Therefore *mazel tov*!
Hearty congratulations!
At least this time
unlike David
there was no one else with a claim!

There again—it has to be said—
Helda is such a quiet girl!
She has suffered from bad headaches

since childhood
so keeps well away from noise:
with Dreidel
in this respect
she has made an excellent choice.
Added to which
süsser Helda
dresses so chastely in those lace-trimmed clothes,
is amazed by everything
gives a look of surprise
and is always saying
"I'm lost for words."

And if she is lost for words
then why go looking for them?
Her husband doesn't try,
so the circle is complete
their understanding perfect
with outright war against empty gossip.

Dreidel and Helda.
Who knows if they communicate by name
or with a few gestures agreed on from the start:
more inquisitive folk
declare
that their apartment
has the atmosphere of a sanatorium
like a home for mystical rabbis.

Even at the *kiddushin,*
while the whole family
in the fifth row
strained
to hear the young man's voice,
it seems that he
at the crucial nuptial question
did not in fact answer "Yes"
but limited himself
to a nod of the chin.
The celebrant
(who apparently even placed a bet on it)
then tried in every way:
"Raise your voice, Mr. Lehman: we haven't heard."

But Helda intervened:
"I heard, and I reckon that's enough."

And so
he had to bless them:
may they go in happiness
and let the celebration begin!

Or rather: what celebration?
The toast, that is all.

A kiss on the forehead.
Greeting to the families.

Helda in her lace
Dreidel with a cigar in his mouth
a photographic plate
to remember the event.

After which
good-bye to everyone:
the bride has a headache.

Mazel tov.
Best wishes and many sons.

16
Eine Schule für Sigmund

Okay, turbulent David
put us to shame
with those antics
among twelve sets of bed sheets.

But could this business
of marrying a cousin
be halfway along the same track?

Sigmund Lehman
has astonished everyone
including his father.

He turned up
with that chubby face
hand in hand with Harriett
Emanuel's daughter.
They looked at their respective fathers
and with a somewhat hesitant voice
announced almost in unison
*"With your permission, Fathers sir,
we would like to marry."*

And she added:
*"He says that if I marry him he'll give up donuts
and so I think he must be very much in love."*

Harriett's quip
—despite its curious touch of irony—
produced not the slightest stir on their lips
Sigmund alone burst out laughing
stopping immediately
since it wasn't perhaps quite appropriate.

*"Dear daughter . . . at one time your cousins
used to smack you,
now they take you as their husband?"*

*"Father sir, smacks are for children
for adults it needs fists.
And there's no tougher fighter than a wife."*
Delightful Harriett
had an impressive way with words:
she would have become a humorist
if only she had been born in England.

There it is: he married his cousin
bought with a plate of donuts.

As for him . . .
What can you say about him?

That their progeny
will be half muscle and half vegetable?
That the world there outside
has a plentiful variety of fauna of marriageable age
and it's crazy not at least to go and look around?
To marry a cousin
is indeed
the lowest point
you can reach
not just in terms of indolence
but
in lack of sentimental imagination.

In any event
they married just the same.
Harriett Lehman became Mrs. Lehman.
No great excitement, not even a change of surname.
Identical relatives
for bride and groom:
we'll save—that at least—
on wedding invitations.

And there it is.

But.
Back from their honeymoon
certain things ought to be clarified.

With Sigmund
the time is ripe
for a certain little chat.

So, sit down.
And without interrupting
listen carefully.

There again
it's good to be honest
once and for all:
it's not enough
to call yourself a Lehman.
That would be too easy.
Running a bank

isn't a job like any other
and much as you are the son of a potato
you cannot forget
you are still the son of a German potato
endowed with a healthy dose of firmness
which is an unmistakable feature
of all Prussian vegetables.
If necessary, then,
let us forget the word *Bulbe,*
and from now on
call it *Kartoffel.*

And then, please, some dignity:
as a leading member
of the family bank
you can't turn up
with candies in your pocket
nor
can you deal with American high finance
going about from morning to evening
with that smile of a country gnome
stamped across your face
with chubby red cheeks
and that round belly bursting from your trousers.
A sense of propriety is required of everyone.
So on this matter
—like it or not—
some thought must be given.

There again
the family
cannot just cast off
those guilty of moral offense:
David Lehman
has been banned
to protect our good name,
but
in all honesty
dear Sigmund doesn't exactly
make us look much better.
So that's that:
the boy has to change.

And indeed.

So as to act
in the most direct
and most practical way,
the matter was left
to his cousin Philip:
for him to find a way
of cutting off the rabbit's
lovely soft ears
putting the horns of a moose
on his head
the teeth of a bulldog into his mouth
and rhinoceros armor over his snout.

Perfect.
Philip had no doubt
about how to proceed:
his cousin required
intensive schooling
—in the German style—
that would teach him a healthy dose
of violence, ruthlessness, cynicism
and therefore
in other words
yes sir
a school that would make a financier of him.

Having identified the crucial points
of a rapid training course
Philip
sought the help
of the only authority
qualified to hold a chair
at the University of Presumption:
Arthur Lehman
the student's brother
ten years younger
but champion of insolence
graduate with first-class honors.

And the family approved the appointment.

So
Philip and Arthur,
appointed
at the meeting of their relatives
to carry out so great a mission,
did everything
with the sternness it deserved.
They discussed it for many hours and finally
drew up a teaching program
for the pupil
with success guaranteed:
in exactly four months
—120 days to be precise—
Sigmund Lehman
would be transformed
at last
into a model of banking insolence.

In first place:
an aesthetic revolution.

Enough of those white picnicking outfits:
a completely new wardrobe
with dark-gray suits
in full New York Stock Exchange style.
Then, away with the parting in his hair:
adopt a new and less childish cut
with burgeoning sideburns
and if possible
a military mustache.
Lastly, with Harriett's help,
enforce a drastic reduction in girth
to entirely deflate the memory
of that jovial plump rabbit
stuffed with sugar and donuts.
Finance is long-limbed.
Finance is sober.
Finance is lean.
And so Sigmund
should be reduced
at least
to a Sigmy
and therefore slimmed down in two respects.

So far, his image.

But his external appearance
however important
—as we know—
is not decisive.

That is why
Philip and Arthur's therapy
was also aimed
most definitely
at the rabbit's mind
providing a treatment
that verged on brainwashing:
"Sigmund, now listen:
all schooling involves study
and study means sacrifice:
and from now on
for 120 days
every morning
every evening
in front of the mirror
look yourself in the eye
as if you were swearing an oath
and repeat
—by memory and aloud—
a list of 120 points
that we teachers regard as essential
and
a good basis
for your final transformation."

"Arthur, I'm not sure I understand:
do I have to say a different rule each day?"

"You have to say all 120 of them
for 120 mornings and 120 evenings.
Philip and I will take turns
as your supervisors
outside the door:
your voice
will have to reach us
loud and clear."

"I'm not sure . . ."

"No more time wasting:
here's the list to recite."

And there, on the eleventh day of February,
he was solemnly handed
in a sealed envelope
with the bank's insignia
the list
on four pages
tapped out on the typewriter
that Dreidel Lehman had never used:

120 RULES FOR THE MIRROR

1. SIGMUND, THE WORLD IS NOT AN ENCHANTED WOOD.

2. NEVER TRUST ANYONE, SIGMUND!

3. TOO MUCH GENEROSITY, SIGMUND, IS COSTLY!

4. SIGMUND! IT IS BETTER TO OFFEND THAN TO SUFFER.

5. ONLY IDIOTS ALWAYS SMILE, SIGMUND!

6. HE WHO IS FEARED, SIGMUND, IS NOT DEFEATED!

7. SIGMUND, YOUR WEAKNESS IS ANOTHER'S STRENGTH.

8. HE WHO SEIZES GAINS, SIGMUND.

9. HE WHO WAITS IS LOST, SIGMUND.

10. SIGMUND, WHAT YOU PUT OFF IS NEVER DONE.

11. ATTACK, SIGMUND, IS BETTER THAN DEFENSE.

12. SIGMUND, DON'T SPARE YOUR ENEMY FOR WHAT HE WOULDN'T SPARE YOU.

13. THE WINNER, SIGMUND, IS THE ONE WHO GETS THERE FIRST!

14. CONTENTMENT MEANS HUMILIATION, SIGMUND!

15. SIGMUND, MODESTY BRINGS ONLY HARM.

16. BETTER TO LIE THAN TO DISAPPOINT, SIGMUND.

17. SIGMUND, ALWAYS CALCULATE FIRST: AFTER WILL BE TOO LATE.

18. ENTHUSIASM, SIGMUND? IT MASKS DECEIT.

19. GIVE UP ONCE, SIGMUND, AND YOU GIVE UP FOREVER.

20. SIGMUND, THERE'S NO PEACE IN WAR!

21. IF YOU DON'T STAND UP FOR YOURSELF, SIGMUND, OTHERS WILL BRING YOU DOWN.

22. FRAGILITY, SIGMUND, HAS A HEAVY COST.

23. COMPLAINING WILL TAKE YOU NOWHERE, SIGMUND.

24. THAT WHICH REAPS NO REWARD, SIGMUND, WREAKS DAMAGE.

25. PRAISE YOURSELF, SIGMUND, AND DISPARAGE THE REST.

26. THERE IS NOTHING, SIGMUND, THAT HAS NO COST.

27. ALLIANCES, SIGMUND, ARE ALWAYS TEMPORARY.

28. SIGMUND, IT IS BETTER TO DEMAND THAN TO ASK.

29. SENTIMENT HAS NO PLACE IN BANKING, SIGMUND.

30. THE HUMAN RACE, SIGMUND, IS NOT A NICE RACE.

31. SIGMUND! ALWAYS CALL THINGS BY THEIR TRUE NAME!

32. HE WHO DECEIVES HIMSELF, SIGMUND, PAYS THE PRICE.

33. IF YOU FALL, SIGMUND, GET UP IMMEDIATELY.

34. IT IS BETTER TO SCREAM, SIGMUND, THAN TO SUFFER!

35. THE ONLY MISTAKE, SIGMUND, IS TO ADMIT YOUR MISTAKE.

36. SIGMUND . . . ONLY THE FOOL EXPECTS GIFTS.

37. LOVE TAKES MORE VICTIMS THAN HATRED, SIGMUND.

38. IT IS BEST TO EXPECT THE WORST, SIGMUND, FOR IT OFTEN HAPPENS.

39. SIGMUND: NO ONE HELPS YOU WITHOUT A REASON!

40. BETTER A TRUE ENEMY, SIGMUND, THAN A FALSE FRIEND.

41. SIGMUND, MONEY HAS NO HEART.

42. ACTIONS ARE REAL, SIGMUND, THOUGHTS ARE IMAGINARY.

43. HE WHO DROPS BY A FOOT, SIGMUND, SINKS BY A MILE.

44. SIGMUND! BETTER TO LIE THAN TO CONFESS!

45. PRIDE IS THE BEST PROTECTION, SIGMUND!

46. IF YOU LOSE, SIGMUND, ALWAYS PLAY IT DOWN.

47. SIGMUND, NEVER, NEVER, ADMIT YOUR OWN FAULTS!

48. Beware, Sigmund: he who offers his hand, hides his knife.

49. The bill to be paid will always arrive, Sigmund.

50. Sigmund! Coins always have two faces.

51. There's no such thing as never, Sigmund: there's only sooner or later.

52. Better to be sought, Sigmund, than to seek.

53. Always choose where you want to be, Sigmund.

54. Sigmund, dignity is personal property.

55. Never take a step backward, Sigmund!

56. Everyone has a weak point, Sigmund. Start from there.

57. Sigmund, what you give never comes back.

58. Always keep the right distance, Sigmund.

59. Sigmund! Remember who you are and forget who you are not.

60. Those who sow affection are ripe for ransom, Sigmund.

61. Fear, Sigmund, is a waste of time.

62. Fear, Sigmund, is energy thrown away.

63. Fear, Sigmund, creates only victims.

64. Fear, Sigmund, is an end in itself.

65. Fear, Sigmund, is a dead loss.

66. Don't expect anything in exchange, Sigmund.

67. Sigmund! Self-criticism is self-defeat!

68. Words, Sigmund, are nothing but air.

69. Watch the path, Sigmund, and you won't slip.

70. Those who think about others end up in trouble, Sigmund.

71. Willpower, Sigmund, is the only weapon.

72. Sigmund! Do you want to make friends of your enemies?

73. Dying of exhaustion, Sigmund, is better than dying of boredom.

74. HONESTY, SIGMUND, IS AN ABSTRACT CONCEPT.

75. THERE ARE ONLY THE EXPLOITED AND THE EXPLOITERS, SIGMUND: YOU CHOOSE.

76. HE WHO WEARS ARMOR, SIGMUND, DOESN'T GET HURT.

77. SIGMUND! THOSE YOU GIVE TO WILL ONLY WANT MORE.

78. DIGNITY, SIGMUND, IS QUICKLY LOST.

79. THOSE WHO PLAY SAFE GET NOWHERE, SIGMUND!

80. SIGMUND, TAKE WHAT IS OWED TO YOU.

81. BETTER TO BE TOUGH, SIGMUND, THAN TO TALK TOUGH.

82. CUNNING, SIGMUND, IS BETTER THAN KINDNESS.

83. THOSE WHO DON'T APPRECIATE YOU, SIGMUND, DON'T DESERVE YOU.

84. THE MORE YOU MATTER, SIGMUND, THE MORE THEY TRY TO BUY YOU!

85. EVERYONE IS FOR SALE, SIGMUND: AT LEAST SELL YOURSELF DEARLY.

86. SIGMUND! TO BE ENVIED IS A STRENGTH!

87. SIGMUND! TO BE HATED IS A GOOD SIGN!

88. THOSE WHO FLATTER YOU TODAY, SIGMUND, MOCK YOU TOMORROW.

89. FOR EVERY BENEFIT THERE'S A COST, SIGMUND, AND VICE VERSA.

90. GOOD LUCK, SIGMUND, CAN BE SUMMONED.

91. BAD LUCK, SIGMUND, CAN BE SENT AWAY.

92. SIGMUND! OTHERS SEE YOU AS YOU LET THEM SEE YOU.

93. IT'S FAR BETTER TO SCRAPE ALONG THAN TO STOP, SIGMUND!

94. IN HISTORY, SIGMUND, THERE'S NO PLACE FOR THE MEEK.

95. THE PAST, SIGMUND? IT'S NOW GONE.

96. KNOW ALWAYS WHERE YOU WANT TO GET, SIGMUND.

97. SIGMUND, TOO MANY QUESTIONS JUST MAKE NOISE.

98. SIGMUND, THERE'S NOTHING ELSE BUT COURAGE.

99. THE MEEK, SIGMUND, WALK HAND IN HAND WITH FOOLS.

100. ONLY IF IT'S WORTH IT, SIGMUND, ONLY IF IT'S WORTH IT . . .

101. THE MISERY OF OTHERS IS NOTHING TO DO WITH YOU, SIGMUND.

102. PEOPLE DECIDE, SIGMUND, THEY DON'T BECOME.

103. THERE IS ONLY ONE VOICE, SIGMUND: EVERYTHING ELSE IS THE ECHO.

104. IT IS BETTER TO RISK, SIGMUND, THAN TO REGRET.

105. IT'S NO USE GROWLING, SIGMUND, UNLESS YOU BITE.

106. AT REGULAR INTERVALS, SIGMUND, COUNT UP WHAT YOU'RE WORTH.

107. TO STRIKE TERROR, SIGMUND, IS THE ONLY SAFE COURSE.

108. SIGMUND! DON'T LET YOUR DEMONS FRIGHTEN YOU: PUT THEM TO GOOD USE.

109. MAN IS STILL AN ANIMAL, SIGMUND, FORTUNATELY.

110. NO ONE CAN TELL YOU ANYTHING, SIGMUND.

111. EVIL MAY WELL BE BAD, SIGMUND, BUT IT'S USEFUL.

112. SLANDER IS STUPID, SIGMUND, BUT SOWING DOUBT IS SMART.

113. SIGMUND, IT IS WISE TO DOUBT EVERYONE.

114. THOSE WHO TALK QUIETLY, SIGMUND, MIGHT AS WELL SAY NOTHING.

115. TRUST OTHERS, SIGMUND, AND YOU COMPROMISE YOURSELF.

116. EVERYONE, SIGMUND, SAVES THEMSELVES FIRST.

117. SIGMUND! IF YOU HELP SOMEONE, A HUNDRED WILL HEAR ABOUT IT.

118. REGRETS ARE SUPERFLUOUS, SIGMUND.

119. THE SHIP SAILS BETTER WITH A LIGHT LOAD, SIGMUND.

120. SIGMUND LEHMAN IS WRITTEN IN CAPITAL LETTERS.

At the end
of the hundred and twentieth day
more or less in mid-June
there wasn't a single Lehman eye
that wasn't watching
the family rabbit:
had such an intensive treatment worked?

Sigmund arrived at the office.
Dark mustache, probably dyed.
Wavy hair, gray at the temples.
Dark suit and London umbrella.
The size of his buttocks had at least halved.

No greeting to the clerks at the desks.
No tip to the shoe shiner.
A stern glance
at Miss Blumenthal
as there was no hot coffee waiting for him.

After which
he sat down
at his usual place.

17
Looking for Eva

Stuck in the snow up to his knees
with a pair of half-split boots
old Jeff
    his back as bent as a hook
    riddled with arthritis
    and what's more, blind in one eye
gives out a sort of yowl
with each shovel stroke:
    "Aiiuuughaaah!"

A deep animal sound
generated from deep inside
for he is racked not just by pain
but the sounds in his mouth are frozen by the ice
even before they emerge,
and all that comes out is an *"Aiiuuughaaah!"*
Agonizing.

But what's the point?
It's useless to complain:
it has snowed all night
and it's Jeff's task
to clear the school entrance.
It will take him two hours at least
so long as his lungs hold out.
So he takes a deep breath
and carries on:
"Aiiuuughaaah!"
"Aiiuuughaaah!"

Between one *"Aiiuuughaaah!"* and another
he hasn't even noticed
that a boy standing
on the other side of the avenue
for at least an hour
is admiring his immense effort.

Standing still and watching him
he morally endorses
each *"Aiiuuughaaah!"*
making it in some way his own
and he would even go to help him
if it were not that at present
he is untutored in the practical sphere.

So that
he limits himself to moral support.
From a distance.

Hands in his coat pockets.
Scarf tight around his neck.
An expression that is supportive
as well as clear-sighted and pitying
for the old shovelman's toil
reveals a problem that, in his view, lies deep down
and the question becomes political:
"What am I witnessing?
What is this man deep down
if not a monument to social injustice?"

"Aiiuuughaaah!"

"Why are people like him
who break their backs shoveling snow
always those worst off
and those who ought to be protected?
He represents a paradigm."

"Aiiuuughaaah!"

"The rich can look after themselves, buy drugs,
get treatment from a good physician
and warm themselves in front of a fire.
And yet, who are the ones
most at risk of falling sick?
Not the rich but this little old man."

"Aiiuuughaaah!"

"Later tonight he'll die of pneumonia
because his house has broken windows,
yet society sticks him out in the snow.
Wealth generates imbalances:
this man believes he is shoveling snow,
in reality he is shoveling our inequalities."

"Aiiuuughaaah!"

"That's how it is. No doubt about it."

Herbert nods.
He takes a notebook from his pocket.
Jots it down
under the heading "Winter rights for workers."

After which
still shaken
he heads along the approach road
to Williams College, Massachusetts.

The reason why
this twenty-year-old from New York
is so feared by the teachers

isn't due to the surname he carries.
Not at all: Herbert would never use it
to instill fear.
If anything he hides it.

The truth is that the boy is a tough nut.
He's not a brilliant student.
He works enough to get by.
And yet to give him low marks
is really not a good idea
for anyone with a minimum of caution:
those who do
find themselves caught unwittingly
up a blind alley
of endless discourses
in which *everything is a problem that lies deep down,*
the question becomes political
and a schoolroom
suddenly becomes Congress:

"If I take the floor in this hall to speak, Professor Maxwell,
it is to defend not my own particular interests
but a general principle.
I will not detain you
over the fact that you have given me a 'C':
I basically accept it, though with reservations.
What I find wholly questionable
—indeed unworthy of this institution—
is the method with which you give out grades:
why, before a class of thirty students
is the teacher obliged by Law
to give out
ten low grades
ten intermediate grades
five satisfactory
three good
and only two commendations?
It is the basic assumption that is wrong,
without taking account of the message it expresses!
Should I be afraid of speaking out in this hall
about an idea of social equality?
I haven't finished, excuse me:
in a truly egalitarian college

the teacher ought to be free of constraints.
Or do we really want to believe that
out of thirty American citizens
one-third are hopeless at their studies?
I haven't yet finished, excuse me:
don't you find that
such a rule
which you are obliged to follow
is—to say the least—antidemocratic?
The implied consequence
however
is that only one-fifteenth of pupils
can aspire to top grades,
and what is this
if not a blatant denial of the principle
that every citizen has a right
—and I say 'right,' Professor Maxwell—
to be treated equally?
I haven't yet finished, excuse me:
let us suppose for one moment
that due to an error
the best thirty students in the college
end up in a single class:
what folly would it be for you to punish twenty
branding them with the marks of blockheads?
I've still not finished, excuse me:
And if in one class
all of them
started whooping about
and burning books,
in what name
would we still be obliged
to honor at least two
with the laurels of State?
And then . . ."

"That's enough, Lehman: for pity's sake!
You've convinced me! I'll speak to the college council
and to Mr. Rutherford, the principal!
We will change the system, if you wish.
And now, can I continue with the lesson?"

"Only after one last observation:
you have given me a 'C'

for my class composition on the subject
"THE LEGACY OF PRESIDENT THOMAS JEFFERSON."
If you now claim that my discourse has convinced you
—and since I have spoken about rights—
don't you think that the facts belie the grade?
I honestly believe I have shown you
how much I embody in every respect
President Jefferson's legacy to posterity.
If then however . . ."

"Fine! Agreed! Lehman, you've won!
Is top grade enough for you?"

"I would consider it fair.
And not for me but for everyone."

There.
What makes
the heir of Thomas Jefferson
unique
is his incapacity to consider something for itself:
everything in him
is immediately projected
onto a social scale
reflecting quite different values.

A serious complication.

There are those who suggest
it is the natural result
of a childhood tormented by questions
and that having risked
trying to confiscate his brother's bed
for this very reason
Herbert Lehman
has radically converted
to an extreme vision of philanthropy.

That's a possibility.

It's certainly true
that this *sensitivity*
makes it quite difficult

to talk to the boy
about even the smallest matters:
How can you ask for a glass of water
when he regards that glass
as symbolizing
the Western system of water provision?
How can you complain about the rain
to someone who immediately tells you about the homeless?
How can you start laughing at a childish joke
with someone who has a fixation
about infant mortality?
And above all
how is it possible
that the blood of a banker
—albeit filtered through a vegetable—
runs in the veins
of someone who doesn't believe
in financial models?

Herbert Lehman
has gone as far
as calling the Wall Street Stock Exchange
a *snake pit*.
And in front of witnesses.

In short
while seeming disinclined
toward a financial career
it can only be hoped
that his path in life
takes him far away
from 119 Liberty Street.
And this thought is shared
by the whole family
including his father, Mayer,
and his brother Sigmund
who, when asked about it,
replied with No. 70
of his rules.

Only Philip seems
strangely unconcerned.

And not because he is moved
by any particular affection.

The point is that dear Philip
believes firmly
in family ties,
including those of relations
acquired through marriage.
And besides,
of all the verbs
we use
in these cases,
doesn't the verb *acquire*
say a great deal
about the commercial implications
that a marriage entails?

Exactly.
Let us say that
in the cost-benefit calculation
of his cousin Herbert's marriage
Philip Lehman
felt
extremely satisfied with the acquisition
and that was enough to endear him
to his thoroughly Democrat cousin.

How this marriage came about
was quite a story in itself
which no one
—including Philip Lehman—
would ever fully discover.

It just so happens, in fact,
that the union between the Lehmans and the Altschuls
proved immediately
deep down
to be a serious problem
becoming a political question.

But in short:
these are facts
of which no one is aware.

Recently graduated
Herbert was drawn
without realizing it
into the most advanced and dangerous of political terrains
namely
that form of exasperated defense of rights
that leads a human being
to go beyond his own bounds
invading the intimacy of others
so that some idea of justice might prevail.

Well.
As often happens
among twenty-year-olds
Herbert Lehman found himself
almost by chance
through friends
intercepting the existential path
of a certain daughter of the Altschuls
by the name of Eve
whose biblical name, to Herby,
seemed not disproportionate to her beauty.
Indeed: he found it entirely consistent.

Playing therefore
the enthusiastic part
of a latter-day Adam
he stepped into Paradise on Earth,
taking it for granted that
they would soon be
plundering forbidden apples.

But it wasn't to be.
For Eden had evidently
already been violated.

The serpent in question
—for this was Satan—
was soon identified
predictably
as one of those wild reptilian characters at the Stock Exchange.
To be precise it was
none other

than the eldest son of the Morgenthaus
true pythons
one of the most prominent families
and a direct rival of Lehman Brothers.

This was a harsh blow to Adam:
his body quivered
with rage
at just the thought
of that fair model of womanhood
being destined to gratify a Wall Street cobra.
Without reckoning on the fact
that Eve had been fashioned by *HaShem*
to be his companion, as Genesis says,
and not to marry the serpent
who plays a mere secondary role
of evil counselor.

So far so good,
being after all the eternal story
of human jealousy.

The problem was that Herbert went much further.

The fact that Eve Altschul
—of such rare beauty—
should be snatched from general admiration
to become the property of a single person
soon struck him
as a social inequality.
On top of this, Morgenthau was a powerful man
who extended the concept of inequality
to that of abuse.
And it was a very short step
from abuse to oppression:
that engagement
was an insult to the American people
and it was time
to put up the barricades (his, he failed to add).

Then
since every legend
has its contradictions

Herbert overlooked
the fact that the victim of Evil
was not exactly a timid virgin,
but an heiress to the Altschul fortunes,
mainstay of the American economy
better known in close circles as the "mastiffs"
confirmation of a not altogether upstanding fame.

In other words
a romantic feud was about to erupt
between the Lehmans, Altschuls, and Morgenthaus
three giants of New York finance
who had more reason to join forces
than to go to war.

Yet this is politics:
the need for conflict.

And Herbert, while not knowing all that was going on,
had certainly already guessed. Deep down.

There it is.
To fight blatant injustice
Herbert embarked
on the first real political struggle
of his fortunate career.
Theodore Roosevelt was an amateur in comparison.
Abraham Lincoln a schoolboy.
George Washington would have asked for private tutoring.

In the first place
a ruthless anticapitalistic campaign
was launched against the Morgenthaus
carried out undercover of course
and keeping the Lehman name well hidden
so that
for many decades to come
socialist mythology
celebrated an unknown popular hero
without knowing
he was a scion of finance.

Meanwhile
as in every war
he triggered a relentless underground campaign
to incite revolt
among those subjugated by the tyrant;
in this case, since
in his view
Eve was a victim of dominant power
(it never occurring to him that she might be happy about it),
Herbert set about pursuing her
every day
and bombarding her
with passionate letters
gifts of flowers
and whatever other political expedient
to stir in her
the urge to rebel.

In this he was helped
by the victim's younger sister
a certain Edith, a kindly girl
more like a young poodle
than an Altschul mastiff
perhaps because she had spent all these years
as an eternal lady-in-waiting
overshadowed by a biblical diva.

In Edith Altschul
democratic propaganda
found an unexpected voice:
the girl was devoted to the cause
stirred by a keen political zeal
and fought with all her might
for the noble moral objective
of wrecking her sister's marriage
in pursuit of a war against finance (and therefore against her father).
Commendable, Edith:
between Party and Family
she chose the former.
Hadn't women, after all,
now won the right to vote?
Her enthusiasm for politics was only natural:
it is always such with new experiences.

And since American politics
rarely abandons its goals,
the pact between Herbert and his deputy Edith
succeeded
after much effort
in producing its first fruits.

It happened one dull summer afternoon.

Months and months had been spent
on electoral campaigning
so that
the results were now expected.

At the umpteenth request
for a brief personal encounter
so far promptly rejected
Eva Altschul at last replied with a glimmer of hope:
she would agree to an interview
so that she could look him in the face
and tell him how much embarrassment
he was causing her.

This was obviously a ruse.
And Edith thought so too:
examining the subtext
is the first talent of a good secretary.

The time was fixed: at seven o'clock sharp.
The place was fixed: the Altschuls' flower garden
as if to say that Eden was welcoming its children back
under *HaShem*'s watchful eye
and in the absence of the serpent.

At exactly seven o'clock
Edith opened the gate
and with repeated warnings of caution
she led Adam in among the camellias
"Come with me: Eve is expecting you."

And there, indeed, was Eve:
she appeared to Herbert among the green rushes
and, as was to be expected,

her gaze was no longer hostile,
leaving hope for an electoral triumph.
Silence reigned in the garden
though Herbert seemed to hear
a chorus
of popular joy.

And yet.

Ah! Politics, what a strange art:
its unexpected leaps and somersaults
are competition indeed for any circus.

That day too, among the flowers,
whoever would have said
that Adam Lehman
finding himself before his Eve
would suddenly have seen her as embodying
the bourgeoisie of high finance
against which he had been battling for months?
Before him, the America of the banks:
so outwardly splendid
so perfect, young, charming
so quick to change allegiance
so voluble
so much for sale to the highest bidder
and while he asked himself
for the first time
what was his concept of beauty
it was clear to him
that in the question there already lay the answer.

Was it worth fighting for Eve?
Was this person who had given herself to a Morgenthau
worthy of his trust?

And since the electoral body
had sometimes to be chastised,
Herbert Lehman
went further:
he left it to itself
for all the significance it might have had.

The party, if anything, had to be strengthened
by closing ranks
ready for future struggles.

And so it was
that Adam left the Earthly Paradise
not with Eve
but arm in arm with Edith.

And while it all took place in democratic vein
—therefore respectful of each person's rights—
the news broke
that the Altschul mastiffs were in league with the Lehmans.

This too is politics.

18
Tsvantsinger

Yehuda ben Tema
in the *Ethics of the Fathers*
says:
seventy years for taking stock
eighty for enjoying the landscape.

Mayer Lehman and his brother
are getting on for seventy
but this taking stock
they haven't yet managed.

Perhaps they have thought of everything
apart from finding themselves
gray haired
handling sheets of paper
on which everything is a calculation.

Now they have more or less understood
that it works like this:

Lehmans decide on what to invest
but rather than put money into it
they get other folk to do so
in the form of a loan:
you hire me your money
I'll pay you back
"in x time, with interest."
But meanwhile
I'll use your money:
I'll give out loans
and I'll gain on the interest.
Loans to industrialists
loans to builders
loans to whoever produces
loans to whoever
sooner or later
brings in capital.

A fine game, for sure.
But this is new, smart economics
very smart
—perhaps too smart—
for two brothers
born over there in Germany
in Rimpar, Bavaria,
where gold was livestock
and they had to hope the cattle didn't die.
But above all
—incredible to say—
the real problem
for Emanuel and Mayer
is that
drinking a glass of water is one thing
but drinking the whole ocean is quite another.
And this ocean is money.
Profits, yes, revenue.

For
the truth is
that Lehman Brothers
is earning incredibly well.
Money is coming in.
A lot of money is coming in.

Too much is coming in, maybe.
And if we end up inundated?

Neither Emanuel nor Mayer
have forgotten that twenty note
which a thousand years ago
down there in Germany
in Rimpar, Bavaria,
was framed
like a picture
hung on the wall:
the first *tsvantsinger*
earned
by Lehmann senior
with cattle.
And next to the picture
there was another
with the hundredth *tsvantsinger*
and another
with the thousandth
and then
enough
for *"a thousand* tsvantsingers
*are a fortune my sons
and* Baruch HaShem*! if one day
you put together that much."*

Neither Emanuel nor Mayer
can avoid thinking
—even if they don't say it—
that 10,000 *tsvantsingers*
come into Lehman Brothers
each day
and you would need
an infinity
of picture frames
of *tsvantsingers*
which
all put together in a line
would form a bridge
from New York
to Bavaria.

Money like rivers.
And more.

It seems now like a vortex
in which millions of dollars
come in through the door
and leave through the windows.
Mayer and Emanuel
no longer understand:
what
exactly
are we making money on?

It's useless talking to Philip:
the bank for him
is a railroad station
through which you pass just to move on
never stopping.
"Dear Uncle sir, dear Father sir,
is it not the same for our capital?
We must not hold on to it
but invest it:
the money comes into the bank
and as soon as it comes in
it must go straight out again."
As for the silent nephew
he simply watches.
It would be a waste of time
asking him to explain,
it would mean
searching for an answer
among the smoke rings of his Cuban cigar.

And if we tried with Sigmund?

Emanuel and Mayer
are sitting in front of his desk.
Time enough to see
that 120 rules are framed
over the safe
between the candelabra.

"Sigmund, we'd like to understand more clearly:
don't you think
our bank is too exposed?
We're investing in markets of every kind
we can hardly remember their names.
If you could enlighten us
about what the bank is at this moment.
In other words
about what we are."

Sigmund lets them speak
without looking up from the accounts
since time is money
and not to be wasted.
Only now does he remove his glasses
and look at them
for a long long time
stroking the skin of his hands.
"I will tell you: the world is not an enchanted wood.
And words are nothing but air.
You ask me to explain more clearly?
Too many questions just make noise.
You ask me who we are?
Sentiment has no place in banking!
I'd like to ask you something myself
if I may.
I will also be tough,
but those who sow affection are ripe for ransom.
Therefore I have something to tell you.
Both of my cousins think it,
even if neither of them
for different reasons
say what they think in so many words.
Stupid: the meek walk hand in hand with fools.
So be it: I speak for the common good.
And then again, evil may well be bad, but it's useful.
Excellent: in these offices, in these rooms,
in case you haven't noticed
we have work to do
the winner is the one who gets there first.
This is what we are required to do: produce.
This we have to do.
For he who waits is lost,

and what you put off is never done.
Therefore
rather than asking me what a bank is
concentrate rather more
on the notion of old age.
Always call things by their true name!
And now, if you'll allow me, I have a meeting."

It is well-known
that rabbits
—when they want to be—
are more ferocious than jaguars
in devouring their prey.

Having first excluded
any negative inference
from their reaction of surprise,
two unyieldingly constructive thoughts
crossed the minds
of the two elderly bankers.

The first
was that the Academy of Cynicism
opened to Sigmund by family decree
had produced
a star graduate.

The second
was that Mr. Bad Rabbit
had probably
seen things correctly:
it wasn't to the bank that they had to turn
but to their own hearts
or failing this
at most
to some kind
of spiritual authority.

And so
they sought out
Rabbi Strauss
who seemed much familiar
with the notion of old age

having now more teeth in his mouth than hairs on his head.
"Dear Emanuel and Mayer,
in order to answer you I would like to reflect
on the meaning of the word age.
What is age if not a place of life
the same as its surroundings,
a territory in which we live?
Every age is a town, a village,
or—if you prefer—a nation
which each of us
must journey through.
And just as every place in the world
has its own climate, its own language
and its own landscape,
the same is true about getting old:
I believe it is like living in a foreign land,
where the rules of the previous countries
are simply
no longer valid.
And as always happens in a foreign land
you have to learn a new language
to call the sun the sun
and the moon the moon:
only then will you discover
that the sun is the sun over the whole Earth
even in a land of exile
and the only thing that changes
is the name given to it.
In other words
the ages of man are like countries:
all is forbidding so long as you're a foreigner
and all becomes congenial
when at last
you become a citizen."

And so be it.
But what does this mean?

Emanuel and Mayer
suddenly
understand
when they bring Elijah Baumann

building constructor
to the notice of the bank.

The two Lehman brothers met him
because there might
"in our view"
be a worthwhile investment.

Mayer thought much about it.
And Emanuel thought about it too.

The same thought, the same intuition:
American industry is growing
therefore more factories
therefore more workers
therefore more immigrants
therefore . . . where will they go to live?
Housing has to be doubled.
To build as much as possible
To create whole new suburbs.
Safe investment: bricks, mortar.
Return guaranteed, short-term deadlines.
Crystalline reasoning:
that Philip himself might have made.
Invest in housing for the workers.
Perfect.
Invest in Elijah Baumann: building constructor.
"I don't know what you think:
we think it has a great prospect. True, Mayer?"

"Absolutely, Emanuel.
And he's a very decent fellow."

Yes.

When Emanuel and Mayer
stop talking
there's a long silence
from everyone.

Dreidel coughs:
he is struggling
with his third cigar.

Silence.

Sigmund removes his glasses
polishes the lenses
puts them back on.

Silence.

Philip sits at the head of the table
almost a dark shadow
against the light that enters from behind
in the room all glass and mirrors
on the second floor of Liberty Street.

Silence.

Dreidel curls his beard.

Silence.

Sigmund pours himself a drink.

Silence.

Philip smiles.

Silence.

Dreidel crosses his legs.

Silence.

Sigmund straightens his tie.

Silence.

Philip folds a sheet of paper.

Silence.

Dreidel tugs at his collar.

Silence.

Sigmund blows his nose.

Silence.

Philip stands:
"Dear Father sir, dear Uncle sir,
for our part there's the maximum respect
for this initiative of yours
and in the name of everyone
I express my gratitude to you for this contribution.
Am I right, Sigmund?"

Sigmund clears his throat
and contemplating the chandelier:
"Only partially, Philip,
for, you see, it just so happens
that the world is not an enchanted wood
and sentiment has no place in banking.
And since for every benefit there's a cost,
remember that one must always calculate first.
Watch the path and you won't slip
and the bill to be paid will always arrive.
So, let us always call things by their true name:
he who deceives himself pays the price.
Well. Building houses? Please!
Do we want to make friends of our enemies?
Do we want to take a step backward?
He who drops by a foot, sinks by a mile.
Homes for workers?
And the benefit? That which reaps no reward wreaks damage.
Without bearing in mind
that our involvement in the building realm
would be something entirely new
unexpected
inconsistent
wrong
disastrous
damaging
and moreover outweighed by the facts:
before investing in homes for Hispanics
do we want to ask where this country is going?
Risk! Risk! It's better to risk than to regret.
Contentment, I say, means humiliation,

and those who play safe get nowhere,
and so I'm sorry: my answer is never!
What counts, gentlemen, is courage!
and since the past is now gone,
we may have given America its railroads
but now it's not enough:
having joined the two coasts of the United States
why don't we aim to join continents?
Pride is the best protection!
Ambition is a virtue!
The idea in short is this:
we establish a consortium of financiers:
twenty, thirty, fifty banks
and we ask the State of Panama
for a hundred-year lease
on a fifty-mile strip of land
between the Pacific and the Caribbean Gulf.
At that point we'll cut the continent in half
from side to side
from ocean to ocean
we'll build a canal that doesn't yet exist
and the whole of the world's commerce
will have to choose whether to pay us to go through it
or sail for days and days
around Cape Horn.
Am I wrong?
That's where tomorrow's money is!
Willpower is the only weapon!
You say no? Out of fear? Ah!
Fear is a waste of time!
Fear is energy thrown away
yes: fear is an end in itself.
Fear, gentlemen, is a dead loss.
I have finished. Or rather, no:
we are Lehman Brothers
and it is written in capital letters."

After which Sigmund stands up
bright red with rage
and, as he leaves, almost demolishes the door.

Silence.

Dreidel puffs out smoke.

Silence.

Philip strokes his nose
with the tips of all his fingers:
"Dear Father sir, dear Uncle sir,
if you think fit
you can however tell Mr. Baumann
to present a written request:
we will consider it
with the attention it deserves."

Emanuel nods.
Mayer too.

But from that day on
the two old men
were no longer seen
in that second-floor room
all glass and mirrors
at Liberty Street.

19
Olympic Games

It all started
on that fateful day
when Philip Lehman
wrote in his diary
in block capitals
DEDICATE MYSELF TO THE TEMPLE.

But it was not the beginning
of some mystical journey.

Nor did it refer to that temple of finance
the Wall Street Stock Exchange

where he already
had plenty of dealings
spending more time there
than he did in his own office.

Under
DEDICATE MYSELF TO THE TEMPLE
were further words
in brackets
of very cryptic meaning:
(MAXIE LONG HAD WON THE RACE).

What possible link could there be
in a banker's diary
between the Temple
and the US sporting hero?

Was Philip Lehman
—long-term benefactor of the Hebrew School—
perhaps planning some masterstroke
by inviting the new record breaker
to the school
to meet the children?

No.
None of this.

Those words
DEDICATE MYSELF TO THE TEMPLE
referred instead
to the unavoidable need
to sort out certain questions
still outstanding
and which
for Philip
had become a mark of shame.

At the same time it related
to a clear commercial maneuver
since a bank
—from Philip's point of view—
had no objective
other than plain and simple success.

And he would achieve it
by watching the fingers of the dwarf.
Of that he was sure.

On the other hand
Lehman Brothers
was already thriving:
the coffers were full
investments excellent and diversified
so that
there was no reason
at all
to feel other than happy with themselves.
So what was the point?
What was agitating Philip Lehman
disturbing his peace of mind
and clouding his thoughts?
What was disturbing him at night?
And above all
what nagging pang
had cropped up one day
almost by chance
and had begun to affect his mind,
becoming an obsession
not to say a torment?

All became clear to him
as often happens
through a dream.

The Paris Olympics
had just started.
In his dream
Philip Lehman found himself in a stadium
beside the course
watching the final
of the 400-meter sprint.
Maxie Long was getting ready for the race
dressed oddly
not in the colors of the American athletes
but instead
in yellow overalls
on which

the name Lehman Brothers
appeared in large letters.
The referee
(who distinctly resembled Rabbi Strauss)
rang a bell
at which the athletes raced off.
The stadium rose to its feet:
the crowd was chanting
everyone repeating
"Maxie Lehman Long!"
"Maxie Lehman Long!"
like a wind
propelling the great champion
urging him to run ever faster
as if he had a Studebaker beneath him
and he was running
running
running
pulling away from his rivals
"Maxie Lehman Long! Maxie Lehman Long!"
running
running
running
carrying Lehman Brothers
miraculously
toward the finish
"Maxie Lehman Long! Maxie Lehman Long!"
when
all of a sudden
Maxie stumbled
as though tripping over his own feet
and skidded flat on the track
forcing the others to jump over or trample him.
"Ohhhhhhhhhh! No!!!!!!!!!!!!!!"
the whole stadium cried
and not only them: the whole of Paris.
Just at the sight of his hero on the ground
Philip Lehman
—though it was just a dream—
could feel his chest on fire
as though four Olympic torches had set him ablaze:
he ran onto the race track
took Maxie Long's arms

hauled him onto his shoulders
and began running like a lunatic
madly
madly
madly
overtaking one after another
madly
madly
and when he had overtaken the last
madly
at breaking point
Philip Lehman
crossed the finishing line
with Maxie Long on his shoulders
in triumph!
Victory! Victory! Victory!
Every single person was shouting
apart from his cousin Dreidel
who confined himself to nodding.
The stadium had gone crazy:
"Maxie Lehman Long! Maxie Lehman Long!"
echoing everywhere
and to this chorus
Philip
dragged his champion
toward the podium.
But he was held back:
the referee
(who distinctly resembled Rabbi Strauss)
gave him a fond embrace:
"Congratulations on your endeavor, Mr. Lehman:
a truly spectacular race.
And now, if you don't mind,
I have to award the prizes to the three winners."

"What do you mean? We have won the gold!"

"No sir, or rather: you've won the race,
but the gold is certainly not yours,
nor the silver, nor even the bronze:
there are no prizes
for those outside the podium.
Begging your pardon."

Hey? What? The podium?
What was this mean trick?
Who dared to snatch his victory?
Maxie Long had won the race!
Maxie Long had won the race!
Maxie Long had . . .

Here Philip Lehman opened his eyes.

Though he wasn't clear about every detail
he was quite certain
that the gold medal
had gone to the Lewisohns.
The silver to the Goldmans.
And the bronze to the Hirschbaums.

As much as to say
that Lehman Brothers
from now on
could win every contest
but would always remain fourth
because
their places
were in the fourth row of the Temple.

And so
a new priority
promptly
appeared in the diary
DEDICATE MYSELF TO THE TEMPLE
(MAXIE LONG HAD WON THE RACE)
and from that moment
nothing was more important to Philip
than closing the distance
—small, of course, but significant—
that separated the fourth pew
from Isaiah Lewisohn's place.

Every move
was carefully planned
and considered:
nothing was left to chance

so long as Philip Lehman
was in the control room,
all the more
since
now
the family bank
had decided to declare war
on the unapproachable gold trio.

For a start
he had to get Elijah Hirschbaum
in third position.

He was a man of advanced age
revered father of an army of daughters
subservient and devoted
often lined up beside the patriarch
so that in society
they were known as
"Hirschbaum's Red Cross girls."

Now
it just so happened
that dear old Elijah
had made such good use
of his Valkyries
as to provide himself
with a very effective
network of family control
over gold extraction
throughout North America:
each of his seven daughters
had been married off
to the owner of an American bank
with particular attention
to those areas
where gold was master.
Once each marriage had been celebrated,
the new son-in-law
affiliated his bank
to the old father-in-law's New York bank
and

in this way
 from California to Klondike
 from Nevada to Colorado
 from Alaska to the Black Hills
the Hirschbaums
—it could be said—
kept their finger on the pulse of the whole market
opening and closing
at their sole discretion
the coveted flows of gold.

About all this
Philip Lehman
was certainly well informed
though the austerity of the Hirschbaum house
allowed almost nothing to be leaked
about the bank's hallowed affairs.

For Philip it was enough
however
to match up the daughters' new domiciles
with the banking news
in the *Wall Street Journal*:
as soon as
yet another financial crisis
erupted in the states of the South
he used it as a pretext to act immediately
and wrote in his diary
once again in block capitals
the following points of reasoning

1. HIRSCHBAUM HAS A DAUGHTER IN TEXAS
2. EACH DAUGHTER IS MARRIED TO A BANKER
3. EACH SON-IN-LAW'S BANK IS AFFILIATED TO THE MAIN
   BANK
4. SO HIRSCHBAUM MUST HAVE A BRANCH IN TEXAS
5. EXCELLENT: WE HAVE THE THIRD ROW

The confident tone of point 5
was due
in fact
to the main headline of the day:
the governor of Texas

in an anticapitalistic fury
had acted rather heavy-handedly
literally outlawing
all bankers in the state
for a period of at least ten years.
Crime: fraud.

Not a day had passed
before Rabbi Strauss
received an unsigned note:
the third row of the Temple
should rightly see itself
lined up in court
A BAND OF OUTLAWS
BANISHED BY DECREE
AND NOT FROM A VILLAGE
BUT FROM AN ACTUAL STATE?
ATTACHED, A NEWSPAPER CUTTING
YOURS FAITHFULLY,
A LOYAL FOLLOWER

And in effect
the view enjoyed in the third row
was a great deal better:
"Incomparable, Philip!" his wife said
before asking why ever
Hirschbaum's Red Cross girls
had been relegated en masse
as though they had caught the plague.
"I honestly don't know, Carrie.
I can't even see them,
where have they been put?"

"There, I think: beyond the tenth row."

"Really? On the border with Texas!"

And he could have added something
about the fact that the Lehmans
deserved their promotion,
but he didn't.

Partly because his wife
felt at that very moment
the first of a hundred and more contractions
with which, six hours later,
she would give him a son.

But apart from this,
his thoughts were already fixed
more than anything else
ahead
well beyond the second row
directly
on the supreme thrones of the Lewisohns.

The fact that in the middle
sat none less than the Goldmans
represented
for Philip Lehman
not the slightest obstacle.

Far from it.
The plan had already been laid.
Simple and perfect.
So that
a smile of contentment
crossed his lips
each time he thought of it:
the Goldmans would serve
as a step
for reaching the Lewisohns.
In other words,
he would use them.
Yes, use. To get ahead of them.

For deep down
—Philip wondered—
what better way is there
of defeating an enemy
than to form an alliance with someone
and
having triumphed
to dispose of him like a scrap of rusty metal?

All it needed was the right opportunity
to bring the long war to an end
and to sign a new pact
with Henry Goldman:
a pact of mutual support
and brotherhood in arms:
alliance with an enemy
was an unavoidable condition
for having no more enemies
but only adversaries.
Under his control.

No sooner said than done.
It was Mother Nature who offered the occasion
with exceptional timing
and this was how.

It's a Thursday afternoon.
There's the promise of a light snowfall.
In the dimly lit Temple
Philip Lehman
comes forward
slowly
clutching a white bundle to his breast
against his dark coat.

Eight days
after the birth
as the Law prescribes
Robert Lehman, called "Bobbie,"
is to be circumcised.
In his veins
not even a distant memory
of Germany
or Alabama
or old New York as it once was
when his grandfather Emanuel
opened the office in Liberty Street.

Philip stops.
He lifts the bundle
then the ceremony begins:

as from today
his son will have a name
and after the *Milah*
he will be in the shade of the Patriarchs.

All would be perfect.
If it wasn't that
another figure enters
dressed in black
he too carrying
a bundle
proceeding down the aisle
until he stops
beside Mr. Lehman.

The new arrival
has caused a stir
among those present:
no one had expected this to happen.

Only in a certain diary
was it fully expected:
FIRSTBORN AT SAME TIME
CIRCUMCISIONS COINCIDING.

Yesterday the *Bar Mitzvah* for the boys.
Now the *Milah* for the newborn.

A remarkable stroke of luck:
facing Elijah's seat
—may he protect both children—
each with his bundle
the two family heads
Philip Lehman
Henry Goldman
find themselves
side by side
in line
upright
proud
without ever looking at each other.

The two bundles are screaming.
The wives—in third and second row—
don't look at each other either.

No one imagines
that something tremendous
and at the same time far-reaching
is about to happen
today in the Temple.

Certainly,
it is hard to break the ice:
Philip manages it
knowing that it's a necessary step:
"Hello Goldman."

The new recruits shriek in unison.

"Hello Lehman."
"Hearty congratulations, Goldman."
"And the same to you, Lehman."

The bundles are drenched with tears of alarm.

"An odd coincidence, I'd say, dear Goldman."
"Very odd."
"A nuisance?"
"Somewhat."
"But inevitable, dear Goldman."
"I agree, dear Lehman."

A piercing squeal from the heirs to the throne.

"On the other hand, Nature cannot be controlled, Henry.
May I venture to call you Henry?"
"Nature doesn't care a damn about the banks, Philip.
No one has any control over her, at least."
"Nor any control over the holy precepts."
"Ah no: nor over them."

A burst of whimpers from the nursery.

"So it's not true what they say, Henry."
"What isn't true, Philip?"
"That the Goldmans can do whatever they like with gold:
there's something beyond their control after all."
"In that respect, nor can the Lehmans do whatever they like."
"So you admit it? You admit you're not omnipotent?"
"Only if you admit it."
"Let's suppose I admit it."
"In that case there'll be two of us who admit it."
"There'll be two of us who admit what?"
"That neither I nor you can do whatever we like."
"Well said. Neither I nor you can reach everywhere."

Loud protests from the latest generation.

"Separately we can't, Henry.
But if, at some stage, we were to join forces . . .
In that case, perhaps . . ."
"At some stage, Philip?"
"At some stage, Henry."
"What are you talking about?"
"About Wall Street."
"Stock market?"
"Stock market."
"Quotations?"
"Quotations."
"Share issues?"
"Share issues."
"Lehman Brothers and Goldman Sachs?"
"Joint financial tactics, Henry:
to set up a partnership, a joint venture.
Our forces—if brought together—would be unrivaled."

Anticapitalistic insurrection of the offspring.

"I would need to think about it, Philip.
Can you give me some time?"
"The length of the ceremony."
"And if that's not enough?"
"In that case I'll look for another alliance.
Someone's already made me an offer, Henry."
"And who might that be?"
"The Lewisohns."

"Swear to me it's true."
"If you swear to me that you'll accept the proposal."
"We'll both swear."
"On what?"
"On these boys of ours."

A chorus of noise from both fronts.

"Baruch HaShem, *Philip!*"
"Baruch HaShem, *Henry!*"

And it is said
that they shook hands
while everyone else
was watching them
from one side to the other
without understanding
why the wolf was licking the bear
and vice versa.

Lehman Brothers.
Goldman Sachs.
Alliance for victory.

Someone leapt out to ask
how
from now on
they could all stay together
in the second row . . .

Herbert Lehman and his wife, Edith,
immediately protested:
isn't democracy all about sharing?

This question was enough, in effect,
to raise a few laughs
which soon
became contagious.
And however much Sigmund shook his head
guarding himself against
any sudden show of affection,
the women began to talk to each other
the old men cautiously poured each other drinks

the boys asked the girls their names
Arthur Lehman made the children laugh,
by telling them how his brother
tried to confiscate his bed.

In short
whatever it was
it seemed like a celebration.

Only the two bundles
never
stopped crying
watched
from an appropriate distance
by Dreidel Lehman
swathed in the smoke of his fourth Havana:
sitting in a corner
—in silence with his silent Helda—
he was not distracted for a single moment,
noting everything with a watchful gaze.

But even this
had been anticipated
in Philip's diary.

As, moreover, was all that followed.

20
Golden Philip

For *Shabbat*
New York now stops.
Shops close
offices empty.
Trading on Wall Street
closes on Friday evening
and that's a good thing

for on Saturday
there'll be no one there.

Nor is Solomon Paprinski
the Wall Street
tightrope walker
to be seen for *Shabbat*.
He doesn't arrive
like every other morning
to stretch his wire
between the lampposts
and he doesn't drink
his mouthful of cognac
there
a few feet from the dark doorway.

New York
stops for *Shabbat*.

Even Monk Eastman
it is said
doesn't send his gang out shooting.

Ever since ships
began unloading
hundreds of immigrants
each day
on American quays
one in four citizens
in New York
has a Jewish surname.
And for months
scrawled on a wall in Brooklyn
are the words:
Jew York

Maybe these Jews
are not like those of the old days.
No sir.
They are like us, but different.
Carrie Lehman wants to make this clear
it's a regular topic

the favorite conversation
every afternoon
when
she entertains
the wife
of Henry Goldman
in her grand house on 54th Street.
It's a ritual, now.
Exactly the same as their husbands
Lehman and Goldman
who go for luncheon
each day
at Delmonico's restaurant.
But not the wives.
No luncheon.
For them, just tea.

"*They tell me the* kosher *butchers*
have a queue twenty yards long.
A little more tea, Mrs. Goldman?
Philip brought it for me straight from England."
"*With all these Jews, they will end up*
giving us rotten meat, just to sell it."
"*I've sent word to the butcher's boys*
that we'll pay extra to be sure there's no nonsense.
A drop of milk in your tea?"
"*One lump of sugar, thank you.*
But the servants are not to be trusted, Mrs. Lehman:
our cook was thieving from us.
I waited for Henry to return from Panama
and had her fired."
"*Our cook has been here six years*
I have no worry on that score."
"*Don't be so sure. Ours was there much longer.*
And the way she treated us!
I shake at the thought of having to employ anyone of color."
"*Oh no! Servants who wander the house cannot be black.*"
"*I've asked around in the Temple but don't have much hope.*"
"*The fact is that these Jews of the last ten years*
are all from Russia or thereabout.
You can't even understand what they say.
And they're poor, dressed in rags!
I've seen some of them in the snow without a coat.

Another cup, dear Mrs. Goldman?"
"With pleasure, dear Mrs. Lehman.
My husband says no more should be allowed in."
"Philip is also convinced of it.
They can't complain then if one in three Jews turns to crime."
"When I read the news in the Times
I confess I'm quite afraid.
Especially if my husband is in Canada."
"Philip is also in New York less and less
but the Jewish gangs don't come up to these parts.
The shooting is down there, in the lower districts.
A little cake?"
"Delicious as always."
"Too kind."
"Tomorrow, however, you shall come to me."
"I'm so sorry my dear but I can't:
tomorrow morning our son, Robert,
will be getting his first horse."

Horses.
Bobbie Lehman
cannot yet talk,
but already has at least ten.

A strange fate
that of horses:
they were once used for pulling carriages,
but now that the streets are full of motor cars
they give them to children!

Maybe one day
we'll all move about in airships
and automobiles will be toys for newborn babes.

The Lehmans
now own three automobiles.
One is used by Philip, dark blue in color
with chrome brass.
The driver is called Gerard
and comes from France
a bright kid.
There again, it always creates a certain effect
having a white chauffeur rather than a black one

to drive you to Wall Street,
especially now that in New York
it seems as if all negroes
are born
ready dressed in their livery.
Gerard, with his blond hair,
definitely adds a touch of class.

The second automobile of the house
is a Studebaker
of the latest kind:
Sigmund gets about only in that
—to save time—
now that Harriett is waiting for him at home with two children.
His driver is Turi, an Italian,
of deceptively dark complexion
who has the tedious habit of always talking,
though Sigmund rarely answers.
Sometimes indeed
he draws the curtain
between the driver's seat and the passenger compartment
to show it's time to hold his tongue
unless he wants to risk his job.
He wouldn't be the first to go.
Yes.
For it's no simple matter
working for Sigmund Lehman.
Over the past few years
he has fired at least three drivers
not to mention the servants at home
and Miss Blumenthal too
who had to leave her post
first for Miss McNamara
then for Sally Winford
and now for Loretta Thompson,
who, to be on the safe side,
is constantly on her guard.

All right
the world is not an enchanted wood
(and sentiment has no place in banking),
but now maybe Sigmund
is beginning to go too far:

fearing that he still hasn't
properly absorbed his Talmud,
each day he makes sure
he puts into practice
one of the 120 rules for the mirror.
In this way, he thinks,
theory will be translated almost naturally
into practice,
erasing
all memory
of the rabbit that once hopped about.

And if an Orthodox Jew
has to respect
all 613 *mitzvot*
to be a good Jew,
then he too
can apply a single one each day
to make himself a tough financier.

Those around him
have therefore begun
to experience at their own cost
the fruits of an inhuman training
marked by the most glaring cynicism,
by the rejection of any altruistic act
as well as continual
self-admiration.

And yet
seeing himself ever more able
to give practical effect
to the dictates of the mirror
has instilled in Sigmund
the pernicious idea
that he has always been
a supreme model
of greed
and therefore object of general hatred.

And so
Sigmund
trusts no one

fears what people say
senses treachery in the air:
it's enough for him to hear one misplaced word
or catch a tiny glance insufficiently submissive
for him immediately to shout conspiracy
for I have my dignity
and anyone who thinks they can do me down is making a big mistake:
my name is Sigmund Lehman
written all in capital letters.

Fortunately
his wife, Harriett,
carries her family blood in her veins
with her own fine capital initials.
Otherwise, and this is sure,
he would already have shown her the door
with the accusation of plotting against him
to steal his wealth.

But since
a man's true nature
even when forced to change
never completely disappears,
Sigmund Lehman's
most angry daytime frenzies
are interspersed
more and more
with sudden nighttime fits of tears
in which a soft furry rabbit
still seems to peak out
from under the banker's frosty pajamas.

These are the situations
in which Harriett Lehman
finds her husband
tender and swollen with tears
in her arms on the pillow
like a little boy with his mother
and hears him
imploring
in a voice of desperation:
"Tell me you still love me."

where the word *still* implies
a full awareness of his recent transformation.

A *"yes"*
uttered by Harriett between yawns
is generally enough
to send him back to fitful sleep
that will take him to morning
when he wakes glassy-eyed
into a world that is not enchanted.

But when
—as sometimes happens—
the medicine is not enough to calm the fever
Harriett is obliged
to invent a story about how
in a few years
—at most—
he and she
will leave the lions' den
hand in hand
to escape from everything and from everyone.
"And where will we go, Harriett?"
"Far away, Sigmund."
"Far away where, Harriett?"
"Onto the open sea, Sigmund."
"Where there are fishes, Harriett?"
"Fishes and seagulls, Sigmund."
"Promise me, Harriett."
"I promise, Sigmund."

"Mum, what's going on? Is Dad crying?"
Harold and Allan ask
rubbing their eyes
peering like two elves
into their parents' room.

"Oh yes, sure: Dad is crying with joy
about the bank's successes
Now you go back to bed, there's school tomorrow."

Exactly: school.
Next day

both Harold and Allan
found a way
of writing in an essay
about how bankers are kindhearted folk:
they cry tears of joy
each time the bank makes money
and since the bank is thriving
fortunately
they cry every night.

Touched by so much sentiment
Miss Ehrman gave them full marks
and felt it right
to let the family read
those joyous accounts of banking bliss.

"Have you gone crazy?" Sigmund began
in no uncertain terms
having promptly summoned the young rabbits:
"Sentiment has no place in banking, you understand?
There's no space for such nonsense.
You have mistaken what you thought to be crying
for a simple inflammation of the eyes.
Tomorrow you will go and tell Miss Ehrman
that you have invented it all, word for word,
you'll ask for a chance to put it right
and you'll change your version of what took place."

These were the beginnings
of the age of communication:
"And from now on I forbid you
to speak of finance in class."

It's a hard life, that of a banker.

And even harder, according to Harriett,
is the life of the one beside him
in the sacred bond of marriage.

Fortunately, the working day
at 119 Liberty Street
is fairly long and her husband

leaves at the first light of the morning
in the Studebaker driven by young Turi.

By the way,
the Lehman family's third and last car
is supposed to belong to Dreidel
though in fact
neither he nor Helda makes much use of it:
too much fuss, too much noise.
When it's not raining
they let Sammy the chauffeur
(a small man of color with a gray mustache)
take Mr. Mayer and Mr. Emanuel
for a ride around New York:
a motorized arm and potato
now that their legs
have begun to act up
and it's better not to take any risk.

The two old men
rarely set foot in the bank
on Liberty Street.
If Sammy strays more than a block
one of the two
calls out immediately
from behind:
"Darn it, Sammy, can't you see it's late?
Where have you taken us? Turn back!"

So he turns back.
What does it matter to Sammy?
So long as they pay him.

But for him
the drive he most enjoys
is the one to the Temple:
during the service
he can spend a whole hour
in the street
laughing and joking
with a good fifty fellow drivers
since all the Jews now have their own cars

and the finest vehicles
stand there together on display
outside the Temple
polished and shiny
like in a showroom.

Sure, a driver has to keep his wits about him:
there are rules
that cannot be ignored.

A few days ago, for example,
Gerard had been persuaded by others
that in half an hour at most
there would be a blizzard.

Last year
it had snowed for five whole days
and when New York decides to turn white
the roads become
a nightmare for traffic.

Gerard wasted no time:
while the service was still going on
he opened the main door,
looked around inside
and hunted
up and down
through the whole congregation
after which
at last
he saw them, the Lehmans,
in the front row, before the platform.
"Pardon me, Mrs. Lehman! Madam!
I think we'll have to leave!
It's going to snow, stop your praying!"

This is what servants are like today:
if you don't teach them, they cause you embarrassment.
And Gerard is no exception,
though he's not among the worst
so that—to make him realize what he's done—
his pay has been reduced.
Significantly.

After all
no language is quite so clear:
money is the only instrument
that governs relationships.

Philip Lehman
is absolutely sure of this
especially now
he has won his war
to control the Temple.

The Lewisohns?
Let them keep the keys for the casket
if there's only gold inside:
that yellow metal may well have its value,
but it's a relic of the past
and stops glittering day by day.

The gold of our times
—Philip has written in his diary—
is that gigantic flow of money
which at any moment
slips lightly
from the pockets of whoever buys
into the coffers of whoever sells!

Ingots? Mines?
Commendable, of course.
But how can you compare it
with the rustle of banknotes
almost invisible
almost imperceptible
which yet becomes a roar
if you imagine it worldwide?

Well yes: the world.
Thinking on a national scale
after all
makes no sense:
commerce has no boundaries
and without boundaries
Lehman Brothers
wants to take control.

With numbers.
With signatures.
With obligations.
With loans.
With bills of exchange.

And so
who would win
possession of the front row?

The Lewisohns
laden with tons of gold
or the Lehmans
who have nothing to weigh them down?
Our power is all numerical:
we stand where we are
through perfect, celestial, calculations.

This is the point:
the Lewisohns' famous wooden pew
—if they don't hurry up and leave it—
will end up collapsing
under the weight of wheelbarrows and hoists
broken in turn
beneath the weight of gold,
whereas we
will whirl lightly
with the greatest ease
and with wealth in our heads
rather than in our wallets.

Having said this:
let's look at the facts.

How much does Lewisohn make?
Six million dollars a year?
Maybe even seven?
Well done Lewisohn!
At the time of the alliance
with its perpetual enemy
Lehman Brothers didn't make more than four.

Excellent. Let's start from here.

Joining forces
with Goldman capital
and the brains of the Lehman firm
we're sure to launch
the decisive attack
on the heart of the system:
ours will be the bank for industry
ours will be the bank for transport
ours will be the bank for commerce
and for the new chains of stores
such as Woolworth
who owes everything to us.

A modern bank
for an up-to-date America

Philip Lehman
has had written
in block capitals
on the immense white wall
of a new skyscraper!

How much does Lewisohn make?
Six million dollars a year?
Maybe even seven?
Well done Lewisohn!
Having acquired control of Woolworth
Lehman Brothers has reached five.
Not enough: full speed ahead!
More! More!
Without ever pulling back!

A bank for everyone
for the prosperity of all

Philip Lehman
has had written
in large letters
on a sixty-foot banner
fixed to the Brooklyn Bridge!

How much does Lewisohn make?
Six million dollars a year?
Maybe even seven?
Well done Lewisohn!
Now that it is quoted on the stock market
Lehman Brothers settles at 6 and 40.
Not enough: full speed ahead!
More! More!
Don't back down!

A bank of today
to finance your tomorrow

Philip Lehman
has had written
in large letters
on trains and on boats and on barges!

How much does Lewisohn make?
Six million dollars a year?
Maybe even seven?
Poor Lewisohn!
Now that it's a gem of Wall Street
Lehman Brothers has hit 7 and 80.
Not enough: full speed ahead!
More! More! More! More!
With no fear of competition!

A courageous bank
ready for every challenge

Philip Lehman
has had written
in large letters
on trains and on boats and on barges!

How much does Lewisohn make?
Six million dollars a year?
Maybe even seven?
I pity you, Lewisohn!

Now that it's on everyone's lips
that Lehman Brothers has hit 8 and 60.
Not enough: full speed ahead!
More! More! More! More! More! More!

Lehman Brothers is in the front row

Philip Lehman
would gladly have had it written
outside the Temple
when the Lewisohns were moved back.

High finance
is sometimes
really funny:
on Wall Street
now that he has beaten the gold giants
they call him "Golden Philip."

"How can those people sit so far back?"
his son asks him
as he watches the Hungarians take their place.

*"Sometimes the horse that starts last
can catch up in the race.
You know that, Bobbie, don't you?
And it also happens to athletes:
Maxie Long was a master at this.
And he still holds the record: there at the top."*
But as he says it
Golden Philip bites his lip.

Don't people say
that up there at the top
there's only room for one person?
In the front row, it's just the same.

It's fine that everyone on Wall Street
is saying Lehman has come off best

from the union with Goldman.
It's fine that Philip
is no doubt entitled to the front row.
That's all fine.

But the fact that they're not out there alone
is what Philip can't accept.

He'll have to find a way.
He'll have to turn the right card.

Meanwhile, patience.

And in his diary
that same evening
Golden Philip
has written:
AS IF GOLDMAN WEREN'T THERE.

21
Shiva

Sitting on a blue velvet chair
back to the wall
the last of the three old Lehman brothers
waits
greets
thanks
the door closes
then reopens: another comes in.

When little Robert
asked him
about his long beard
he told him
this is what they once did
over there in a place called Rimpar
and this is what they also did for Uncle Henry, in Alabama.

Robert then
drew
on a sheet of paper
lots of people with beards down to their feet
—even women—
—even the dog—
and showing it to everyone he said:
"This is Rimpar, in Alabama."

Robert likes drawing.
And if they ask him
what he'll do when he grows up
he replies:
"Painter!"
At which his mother, Carrie,
promptly smiles
well knowing
that in her husband's diary
this wasn't exactly the plan
and corrects him:
"Bobbie! You mean to say banker painter."

For the moment
however
Bobbie Lehman has no interest
in his professional future:
he looks around him
at his father and all the others
who have been doing strange rites
for three days.

For the Lehman family
has decided it will follow all the rules:
Shiva and *sheloshim*
as they did over there in Europe,
all the rules
as if we were Bavarian Jews.
Not to go out for a week.
Not to prepare food:
to ask neighbors for it, receive it and no more.
They've torn a garment, as prescribed
they ripped it to pieces as soon as they came back
from the burial

at the old cemetery.
And they've also recited the *Qaddish*
every day
morning and evening
the whole family
children in the front row
ever since mourning began.

Now
in a whisper
with tired eyes
sitting on a blue velvet chair
back to the wall
the last of the three Lehman brothers
waits
greets
thanks
the door closes
then reopens: another.

They have closed the body in a dark coffin
with no handles
with no decoration
with nothing
just like Henry's
half a century ago.

The offices at 119 Liberty Street
with their windows as high as the chandeliers
stay shut today.
Today like yesterday and the day before.

The Lehman Brothers offices
at 119 Liberty Street
have been there nearly fifty years
and have never stayed shut for so long:
Even on Wall Street
at the Stock Exchange
the flags are down, at half-mast.
"Funny"—old Lehman thinks—
for
he and his brother
hadn't set foot in there for a long time;

now that all they talk about in there
is shares and bonds and stock markets.

Sitting on a blue velvet chair
back to the wall
the last of the three old Lehman brothers
now
waits
greets
thanks
the door closes
then reopens: another.

The crowds
—all the Jews in Manhattan—
have been queuing now for hours
at the front door of the house:
they saw the news in the *New York Times*
which put it on page one.
"Funny"—old Lehman thinks—
for
he and his brother
didn't read a single page of the newspaper
since all they write about now
is shares and bonds and stock markets.

Crowds silent.
They go in two at a time
into the large house on 54th Street,
where the blinds today are left down:
the street
will not be brightened
by the light of the enormous chandeliers
that run
—to Carrie Lehman's delight—
not on gas but electrical current.

Crowds silent.
They go in two at a time.
There's also Solomon Paprinski
the tightrope walker of Wall Street
who in twenty years
has never fallen
from his wire.

All as the Law prescribes
all as it was in Rimpar, among those Bavarians,
even if
now
there is only one
who actually remembers how it was.

22

Horses

A as in Antares
B as in Brandon
C as in Calypso
D as in Dakota
E as in Eagle
F as in Felix
G as in Gypsy
H as in Hister
I as in Isidoro
J as in Junior
K as in King
L as in Lucky
M as in Melody
N as in Nigel
O as in Olympus
P as in Pepper
Q as in Quebec
R as in Rubir
S as in Silver
T as in Tango
U as in Ulysses
V as in Velvet
W as in White
X as in Xoros
Y as in York
Z as in Zagor

Bobbie
has learned the alphabet
from horses in the Lehman stables.

Though still only seven
he's already crazy about them.

Since that very first time
when Philip and Carrie
took him to watch the races:
Bobbie never once
took his eyes off the race,
he didn't close them
even when the horses raced past
raising a cloud of dust
in front of upper-class seats
and from that day
he hasn't done a single drawing
at school
in which there isn't a horse.

The boy knows each breed
can distinguish a Barb from a Scot
and an Arab from a Thoroughbred
he knows the value of one
and knows the value of another.
For now, here in New York,
since the arrival of the new century
the watchword is *value*.
Everything
has a price
everything has a quotation.
Everything in New York
carries a price tag
like shoes in shop windows
like fruit on market stalls
but the thrill
the real thrill
lies in the fact that
the price
can
must

always
alter
change
change
change.

There:
just as Bobbie Lehman loves horses that race
his father, Philip, loves prices that change.

Sure:
it's easy to sit on the terraces
and follow horses at a race course
through binoculars: you just have to watch.
It's more difficult to follow the course of prices.
But Philip Lehman doesn't lose heart
and is already starting to invest
in the financial training
of his heir:
"Do I have your attention, Robert?
If you'll follow me and stop drawing,
I have something much more interesting.
Our game today is called stock market values.
How does it work? Simple.
Once upon a time, Bobbie, there was an umbrella.
The umbrella costs three dollars.
But if the New York Times
were suddenly to announce
bad weather for two months
then do you know what would happen?
Umbrellas would sell like hotcakes
and their price would go up
because no one wants to get wet
and, so as not to get wet, they are ready to spend.
Do you like our game? Good.
Now suppose that all of a sudden
word starts going 'round
that umbrellas attract lightning . . .
Who would want an umbrella anymore?
A raincoat is a thousand times better . . .
And so then the price of umbrellas would go right down.
Perfect, Bobbie dear: that's all there is to it.
The bank that carries your surname

is just the same as the umbrella, did you know that?
On the stock market we're being checked out all the time:
those who believe in us will buy a small piece of your surname
which they can then keep or sell.
(it's called a 'share,' Bobbie, make sure you remember that).
If the bank is healthy, if it's strong
then its shares are valuable
and no one will want to get rid of them.
But if the company slips up
—because word goes 'round that it attracts lightning!—
then anyone with shares in it will want to sell them
to get their money back.
This nasty thing is called a crash.
Like a horse
which, if it stops winning, drops in value
but, if it has a great victory, it's worth a fortune.
Is that clear? Well, Robert,
I would like Lehman Brothers
to become
a great stable
with horses that win all the time."

Bobbie has heard it all
not missing a word.
And he also thinks he has understood.

Then
just once
he tried to draw the stock market,
but the sheet of paper was left blank.
Then he tried with the bank
in vain.

So he drew a horse.
With an umbrella over it.
And he wondered whether that
might seriously be a bank.

Good question, Bobbie.
You're not the only one
in this house
to ask this.

Perhaps grandfathers come to resemble children
but the oldest surviving Lehman
is continually asking
where
in his family
this great passion for horses comes from
seeing that over there in Rimpar, Bavaria,
with all that livestock
there was no one who raised horses.
But then the old man stops:
this is a typical thought of his—being a good arm—
because he ought to know by now
that 1 + 1 in New York never makes 2
and here the certainties of life
are swept away by the wind.

There it is:
Emanuel sometimes thinks
that if the bank today
had to choose a trademark
it would probably choose a horse.

For this reason
he wasn't so surprised
when he asked
his grandson Bobbie:
"What will you do when you grow up?"
and he replied:
"Jockey!"
At which
his mother, Carrie,
promptly smiled
well knowing
that in her husband's diary
this wasn't exactly the plan
and corrected him:
"Bobbie! A banker jockey."

And if Philip hadn't been at the Stock Exchange
she would have heard him correct her
in block capitals:
"A FINANCIER JOCKEY."

Yes.
Now
for several years
at least
—ever since Uncle Mayer's passing—
that signboard with the word BANK
feels too restrictive for Philip
like a tie around his neck.
And it makes no difference
that the sign is no longer made of wood
but is all glass and wrought iron,
designed in Liberty style
by a proper architect.
For Lehman Brothers,
which is quoted on the stock market
which issues securities and distributes shares
offering advice
and maneuvering markets,
those four letters B-A-N-K
are almost an insult.
Philip would like to change its name:
he dreams of
LEHMAN BROTHERS COMPANY
and
each time he arrives at the front door
of 119 Liberty Street
he seems to see the sign already there.
But then?

Then he always has something else to do:
his day is chock-full like his diary
and he often thinks he has some divine power
like Moses, like Abraham
for he never once feels tired.

This
more or less
is what he thinks
as he looks at the black and gray prints
—not at all consoling—
that hang on the walls of Bobbie's bedroom.

A week ago
in fact
the Council of Elders at the Temple
decided
to reward their benefactors
with a token of gratitude
and have presented the Lehmans
with a fine collection of prints
each framed separately
that portray
the great prophets
and King David with Goliath
and Noah with the Ark
and the Tower of Babel
the Golden Calf
and Ezekiel among the bones of the dead,
in short
an impressive biblical gallery
containing a verse
beneath each picture.

The problem is that these prints
are done in such dark ink
and in such shocking detail
as to seem
more than anything
like a punishment for lost souls.

Nonetheless
there's something powerful about them:
Philip finds them instructive
because for him
the history of Israel
is family history
where he clearly sees himself
as patriarch.

He has therefore given instructions
that the whole collection of prints
so dark
so disturbing
is to be hung over Bobbie's bed:
these will be the last scenes he'll see

each night
before he goes to sleep.

Whereas Philip
on his office wall
has hung Maxie Long
the Olympic athlete of bygone years
in a portrait with a lifeless gaze.

And Philip thinks he knows
where that opaqueness comes from:
now that you've broken every record
what medal is there to seek?
A moment comes
when even the greatest climber
finds himself on the peak
of the world's highest mountain . . .
And then?
At that point
what else can he aim for?

In a word
Philip Lehman
feels all of this.

And has also written
in his diary:
BIG PROBLEM: CAN NEVER GET THINGS WRONG.

For him, it has become an obsession.
He's constantly putting himself to the test.

He opens the pages of the *New York Times*
and picks an article at random
after which
he starts to order each detail
and notes down his prediction:
he never gets it wrong.
The career of a politician?
Philip studies the facts, and gets it right.
The future of an industrialist?
Philip studies the facts, and gets it right.
The success of a patent?
Philip studies the facts, and gets it right.

His son, Bobbie,
never imagines for a moment
that this is the only reason why he loves horses:
to bet on the one that's going to win
and to see that his intuition
is never wrong.

He has even been seen
entering
the boxers' training club
on Long Island.
And not because he likes boxing: he hates it.
He has to put himself to the test.
He sits in a corner.
He watches them training.
He listens to what they say.
Then he pulls out
his diary
and writes "TOMORROW GRIFFITHS TO WIN."

They come to his office
from morning to evening
proposing
investments of every kind:
airships, gliders,
automobiles, city transport.

Each time Philip
asks for all the necessary facts
shuts himself in the drawing room at home
till late at night
and before falling asleep he knows what to do.

"Mr. Lehman, a leading bank
such as yours
cannot but give careful consideration
to the seven-figure revenue of the cruise sector:
we offer accommodation to customers from every sector of society
—arranged, of course, in separate classes—
on transatlantic liners of exceptional quality
in which nothing is left to chance
from the door handles

to the livery of the last waiter
and trays of lobster are served
with plentiful supplies of French wine and caviar.
The modern world is expanding fast
and you are its driving force, Mr. Lehman:
now that you have hoisted your flag
over the farthest reaches of the United States,
will you miss this chance, I ask, to tame the oceans?
The name of a bank is not ink
and may even be written on water.
Can I possibly be wrong? You'll have no regret
in financing my floating Jerusalem."

And though
it was true that the name of a bank
could without a doubt
be engraved in seven figures on the waves,
Philip Lehman
thought that perhaps
to have it written on a boat
was not his highest ambition.
Let others go ahead and do it.

And he didn't finance it: the *Titanic*.

23
Pineapple Juice

Bobbie is doing well
at college:
he has very good grades
especially in art history
and plays on the polo team.

Philip and Carrie
go to watch a match
in which Bobbie scores ten goals.

And yet Carrie alone is truly delighted.
Her husband, no.
For some time he has been so distracted.

Curious, at times, how men's minds work:
the family coffers are full
the stables packed with horses
they sit in the front row of the Temple
and yet
for some time
an air of disquiet
wafts through the rooms
of 119 Liberty Street
affecting the mood
and the diary of the Golden Man.

For a start: Dreidel.

Philip couldn't fail
to notice
a certain change
in his cousin's long silences:
now on the verge of fifty
swathed in cigar smoke
he
had taken to wearing a thick pair of dark glasses
whose effect
on his face
was to silence even the expression of his eyes
—Dreidel's only remaining form of language.
If Philip and Sigmund had imagined
until then
that they had some means of interaction
through learning to recognize the lexical value
of a frown, pursed lips, convulsive blinking, or a reddened face,
this dictionary suddenly became useless:
their cousin's contribution
was limited
more and more
to the role of witness
performed with hieratic presence
save for crucial moments
when his vote

—for or against, with no discussion—
was expressed through a minimal nod or shake of the chin.

And what was more,
during meetings
the chair on which Dreidel sat
was turning into a place of torture:
he had developed the habit
of scratching
furiously
at its leather arms
with his fingernails
like an animal in a cage
and scraped the heel of his shoe
constantly
against the leg of the table.
Meanwhile, incapable of sitting still,
he wriggled
convulsively against the back of the chair
with spasms
so sudden
that several times he burned his hands
on the tip of his cigar.

Dreidel
more than ever
seemed to harbor
some restless form of pent-up agitation
which
—they felt sure—
would soon produce that extreme rush of poison
that the hornet had been storing up for years.

And this worried Philip.
To the point of distress.

All the more since Dreidel's wife
        invited to celebrate
        the recent purchase of their foal Hidalgo
        with a pineapple juice
seemed quite unworried
about her husband's imminent explosion:
she listened of course to Philip's concern

understood his tone of anxiety,
but was perplexed
more than anything
when
her consort's throes
were described
in detail.
Her only comment was *"I'm lost for words"*
and when asked to offer a little more help
she simply smiled: *"Discuss it yourselves, he has said nothing to me . . ."*

As he watched the prances of their new Hidalgo
Philip pondered for hours
on this almost insulting response:
might she and Dreidel be in league
to make a mockery of the family business?
Or did that mysterious phrase *". . . he has said nothing to me"*
suggest he had in fact said *something else* to her?
And so
did he actually talk to her
reserving his silence just for them?

Frankly
he wasn't sure
which explanation to prefer.

The first terrified him
for its affront to family ties.

The second upset him just as much
—perhaps even more so—
for it was the exact opposite of his own situation:
how many times had his Carrie
complained
about having to live with a taciturn husband,
who practically never spoke,
despite the news she heard
of his great success as a public speaker?
How many times had Philip returned home
with the feeling of not having enough breath
—and not just breath: not even the desire—
to say as much as good evening?

Once, indeed,
after Bobbie had been promoted
to captain of the polo team
(and given the title *Silver Falcon*),
Philip listened distractedly as Bobbie explained
the whys and wherefores
and finally
only at the end of the long story
did Philip pat him on the shoulder and say:
"Well done Bobbie! It's such a wonderful sport, baseball."

If he had to choose
which Philip deserved a medal
the father/husband or the banker/financier
he would choose
without a doubt
the Golden Man of Wall Street,
and certainly not that part-time being
that he became on his arrival home.
This was fact.

And now
the idea that his cousin
might be withholding from Liberty Street
all his faculties of communication
and reserving them for the bridal chamber
was, to his mind, unthinkable:
how could anyone even think it?
Placing his role of husband before that of banker?
How could anyone row against the family fleet
in the name of something so limited
as the perimeter of one's own existence?
This would be enough
to make Dreidel in his eyes
eligible for instant dismissal.

This whole reflection
took place during Hidalgo's leaping and bounding
tamed by the jockey
with masterful ease.

Maybe this is why
Philip

wrote in his diary
simply:
KEEP HOLD OF THE HORSE'S REINS.

Sigmund, for his part,
had no interest in the problem:
after his father's death
he had carved out
his own area in the bank
and was acting
so to speak
in almost complete independence
steering clear of the others
and hiding himself
behind a glacial mask
of bitterness and antagonism
whose price
was measured by Harriett
in gallons of nightly tears.

Whereas by day
his liturgical observance of the 120 *mitzvot*
had made him colder
than a piece of metal.

And it was
with a metallic sound
that Sigmund knocked
one morning
—in the month of November—
on the door of his cousin's office.

But note:
not on Philip's door.
On Dreidel's.

The words *"Could I ask you a question?"*
murmured quietly from the doorway
sounded already so bizarre,
partly because
no one
anywhere in Liberty Street

expected advice
from the sphinx in dark glasses,
and partly because the question
came from whom? From him?
From that Sigmund
who for four months
in front of the mirror
morning and evening
was convinced
that he could and should despise the world?

Dreidel however
gave no sign of dissent.
He studied his cousin
from a distance
searching for some meaning
that he couldn't find.
Nor, much as he looked,
could he find any bunny tracks.

Sigmund meanwhile closed the door,
making sure there was no one in the corridor.
He approached the desk
penetrating the blanket of smoke.
Sat down.
And moved his seat forward.
Of all possible opening lines
he chose the most unlikely:
"Do you like fruit?"

And not satisfied, he repeated it.
"Do you like fruit?"

Two. Three times.
He detected a hint of agreement
only on the fourth attempt.

In the long silence that followed
Dreidel
never once took his eyes off his cousin.

Was he mad?

Or was this sudden horticultural zeal
due
to ill-concealed grief at the loss of his father?

There was, of course, another explanation
but for the moment
he didn't even want to consider it.

Also because
Sigmund got there first:
"So that makes two of us, Dreidel,
because I like fruit very much indeed.
I've come to talk about it
because the world is not an enchanted wood
and in war, dear Dreidel, there's no peace.
Philip, no, you know? I fear he doesn't like fruit.
In fact, I'm pretty sure we're the only ones in this, me and you.
Eh! Philip likes arithmetic,
he likes doing conjuring tricks
with shares on the stock market: Up! Down! Up! Down!
And so, I don't want to go knocking on his door:
he wouldn't understand. Or perhaps he would,
but in his own way, which I don't like.
He thinks in terms of money. For me, it's influence.
I'm not interested in those who greet me on Wall Street
I want control over those who sit in Congress.
Our parents have left us a fishing boat
I want it to become a whaler
a ship on the open sea
one that has no fear of monsters.
And since pride is the best protection,
I'm here to propose an agreement.
An agreement—seems strange, eh?—in the name of fruit.
Or rather: of the United Fruit Company.
You know what I'm talking about, huh?

Dreidel gave out an enormous puff of smoke,
hoping that by belching more cloud than a chimney
would enable him to disappear as much as possible.
Meanwhile
he set his facial muscles
so as not to indicate the slightest approval:
he knew exactly what was being talking about

but preferred to let Sigmund explain
if only
to hear the metaphors.

"United Fruit deals in bananas, coconuts,
avocado, mango, and a load of other delicacies
that don't grow here . . .
It's a worthy enterprise, Dreidel.
I'd even say benevolent:
we buy tons of fruit
from woebegone countries in Central America
and we pay them what is right,
I don't mean a market price
but what is little for us is a lot for them.
Having said this.
As we know: everything has its price
and only fools expect gifts . . .
Exactly. So I'll come to the point, my friend."

Dreidel gave out another puff of smoke,
limiting himself
then
to the thought
that he had been moved
so swiftly
from the status of blood relation
to the more ordinary rank of common friend.
Clearly more appropriate to the circumstance.

"We have to be single-minded:
regrets are pointless.
So I will speak plainly:
United Fruit is an excellent investment.
Not because I have any liking for pineapples
nor for those fruits from Puerto Rico.
Here we are financing the farmers
for appearance only:
by controlling the market
we are controlling them politically.
Guatemala, Honduras, Cuba, Nicaragua:
we have a hold over them, you understand?
Private property, we'll make it ours,
and since it's best to expect the worst

if one day there's a need, then we're already there,
ready to do anything."

At this *anything*
emphasized with its whole range of implications
Dreidel
exhaled a tall plume of smoke
similar to a spout of water from a sperm whale:
as much as to send out the message
that Moby Dick had not been killed
and the whaler might still miss the target.

"What counts is courage, my dear friend, and I have it.
Well. Lehman Brothers cannot say no:
there are only the exploited and the exploiters
and we cannot remain with the first
even if we win on the stock market. Far from it . . .
You know what it is? The milch cow of Wall Street
might be full of milk,
but do you want to spend your life getting yourself milked?
America is using us
and I want to keep my dignity:
I want to be the one who pulls the levers.
The politicians are asking us for help . . .
If we do it,
not only will we be milking the cow
but we'll be in charge of the cattle shed.
Our name, after all, is Lehman Brothers
and it's written in capital letters."

Though flattered at being a member
of a circle of capital letters
Dreidel made no reply,
remaining impassive.

And he hoped that his nonresponse
was as good as a reply,
saving him from the muscular fatigue
of moving his chin.

After an hour
of the most remarkable flat calm
Sigmund

sensed his cousin's meager vegetable propensity:
took a deep breath
in the tobacco-filled air
stood up
and
once out of the room
walked the length of the corridor
to Philip's office.

The fact that he hadn't closed Dreidel's door
was clearly
no coincidence:
the cards were now on the table.

He knocked
waited for a reply
then opened the door.
Dreidel only heard him
ask: *"Do you like fruit, Philip?"*
after which
he disappeared inside.

It is said that horses
can sense
imminent danger.

No one will ever know if it's true.

Yet
a few days later
the most recent arrival at the Lehman stables
suddenly took fright
kicked madly
and broke its reins
unseated the jockey
jumped the fence
hurtling full tilt toward the wood,
terrified
with panic in its eyes
for no reason.

They had to put it down
owing to the injuries it had suffered as it fled.

"*Fear*" Sigmund remarked
"*is a waste of time and energy.*"

"*And of money*" Philip added.
"*Hidalgo cost me $400,000.*"

Money thrown out of the window.

24
Babes in Toyland

Yehuda ben Tema
in the *Ethics of the Fathers*
says:
forty years for growing shrewd
fifty to be prudent.

Sigmund Lehman
cannot say whether he's reached the end
of that age of shrewdness
but feels he has entered
that of prudence:
to tell the truth,
if he could discuss it with Yehuda ben Tema
he would ask
at what age in life
he might hope for a minimum of clarity.
Frankly, that's what is missing.

Often he sits at the table of a restaurant,
by a large window
and spends his whole lunchtime
eyeing people in the street.
He's not interested in how they dress.
What matters is whether they are alone or with others.
If he stares at them—one by one—
it is only in search of a Sigmund Lehman.
Another self.

To see him walking.
To follow him as he talks.
To witness his every gesture.

And maybe, who knows, to understand at last
who it is who dwells inside you.

There again
Sigmund lost the thread
quite some time ago.

Born a rabbit
and transformed into a cobra
thanks to the *mitzvot* of a banking Torah,
he has been wavering
now for years
between the opposite extremes
of a double character:
frosty while awake
desperate at night.

At first
he had hoped
it was a temporary inconvenience
perhaps the price to be paid
for having moved too fast
with no intermediate stage
from fearing to being feared
from quaking to making others quake
and above all
from being mocked to mocking others.
It hadn't been an easy passage:
he was now paying the price.
And hoped it would soon pass.

But he was wrong.
Over time, the thing grew worse.

All the more since
Sigmund
meanwhile
was convinced
that his mood swings were inevitable

and as such had to be accepted with resignation,
one of those natural hazards to be found in any profession:
the feeling of anxiety that gripped him
was to a banker
what calluses are to a typist
or burns to a fireman.

Night after night
his crying fits
became uncontrollable,
lightened only
by the matrimonial idyll:
forced to share her husband's insomnia out of domestic solidarity
Harriett
recited for her (nonpaying) audience of one
her script about their escape to the open sea:
"I promise you, Sigmy: they'll never find us."
"When shall we set sail?"
"Sooner or later."

And in saying
sooner or later
Harriett began to ask herself
whether the purpose
of her husband's tears
wasn't to create an ocean of his own
on which he alone could sail.

But as sometimes happens,
a glimmer of self-love
saved Sigmund from the brink of disaster:
if he couldn't entirely kill
the rabbit he carried within
he reckoned
at least
to offer it some assistance
and there were occasional opportunities
for his midnight tears
to find a daytime outlet.

Clearly it wasn't easy.
Partly because sentiment has no place in banking,
and partly because it had cost so much

for him to build a reputation for ruthlessness
that it couldn't be thrown to the wind
with blubbering during office hours.

Sigmund therefore had
seriously
to ask himself
on what social occasions
was the unimaginable absurdity
of a banker in tears
not merely permitted
but perhaps even applauded.

Fortunately
he could think of several
that proved exceptionally useful.
And for him crucial.

Firstly funerals.
For after all
wasn't Lehman Brothers expected
to be a friendly bank
to offer sympathy and support in the darkest hours
not just for the Nation
but for every single investor?

Funerals of interest from a promotional point of view
related to three types of corpse:
1. American soldiers
2. those who die rich with no heirs
3. well-known artists or illustrious figures

In these select circumstances
even the most hardheaded bankers
forced themselves to shed a tear
as they threw a handful of earth onto the coffin
and if he managed it
drew unanimous approval from those present:
"Have you seen? He's such a sorehead, but he's grieving for us!"

Sigmund's two partners
in this respect
were totally ill-equipped.

They had tried, of course,
to attend the occasional funeral,
but without the desired result:
Dreidel closed himself in his own silence,
however admirable for a funeral,
but yet
from which
he was incapable of uttering
a simple word of condolence
whispered into an ear.
And this was generally not appreciated.

Worse still was Philip
literally incapable
of adopting
even the slightest hint of emotion:
his expression—a mocking smile—
was irrepressible
and this made his presence at deaths
counterproductive.

Not so for Sigmund.
He proved to be an excellent weeper.
Especially when America
had to start reckoning with gangsters
and the streets were paved with corpses:
Lehman Brothers was much involved.
"Have you seen? He's a profiteer, but look how he suffers."
And in fact he wept copious tears,
gratifying for the next of kin
and of much relief for the man himself.

To funerals he then added theater attendance.
Sigmund
had never been
a music fan
nor did he ever think
a bank would discover
any interest in theaters.

But since certain wives
not infrequently
play a role as financial consultants,

it was his Harriett
who took him for the first time
to Broadway.
The intention, in truth,
was more about entertainment than banking,
but there it is:
as they watched
the triumph of *Babes in Toyland*
—seated at the Majestic—
Sigmund
noticed around him
a strange symphony of handkerchiefs.
It was the moment when the rich miser
seems about to kidnap Little Bo-Peep
snatching her from the piper's son:
as though it were he, Sigmund, onstage
dressed up as the mean financier.
And what was more:
didn't Old Barnaby
seem to portray half of Wall Street?

Yet, the miracle.

Sigmund looked around.
The top financial bourgeoisie
of New York:
not only were they not offended
but they were all in tears.

It was like receiving a surprise gift:
the floodgates opened
and he joined
the general distress for the fate of Bo-Peep
victim sacrificed on the altar of capitalism.
From two rows back he heard someone say:
"Have you seen? He's a shark, but he's crying for Bo-Peep!"
And he was exceedingly happy.

Broadway theaters
in effect
when he came to think of it
weren't all that bad as an investment:
they were always sold out

and the entertainment machine
never stopped for a moment.
And what's more, now that America
was so infatuated with work
wasn't it time
to think of leisure?
It could be turned into a business
with piles of money to be made
from amusement.

Sigmund set to work
and pursued it with much care:
at the theater five nights a week
with swollen eyes
soaked handkerchiefs
and while at first he preferred melodramas,
he was happy to stretch to comedy
when he heard someone in the street say:
"I laughed this evening until I cried."

He cried through the operas at the Metropolitan.
He cried through the musicals at the Princess.
He cried through the comedies of Florenz Ziegfeld.

He also cried
—this time with delight—
when a theater
for the first time
used electrical current
to light the street sign
with sixty-four bulbs.

For a moment he even imagined
the words LEHMAN BROTHERS
flashing in bright-colored lights
as if it were a revue.
And he found it a touching idea.

In short
with great professional spirit
frosty Sigmund Lehman
—known on Wall Street as the terror of secretaries and chauffeurs—
cried buckets of tears

dividing his time
between funerals
theater first nights
and charitable events.

The last of which
was perhaps his masterstroke.

It just so happens
in fact
that a strange fashion
began to sweep the offices of the Stock Exchange:
banks
that investigated every way
of draining American salaries
had been gripped
by a sense of social conscience
and had been competing for some time
to see who could make the largest gifts
to widows, beggars, and cripples.

The return in terms of moral probity
was remarkable.

Yet
in Sigmund Lehman
this brought on
a matchless burst of tears:
while for other banks it might raise the doubt
that the altruism was self-serving,
no one ever harbored a single doubt
on seeing the most ruthless of the Lehman cousins
so touched
so moved.
And therefore
on with the hospitals
on with the orphans
on with the deaf and dumb
on with kissing little old ladies
and diplomas for the illiterate.
All, of course, duly drenched.
And not just with champagne.

With such a galaxy of opportunities for tears
Sigmund hoped against hope
that he had squared the circle.

And
—as compensation—
he strove to harden his crimson mask
allowing his cynicism each day
to strike bold scimitar blows,
convinced
that these outbursts
would then be quenched
by floods of tears.

But it was not enough.

For an unexpected element
crept into the story
in the innocuous guise
of his two sons.
Harold and Allan.

They were two unusual creatures.
Destined for the new century, Harriett thought,
when she began to notice the first traces
of a strange electricity about them.

From their earliest childhood
they were marked out—from all other children in the world—
by a remarkable intelligence, well above the norm.
Excessive, without doubt.
And troublesome.

Their perspicacity was overwhelming:
nothing could be hidden from them
and even at the age when children play games
these seemed not like two young boys
but two authorities from the modern Pantheon
already eligible for Nobel prizes.

If they were playing with toy trains
theirs was a railroad engineering system.
If they were coloring with crayons

their models were seventeenth-century Mannerists.
They viewed the mysteries of the world
—of general fascination for every creature—
with the skepticism of a speculative philosopher
and even in the way they spoke
they quickly assumed
the cool confidence of public speakers.
Their mastery of language was irksome.
Its pertinence precise.

There.
The delicate situation
in which Sigmund found himself
did not exactly help.

The children's eyes could fathom him
leaving no means of escape
and he
on returning home
would have gladly looked forward
to a minimum of childish innocence,
seeing that for the rest of the day
the world was not an enchanted wood.
Instead, he was given no such allowance.

The boys were not yet ten
when they stopped him
unexpectedly
at the drawing room doorway
just as he was leaving:
"Do you want us to become like you
or can we model ourselves on someone else?"

And that was just the first
of a long series of questions
protracted over years
yet with no unkind intent:
Harold and Allan
were merely
assessing matters
with an unrelenting,
objective,
twentieth-century gaze

as if the age of dreams
had died out with the dinosaurs
and their century was called "reality."
Sigmund couldn't help thinking
now and then
that between him and his sons
there was the same difference
as between a drawing and a photograph.

"Did you choose to work in a bank
or was it the bank that chose you?"
Harold asked him at the age of twelve
as they were eating some chicken
(which, for Sigmund, immediately went down the wrong way).
And he didn't even have to answer
for Allan did it for him:
"I didn't choose to be called Allan
I didn't choose to be born
I didn't choose to be a boy
I didn't choose to be Jewish
I didn't choose to live in America:
the most important things are not chosen, Harold,
you're saddled with them, and that's it."

"And so all this freedom, where is it?" his brother protested.

"You can choose between boiled chicken and roast chicken."
Allan said, pouring himself a drink (still just of water).

For Sigmund
family lunches
gradually became a kind of torment.

At the age of fifteen
while they were playing with Sigmund
at skimming pebbles over the lake in the park,
it was Allan who launched another attack:
"Have you ever thought that if you're in charge of a bank
it's only because of your surname?"
Sigmund instinctively reacted
by aiming his stone
at the head of a duck,
but not even the consequent flap of wings

stopped him from hearing Harold:
"Maybe he'd prefer not to have the surname or the bank."

Could the little boy be right?

And so
bedtime tears
became daily
(and not those of children, but silent tears).

With adolescence
then, as was obvious,
the phenomenon showed no improvement.
On the contrary, if that were possible,
it acquired further undertones
of devastating effect.
The two alternated
in a grueling team game
that ultimately witnessed
their father's elimination.

Harold, pondering on his childhood,
asked: *"When we were young,*
you always told us that Lehman Brothers
is doing good to all American citizens.
Children are always told ridiculous stories,
so I don't criticize you for this.
But today, in all honesty: do you actually believe it?"

Or Allan, in rabbinic vein:
"If the Almighty had ten dollars,
do you reckon he would give them to Lehman Brothers?"

Harold, with infinite tact:
"Who knows if Granddad Mayer would say you're smart."

Allan, with fake kindness:
"It can't be said you didn't try."

Harold again, with a scimitar blow:
"But do you seriously respect Uncle Philip?"

And lastly, as in every war,
the final
decisive
sweeping attack
by both armies
all guns blasting:
"Last night we heard you crying.
How long do you think you can carry on?
Maybe you should ask yourself a question.
And not just for your sake: for everyone else's.
Look, even if you pull out
the bank carries on just the same."

It is filial love
that sustains fathers
and encourages them on their long journey.

So that
after much waiting
the rabbit
timidly
emerged from his burrow.

He dried his eyes
sniffed the air
put on his life vest
and holding Harriett's hand
began to swim.

25
Model T

Yehuda ben Tema
in the *Ethics of the Fathers*
says:
fifty years to be prudent
sixty to be wise.

Philip Lehman
is not sure whether wisdom has anything to do with dreams
but the fact is
that at night he dreams.
And he always dreams the same thing.

It starts like a game.
In the garden of an old house
there is Philip and his father, Emanuel.
The sun is dazzling.
It's the festival of *Sukkot*:
the hut
will have to be finished by this evening
with its roof of willow branches
and leaves and festoons.
This is what they did each year
at one time,
just as it was done over there in Germany
in Rimpar, Bavaria.
The sun is dazzling.
Emanuel has already built
the whole hut:
now the roof has to be decorated.
"It's your turn, my son:
make this sukka
into the finest sukka *you can*
and I'll watch you."
Philip steps forward.
The sun is dazzling.
He climbs a ladder:
puts sprays of ivy
on the roof
—*"Well done Philip!"*
and palm leaves
—*"Well done Philip!"*
and branches
—*"Well done Philip!"*
and fruit
—*"Well done Philip!"*
and garlands
—*"Well done Philip!"*
but then his brothers and sisters
arrive in the garden

"We'll make the roof even finer, Philip!"
and they bring
other shoots
—*"More, Philip!"*
other leaves
—*"More, Philip!"*
other branches
—*"More, Philip!"*
other garlands
—*"More, Philip!"*
but then Jews from the district
arrive in the garden, a crowd
and they also have leaves
branches
whole trees
and the roof of the *sukka* becomes enormous
becomes gigantic
—*"It's all going to collapse, Philip!"*
but then the whole of America
—whites, blacks, Italians—
arrive in the garden
carrying stones, sticks, logs
—*"It's all going to collapse, Philip!"*
—*"It's all going to collapse, Philip!"*
—*"It's all going to collapse, Philip!"*
—*"It's all going to collapse, Philip!"*

Ever since his wife, Carrie,
has been sleeping in another room for peace and quiet
there is no one
to hold his hand
when Philip falls
plummets
down
under the *sukka*
knocked over
cut to pieces
by the gigantic collapse.

A secret.
Not to tell anyone.
Not even to write down in his diary
because block capitals

don't work with dreams
and the dwarf's hands have thirty fingers.

And then what do you do?
How can you go 'round saying
that the genius of Lehman Brothers
wakes up terrified
instead of sleeping soundly
now that everyone
but everyone
in the United States
has been caught up
in the fashion for the stock market?

Wall Street
is jubilant
always on the up.
Always a + sign
in front of that index
invented by
Charles Dow and Mr. Jones
putting together
the performances
of the top thirty industries
in America.
Always a + sign
for the Dow Jones Index.

And how could it be otherwise?
Everyone in America
but everyone
is investing
in bonds and shares:
"I'll buy 200 International Steam shares!"
"I want 300 for General Electric!"
"400 for Gimbel Brothers!"
because
who doesn't want to get rich
buying shares
for industries with the wind in their sails
that triple their profits
in two three years
and so:

"Americans, buy today:
you'll have a capital tomorrow!"
to the point where
even the Temple *shammes*
the old man who lights and snuffs out the candles
brother of the tightrope walker
turned up
one morning at the counter:
"I've a load of money and want to make an investment.
Call one of your bosses for me."

Exactly.
Let's stop there, at these words
and this old man with greasy hair
who demands to see *one of the bosses*.

Since along the path in life
there are always many junctions
(and the life of a bank is no different)
the old *shammes*
so anxious to invest
finds himself without knowing it
with three extreme possibilities.

The first is to find himself before a wall of smoke.

The second, more reassuring, is to come up against Philip Lehman.
And in this case, the conversation would go like this:

"Baruch HaShem Mr. Lehman!
I have 10,000 dollars in my old bag
but I want them to be turned into at least 20,000:
they tell me that you multiply money.
And so: what can I invest in?"

"Dear Mr. Paprinski:
there are hundreds of shares
that will double their profits in a few years.
Do not ask the question
how they invest your money:
it's a question with little meaning.
Not even we are in a position to tell you that!
Let us say, for example, that you have a piece of land:

you go to a good farmer
and you tell him to cultivate it, to produce a good crop. Yes?
At that point, what does the farmer do?
He takes a spade and a rake
and plants a little of everything:
fruit trees, vegetables, salad.
After which—a year later—
he comes and hands you a fine amount of money.
Why do you want to know whether that money
comes from apples, from tomatoes, or from carrots?
It's enough for you to say 'my field has made money'!
The same is true of your savings:
give all your cash to Lehman Brothers
and we'll invest it
in everything that earns money."

This is what Philip would tell him.

And it is highly likely
that after this fable about agriculture and banking
the good *shammes* would hand over
the whole of his 10,000 dollars
to be invested in shares.

But now
let's take one step back.
And let's imagine that the *shammes*
doesn't meet Golden Philip
but the third head of the bank
the recent replacement
for a rabbit who has fled for the open sea:

"Baruch HaShem, *Mr. Lehman!*
I have 10,000 dollars in my old bag
but I want them to be turned into at least 20,000:
they tell me that you multiply money.
And so: what can I invest in?"

"Yours is a complex question, Mr. Paprinski.
For the problem here lies deep down
and the question becomes political:
I could tell you indeed to give us your money
so that we invest it for you in the stock market . . .

But it just so happens that Wall Street
creates strange mirages at times. Dangerous.
I remember that years ago, I was a young boy,
my mother, Babette—good soul!—decided to move some furniture
from her bedroom to the floor below.
As it was heavy,
she called in a couple of laborers
two brothers with broad shoulders,
Kildare was their name: I remember them well.
Toby and Johnny Kildare.
Well: they heaved the furniture onto their backs
and went downstairs a step at a time
without wavering, you understand? A real marvel.
They were so good
that my mother had them carry down
a six-foot pendulum clock as well
and then a table, and then a sofa
and the statue of Juno
and the one of Mercury:
the Kildare brothers would have shifted the world.
It was no problem for them:
they knew they had strong backs.
Maybe they were too sure of themselves
and this was the trouble:
when my mother showed them
a grand piano
which came—just think—from Alabama,
the Kildares didn't say no,
but halfway down the stairs . . .
Have you ever seen a piano fly?
It's quite an experience
not easy to forget, Mr. Paprinski.
And even the shoulders of Wall Street
however sturdy they might be
are not of marble, nor do they last forever . . .
I advise you to take care of your dollars,
put them safely into a savings account
you can have them back at any time
just as they are
and without the minimum of risk."

"But in this way I won't double them."

"Of course not. But you know what the point is?
If my mother
hadn't wanted to shift her piano
she could have played it until she was seventy."

This is why
rather than jumping for joy
Philip Lehman
tormented by nightmares
now
sleeps in an armchair
with a heavy feeling
of being alone:
the real problem deep down
is that Herbert is rowing against the tide
and the question is becoming . . .

Oh dear, politics.

Herbert's sacrifice to his ideals
has driven him to the point
that he and Edith have adopted a son.
His name is Peter.
And in all likelihood he comes from humble stock.

Philip hates politics
wholeheartedly.
Because that mass of people who decide with a vote
seem to him so inept.
They should at least pay to vote:
a dollar for each ballot paper.
Even a cent.
But totally free . . .
It's unthinkable.

Philip Lehman
also has these thoughts
during his long nights of insomnia,
made even more disturbing
ever since the roof of the *sukka*
in his nightmare
is no longer covered with branches and leaves
but with canvases, paintings, watercolors, portraits:

they are being unloaded from a ship
each artwork under the arm of a jockey
in the saddle of his horse
and directing operations
it's him, his son, Bobbie.

Ever since he graduated from Yale
with top grades
the boy
has been traveling the world
cultivating a passion for art collecting.

And so
each month
a letter from Europe
arrives on Philip's desk
in which the boy informs him:
"I'm about to buy a Rubens:
if only you knew how beautiful it is, Dad!
With your taste for art
you cannot possibly say no.
Shall I get it? Send money, Dad!"
And the same for Monet.
"Send money, Dad!"
And the same for Goya.
"Send money, Dad!"
And the same for Velázquez.
"Send money, Dad!"
And the same for Bramante.
"Send money, Dad!"
And the same for Rubens.
"Send money, Dad!"
And the same for Canaletto.

And so it's no surprise
if now in the dream
Bobbie is shouting to his jockeys:
"Put the pictures on the roof, guys!"
and it seems he can't hear his father's voice
shouting at him
"Stop, Bobbie! What are you doing?
Can't you see it's all about to collapse?"

"I've bought a Rubens:
look how beautiful, Dad!
Haul it onto the roof, guys!"
"Stop, Bobbie!"
"This is a Rembrandt
I bought it from a gallery:
heave, heave, onto the roof!"
"Stop, Bobbie!"
"Voilà: Monet! Hup: onto the roof!"
"Stop, Bobbie!"
"Voilà: Velázquez! Hup: onto the roof!"
"Stop, Bobbie!"
"Voilà: Cézanne! Hup: onto the roof!"
"Stop, Bobbie!"
"Voilà: Degas! Hup: onto the roof!"
"Bobbie!"
"Bramante!"
"Bobbie!"
"Perugino!"
"Bobbie!"
"Canaletto!"
"Bobbie!"
"Renoir!"
"Bobbie!"
"Pontormo!"

And having finished with painters
he starts on sculpture
full on.

What can a poor man do
to get to sleep
persecuted
by a sadistic son
who mistakes the roof of a hut
for the Louvre?

This nocturnal *Sukkot*
with its horses and art collection
has become more efficient
than an assembly line.

Well yes.
For among other things
it just so happens
that one fine day
Philip Lehman
felt the need
to do what his father once did:
to physically touch
go and see
understand
—for himself—
what
those wondrous
amazing
American industries
the envy of the whole world
really are.

Highland Park Plant.
Mr. Philip Lehman
has an appointment
at 10:00 a.m.
with Mr. Henry Ford.
And who cares
if he's an anti-Semite:
we're bankers, not rabbis.

The new Ford Model T
will be assembled
before his eyes
in exactly
ninety-three minutes.
Watch in hand
Henry Ford is about to kick off.
Conveyor belt.
Workers ready.
Each one in place.
Each one equipped.
Ready?
Steady?
Go!
four-cylinder engine
93-92-91-90

rear drive
89-88-87-86-85
engine transmission with bearings
84-83-82-81-80
side valves
79-78-77-76-75
two-speed gear-change
74-73-72-71-70
reverse gear
69-68-67-66-65
cooling system
64-63-62-61-60
thermosiphon radiator
59-58-57-56-55
steel chassis
54-53-52-51-50
single leaf spring
49-48-47-46-45
ammeter
44-43-42-41-40
starting handle
39-38-37-36-35
drum brakes
34-33-32-31-30
pedal control
29-28-27-26-25
flywheel magneto
24-23-22-21-20
petroleum carburetor
19-18-17
fuel tank under the seat
16-15
upholstered seats
14-13
velvet trimming
12-11
matte black body, the same for all,
10-9
single dynamo for headlamps
8-7
tempered steel wheels
6-5
wooden spokes, as for carriages
4

brass fittings
3
Ford nameplate back and front
2
horn
1
ready
for sale
will do fifty miles
on one gallon of gasoline.

Philip Lehman
is speechless.

He turns to look at Henry Ford
smiling with pride.
He looks at the faces
of the workers
each in their place
ready to send off
in ninety-three minutes
another Model T.

The fact is:
from that day on
ever since that visit to Henry Ford
an enormous
highly efficient
assembly line
now appears
in Philip Lehman's dream:
his son's artworks
are no longer brought in by jockeys
but on a conveyor belt
sorted by Ford workers.
As far as the eye could see.

And the *Sukkot* hut
under siege
collapses
each night
in ninety-three seconds.

26
Battlefield

For many years
there has always been fresh fruit in the Lehman house.
And also in the rooms of the bank:
whole trays piled with bananas and pineapples
laid out on the glass tables.

Only in Dreidel's office
is there no sign of them:
they wouldn't survive in the smoke-filled atmosphere.

Each time Philip
walks into that room
he wonders
whether the impact on his lungs
is so very different
to what soldiers felt
over there in Europe
when the Germans used Yperite.
They call it *mustard gas.*

*"A deplorable use of chemistry
applied to the art of war."*
Philip Lehman remarks
as the latest model of gramophone
wafts chamber music down the corridor.
That crackling
accompanies the staff
from morning to evening
in the background
as though it were attempting
from far away
to cover the sound of gunfire
on the other side of the ocean
over there in Europe.

They are killing each other like beasts
on the old continent:
the Habsburgs against the French

the Ottomans against the English
and the Prussians quite certain of victory.
Let them get on with it.

*"It makes no difference to us
for the moment"* Philip remarks
"we don't have so big an interest in Europe."

The one who disagrees with this assessment
however
is his cousin Herbert,
who's becoming ever more abrasive
verging on the offensive:
*"In your trifling position of banker, dear cousin,
do you really imagine that a war in Europe
can have nothing to do with us?
Simply because there's an ocean in between?
The planet Earth has changed, we're no longer in the 1800s . . .
Here the problem has become deep down:
we are all in a single system.
The question is a political one, Philip:
there is nothing that doesn't concern the whole world."*

*"Why not then read the Chinese newspapers, Herbert?
Why don't you learn the Indian language or that of the Maoris?"*

"Are you being sarcastic?"

*"Not at all: I'm inviting you to be practical:
a banker, believe me, is a practical being."*

*"Practicality means looking things in the face:
a war without precedent has broken out in Europe
and you treat it like a neighborhood brawl?"*

*"My hair is turning gray
not like yours:
I think I know what I'm talking about."*

*"The problem lies deep down:
you bankers always think you know what you're talking about."*

"May I remind you that you are also a banker?"
You sit with Dreidel and myself at the head of Lehman Brothers."

"I was just trying to say that I'm not a banker like you."

"I detect a slight hint of disdain."

"You are wrong: it's not a hint, nor is it slight."

"Remember I'm getting on in years."

"Remember I have a university degree."

This is the tone of the daily altercations
between Philip and Herbert.

And after all
how could it be otherwise?
They have practically nothing in common.

Or rather: they have one thing in common.
Used—not surprisingly—used each day
as a final means of pacification
when arguments become too heated:
"You are an exploiter of the masses, Philip!"
"And you are a pettifogging idealist, Herbert!"
"You shouldn't be running a bank but a slaughterhouse."
"If you don't like my methods, then vote against me."
"In fact I do, and I'll carry on doing so as long as I can breathe."
"And as long as I can breathe I'll tell you that you're wrong."
"A great prospect."
"It will carry us to ruin."
"Not too soon, I hope: shall we have a whisky?"
"I'll never say no to a whisky."

Whisky is the nectar of the gods:
high finance drinks rivers of it.
And no banker's office is ever without
a cabinet chock-full of liquor.

This is what happens
more or less every day

between Philip Lehman, son of Emanuel
and Herbert Lehman, son of Mayer:
fighting
as never before
between a Lehman, always in block capitals
and a Lehman always ready to kick like a horse,
swords drawn
between the son of an arm
and the son of a vegetable
irreconcilable
but
promptly
reconciled
by a single malt whisky.

Even today
with a glass in front of them
the three Lehman partners
have discussed
the words of President Wilson:
"The war is not our business!
We do not hunger for supremacy
the United States are for peace
we're not crazy
like the German people."

Everyone today is talking about these words.

Including probably the Goldmans
to a couple of outsiders.

For Philip, they are always on his mind:
"They tell me Henry Goldman's automobile
is decorated with a G in pure gold.
Did you know about it, Herbert?"

"Bankers like you and Goldman
need to spend their money somehow.
I would invest it in more decent factories,
while others put it into gold trinkets.
I wouldn't be surprised if you had an L made.
Or rather: perhaps the whole name PHILIP."

"I appreciate your sense of humor, Herbert.
I'll pass your criticisms on to Goldman and Sachs."

"When they get back."

"Why? Have they gone off?"

"Yes sir: to Germany. Didn't you know?"

"That's news to me . . .
the Goldmans doing business with the Germans . . ."

"Don't you see? The problem lies deep down:
you bankers really cannot
separate the mercenary aspect from everything else:
perhaps he's just traveling for pleasure!"

"Perhaps he is. Perhaps not.
Good old Goldman: guten Deutschland . . ."

Exactly: the Goldmans.

Some wars are fought with guns.
Others are wars of silence.
The continuing war between Lehman and Goldman
was of the latter kind:
allies in appearance
enemies in substance.

Now, it's very strange how sometimes
just a few words
are enough to light the fuse
which sets off the bomb.
That phrase from President Wilson
about crazy Germans
produced a similar effect
in the golden mind of Philip Lehman
who without realizing it
busily set to work:
the war that has erupted in Europe
might have its advantages
even though it's far away.

Let us suppose that a generous
loose cannon
were suddenly to be fired
in a westerly direction
and with the help of a fair wind
—having crossed the entire Atlantic—
made a perfect hit
striking only
the offices of Goldman Sachs.

He wasn't interested in them collapsing into a pile of rubble:
he just wanted them to be out of action
to lick their wounds
for a year, maybe two.
Three at most.

Yes.
Definitely:
the Germans' demonic war
might be of help to him
if used wisely,
if word got 'round,
since high finance now
depended above all on gossip.

Or rather: on getting *others* to gossip.
Which is not the same thing.

To put the idea into practical use
his son, Bobbie,
was of great assistance.

There is something heroic
about that unique moment
when a son for the first time
proves to be helpful
in a father's scheming.

When the son is destined to become "King of Wall Street,"
then such a transition is all the more significant.

In a letter from Paris
Bobbie informed him

that he had spotted a seventeenth-century Madonna
but this time
"you don't have to send me money, Dad:
I need more time."

The reason for this delay
was explained to Philip only six months later:
his rival bidder was a rich Portuguese
and Bobbie was convinced
he wouldn't manage to buy it.
But he took careful notes
and discovered his rival was
more of a mercenary than an art collector.
And so, having persuaded the gallery
not to put the painting straight onto the market,
he arranged
in the meantime
to be invited to social events and dinners
with the specific aim
of harming his enemy's credentials.
Having won his scalp in terms of reputation
he gained his victory
on the battlefield:

"I have Our Lady of Sorrows in my grasp:
now send me money, Dad!"

Sometimes, you can learn so much from children!

Philip thought along the same lines.
But did so
quite simply
on a larger scale:
it was no longer like the old days
when his Uncle Mayer ruled over cotton
armed with a slice of cake!
In the New York of high finance
everyone moved on a megaphone
called "Press."

Anyone with influence over that mechanism
could hope to win any war.

After all, Philip asked
in his diary:
1. WHAT ARE NEWSPAPERS IF NOT COMPANIES?
2. WHAT DOES A COMPANY FEED ON IF NOT MONEY?
3. LEHMAN'S WORK IS INVESTING MONEY IN COMPANIES
4. CONTACT PROPRIETORS TOMORROW MORNING

The three press barons were most cordial:
not very different in manner
from those of the petroleum market.
The only difference was the type of product.
Their objectives being otherwise the same.

Philip was very clear:
Lehman could see large profit margins
from a widespread newspaper circulation.
"THE NEW YORK TIMES"
"THE WASHINGTON POST"
"THE WALL STREET JOURNAL"
what were they, after all, if not instruments to exploit?
And at the same time,
with the thrust of a bank like Lehman
how much bigger could they grow?
"I dream of a future when everyone in the street
—and even in China, even in Australia—
will have a newspaper under their arm.
If this happens, you will be very happy indeed.
And I, as a bank, will be just as pleased."

Wasn't there a mutual gain in this?

The press barons looked at each other:
now it was clear why this man
bore a name that could be measured in karats.
And they decided that, yes, they could sign.

Just as they were getting up to go
however
Philip Lehman
brought home the real result:
"And what do you think, gentlemen, about the war in Europe?"

"We think what everyone thinks, Mr. Lehman:
we fear the madness of the Germans."

"Oh no, gentlemen, surely not: I don't agree.
Prussia doesn't have the money to fight a war for very long.
Banks are needed, behind the armies, that's clear."

"Ah yes, that's true.
Are you familiar with German finance?"

"We no longer have any links with Bavaria.
But the Goldmans, I know they do,
they went back there only yesterday: I'll ask them
and then I can let you know."

A seed, when dropped into the ground,
generally needs some time
before it germinates.

In this case it was extremely fast:
"THE NEW YORK TIMES"
"THE WASHINGTON POST"
"THE WALL STREET JOURNAL"
took no more than five working days
to voice a doubt
loud and clear:
was someone using American money
to finance German guns?
And Goldman Sachs, first and foremost, what side were they on?
Why these trips
"too often" onto Prussian soil?

Philip himself
was truly amazed
what effect this discovery had:
soon
almost everyone
on Wall Street
turned the other way
when they saw a Goldman.
What was this, other than victory?
What was this, other than justice?

It would have been
an excellent result
if the Great War
were limited to this contribution
to the family bank.

This was not to be.
And events moved differently.

Not long after
on an average rainy evening
at 119 Liberty Street
Philip Lehman
Herbert Lehman
and an entity wreathed in smoke
sat around a table
facing each other.

Philip ended his long discourse
making it clear
that his last word was followed by a full stop
and that there would be no more.

So he leaned back
and waited for his cousins
to vote on his proposal.

This time, however, there was no doubt:
the question really was political . . .

"What will the other banks do?" Herbert asked.

*"Kuhn Loeb, J. P. Morgan, and the Rockefellers are ready to start:
they already have contacts in England."*
was the reply
while the curtain of smoke around Dreidel
began to resemble a London smog.

*"So far as I'm concerned, I have strong doubts:
the problem here lies deep down,
I ask whether a bank can, ought (or even wants to)
finance an army at war."*

"To turn back, Herbert, would be cowardice."

"I am putting the question in ideal terms!
You are calculating the profits!"

"You always put the question in ideal terms
which is why you are continually wrong.
I, on the other hand, keep to the facts. To the facts alone."

"Enlighten me from the height of your wisdom."

"Perfect: the Germans threaten to support Mexico against us:
they'll help them to take back Texas.
There: this is a fact. Not an ideal: a fact.
And I'll remind you that Lehman has petroleum and railroads in Texas.
Second fact: their submarines are targeting us daily,
the Lusitania is already sunk.
And this, Herbert, is not an ideal:
or do you want to know exactly how many died?
The third fact is that if we leave everything as it is
we'll still come out of it badly:
if the Germans win, they'll control half the world,
but if we enter the war, we'll be in charge.
Facts, Herbert: these are all facts."

"You take it for granted that we will win the war:
I would describe it as a mirage. Not a fact."

"And you're wrong again. Because now
the United States has only a few soldiers.
But with the massive involvement of the banks
there'll be a million within a year.
With a million soldiers, the war is won.
It's a splendid fact, dear Herbert."

"Extraordinary. Marvelous.
To hear you speak is a rare treat, Philip:
we are on the very brink of a precipice.
You could finance a war
with not the slightest hesitation
and we are talking about a world war!"

"And so, in a word, are you against?"

"The argument is vast:
it would take a month to study it in depth!"

"And instead, I'm giving you a few minutes:
President Wilson is asking for support
and we can't tell him
that Lehman Brothers needs more time
than the Capitol to decide."

"I'm asking only to look at the facts
I'm asking to consider and reflect
I'm asking to interpret in my own way
what we've been requested to do
as members of the whole of humanity."

"You're a banker, Herbert, you're not a rabbi."

"And you're a warmonger."

"Wrong: the military people are the Prussians, not me.
Do you want the Germans to rule the world?"

"Not at all."

"Then the Germans have to be fought,
and not with words, but with grenades."

"And with our money?"

"With the American economy, Herbert,
of which Lehman Brothers has the honor to be a part."

"I can't reduce the question to a simple yes or no:
there are a thousand problems deep down,
which you Philip refuse to see.
If the state seeks the help of a bank to finance the army
then what can the bank ask in return? Laws? Regulations?
Do you understand how it creates a dangerous precedent?"

"This is just a lot of words."

"Without adding that up to now
the money in bank savings was invested in growth,

whereas now you want it used for killing:
don't you think in theory
we ought to ask each of our customers
if they agree to their money being used like this?"

"I ask you not to lose yourself in idle chatter.
Words are a waste of time, Herby,
they are like diluting whisky with water.
Therefore, less hot air and more substance."

And Herbert would have replied
by pouring him a pure malt whisky,
except that he didn't get the chance:

"May I speak?"
uttered Dreidel
stubbing out the whole of his cigar.
He stood up.

Took a notebook from his jacket.

Cleared his throat.

And this was what he said:

27
A Lot of Words

So to begin.

In Alabama, when I was born,
(well over half a century ago)
there was a black man who always wore a hat
we called him Roundhead.
He had a cart with two nags,
and he went up and down with it
carrying cotton.

One day—I wasn't yet five—
he took me with him on the cart
and we went together to the plantation.

Word had got 'round that I was a champion with numbers:
at the age of four I already counted so well
that even my mother was amazed.

So before we set off
Roundhead pointed his finger at me with a smile:
"Now that you can count, master,
you have to tell me how many carts, how many horses
how many dogs and how many children we see
along the road from here to Sweet Hill!"

I know now that he was joking.
But a child?
He can't tell the difference between jokes and serious stuff.
So I accepted the challenge:
I liked counting, I was a phenomenon.
And so, while Roundhead was holding the reins
I kept my eye on the road:
1, 2, 3, 4 carts
20, 30, 40 horses
8, 9, 10 dogs
50, 55, 60 children . . .

That day
Roundhead
obviously had some kind of torture in mind for me
because along the whole ride
he was singing a psalm
never stopped for a single moment.

I managed to hold out
with all my might:
he was singing, I was counting.

As soon as he stopped the cart in the yard at Sweet Hill
I was the one who pointed my finger at him:
"I've counted them all! I know the exact figures!"

He took it badly: he wasn't expecting it.
But so as not to keep silent, he said:
"Master, I hope you ain't lying,
for in my religion—and in yours too, I believe—
making things up is a serious sin . . ."

"I swear it's all true!" *I yelled:*
"There's 43 carts
90 horses
21 dogs
and 78 children.
79 with the one who waved to us from the well."

Roundhead smiled.
And without imagining the consequences
he threw out an idea
one of those destined to sink deep
into the guts and farther down
to end up with all that stuff
that you can't or don't know how to deal with:
"But Master, how can I know whether you've lied . . .
Because them that drive the cart, you see, they don't count the other
    carts
them that whip horses don't count the horses that go past,
and them that think about avoiding dogs and children
can't spend their time counting them.
And then, you heard: I was singing the psalm
and only them that keep silent can occupy themselves with numbers.
You understand what I said, master?"

And I certainly had understood.
Of course I had understood.
Maybe I had understood too well.

So that that evening
the carts had risen to 116
the horses to 320
the dogs to 98
and the children to 204
not taking into account
17 pregnant women
11 soldiers

7 beggars
a couple of barbers
and so on
with extreme precision.
Relentlessly.

By now
the whole of humanity was dividing into two:
those who sing while they drive
and those—quiet and reserved—
who count carts, horses, and everything else.
I was part of the latter.

All of a sudden
in short
I could see clearly before me
my role as universal counter:
I would watch the world go by
keeping count
never letting my mind wander
never losing the thread.

It mattered little or nothing to me
that as the years passed
I met no one else who could do the same:
everybody climbed onto their carts just to drive them
no one handed the reins over to another
no one apart from me.

And what was more
the disturbance around
—like Roundhead with his psalm—
was devastating.

For me it was a further reason
not to give up:
let them talk
let everyone talk
but—for my part—I counted.
1, 2, 3, 4,
170, 1,300, 4,000 . . .

For me it was numbers
instead of letters.
But I wasn't complaining.

For over sixty years
I have never stopped counting.

I've had some tough moments, of course:
anyone born with an instinct for sums
comes face-to-face on certain occasions
with the ultimate, most dreaded enemy:
with the sudden feeling
of being minuscule
compared with the material to be counted.
Well: that's not easy,
and sometimes it's pure terror.

It happened to me once
in front of a crystal bowl
crammed full of grains of sugar:
impossible to count.

And then once,
at the start of the Civil War:
the square was full as never before
heads, hands, hats, flags.
I lost count.

And if you lose it,
it's not easy to start again.

Up to the age of twenty
I used to count other people's words as well as real objects,
but of the two, I preferred the second:
I was at that stage of life
in which whatever passes in front of you
seems more important
than what you're thinking.
Then, as we know, everyone changes.
We discover that inside is much worse than outside
and at that point let the dance begin:
you're among grown men.

It usually takes time
to realize this.

The real turning point, for me, was dramatic:
I was with your fathers
on a business trip to Oklahoma.
There too I was severely tested:
the effort it required to count the drills
and distinguish them from the oil wells
and the wells themselves from the tubing
was all sabotaged
by the barking of an animal
who for the whole time
never stopped irking me.
But it wasn't this that caught me out:
I wasn't an amateur.

The crucial point was more subtle.

When I heard that the animal and I had the same name
it was like heaven breaking open:
how could a small identical sound
be used to describe a genius at sums
and an animal that couldn't count?
At that very moment a thought came to mind:
"Some order has to be brought
to the chaos of words.
Some light has to be brought
to the pitch darkness of speech."

And to mark the beginning of my new mission
I literally brought light
by setting the black oil ablaze.
They shouted fire,
and it certainly was:
luminous, clarifying.

For me it was a fundamental step.

That evening I stopped counting things
and began to count words:
there is everything in words.

And Roundhead was quite right:
those who drive the cart
have a head only for driving.
Now I know that those who talk
do nothing but talk.

I write my numbers in these notebooks:
I have no end of them.
And you are there in all of them.
Without exception.

Constantly
for years and years
I've been listening to what you say
And I've written down the numbers.
Not feelings: numbers.
What did you say, just now, Philip? Facts.
Words are also facts.
And they are facts more than facts.
It's a fact that you use them.
It's a fact that they produce an effect.
Better than watered-down whisky.

In these rooms
over the last thirty years
I ask you: what words have echoed around?
What language have you all been speaking?

The first year I spent in here
there were three words on everyone's lips:
21,546 times you said EARNINGS.
19,765 times I heard INCOME.
17,983 times RECEIPTS.

Over the past few years
none of these words
is at the top of my list any longer.
The first place has been taken 25,744 times by INTEREST.
and after that, 23,320 times you said PRODUCTIVE.
And this, dear cousin, isn't just hot air,
this I believe is substance.
Because EARNINGS, INCOME, and RECEIPTS
are money that comes in: you see them.

Uncle Mayer and Uncle Emanuel
marked up the RECEIPTS every evening.
And INTEREST, on the other hand? Where is it? Do you see it?
You're continually talking about "HAVING AN INTEREST" . . .
And when you say it, you mean that the bank is not cut out:
you want to know that our name is included,
in whatever—and I mean: whatever—deal.
One day, if they tell you that a cholera epidemic
is setting off some commercial effect
you'll would want to get sick with cholera
just to say "I HAVE AN INTEREST, I'M INVOLVED."

So far as I'm concerned
I prefer not to get cholera.

But there's something else.
Over the last year alone
3,654 times you've used the verb IMPOSE
whereas before you used to say GAIN, SUCCEED, ACHIEVE.
2,978 times you've said EXPAND
and 2,120 times CONFLICT.
I noticed you used to say COMPETITOR,
now you talk about the ENEMY.
You used to say INSTRUMENTS, now you say WEAPONS.
I wonder whether already
you might have been at war some time
even if now you're asking our permission to actually proceed.
Aren't these all facts?
Or is it watered-down whisky?

All this, of course,
regards the words I have heard you use:
not those you will use from tomorrow.

For, my dear cousins,
since it's a lifetime that I have been listening to you talking
I think it's appropriate to ask you one thing.
And basically one thing alone.
Because it's the most important
of all questions that a human being
can ask himself:
what words would you like to use?

If this were the notebook for tomorrow—or for ten years' time—
what words would you like not to hear yourselves say?

The mouth follows, it is not independent.
The lips receive their salary.
Each person utters the sounds they choose.

And so
you decide what to say.
And what not to say.

Which words you will reject.
Which words you will banish.

This bank
which carries our name
can decide for itself what language to speak.

There.
I have nothing more to say.

*

After which
Dreidel went silent.

It was late night.

He opened the door
and disappeared along the empty corridor.

From that day
he has never been seen again
at Lehman Brothers.

Book Three
Immortal

1
Czar Lehman

Who knows whether our money
has destroyed Rimpar.

Herbert Lehman can't stop thinking about it
now that the newspapers
bring news each day
of the fighting in Europe.
"Have you seen the papers, Philip?"

"I've seen them, Herbert."

"And you're not worried?"

*"If I really have to worry
I'd rather think about the revolution in Russia:
I don't much like the idea of people taking power."*

*"We're laying Europe to waste!
And it will be the first time that a war
will be fought first with banks and then troops.
Don't you see that this will create a precedent?"*

*"Let me correct you, Herbert:
wars have always been fought with money,
for the simple reason that weapons don't grow on trees."*

"So you're trying to tell me war is profitable for a bank?"

*"War is like fever, dear cousin:
it's a nuisance but it purges the body.
And when your temperature returns to normal
you feel a thousand times better than before."*

"You manage to think up some monstrous ideas."

*"I see the crude reality, you interpret it.
That's the difference between finance and politics."*

"So you're telling me I'm a fool?"

"No, I'm just offering you a glass of whisky."

Ever since Philip and Herbert
have been left to run the bank alone
alcohol has begun to play a central role:
it provides the only possible point of agreement
between finance and ideals.

Meanwhile, each night,
Herbert dreams about a fleet of planes
all bearing the name Lehman Brothers:
they fly threateningly
noisily
over the bank
and all at once
they bomb New York
with shells of solid gold.

When Herbert wakes shouting *"To the bunker! To the bunker!"*
his son, Peter, looks at him as though he's mad:
*"We don't have a bunker in the house, Dad,
we don't even have a cellar."*

Philip, in the meantime,
dreams that a crowd of Cossacks
with tall fur hats
and Bolsheviks in uniform
are laying siege to Liberty Street
shouting *"Death to the czar!"*
and Philip fears it's he who is Nicholas II.
There again
the czar still had a capital
of 900 million dollars.
Part of it invested in Lehman Brothers too.

What Philip cannot understand
however
is a small detail in his dream:
why
does a silver falcon
suddenly swoop down from the sky

seize him by the shoulders with its claws
and carry him to safety?

They say that some guy, in Europe,
—a Jew, one of ours—
has got it into his head to interpret dreams.
It seems that everything, at night, has a meaning.
He's written a book about it too.

Philip Lehman
has read it with great care.
But he hasn't understood a word.

Or rather: Doctor Freud doesn't write at all badly,
but Philip was hoping to find himself
holding a dictionary
that would teach him to take his dreams—exactly as they are—
and transfer them one by one
in block capitals
into his diary.
But no.
Thick mist.

The silver falcon remains faceless.

Now,
it is curious how
human beings sometimes realize
all of a sudden
that they have underestimated some point,
taking it for granted
to such an extent
that they don't even ask themselves
whether there's any need to check it out.

This happened to Philip Lehman
when Bobbie—at last—returned
to American soil,
after the kid—with youthful zeal—
was determined, come what may, to join the army
to *"defend European art."*

Exactly.
Not to defend our interests.
But to *defend European art.*

There again,
in the last years before the war
Philip had never sought to interfere,
to tell Bobbie to forget his hobbies.
On the contrary: the idea of leaving the bank
one day
in the hands of a dandy heir
with a passion for horses and art
seemed like a masterstroke
as well as a contribution
to the field of sport and culture
to the whole world of finance.

Had he gone too far?

Bobbie, now he came to think of it,
never mentioned financial matters.

He had graduated from Yale, yes sir.
But he never talked
about his ideas on economics.
And even if the conversation
happened
to touch on his university studies,
it seemed to provide an immediate opportunity
to talk about his achievements
on the university polo team
which he had captained.

Yes. He was glad to talk about that.
As well as art.
And about horse racing.
And sometimes about biblical stories
seeing that for years and years
he had grown up in the company
of that frightening series of prints
punitively
hung on his bedroom wall.

And so
could it be any surprise
that those bearded prophets
    those burning bushes
      those seas that parted between the waves
      those monsters killed by slingshots
by dint of contemplation
as the last image before sleep
had been etched upon his mind
to such a point
that they gave the impression
of being some small part of him?
So that
not infrequently
at night
he dreamed
that he had to build an Ark
or had to kill Goliath
if he wasn't being swallowed by Jonah's whale . . .

Childhood, after all, leaves its mark on you.

Well,
having descended, come what may, into the hell of war
(something he was granted as if it were a childish whim),
Bobbie
was not perhaps aware
of having put his father at serious risk:
a horse destined to win on racecourses 'round half the world
cannot be sent into the mud of Argonne
dodging grenades and machine gun fire.
And if he'd died?

There it is.
Fashions are fashions, and young men often succumb.
He wanted to play the young soldier? Let him do it.
After all, each of us has played our childish games.

And luckily, he returned unharmed.

But it just so happened that the war—the real one—
was yet to begin.

After a long family dinner
in which Bobbie
when asked about what he thought of the Stock Exchange
answered
praising a collection of Expressionist paintings
displayed on the ground floor of Wall Street
Philip Lehman
finally raised the question
about whether his son
apart from his success in world war
was also ready to succeed in banking.

After all, he said,
he had invested much in him,
as a father of course
but also as a banker.

And every investment, we know,
has a purpose.

So
next day
with great composure
on one of those days best forgotten
his father decided to have a word with him.
And not in the drawing room at home.
But in his office at the bank:

"My dear son
of the many ways in which I could begin this conversation
I'll tell you that I have chosen a metaphor.
And it's your passion: the sport of polo.
At each round of the game you change horses.
It's the most important rule, if I'm not mistaken,
and this is what makes it a sport for the few
since those who play need five, six horses.
Excellent. Let's move on.
Lehman Brothers
which passed from your grandfather to me
is not so different from the game of polo:
it requires not one but several horses
ready to enter the field.
And this is why

I think it is right to bring you in
very soon
my dear son
into the heart of the bank."

"Into the bank, Dad?
Quite honestly, I'm not sure it interests me."

Philip Lehman
had the distinct feeling
that he hadn't properly understood.
And with extreme courtesy
with not the slightest trace of unease
he reformulated the offer:

"My dear son Bobbie,
your father took over this bank
when it was running on zero-points:
I have made it into a monument
and more
I have made it into a model.
We are the sap that brings life to the tree,
if we were to stop just for an instant
the system would immediately collapse.
And so, those who carry the name Lehman
are appointed to perform great deeds
and like a jockey, Bobbie,
always ready to take the field."

Philip smiled,
he had chosen the horse racing metaphor
to please his son
who did indeed seem touched:
"All of this is very nice."

"It is. You are predestined, Bobbie:
Your place is here, beside me.
And one day behind this desk."

"Thanks, Dad, from the bottom of my heart,
but as I said: I'm not interested."

Philip Lehman
had the distinct feeling
that he hadn't properly understood.
He took a deep breath
and returned to the fray:

"My dear son, my dear Bobbie,
you're an intelligent boy.
In all honesty, tell me:
when Noach built the Ark
do you think anyone asked him:
'Do you want to do this?'
And then Elijah? And Jeremiah? And Jonah?
Do you think anyone ever asked them
if they were interested in being prophets?
And King David? He was sent against Golyat
without anyone asking his permission . . ."

This time too
he had chosen the biblical metaphor
to stir his son's patriarchal pride
but failed to produce the desired effect:

"But that was HaShem, *Dad, if I'm not mistaken . . ."*

Philip kept calm,
and tried another metaphor dear to his son:
"If you were a Giotto, a Botticelli, a Guercino,
do you think you could choose whether to paint or not?"

"Precisely, Dad: this is the point.
I don't think I have a talent for business."

It was therefore time
for the language—dear to his son—of military discipline:
"I'm ordering you on a mission,
and the mission is a duty for whoever is drafted!"

To which he answered, innocently:
"I've never been drafted into the bank, Dad."

At which point
Philip

ignoring the cramp he felt in his gut
and trying hard to find a point of compromise,
with the paternal weapon of mildness:
*"That's enough! You will be a banker!
It's been decided, it's my wish and my desire."*

*"It's not that I don't want to: it's that I can't
and if I can't I mustn't.
So go and look for someone else."*

There.
This caught Philip
straight on the rebound.
So that for the first time
(not just that afternoon but in his life)
he had no answer.

And this was bad.
For his son had more to say:

*"Of all the people I know in this world, Dad
I regard myself as the least suited for that job."*

There are certain moments
in the relationship between father and son
when they find themselves at the crossroads
between victory and a sentence of death
and more often than not
the prospect of choice is far from clear.

Philip Lehman
on the other hand
saw the alternative as though it were written.

He stopped at that crossroads
contemplated the two roads
could clearly see the two horizons.

And with no hesitation
made his choice.

2
The Arthur Method

The perfect geometry
of the decoration
is of crucial importance
for today's *kiddushin.*

The Temple has even been divided
into two semicircles.
The corridor divides them in half
like the diameter of a circle
and on both sides
arranged symmetrically
are 60 places for adults and 22 for children.
The women are invited not to choose
hats that are too cumbersome
so as to even the distribution of volumes.
This so far as the congregation is concerned.
The ceremony itself will take place
along a horizontal line
outside the semicircles
but at a right angle to the diameter of the Temple.

As she arrives
with her silk veil
who knows whether in some corner of her memory
the bride
will still remember
the time
when a little Lehman
trampled her favorite bow of ribbon in the mud
hurling a few choice insults at her.

This detail is by no means incidental,
since that little boy
will soon be her husband,
thus closing various cycles of time and space
—and business too—
into an ellipse.

In particular
this last aspect
(crucial for Philip
but welcomed by the family as a whole)
is quite apparent
since those to be joined in marriage
will be no less
than a Lehman and a Lewisohn
or rather
a kind of agreement between Olympic champions
a pact between the Kings of Wall Street and the Lords of Gold
a bond between the front rows of the Temple
and—why not?—
a slap in the face for the Goldmans
who indeed are nowhere to be seen.

Lehman-Lewisohn.
Two Ls that become three by adding *leaders*.
Arthur and Adele.
Two As that become three by adding *arithmetic*.

Since arithmetic
has played an essential role
in the very construction
of this marriage.

And how could it be otherwise
for
nothing now
in the life of Arthur Lehman
is without its mathematical implications?

Known since childhood
for his somewhat polemical nature
Arthur
has distinguished himself on growing up
for a series
of true masterstrokes of cunning.
With a generally abrupt manner
—and always personally justified—
he has acquired a name over time
for operations that have become

to say the least
legendary:
—he managed to steal from the pockets of his brothers
getting them reimbursed from the coffers of the bank
—he persuaded his sisters to mortgage their toys
—he terrified Sigmund by calculating more or less
how many tons of donuts he had scarfed in a year
—he even went as far as setting hourly charges
for pushing his Uncle Emanuel's wheelchair in the park.

And though each of these marvels
was attributed at first
to a natural chutzpah
(and to that sour aftertaste
typical of Bavarian potatoes),
by his early youth
the boy began to look at himself from outside
overcoming
the hasty prejudices of relatives:
he was not his cousin David.

And the more he thought about it,
the more his shrewdness
seemed to him to conceal something other
than a simple diploma in guile:
in it he saw
instead
some vaguely scientific bent
so that
anyone who thought his talent
could be confined to that Indian reserve
where family eccentrics are often consigned
was making a big mistake.
Let them even laugh at his whimsy:
they would pay so much a kilo for it
in a few years' time.
just to have it back.

And in short
as often happens
to those of true worth
Arthur decided for himself.

He didn't know exactly *what*,
but he accepted the challenge of *something*.

In the meantime
as he waited for the gas to take a solid form
he placed his surname in parentheses
and made an appointment with his relatives
for a day not yet fixed
—still far away but nonetheless certain—
on which they would search him out at the acme of his success.

Now,
in families
as we know
a set period of time is allowed
(by ancestral decree)
in the name of pity and compassion
to those who seem affected by pathological ambition.
At the end of which
they are required to opt for more ordinary shores.
This space of time
traditionally a couple of years
is viewed
to varying extents
with that mixture of mirth and disapproval
that in many cases would have discouraged even Charlemagne.

In Arthur's case
however
the quarantine passed much sooner
—or, one might say, immediately—
as soon as the boy
had focused on the starting point:
his whole edifice rested,
after all, on a single word.
Or rather: on a clutch of numbers.

It so happened that
at the crucial point in his youthful advance
Arthur
came across a notebook
with marks from 1 to 10 he had written crudely as a child

and couldn't resist being struck
by how many combinations
could in theory be created
from those simple scribbles in black ink:
mathematics governed the universe
and by keeping it in his grip
nothing could escape him.

This was the starting point.

An illuminating example of how at times
a momentary intuition is enough
to give a whole meaning
to billions of attendant moments.

It is generally a lyrical experience.
Arthur took away the poetry
describing it in a more prosaic way:
"I will win and I'll win with numbers."

Arthur Lehman's
project in life
was therefore
that union between science and dominance
which generally proves inauspicious,
leaving us to hope
that Pythagorases remain as Pythagorases
without choosing the surname Bonaparte.

In this case
at least
fortune ordained that there were
no military implications
but that any consequences
—if worst came to worst—
would be merely financial:
and, since the two realms
were still distinct (though not for long),
humanity as a whole came out of it unscathed.

For Arthur it was an exciting step:
with the help of those ten numbers

he could assure not only his own future
but also that of the family bank
being immediately certain
that the concept of gain
was none other
than an algebraic secret.

In the years to come
therefore
he devoted himself wholeheartedly
to the endless acrobatics of numbers:
he worked away, almost to the point of exhaustion
often night and day
until his head ached.
He devoured equations, logarithms, and prime numbers.
He became a master of theories:
he felt not the slightest intimidation
before whatever kind of problem.
And we are talking not just of arithmetic.

On the contrary,
the crucial point was exactly this.

In him the science of calculus
was like those rivers
that promptly burst their banks
causing damage.

And while his brother Herbert
resorted to politics
even in his choice of soup,
soon
there was not a single aspect
of Arthur's human existence
that wasn't mathematically dismantled:
all of which appeared to him
(and gradually more so)
as a chaos
that can be organized only through numerical logic,
as necessary to the order of things
as education for the redemption of savages.

If Arthur was invited to a restaurant,
he couldn't answer a simple question
such as *"Did you enjoy the meal?"*
without resorting
to a particular formula:
having given the value X_Q to the overall quality of the experience,
it would be calculated from the sum
of I (ingredients) and S (level of service)
from which he would deduct
a factor M (his mood that evening).
All divided, of course, by C + C + C (cost for each individual course).
So that his definitive answer
amounted to a:

$$X_Q = \frac{(I + S) - M}{C + C + C}$$

What was more
he subscribed
to a universal religion of economics
that considered all things
as being part of a cost-benefit system
where everything (even the air)
was nothing but an accounting entry
written into the great ledger of the Supreme Bank.
And so he proposed
his own very personal existential synthesis:
given that planet Earth
was a composition of resources
(and therefore a patrimony P),
then each human being
if only through the act of breathing, walking and eating
    (PB + PW + PE)
was spending some of that shared capital,
using it for themselves (Pi)
and depriving others of it.
At the same time, however,
individuals through their labor (L), their contribution (C), and their
    procreation (Pr)
were also providing a social benefit (B) for others.
And in this way
by giving each item an indicator from 1 to 100
it would be possible to quantify an X_{sr}
indicating none other than the Socioeconomic Role of the Individual.

$B = L + C + Pr$

$PI = PB + PW + PE$

$X_{sr} = (L + C + Pr) - (PB + PW + PE)$

It was at this stage
verging on psychosis
that Arthur Lehman (AL1) met up again with Adele Lewisohn (AL2),
finding her radically different
from how he remembered her in the past [AL_2 (t=now) ≠ AL_2 (t=then)].

She
having survived the trauma of the bow of ribbon (Tb),
had developed over time
into a female algorithm
of not insignificant appeal [AL_2 (t=now) = f AL_2 (t=then)],
whose charm produced in Arthur
not the slightest effect [f AL_2 (t=then) ∉ AL1].

What struck him most about her
was the fact that she danced (fj).

Not that he particularly liked dancing.

But it so happened that one day (D)
during a chance encounter in the park (Dp),
she saw him looking so strange
that she would never have thought
even in her wildest imagination
that he was calculating the influence of birds (Xb)
on the economic system of green spaces (GS).
She thought he had some nervous disease,
didn't rule out the aftereffects of smallpox.
And she was so touched
by her memory of Arthur as a child
that she made the first move
inviting him
to her afternoon dance class (Dd)
at a famous New York theater (T).

Sitting in the stalls (S)
at yet another crossroad of life

•

AL1 saw his idea about mathematical order
unexpectedly
take form
onstage:
every human being walks
but no one would ever count their steps
or the opening stages of a gesture.
Whereas dancing demanded it
creating perfect harmony . . .
All was clear to him:
ungainly movement was to the *rond-dejambe*
what wild commerce was to finance
and
economics was the dance of the people!
As for him,
he would be its choreographer!

But who
could share
a tortuous journey with him
on this chaotic earth
if not AL2, priestess of ritual?
In her
whom he adored for her *allongé* and her *port de bras*
he felt an intense love for every detail:
he loved her language of order
and that control even over her little finger
accepting the rigor and rules
of a superior system of numbers
in which there was no place for chance.

What a shame that in that system (x)
it was not only chance (C) that was excluded:
feelings (FF), vehicles of disorder,
were not to be considered either:

$$(C + FF) \notin x$$

And indeed, they even became a threat.

AL1 realized this in the worst of ways:
having decided
to propose immediately

and organize the marriage as soon as possible,
he
on finding himself before the girl
saw the ground open beneath his feet:
every attempt at wooing her
died upon his lips and although truly smitten
he was literally incapable
of articulating a completed sound
apart from a devastating
"Now that I look at you . . .
Your eyes are not symmetrical."

It goes without saying
that such a compliment
was greeted by AL2 with a symmetrical reaction,
so that she immediately ordered
the theater doorman
not to allow him into the hall
for any reason in the world.

AL1 recovered from the blow.
Had he become so hardened
by all those years spent among numbers
to the point of being incapable
of the slightest impulse?

And yet, he thought,
something didn't add up:
if the technical objective of human love was to build a family (F),
then why
did social customs
still require
so much terrible wastage of time in courtship (Tcort)?

It wasn't he who was wrong:
it was humanity that had lost its way.
They couldn't complain then
if their lives slid by
in a flash:
their time, like all resources, had to be better used.

Then, in this regard, he focused
on a particular fault of the female sex

which was too concerned about the (anti-economic) goings-on
    around the ritual of love
and he dreamed, with eyes shut, about a future world
in which
without too much beating about the bush
Alpha could ask Beta: *"I want you. Do you, yes or no?"*
and if the answer was *yes*
they got straight down to the question of procreation.

However magnificently she danced
(and dance, for AL1, was pure engineering)
AL2 didn't seem to hold the same view
and each time he appeared in the street by the theater
as rigid as a scarecrow
and with his mouth frothing with saliva
she always preferred to walk straight on.

And so as not to meet him in the future
she even went as far as giving up dancing
devoting herself with equal success
to another old passion for the classical harp (CH).

This change, in reality,
had not the slightest effect
since AL1's blackboard
already displayed in algebraic terms
the equation between dance (fj) and music (M)
and therefore its symmetry with finance:
if dance harmonized movement
the music score did the same with noise,
and a bank with the wild orgy of barter:
for him, a symphony orchestra
didn't seem so different
from the board of Lehman Brothers.

So he came to pursue her
even outside Tin Pan Alley
where she recorded three times a week (3d × RCA = AL2),
and where three times a week
the theorem remained unresolved:
"Madam! Is there anything I could do for you?"

"Buy Tin Pan Alley for me
and stick a bow of ribbon on it!
Oh, sorry: I was forgetting,
you trample those in the mud."

"Is there nothing cheaper?
Thrift is a virtue . . ."

"Then be virtuous: save your money
and save me the hassle."

All this warfare
took place
every three days
in the tree-lined avenue of Tin Pan Alley
along which the sweet harpist walked
not stopping for a moment
while ALı
to save energy
spoke to her from his automobile
lowering the window
and driving at a crawl.

He made an exception only once
on the afternoon
when having got out of his Model T
he planted himself in front of her
preventing her from reaching the artists entrance
and having yielded—against his will—
to the need for a minimum of romanticism (R)
he made a promising start:
"May I read you one of my poems?"
and on receiving her almost immediate agreement (Y)
(he needed little encouragement)
he began to read her a sonnet (S)
with the same rush of emotion with which one might read a railroad
      timetable (RT).
But apart from this,
he was turned down for quite a different reason:
"You haven't written this poem:
it's by Emily Dickinson."

"Pardon me: what the devil are you talking about?
If I had offered you flowers,
would you have refused them because they weren't from my garden?
You would have taken them for sure, since I had bought them.
And if I were to give you a ring (it's a theoretical assumption)
would you return it because I hadn't forged it myself
and had merely bought it from a jeweler?
Well then, I bought the poem from a bookseller.
Being a saleable asset, it can be purchased.
And on being purchased it can be passed on to others
just the same as flowers,
just the same as the ring.
So what are we talking about? I'm entitled to use it.
Miss Dickinson, a professional in matters of poetry,
has put her product on the market
which I am making use of today, having need of it.
And please note: I didn't get the poem free of charge
I paid 3 dollars 25 cents,
to which is added the cost of my time
absent—in order to be here—from a more profitable activity.
Having said this: I believe in you as a form of investment
so long as we remain within certain bounds, you understand?"

"And if not?"

"Do not worry, Miss Pirouette: I will seek no reimbursement."
And with these words
he seemed to have delivered a true masterstroke of poetry
to outshine even Emily Dickinson.

But one fact was clear:
that the male notion of poetry (P♂)
didn't tally with the female notion (P♀),
and indeed
the former could even
border on the subset of insults (I).
At any rate, poetry as a whole (P)
from that day on
in ALı's eyes
was a product of doubtful utility.
And as a consumer he felt disillusioned.

Where did Arthur's method
prove effective?

In the fact that he didn't give up.
And not because the musician appreciated his tenacity.
What saved the scientist
was his extreme act of faith
in the all-powerfulness of mathematics:
to transform the most implacable foe of logic
into a logical formula.

So having taken his courage in both hands
he put down in writing
on a sheet of paper
that Love (L)
depended on two factors alone:
Instinct (IN) and Megalomania (MEG):

$$L = f(IN, MEG)$$

and while the first was impossible to influence
there was room for maneuver on the second
which, after all, was commonly found in high finance.

He pondered carefully on the effects and countereffects.
He studied the proposition, examined the formulas.

Finally he decided.
And having gone to see his cousin Philip
he proposed a twenty-year investment
with a very ample profit margin:
he was more than certain
that America's future lay in music.

"What's got into you, Arthur?
You want us to put money
into theater orchestras?"

"Oh no, Philip. Not just that.
I'm thinking much farther than Broadway.
I've got big ideas:
pure megalomania."

"I'm listening."

"I've heard some talk about a certain Edison.
And about a certain Tesla: two inventors.
They're at war with each other over a patent.
Just think of having an apparatus at home
—in every home—
which you switch on and you hear
simultaneously
the same music they're listening to in Minnesota.
This miracle, Philip, is called radio.
A harpist plays in New York and millions can hear her.
The radio takes you into drawing rooms, kitchens.
You decide what you want to listen to
even in bedrooms,
in attics, in bathrooms.
There's a whole mass of people in the world
just waiting to switch on and listen."

"Don't you think you're exaggerating?"

"Yes, fortunately, of course.
A good investment, Philip,
always depends on two factors:
Instinct and Megalomania."

And only at that moment did he realize
in effect
that every investment
was also a test of love,
so that he pulled out the sheet of paper with the formula
and showed it to his cousin:

$$L = f\,(IN, MEG)$$

"And what does the 'L' stand for?" Philip asked.

"You're asking me? It stands for Labor. What else?"

3
NOT

The chapter that was about to open
was NOT the simplest.

A real scourge
—NOT definable in any other way—
was about to wreak havoc
from Alaska to New Mexico.

The war in Europe had been fought and won,
but the bombs about to strike them
so ruinously
were NOT German.

Was American aviation
NOT the innovation of the Great War?
Well.
Torpedoes and missiles
crammed full of NOTs
were now about to be dropped
over American skies
by a fighter-bomber
flown NOT by an air force pilot
but by a glum-looking senator
with a NOT ordinary mustache
by the name of Andrew Volstead.

NOT that the Lehmans were great drinkers:
rivers of liquor did NOT flow
in Liberty Street,
apart from Philip and Herbert's
conciliatory whiskies.
And yet the Volstead Act
did NOT go unnoticed there either.

And NOT because the American distilleries
were almost all Jewish:
this was NOT the point.

It was, if anything, that the deluge of NOTs
suddenly raged like a hurricane
and there was NOT a single person
who was NOT thoroughly drenched.

Put down in writing
by the ardently Christian Volstead,
the NOTs were now state law.

Written in large block capitals
so there was NOT anyone
who could NOT see them,
they found their way everywhere:
you did NOT escape them in drawing rooms
you were NOT safe from them in kitchens,
you could NOT forget about them in bedrooms
and bank offices did NOT make any exception.

Like a drum in the brain
the beating of NOTs had become tremendous:
you were in danger of migraine
if NOT literally of madness.

The Lehman's bank was NOT any different
and was full of it, up to the ceiling.

All the more since the atmosphere was NOT calm:
ever since a spinning top was NOT any longer to be seen,
the bank was run
NOT by three but two:
Philip and his cousin Herbert,
bound together until now
NOT by anything more
than a now forbidden pact with whisky.

In its absence
their coexistence had become sober but NOT calm.
Or rather: there was NOT a single remnant of peace
and the LEHMAN BROTHERS sign
purporting brotherhood
might become LEHMAN NOT BROTHERS
to judge from the yelling audible even in the street.

In the end, was it NOT ludicrous?
While a day did NOT pass
without the mustached pilot NOT boasting
about his thousand NOTs
with which America would NOT go to ruin,
now
it was Lehman Brothers
that risked ruin.

Ever since throats had been left dry
the battle between cousins
was destined NOT to end.

When were they NOT at each other's throats?
And though there was NOT a drop of alcohol
their conversation was intoxicated with NOTs:
"Do you NOT think, Philip
that it is NOT a good idea
to make the bank NOT a place for saving
but a slate of figures
that do NOT mean a thing?
Lehman can NOT become a branch of Wall Street!"

"I do NOT agree, dear Herbert.
You do NOT like the stock market, and this is NOT new.
But is your opinion NOT prejudiced?
If you do NOT mind: what is the world after all, if NOT a market?
Human beings can NOT live without money.
Do they NOT feed themselves with money?
Do they NOT dress themselves?
Do they NOT move about?
Do NOT tell me that you have NOT considered it:
NOT a single aspect is NOT governed by buying and selling.
So I do NOT understand: what is there that you do NOT like?
Wall Street is a temple of business—it's NOT anything else
there's NOT a single place in the world where bartering is NOT done:
even among people NOT civilized,
who is NOT going to offer six dates for a pineapple?
And if the dates are NOT ripe,
does this NOT change the nature of the agreement?
Even if you do NOT like it, dear cousin,
trading goes on everywhere, NOT just in the Stock Exchange.

Wall Street is NOT any different from a synagogue:
HaShem does NOT exist in there alone,
and if you destroy the Temple, He does NOT care after all."

"Do NOT pretend NOT to have understood: I'm NOT falling for that:
I do NOT accept that the bank does NOT care about people,
I do NOT want to close myself up behind the doors of the Stock Exchange
and I'm NOT interested in financier's clubs!
What is more, Philip, let us NOT forget:
This was NOT what our fathers had in mind:
it is, I think, a detail NOT of secondary importance."

"You and I do NOT understand each other
I do NOT know what else to say!"

And having said this—NOT thinking what he was doing—
he went to look for a bottle in the drawer
which he did NOT find.
So that he continued, alas:

"You do NOT accept the idea that the present is NOT the past.
Our parents did NOT talk about shares, I do NOT deny it.
But only because shares did NOT exist!
NOT for any other reason, Herbert, NOT for any other reason!
I do NOT doubt that our old men
NOT being ingenuous
would NOT have hesitated about investing in the stock market today:
talking about a 'share' is NOT any different from talking about 'money'
let us NOT talk the language of yesterday.
Are the streets filled with vehicles, or are they NOT?
Do you NOT want us to sell any more automobiles
just so as NOT to deprive coachmen of their salary?
The twentieth century is NOT to be approached like this, Herbert,
and it should NOT be me who is saying such things
seeing that there's NOT a single dark hair on my head.
The truth is that you do NOT believe
in the role of a bank, do NOT deny it."

"Do NOT make me say what I do NOT think:
it is NOT respectful, apart from NOT being correct."

And in shouting the last word
he waved to a secretary

to pour them a drink, but she did NOT move.
So that he continued, alas:

"You insist in NOT wanting to understand the point:
here it is NOT a simple matter of words.
You do NOT use your personal wallet:
you use money that is NOT yours, but other people's."

"It's NOT other people's: call them customers."

"Investors, if you do NOT mind."

"I do NOT understand where you want to go."

"NOT too far."

"I do NOT have time to waste."

"Do NOT worry: I'll be brief."

"And I hope NOT far from the point."

"Let us NOT ignore the fact that they give us their money
because it's NOT safe to keep it at home
and do we NOT in fact lock it away in a safe?
Tell me what it is, if NOT comic:
this money that they do NOT want to risk,
do you NOT use it for betting at poker?"

"I have NOT sat at a poker table, ever."

"And betting on shares, is it NOT the same thing?
What is it you do in Wall Street if NOT gambling?
All right: you do NOT have a hand of cards
but just stocks, shares, or I know NOT what else."

And after this last rebuke
he went to a cabinet and took two glasses
which would NOT be of any use.
So he continued worse than before:

"You are gambling, Philip: does the stock NOT increase, does it NOT fall,
if it goes up, have I NOT gained, if it goes down, how much have I lost?

You say then that I do NOT believe in the bank?
I do NOT have anything to say if the bank makes a loan.
I do NOT object to loans, transfers,
I do NOT even have anything against investments
provided you show me it is NOT speculation."

"I do NOT want to count zero-points!"

"And I do NOT want to swindle people!"

"You do NOT know what you're saying, Herbie!
It would be laughable, if it were NOT such a serious matter.
You pretend NOT to see that there is NOT a single person
when he brings money in, NOT just to us but to any bank,
who does NOT want to see it grow:
he is NOT interested in keeping it safe, believe me.
No one is satisfied, it is NOT human.
At the counter they ask 'can you NOT make money for me?'
You who talk so much about people, you do NOT know them:
There is NOT a single magnet as strong as profit."

"Precisely: I do NOT stoop so low."

"And I do not ask you to.
But the fact remains that you are NOT a prophet: you're a banker!"

Herbert did NOT reply to these words.
As for Philip, he did NOT ask him to do so.

Each of them withdrew to their room
NOT without cursing
those who had prohibited whisky
so they satisfied themselves with the gesture
and knocked back a whole glass,
forcing themselves NOT to think of it as milk.

From that day
Herbert did NOT give himself a moment's peace.

there again, it is NOT rare
that that which we strive NOT to see
suddenly appears clearly before us,
with such force that we can NOT ignore it any longer.

His own situation was NOT so different:
however hard he tried NOT to admit it,
his cousin deep down
was NOT wrong.
Was he perhaps NOT in the right place?
How could he NOT see that the problem was deep down
and there were NOT any solutions
if he did NOT take up politics?

This time he did NOT ignore it.
And he asked himself the fateful question he had NOT asked before:
"Why am I here and NOT somewhere else?"

Where this somewhere else was NOT
a place on Earth NOT specified
but the Corridors of Power.

There. Right.
In his NOT perfect guise as banker
Herbert did NOT ignore the question:
why was he NOT mayor?
Why was he NOT running for Congress?
Why NOT hope to have the title of governor on his door?

Certainly, man is NOT a simple machine.
And when he has a destination in mind
he can NOT manage NOT to complicate the route.

Herbert told himself it was now too late
(NOT the most infrequent of alibis).
Then added that he had NOT had the opportunity
(this too NOT any more than an oft-repeated phrase).
He concluded in the end that, if he could, he would NOT pull back:
generally the most cowardly way of saying "I'm NOT going to do it."

But it's NOT easy NOT to admit what one really wants.
It's NOT surprising that Herbert began to dream
each night
about the great hall of the American Congress
where however it was NOT congressmen who sat
but only bankers, NOT excluding him.
And when everyone began pulling from their bags
bundles and bundles of banknotes

it was NOT long before the hall was full,
like a bank safe, to the point of suffocation
so there was NOT a night when Herbert did NOT wake up shouting:
"Onto the roof! Onto the roof! Onto the roof!"

His son, Peter, looks at him as though he were crazy:
*"There's no way of climbing onto the roof, Dad.
We're on the ground floor and we have no attic."*

It was NOT easy to tell a child
that dream houses have an architecture all their own.
Especially if you are NOT feeling at ease.

Chance, however, was NOT against him.

For a surname like Lehman
was NOT so unattractive for politics
as politics itself came to realize.

Herbert for his part
kept it secret for some time,
though NOT hiding it from Edith,
finding in her NOT just an ally but an encouragement:
there was such a storm of opposition to be fought
that people like Herbert were NOT only useful, but vital.

To his cousin Philip however
Herbert decided NOT to speak:
he was afraid—NOT wrongly—of doing him a very great favor
almost as if he'd been able to read
that diary all in block capitals
in which he had once written
HERBERT IS A RESOURCE.
Except that he had then added beneath it, more recently:
BUT OUTSIDE OF HERE.

Having said this,
certain vocations can NOT be deferred.

So that it was NOT long
before Herbert knocked on his cousin's door.
He asked whether or NOT he was interrupting

and on NOT receiving a positive response
he sat down NOT far away
from the old liquor cabinet
(he was NOT yet reconciled, poor kid).

Philip meanwhile
had already guessed everything, and could NOT ask for more.
Did other New York banks NOT have just one president?

He pretended all the same NOT to be expecting anything
and even humming to himself
did NOT raise his eyes from the *Wall Street Journal*.

It was Herbert who broke the silence,
NOT beating about the bush:
*"Philip! I'll NOT hide from you that the party has made me an offer.
And I wonder whether I should NOT accept."*

Philip was NOT ruffled in the slightest.
And so as NOT to remain totally silent, he said
"The choice is yours, my dear Herbie, I will NOT interfere."

It was that *my dear* that did NOT convince Herbert:
the fact that his cousin would NOT stand in the way
did NOT reassure him deep down.
So that he was NOT satisfied with his approval:
"Do you NOT think that the bank needs all of us?"

Philip was NOT an amateur.
He could have pretended NOT to understand.
Or he could have preferred NOT to reply, with a smile.
Instead he chose a NOT obvious maneuver:
*"I am NOT so crazy as to let America lose you
simply because I do NOT want the bank to lose you."*

NOT bad: a patriotic stance.

Which did NOT displease Herbert:
"So I should NOT feel guilty about it?"

Here Philip could NOT control his lips.
He saw the approach of victory, and could NOT contain himself:

"There is NOT anything more important, Herbie,
than NOT to shy away from the great call."
He attempted a smile, NOT managing to form one.

Herbert realized NOT without annoyance
that his cousin was NOT claiming anything other than
a crown on his head
and NOT that of a king but of an emperor.

And so as NOT to give him such satisfaction he added:
"Of course, I do NOT want to cut myself off altogether:
I do NOT forget that this is the family bank."

Philip did NOT bat an eyelid.
And so as NOT to confirm his reputation as a man of ice
he gave out a sound NOT unlike a grunt:
it was NOT approval
and NOT disagreement.

But NOT a moment passed
before a doubt came to his mind:
might it NOT seem that he was holding him back?
So as NOT to create any misunderstanding, he therefore explained:
"For my part I'll NOT keep you in the dark, in any circumstances:
and even when you're NOT here, I'll behave as though you were."

And on this point, Herbie did NOT have any doubt:
he risked leaving him NOT just the reins of the cart
but the keys to the stable, which he would NOT have seen again.
Fortunately, however, he was NOT stupid.
He therefore chose NOT to say what was in his mind
but let his stomach—if NOT to say his liver—speak
and NOT without surprise he listened to himself as he said:
"My father's family can NOT be allowed to go hungry . . .
And luckily I am NOT the only son . . ."

Philip was NOT expecting this blow.

Arthur's name had NOT ever appeared in his diary.

And he did NOT keep back a look of disapproval.

He consoled himself with the thought that a Lehman in Congress
was NOT an inconsiderable success
and that Arthur, after all, was little more than a boy.
So he concluded that the arrangement might work,
and could NOT restrain his enthusiasm:
"*Let's celebrate?*"

"*I do NOT know what.*"

"*You're future career. I'm NOT in doubt: it will be sensational.*"
And NOT having whisky,
they drank a toast with lemonade.

4
One William Street

Solomon Paprinski
the tightrope walker
stretched his wire
this morning
from lamppost to lamppost
straight
taut
then jumped up
and when he began to walk
almost lost his balance
shook
stationary in the air
then recovered.

His son Mordechai
a kid with green eyes
future tightrope walker
is always there watching his father
below the wire.
This morning
when Solomon almost fell

his son moved forward
as if to save him
but Solomon glared
from up there:
a tightrope walker
who hasn't fallen in thirty years
has no need
no sir
not for kids
nor for shots of cognac.

Just as well
because
a small bottle costs a fortune:
contraband alcohol
—according to the *Wall Street Journal*—
is pulling the underworld apart.
It's a greedy business:
fought over
by Italian gangs
—deft with knives
good at threats
formidable corrupters of police—
Irish gangs
—perfect with explosives
quick to vanish
masters at getting past customs—
and most of all
Jewish gangs
—close-knit
owners of distilleries
extraordinary at working their way in.

America
is now ablaze.
Great department stores
go up in flames
those of Sears, Roebuck & Company
those of Woolworth
all financed by Lehman.

America
is now a battlefield

torn to pieces
far and wide
by fire sirens
and flaming wrecks of vehicles.
Yes, vehicles.
Who knows
what Grandpa Emanuel would have thought
if rather than going
up there
to join his brothers
he had seen the United States
now streaked with railroad tracks
and crazy
no longer about trains
but about these motor cars
that at first belonged to the wealthiest
but are now sold to anyone
even to bakers.

Streets chock-full
of great hulks
all smoke and noise
with headlamps like eyes
and bulging with gasoline;
so that oil has gone sky-high.

Philip always thinks about it
each time he reads and rereads
the Public Purchase Offer
for Studebaker
which Lehman Brothers
is launching on the stock market:
a wide range of shares
for any bidder
    from financier to barber
    from millionaire to *schnorrer:*
BUY STOCKS AT A GOOD PRICE
and you too
in your own small way
will be
part-owners of an automobile company!
The aim is close, within easy reach:
to fill

American streets
within ten years at most
with exhaust fumes
and the spin of distributors.
Full speed ahead
no one
can be without a car,
there's business to be done:
drive
drive
drive
grip the steering wheel
of these splendid bodies
all iron
full of oil
and drunk on gasoline.

For them, drunkenness is allowed, for sure.
No confiscation of fuel tanks, hurrah!
Even though no one
drinks fuel oil
to celebrate.

Arthur Lehman
turns up each morning
driving his own car:
arrives at great speed (S)
to the new office
at One William Street (OWS).

As he darts through the streets of New York
Arthur cannot stop thinking that
in the end
every human being (H) he sees passing
—on the trams or sitting in a park—
is nothing more than a debtor to Lehman Brothers (LB).

It's an obsession, certainly.
But gratifying.

If you put together all Lehman investments in industry
and those on new patents
plus bank loans

as well as charitable works,
Arthur Lehman is sure
that every American
owes his bank
a lump sum figure
of somewhere around 7 dollars and 21 cents.

It seems incredible
but along the streets
Arthur no longer sees pedestrians
but walking numbers.

Those 7 dollars and 21 cents are everywhere:
they fill the theaters, the restaurants
they swarm onto ships and trains.
Those 7.21s also go to church
and pray to a God (J) who in moral terms
is comparable to
—or, at most, one step above—
Lehman Brothers:
He's the creator of 7.21s, but we are their financiers.
He's the inventor of the race, of course.
But if it were not for the bank
who would give 7.21s any scrap of existential meaning?

Arthur
as a partner alongside Philip
feels appointed therefore
with a supreme anthropological mission:
7.21s
plead through the look in their eye
not to be abandoned.

Lehman is, after all, a magnanimous divinity:
7.21s wanted cloth, and we gave them cotton.
They wanted to drink, and we gave them coffee.
They asked to travel, and we gave them trains.
And when they said *"Faster!,"* we created motor cars.

Speaking of which
Bobbie will be getting his own automobile
on his next birthday:
it will be a present from his father

since the future genius of Wall Street
cannot go on foot.

This decision is one of a series of measures
decided by Philip perfectly independently
in the personal confines of his diary:
THE BANK WANTS BOBBIE.

It was entirely irrelevant
that the notion was not reciprocal.

Now, it is well known that sometimes
between a father and a son
strange understandings can be created
based on the unsaid.

Ever since Philip had asked his son
in no uncertain terms
about his professional intentions
no further word
had been spoken on the matter
between the two of them:
all seemed perfectly clear
with no further need for explanation.

And so
an abstract contentment had settled on the two Lehmans.

Philip, for his part,
was necessarily convinced
that his son,
after his resistance that day,
would naturally give in.
And his smile was borne on this certainty:
the idea that the blood of his blood
could refuse to run the bank
seemed to him so inconceivable
that he had slowly dismissed it as the whim of a twenty-year-old
destined to be reabsorbed
—through natural more than filial law—
in the more prosaic ambition of an adult Bobbie.

In short, Philip had decided
—like any good banker—

to invest in his future
overlooking current risks:
Bobbie in his eyes
had become
the imperfect prototype of a perfect future son
in whose name
he had to excuse every passing defect.
It was, in the end,
a simple process of rapprochement.
To be encouraged
with the certainty of success.

Bobbie, for his part,
was unaware of all this.

And not because he dreamed
of any sort of idle life.
On the contrary
he was truly convinced
that his father had promoted him to "Lehman family representative."

The difference was substantial:
having decided he was unfit
to wear a banker's hat
Bobbie felt he was the natural candidate
for the role of warrior, yes, but in society.

Who better than he
to advertise the new face
of a bank that appreciated art,
that was a generous benefactor
and diplomatic in the game of respect?

"After all," Bobbie thought,
"for all the rest, there's always Arthur . . ."
and not surprisingly he gave a satisfied smile
each time his father
publicly lauded his cousin's equations.

The new office at One William Street
would therefore be
—in a still-distant future—
the scene for a new structuring of the family's bank:
Arthur Lehman seated like a monarch on the throne

and Bobbie immediately below
happily content to play the chamberlain
or even the master of ceremonies.

Oh, the dangers of silence:
it wasn't just Bobbie who was firmly convinced
that this—and this alone—
was his father's hope,
but even Arthur
felt quite reassured
through certain attitudes of his cousin (B)
that he was destined to hold the scepter (S).

And with this mutual certainty
peace reigned:
Philip smiled
Bobbie smiled
Arthur smiled.

May God bless that postwar moment.

Which, as we know,
can also be the precursor of another war.

Indeed it can be, without a doubt.
The only difference is in how it is viewed.

5
Roaring Twenties

"Ah, of course! Then there's Irving."

These words
had been heard
in the Lehman house
for over thirty years.
Though fairly intermittently.

Let us say that Irving
was remembered more or less
once
every five years.

After which
the mist returned
and this son of a potato
vanished entirely
not just from conversation
but also from recent memory.
He became
so to speak
absorbed in a cloak of silence
exactly like the two vowels of his name
overwhelmed by a mass of consonants.

There again
an almost mathematical law
dictates that in every numerous family
there is one who slips into the background.
Generally the quietest character
or the one who gives least cause for thought.
By way of reward, he is forgotten.

It's a form of ancestral equity
against which complaint is worthless:
just resigned acceptance.

In Irving's case, for sure,
his nature didn't help.

Ever since he was a child
he had tended naturally to remain,
so to speak, in the shadows.
And not because he was moody:
on the contrary, he was quietly cheerful,
even-tempered, unflappable
tending neither in one direction nor another
and in this flat calmness
there was not the slightest trace of apathy.
Irving represented the epitome of moderation
and anyone observing him could glean

an otherwise indefinable sense of "average humanity"
light years away from mediocrity or compromise.
Quite simply: he stood in the middle.
And, moreover, it suited him very well.

Now
a great social merit should be acknowledged
in such types of individual:
they enable those who live around them
to gain a clear picture of the word *normality*.
This is no small contribution
commendable above all when it comes to youngsters.

Thanks to Irving
for example
it was possible to formally proceed
in identifying shortcomings and eccentricities
in the behavior of each of his brothers
whose excesses were labeled
with the words *"Irving wouldn't do that."*

Though he himself was only four or five years old
he was chosen therefore as an early paragon of life
whose daily example
inevitably
became
a lesson to all.
One might even have thought
that he wasn't the product of Babette's womb
but of a technological laboratory
assembled by the most advanced parental engineering
as an automatic machine for educational ends.
A *Golem* child, in short.
The quirks of New York Judaism.

In any event
for little Irving
a gilded determination soon developed:
in the eyes of his brothers Arthur and Herbert
whatever he did
tended to be the *right path*
rightness meaning
not so much the respect for a moral idea

as the implementation of every possible and imaginable restraint
against the destructive rashness of children.

And indeed.
Irving did not shout.
Irving did not run.
Irving did not sweat.
Irving did not jump.
Irving did not fight.
Irving, in the broadest terms, did not rebel
accepting
with submissive composure
the limits imposed by human coexistence.
This made him a civilized child.
Or, if you like, a fifty-year-old who played games.

But, as we know:
human society is cruel.

Not only because the voice of judgment
draws the hatred of those being judged.
There is generally more to it.
And in this case there was.

As often happens with great moral authorities
young Irving
ended up becoming more of a concept than a human being.
His consistency was such
that *Irvingness* was created in the family
and this
gradually
took the little boy's place
with all the consequences that followed.

For a noble rank of morality
inhabits minds and edifies hearts
but is entirely devoid of material needs:
Irvingness required no food
felt neither hot nor cold
nor were more trivial desires expected of it
such as a lollipop, a ball, or a cap.
Without taking into account
that an entity is made of air

and as such
isn't even visible with spectacles.

Irving paid the price for it:
he discovered just how hard it was to be ethereal.

"Ah, of course! Then there's Irving" parents and uncles used to say
only then to realize
that Irving meanwhile was no longer there
forgotten who knows where.
In a garden?
At the Temple?
At the station?
Once even at a zoo
where, three hours later,
luckily, he was found
—perfectly calm and unruffled—
in conversation with a pair of macaques.

As he grew up
this straightforwardness of his remained unchanged.
On the contrary.
The pureness of his normality
gradually became a matter of conscious choice
and developed into pride.

Irving had no excesses, and was proud of it.
His plain—even during the restless years of youth—
was completely horizontal
absolutely level:
in his conversation and in his clothing
in his political positions and in the most ordinary choices
he adhered no more no less
to the most predictable profile of the American middle-class man.
But with what happiness.
Even at mealtime
his tastes were excruciatingly ordinary
and in tune with the masses.

A generous heart beat inside him
in unison with the vast majority of Americans
and this was all the more surprising
since he

made not the slightest effort to conform:
it came entirely naturally.

It would have been great
all the same
just for a change
to hear him say something out of the ordinary, like
"my favorite fruit grows only in Japan"
but such a hope was in vain
and unfailingly
he praised
the deliciousness of yellow apples.

There it is.
Each to his own.

Not that there was anything wrong about it.
After all, this had useful implications too.

For a start
his cousin Philip
not infrequently
used Irving as a commercial thermometer:
In what direction was the middle class moving?
Would it prefer transport by road or rail?
And did it favor gas or electricity?
The young man's opinion
—periodically subjected to appropriate sessions of interrogation—
served like that of an oracle.

So much so that
for all practical purposes
he was the only cousin
who kept himself well away from the bank,
by which he was therefore not influenced in the slightest.

Yes: Irving had opted for an entirely different job.

His choice
had been only partially influenced
by an understandable touch of revenge
seeing that his assortment of relatives
had too often

forgotten him in the most improbable places.
Could he now join the family board
after a childhood of roving?
(a condition, moreover, that had fueled in him
a unique form of independence)

But he had something quite different in mind.

Having been accustomed
from his earliest childhood
to being held up as a wondrous point of mediation
he was convinced at last that it was true
and felt nothing other
than to interpret nature's gift as the sign of a mission:
he would use his natural equidistance
to emerge from himself
and enter the souls of others
examining their motives, reasons, and wrongs.
So that, since psychoanalysis was still in its infancy,
he resorted to jurisprudence.

Certainly, if Dr. Freud had applied himself a little earlier
he would have found in Irving
a most worthy heir
since from his earliest judgments
the humanity of Judge Lehman
was admired by all:
a new Solomon was roaming the courts of New York.

The fact remained
of course
that Philip Lehman still used him as a guinea pig:
the more Irving penetrated
the thousand human cases of the criminal labyrinth
the more his understanding of human beings
drew an interest
beyond the legal implications:
Philip was interested in the commercial aspects.

Irving, for his part, had no reluctance to answer questions,
not imagining for one moment
that certain pleasant chats were pure marketing:

"Dear Philip, have you read about this genius from Chicago?"
he asked one day at the fireplace.

"Who exactly are you referring to, Irving? I missed that one."
his cousin immediately pricked up his ears, feigning disinterest.

"There's a remarkable fellow everyone's talking about:
dresses rats in dungarees and then makes them sing.
He's truly marvelous, Sissi and I adore him."
And first thing next day
Mr. Walt Disney was contacted
to the great delight of Sissi Strauss.

Sissi had been Irving's wife
for quite some years.
A very normal union, theirs.
A very normal love.
Very normal matrimonial bliss.

Perhaps because there was no living creature
on the face of the earth
more similar to Irving:
the more he championed *"good yellow apples,"*
the more zealously
she discouraged green ones.

And yet how much tenderness
in the perfect American couple!

It had all proceeded
from the very start
with a disarming linearity.

Such was the explosion of passion:
he had seen her at the Temple
had joined her at the end of the *Haftarah*
and asked if she happened to be the daughter of Nathan Strauss.
She replied *yes.*
He replied *good.*
She replied *that's right.*
He replied *good.*
She replied *good-bye.*

This was the start of the relationship.

Not even a month passed
however
before Irving
at the Temple once again
made the most unexpected declaration of love:
"Today, Miss Sissi, you are the most beautiful young lady in the Temple."

And apart from the fact
that the only women in the Temple that day were elderly
the girl appreciated it so much
as to reciprocate:
"And you too, Master Lehman."

Having therefore reached a first exchange of pleasantries
all that was lacking was a plan of intent.
And this was achieved, promptly,
on the stroke of the next month:
"Miss Sissi, I would like to offer you a drink in some quiet corner."
"I gladly accept, Master Lehman."

Mazel tov: the orangeade was indeed propitious
evidence that America
had not entirely wilted under prohibition.

Perfect.
What else was there to do?
Ah yes: little else, after all.
Engagement, rings, kisses: all in convenient haste.
The wedding was fixed shortly after
and took place on the happiest of occasions
in the happiest of Temples
and with the happiest of smiles.

As for the domestic life that followed
it was—no surprise—a triumph of happiness.
Barbecues in the garden.
A single white dog.
A maid called Trudy.
Floral upholstery.
A vase of flowers on the piano.
A mat in the veranda for wiping shoes.

Embroidered curtains at the drawing room window.
The words *Sissy & Irvy* on the door.
But above all
an ever-careful ear
for what *distinguishes a modern house.*

There.
This was of great assistance
for the expansion strategy of Lehman Brothers:
"Our task, after all"
Philip remarked as he studied Sissi and Irving
"is quite simply to respond to some wish
even before there's any demand for it:
we fulfill America's dreams
a moment before it reopens its eyes."
And it was true.

Since Sissy & Irvy always got there first,
listening to what they were buying
was like looking into the book of tomorrow:
"Sissi and I are getting an electric toaster!"
"Do you want to see our refrigerator, Philip?"
"I've bought Sissi an electric iron!"

To such an extent that Philip delighted in it
and began thinking one step ahead:
what if Sissy & Irvy's model
were applied abroad?

After all, ever since the Allies
had sorted out
the First World War
reconstruction had also become an international money-spinner.
And hadn't Irving's father, Uncle Mayer,
founded the bank
on the ruins of the War of Secession?
The aftermath of every war
—as we know—
always provides an opportunity.

Maybe yes.
Maybe we could try:
we were a world power, after all.

And as such, why not imagine
a planet Earth in American style?

For sure, it needed a good start.
And the oracle was consulted in this regard
in a conversation destined not to be forgotten:
"You're reading the papers, my dear Irving?"

"Oh yes, Philip. Every day. Interesting."

"And in Europe, tell me, what's going on?"

*"Germany has no money for its war debts:
if it doesn't get help, it will go bankrupt."*

"Do you reckon there are families like ours there in Europe?"
And he only said *ours* so as not to seem insulting:
he should have said *"like yours."*

*"I reckon an electric toaster heats bread in Paris too,
and a refrigerator goes just as well in Berlin.
And then electric irons:
you reckon a Londoner doesn't want his shirt free of creases?"*

*"The point is this, Irving:
will they have the money to buy them?*

"If they don't, they can ask for a loan."

His cousin was smart, after all.
He could have made an excellent banker.

Philip saw ahead, as far as the eye could see,
endless mountains of electric toasters, refrigerators, and irons.
The future had just one name: PAYMENT BY INSTALLMENTS.

The everlasting dream: to have now and pay later.
When? No hurry! Then!
Clearly with interest.
There was no one in the world
who, just to *have*, was not prepared to *lose*
and a gigantic flow of money
could sail off from New York to the Old Continent:

they would get it back three times over.
They just had to risk.
Everything was risk, after all.
They just had to risk.
They just had to risk.
They just had to risk.

"You'll all end up in court" was Irving's remark.
"And don't come looking for me then."

6
Peloponnesus

Harold and Allan
sons of a rabbit lost in the open sea
have never seemed like two little orphans.

On the contrary.
There's a general feeling
that they've compensated for the absence of Dad and Mom
by immediately becoming
in one fell swoop
absolute paternal and maternal authorities.
That is to say: there are those who
as they grow up
see their parents in a different light
and those who put them on a boat for Honolulu.
Different approach, identical aim.
Problem therefore solved.
Full stop, new paragraph.
Onward.

Harold and Allan are now twenty.
And they're ready for battle.

As time goes by
their lucid and cutting way with words
has become even more blunt

and the two never open their mouths
without inflicting some lacerating injury:
to those begging money in the street
they are capable of replying:
"We don't finance those who've got it all wrong."
and if the rabbi complains
about not seeing them so often at the Temple,
he might catch them saying: *"Like you in the bank."*

Small remarks.
But deadly.
This is their motto:
too much talk is wasted energy.
A negation of the concept of economy.

Harold and Allan
are the ambitious face of high finance.
Of that kind that seeks no compromise
mature offspring of the 120 *mitzvot*
among which *"sentiment has no place in banking."*
For the sins of the fathers fall upon the sons
together—and this seems sure—
with certain small lessons
not perfectly understood
    by those who have brought you into the world.

There.
Exactly.
The two brothers
have produced at last
the maximum essence of cynicism
which Sigmund used to dilute with tears.
The marvels of genetics.

Just think how their grandfather Mayer
even took the medal for *Kish Kish*
at a time when it seemed that the basis for commerce
was a broad smile and courtesy in relationships!
Today it needs something very different.
The market is power, and power means tight lips.

And in this, these two are champions.

When Charles Lindbergh landed
after his lone flight across the Atlantic,
Harold was the first to shake his hand:
"*Thirty-three and a half hours, a remarkable feat.*"
to which Allan immediately added:
"*costing hundreds of thousands of dollars:
not exactly economical, a flight for one person alone.*"
And Harold nodded.

Because the two always complement each other.

One a Republican.
The other Democrat.
And yet in perfect agreement.
As though in that fraternal union
there was much more than a pair of Lehmans
but the whole of America
aware of all its power.

One blond.
The other dark.
One bearded.
The other clean-shaven.
One high-pitched.
The other baritone.
Harold and Allan
of contrasting appearance
move about like two armored tanks
fighting off all resistance.

There again, how can they be blamed
if they are born in a superpower
whose hand extends across the whole world?
Might this allow them a minimum of arrogance?
Or do we want to pretend we are like everyone else?
Come on!

These are the most recent points
of their life story:
for a start
they graduated with top grades.

In reality, the last exam wasn't so perfect
but Professor Torrel
saw them glaring at him
and when he heard the words
"Lehman funds the college, and its salaries"
he had no doubts about an upward adjustment.

Soon after graduation came the wedding.
This too arranged in tandem
without breaking the fraternal harmony:
Harold has chosen Bibi.
Allan has picked Tessa.
Harold courts Bibi:
    "I find you pretty, even if you're not entirely so."
Allan courts Tessa:
    "With you I get less bored than with other women."
Harold woos Bibi:
    "I'd have preferred you blond."
Allan woos Tessa:
    "Now I come to look at you, you're really not so tall."
Harold gets engaged to Bibi:
    "They've told me I have to give you a ring."
Allan couples up with Tessa:
    "This is gold, my girl: get it off your finger and lock it in the safe."
Harold proposes to Bibi:
    "It's worth you marrying me, you'll not do any better."
Allan offers himself to Tessa:
    "You're getting the best deal out of this wedding, but I won't object."
Harold at last takes Bibi:
    "Now that I've married you, let's see how you behave."
Allan at last takes Tessa:
    "You're now a Lehman, you do realize that?"

Problem therefore solved.
Full stop, new paragraph.
Onward.

There's now the question of working out
what role these brothers can play in the bank:
there again, just to be clear,
could Uncle Arthur really fail to notice
two characters like these?

All the more since they seem perfect
for resolving a substantial problem:
though Arthur feels he has
the secret of banking algebra within his grasp,
what escapes him
is how to give practical effect
to the pure theory of calculus:
Harold and Allan could play the role of soldiers
instructing their dear uncle in the science of war.

And if Arthur was already certain of this,
today he had a clear demonstration.

It has already been mentioned how
Arthur no longer saw human beings inhabiting planet Earth
but ravenous hordes of 7 dollars and 21 cents:
what he sometimes finds irritating about them
is that the 7.21s
are often guilty of ingratitude.
And this is not very nice.
Today, for example.

Uncle Arthur is traveling
in the company of Harold and Allan
on a business trip to far-off Nebraska:
Lehman's interests stretch as far as here,
where we finance those who drill the mountains
in every corner
just to find a few drops of oil.
For there's half the world to get moving.

And since mathematics has its own fine fuel tank,
the three Lehmans are on the lookout for some decent food
after hours traveling in the middle of nowhere.

Then the mirage.

Appearing there at the roadside
a providential diner
open 24 hours a day:
a Greek diner
"PELOPONNESUS"

run by immigrants
opened six years ago.

The owner
Georgios Petropoulos
behind the counter
—olives and cheese—
with his oil-stained apron
and a three-year-old son in his arms
is trying to tune the radio
but with no luck:
among capers and sardines
there's no signal.

Among olives and capers,
this morning
in the middle of Nebraska
is not going well.
A bad Thursday.
Partly because it's Thursday
who knows why
customers aren't coming in.
Partly because this child
just three years old
won't stop whining
whining
whining
still?
Whining
whining
*"Αν κλάψεις πάλι, εγώ . . ."**
his father yells as though the child were likely to stop on command.

The three Lehmans sit at the counter.
They'll eat just olives and cheese: there's nothing else.

Meantime, the child cries more than ever
and his father is trying to find the frequency:
Georgios Petropoulos
wants
for sure

---

* "If you don't stop crying, I'll . . ."

to hear the news.
He always listens in
ever since those years
when every morning
they broadcast news
about the Ku Klux Klan
who even there at Kearney
yes sir
used to burn down Greek diners
at night.

And there, suddenly:
the news headlines:
*"The Lehman Brothers bank
has signed its divorce from Goldman Sachs."*

At this news the child cries louder
and the cook curses in his language
hurling a couple of olives against the wall
as though they were bullets.

Arthur peers in front of him
at that couple worth a total of 10 dollars and 81 cents
(since children count as half):
how dare they insult an institution?
"Excuse me, sir: you have something against the bank?"

"Pardon me?"

*"I had the impression you were somewhat upset
when the radio spoke about Lehman Brothers."*

*"And of course I'm upset! Lousy Jews!
To build this place up they gave me a loan
and it's six years that I've been paying a fortune!
I'm not paying them anymore, I've decided! Lousy Jews!"*

The mathematical formula of the curse
was about to lead Arthur
to the equation of an equal and consequent anger.

Luckily his nephews were there too.
"Is that child your son, dear sir?"

Harold immediately began
without even looking up from his plate.

"Of course, it's my Pete."

"We imagine that Pete will take over your job as he grows up"
his brother continued, he too without looking at him:
"Do you think Pete's business would do well
if he served food to his customers without making them pay?"

The Greek made no comment:
he merely frowned,
surprised more than anything by the fact that the child
—at the sudden mention of his future in the world of catering—
had completely stopped his wailing
and was studying the boy with the greatest attention.

Harold continued:
"Because the fact is that we have eaten today
and even though the quality is execrable
by the law of trade we will be obliged to pay.
Indeed, to be exact: how much?"

"7 dollars and 21 each" the Greek answered straightaway.

Arthur was about to protest.
But he was stopped by Allan:
"Let us now assume, dear sir,
that your son Pete becomes a banker one day.
Indeed, let us go further:
that he might work at Lehman Brothers."

"Never!" the Greek yelled
even though the child seemed to be nodding.

Harold ignored him:
"In that remote case, quite honestly:
in what would his occupation of banker consist
if not in obtaining the payment of interest on the loan he grants to you?
Interest for the bank is the same as what $7.21 is for your cooking.
Therefore, esteemed sir,
if you are really saying that you will pay no longer

then—as we ourselves, unluckily for you, are the Lehman bank—
we will be entitled to get up now
and leave here—we too—without paying anything to you."

The child emitted a sound much akin to agreement.

And the Greek took note.

The Lehmans paid $7.21 each,
with the reasonable certainty that they hadn't lost a debtor.

They got up
wiped their mouths
and
with cool confidence
left the Peloponnesus behind them
climbing back up Mount Olympus.

7
A Flying Acrobat

And to think that at one time
people in Wall Street
looked up only to watch the tightrope walker.

Solomon Paprinski
isn't too happy
about having partly surrendered control of the air spaces.

Goodness knows what he would say
if he knew it was he who had prompted the investment.

Yes.
For chance would have it
that Lehman Brothers' entry
into the airplane market
had been a very delicate question

begun almost as an amusement
and destined to have an importance
inside and outside the bank.

These, in short, are the facts.

Bobbie Lehman
who generally kept well away from Wall Street
had met his father one day
not far from the Stock Exchange
to examine a few paintings.

Or rather: this was the excuse,
thought up by Philip Lehman
to drag his son into the den of high finance.

His aim was of no little significance:
to present the bank's future helmsman
to the most important members of the Stock Exchange
hoping that a love at first sight
might cut clear away
all remaining uncertainty.

So having attracted his son
with the tempting bait of a pair of Flemish masters
Philip
could hardly control his excitement:
at least ten leading business figures
waited impatiently to test out the mood and knowledge
of the next Mr. Lehman Brothers.

Bobbie arrived in white suit and white tie
immaculate
and looked every bit like a Paris art dealer
who had ended up by mistake in a bankers' haunt.

The contrast was in no way lessened
by the presence of Arthur
perfectly marshaled in financier's uniform:
black suit (BS)
double-breasted (DB)
black tie (BT)
rounded spectacles (2S) of a confirmed mathematician

and a black pencil (BL) stuck in his hand
to note down the listings of the day.

For his part
Arthur was unaware
of the reason for bringing Bobbie to the Stock Exchange:
he imagined it was a simple sightseeing tour
and in this spirit regaled his cousin
with anecdotes and remarks on customs.
Arthur felt very much at home
happy to show his place of work
to a cousin who happened to be passing by
and who lacked any knowledge of the sector.

They sat down in a large room
with dark upholstery.
Just one window recounted the world outside
open wide at the very same height
that Solomon Paprinski was balancing on his wire.

Philip and Arthur sat at either end of the table,
Bobbie between them.

Around the other sides
sat ten committee members, ready for the examination.
For this, after all, was the purpose.

Philip stood up
in almost ceremonial manner:
"*Gentlemen, I present my son, Robert,
ready to answer your questions.*"

Bobbie nodded, and added a "*With the greatest pleasure.*"
For, despite the disturbing emergence of that *Robert,*
he had no reason to lose his smile:
he was waiting for the arrival
at any time
of the paintings to be examined
and there wasn't a single moment
in which he doubted that those before him
were not gallery owners, critics, and collectors
with an interest, like his, in the art market.

On the other hand
the one to whom all had suddenly become clear
was his cousin Arthur
who well knew
the identity of the ten sharks gathered in that room
and felt a genuine quake of terror (Tx).

The first of the ten
began to speak straightforwardly:
*"So, Mr. Lehman,
what in your view is the market situation?"*

Bobbie smiled,
like a master just waiting for the question.
After all, in the last month alone,
he had attended thirty or so auctions
from Bordeaux to London and Frankfurt:
*"I think I can say that our sector
is in feverish activity: everything's on the move, since the war,
and fortunately for us in America
the situation for many Europeans is not so florid
so we find we can make the best offers."*

There was a unanimous murmur of approval
while Philip gestured assent with his chin, his neck, his fingers,
in a true blaze of muscular energy.
Arthur meanwhile broke into a cold sweat (CS).

The second member spoke sternly:
*"Am I wrong or is this a proposal for large-scale buying?
Since Europe is in crisis, ought we to be taking advantage?"*

Bobbie smiled again:
*"With all respect: yes, that's what I think.
An opportunity like this won't present itself again.
If we want to establish ourselves in this sector of ours
we can't hold back."*

A third voice rose from the far end of the table:
"I'd like to understand more clearly what you are referring to."

Bobbie showed not the slightest irritation:
"It seems so clear, quite frankly:

until a few years ago
we felt the superiority of the French, of the Germans, of the Russians.
Not to mention the English.
I've spent whole years in Europe:
I can testify from personal experience
that—so far as my own satisfaction is concerned—
not infrequently the best deals
were all in marks, sterling, francs, and rubles."

A blond Viking nodded: *"Especially in marks."*

Bobbie continued:
"In Europe they know that Lehman
was one of the first to invest dollars in this sector.
There was us and a few others, then I can say we outdid them."

The Viking was elated:
"I agree, I approve, and I associate myself without hesitation:
we can alter the axis of the whole market
bringing it at last to this side of the Atlantic."

It was now the turn of a small thin man,
swamped in his own double-breasted suit:
"For the future, therefore,
must we expect Lehman
to expand its range of action
not just in America
but on an international scale?"

Bobbie stretched his arms wide: he seemed to be among amateurs.
"With all due respect: America? In our sector?
Come, it's of little importance.
The real business is done far away
and I imagine you know.
I, with the agreement of my father, Philip,
went to Europe immediately after Yale
and I realized from the very first day
that the only problem was knowing where to start."

Philip didn't let the opportunity slip
and, laughing like a drunkard, he remarked:
"He used to write, I remember, 'send money Dad!'
And straightaway I provided the capital!"

Bobbie at this paternal encouragement
grew bolder still:
"But let me point out
that this new American role
cannot be simply a predominance;
we also have duties
that can benefit all the people of the earth."

At these words
an old man with wild eyebrows
banged the knob of his walking stick on the dark wooden table:
"I detest these philanthropic gestures:
it's money all the same! It's business all the same!"

Bobbie stopped his father from any mediative effort
by responding immediately:
"No sir! If this were so, we would buy to resell,
and would sell to then perhaps rebuy!"

The old man protested again by banging his stick:
"And isn't that what we do?"

"Not on behalf of Lehman, my dear sir:
I like to think we are not traders
but people inspired by a mission."

"And what might this mission be? Let's hear it!"
began a young buck glittering with gold rings.

Bobbie replied without even letting him finish:
"To make the world better
since what are we investing in after all?
In man's ingenuity, in his genius,
in his extraordinary capacity to create."

A smartly dressed young man with mother-of-pearl teeth
jotted this phrase in his notebook
whispering to the one beside him: *"I like the way he talks."*
And the other: *"At least there's some vision."*
Bobbie now bristled with pride:
emerging from within was a comradely zeal
that he was neither able nor willing to repress
along with the memory of his military glories:
"I, gentlemen, have even fought for this

putting my life at risk
but I would do it again tomorrow!"

A warrior at the Stock Exchange!
A Homeric banker!
The enthusiasm became uncontainable.

The only one not to have spoken so far
was a gaunt middle-aged man
who had spent the whole time
endlessly stroking his fingers
as long as spindles.
Now, however, he felt he should make himself heard:
"If it is appropriate for me to ask, I'd like an example
of this great urge of yours—highly personal, I have to say—
to invest in humanitarian terms.
I do not see around us
all this burgeoning of intuition."

In a long silent pause
Bobbie looked at him as though he felt offended.
Then announced:
"Quite honestly, I don't know whom I'm speaking to."

And the reply came immediately:
"That's very strange. A Lehman ought to know very well.
In any event, I'm Rockefeller."

"Ah! No less!" Bobbie retorted, furiously:
If I'm not mistaken you swiped a triple deal from me
last month in England!"
(for the Rockefellers had indeed managed
to get their hands on three late Imperial Roman altars).

"Simple law of the best bidder!"
Rockefeller replied
referring to a triple purchase of Swiss banks.

"Is a Rockefeller asking me what is pure genius?
With respect, I see it wherever I set my eyes.
Here, for example:
look there, outside that window . . .
He is no more than a tightrope walker, after all.
But in the frame of the window, he is a true picture:

humanity is no longer satisfied with walking on the ground,
but is competing with the birds for air space.
This is pure art, Mr. Rockefeller.
If for you it is only a question of money
then I believe that you and I don't have much to say to each other.
Begging your pardon: I have here somewhere
two Flemish masters that await me.
Am I not right, Dad? I'd like to go."

And without adding more, he left the room
in such haste
that everyone wondered who were the Flemish financiers
who had come from Europe to meet him.

Before they could ask him
however
the old man with the eyebrows
waved his stick at Philip:
"Devil of a Lehman: you hadn't told us anything!
Competing with the birds for air space!
Civil aviation!
Your son wants to fly humanity up and down the planet?
A sensational idea: pure art, he's right!
Rather than using airplanes just for war
let's use them to move ourselves about for pleasure!
My bank is prepared to support you in the deal."

"We too!"
"May I join in?"
"I offer a third of the capital!"
"Very smart, Lehman!"
"A textbook success!"

While all these voices were echoing 'round the room,
Philip could barely hold back the tears:
a baron's baptism had just been performed.
And so, with paternal pride,
he uttered a phrase that turned into a shout:
"Talk all of you with Robert, not with me!
Talk with him tomorrow!"

Well.
It was here that Arthur Lehman's

own mathematical dose of tolerance (TL)
reached a definite end.

He could expect anything from his cousin.
Anything apart from seeing him emerge
without warning
as a claimant to the throne.
And then what shred of good sense did he have?
Hadn't Bobbie always been a wastrel?
Okay, he had graduated from Yale
but who had ever heard of him discussing finance? (BY ≠ FIN)
Through what algebraic formula
was old Philip
now wanting to promote him in the bank?

Yes. All this whirl of question marks
exploded like a volcano in Arthur.

And as often happens with human beings
anger doesn't always go hand in hand with logic (A ≠ L)
so that
this was what he yelled:
"Well done! That's it! Go on! Why not?
You want to fill the sky with airplanes?
They'll go crashing into skyscrapers!"

"I heartily hope not"
came the immediate reply from Louis Kaufman
who was financing the Empire State Building.

"It's a mathematical certainty!"
Arthur said or thought
(this was never clear)
before slamming the door.

In any event
this was how Lehman Brothers
began investing in Pan American Airways.

And apart from this
it was how Bobbie Lehman
without realizing it
rose from chamberlain to heir to the throne.

8
Business in Soho

Since that day a few months ago
Philip is always smiling.

Once again he feels
he has turned up the right card.

It matters little that his son, Bobbie,
on the other hand
has sunk into a leaden silence
and often bites his lip until it bleeds:
the boy has the feeling
he has entered a strange game
whose rules and field of play he cannot figure.

And why then does his cousin Arthur
no longer speak to him
nor even say hello?
A mystery.

Bobbie watches all this
with resigned melancholy.

No one explains things clearly.
No one tells him what they expect of him.

Even Harold and Allan,
potential masters of ruthlessness
limit themselves to a
"Are you getting ready, Bobbie?"

"For what?" he asks biting his lip.

"For the worst" comes the reply
seasoned with one of those smiles of compassion
that nurses reserve for the dying.

Now
it is well known that each human being

has their own particular way
of exploring the lowest depths
of their own inner ocean.

There are those who go off into the mountains
those who climb to the top of a cliff
and those like Bobbie Lehman
who venture alone
on foot
into working-class districts.

It matters little
that his cousin Irving has strongly warned against it:
*"Two out of three villains that I sentence in court
come from those districts
where you go wandering!
They are training grounds for criminals.
One of these days, dear Bobbie, you'll find yourself
with a knife right in the middle of your chest.
You kids have this obsession about risk.
You'll all end up in court, and then don't go looking for me."*

"I, on the other hand, approve of this type of tourism!"
retorted Herbert the democrat:
*"Just by feeling the suffering
of less-privileged classes
we can plan a path for redemption!
People must stop pretending not to see!
The middle class is proudly blind!
Congratulations, cousin: you have my approval and my encouragement.
And I say more: I'll follow your example."*

Bobbie didn't have the courage to tell him
there wasn't an ounce of altruism
in those wanderings of his.

Or rather: he was about to explain
but was preceded by Peter,
Herbert's high school son
who had grown into a beanpole almost six feet tall:
"You have my deepest respect, Bobbie."

It's always dangerous to destroy a model for an adolescent.

So it's better to say nothing:
let them think his visits to Soho
grew out of a social concern.

Whereas
ever since he was a boy
a strange form of calm
fell over young Lehman
at the mere sight of those
cramped and noisy slums
drowned like sardines in their rotting stench.

Bobbie walked slowly
not missing a single detail
enjoying the pleasure of not feeling rich
but of sensing
that another path was yet possible
far away from money and from the Stock Exchange
far away from such an awkward surname
far away
in short
from all that took away the thirty-year status
which made him Robert son of the great Philip Lehman.

If someone then looked out
from a window
in one of those hive-like houses
he felt a splendid and heartwarming relief
when he saw that a smile—on those dirty faces—was not at all
     impossible.
And his eyes even reddened with joy.

The fact is
that Bobbie's visits to the vaults of hell
became more and more frequent.
Until the day we are now describing.

Life, at times, is funny:
surprise lurks nearly always
among the recesses of normality
where you least expect it.

That evening
in fact
Bobbie Lehman was walking with his head down
under a light rain.

His coat lapels up over his face.
His hat tight over his eyes.
Almost as if he wanted to disappear.
Not from others: from himself.

He was about to leave
the last block of Soho behind him
when several wild shouts
reached his ear.

They came from an inner alley
a kind of gorge between high concrete walls
closed on either side and above
by a metal roof and rusty steps.

Life, at times, offers an alternative.
Bobbie therefore had to choose
between continuing on toward the driver who was waiting for him
or stopping at the beginning of that passageway.

He chose the second.
And more: he moved
a few steps closer
to that metropolitan lane
driven partly by curiosity and partly by a civic instinct
seeing not only that the shouts didn't seem to diminish
but merged with a background sound
more resembling a human cry
than any animal call.

Bobbie looked about.
The path was almost empty.

He paused for a moment
restrained the hero's fury
and urged himself to be cautious.

And only when he heard
another shout of *"Megöllek!"* *
did he decide to let his lower limbs loose
in an unprecedented display of courage.

Once inside the stinking hole
Bobbie could see
only cats around him
scurrying frantically
after which he glimpsed at the far end of the alley
a sign in Hungarian
above an open door.

"Megöllek!"
a man shouted
from inside the workshop
and Bobbie distinctly heard
the plaintive cries of a child
the likely object of paternal rage.

Once again Bobbie was faced with a choice:
he thought of the route he could take to find a policeman
or
could continue on with all the risks involved.

And once again he rejected the more cautious path
and rushed inside the building.

Laid out on a workbench
were various chisels:
the Hungarian was making table lamps
which filled the shelves up to the ceiling.

In a corner of the room
a corpulent man with sand-colored apron
was repeatedly kicking and slapping
a fragile being
that looked more like a frog than a child
crouched between crates
protecting itself with its arms.

---

* *"I'll kill you!"*

Bobbie summoned all the breath he could find:
"That's enough, or I'll call the police."

At these words, the shoulders of the craftsman
swiveled 'round as though on a hinge
revealing
the absolute predominance of two round eyes
under a mop of red hair:
"And what do you want? A lamp?"

Bobbie was caught unprepared:
"I'll buy a lamp, if you leave the child alone."

*"I've no lamps to sell this evening
since this scoundrel hasn't lacquered the metal!
I told him to do it but he hasn't!
And now you're asking me for a lamp
and I can't give you one! Should I not kill him?"*
And he aimed a kick which the child jumped to avoid.

"But if I pay you for the lamp all the same?"

He went silent.
All of a sudden the discussion turned
to a fundamental law of craftsmanship:
*"I don't sell lamps unfinished.
Are you going to pay for stuff half finished?"*

Bobbie searched for a more confident tone:
"I'll pay for the lamp if you stop beating him."
And he pulled out his wallet as proof of intent.

The runt, meanwhile, watched him from below.

"How much do I owe you for an unfinished lamp?"
Bobbie ventured, optimistically.

"I sell them new for eight dollars" the Hungarian said
adopting the manner of a bookkeeper
(if only because the other had a whiff of higher stock)
and after pretending to do a few sums, he made the offer:
"7 dollars and 21 cents: it's a good price."

Bobbie started looking for the money. And meanwhile:
"For 7 dollars 21 you'll sell me the lamp
and the promise that the boy is safe."

"Ah! Safe! That's very nice! What's that got to do with it?
He has to work, because we all work in here!
And I've decided his job for me is to lacquer the metal!"

This was the third choice of the day:
Bobbie could close the deal at 7 dollars 21
or
follow an uncertain path
like Mallory and Irvine who on climbing Everest
lost their way on an icy ridge.

Maybe it was the thrill of taking a risk.
Or maybe it was because that story
of the runt
stuck down there
lacquering metal in his father's workshop
seemed in the end so familiar
that it was worth any price to help him.

And so:
"How many lamps do you sell each day?"

"Oh, it depends! How can I put it?
Five if it goes badly, double if it goes well."

"So an average of seven lamps a day."

"You can even say eight, let's not be mean about it."

"Which makes sixty dollars, more or less, if I'm not mistaken."

"And you're not mistaken" the Hungarian said, taking a seat,
since the matter was becoming interesting.
He gestured to Bobbie to sit down
but he didn't move:
"How many of you work in this place?"

"Me, the boy, my wife, and my five sisters."

"*Excellent. Since there are eight*
each of you produces one
of those lamps you sell each day.
So each contributes to the business
eight dollars every day
forty-eight a week and more or less 200 a month.
In a year that is 2,400. How old is the boy?"

"*Seven!*" the runt shouted
jumping out as though he had been bitten
and up to the table.

Bobbie prepared for the grand finale:
he wiped a trace of sweat from his brow,
savored the last silence, then:
"*With 30,000 dollars I will indemnify you*
totally
for the child's work over the next eleven years.
You leave him in peace:
he will do as he wishes.
The money I'll give to him, of course, not to you:
each month he'll give you the amount he owes you.
And it will be as though he has done his duty.
If you beat him, I'll stop paying you, and that's a fact.
Do you have anything to say? Don't you like it?
It's an offer: take it or leave it."

The Hungarian stared at his son.

Then scratched his ear.

"*7 dollars 21 for the first lamp, however . . .*
That's not part of the 30,000, is it?
That's separate, it came before the agreement."

Bobbie smiled:
"*I'll give 30,000 dollars to the child, and 7.21 to you.*"

"*It's a deal, sir.*"

"*It's a deal.*"

They shook hands.

Bobbie paid as agreed.

And having raised his lapels, he returned the way he came.

As for the runt
he didn't even say thank you.

9
The Fall

Solomon Paprinski
is now seventy.
And yet
over the fifty years that he has walked the wire
in front of Wall Street
he has never fallen.

Philip Lehman
is also getting on for seventy.
And yet
for the fifty years he has run Lehman
in Wall Street
he has never fallen.

Solomon Paprinski
can manage
for the moment
without his tightrope walker son
just as
he has managed without cognac.

Philip Lehman
can manage
for the moment
without his economist son

just as
he has managed without whisky.

Between
Solomon Paprinski
and
Philip Lehman
however
there's a small
trivial
difference
and it's a diary
written in block capitals.

LEHMAN CORPORATION.
is the last note in it.

It sounds so good.
Philip Lehman's idea.
Pure finance.
Lehman Corporation.
Which means: *Investment Funds*.
To invest money just to make money.
No brand-name to finance
no industry to launch
no market to explore:
money for money.
Pure adrenaline.
It's the excitement, the continual excitement.
The excitement of risk.
Of the kind that keeps you awake at night
for Philip Lehman
doesn't sleep now
ever since
in his nightmare
the *Sukkot* hut
has a gigantic sign on the front
with HOLDING written on it
and whoever passes below
no longer has a human face
but a large + where its skull should be.
Maybe this is because America

is a horse that is racing madly
on the Churchill Downs racetrack
and Philip Lehman
with his gray hair
is its jockey
who every evening signs his accounts
always in profit:
+
+
+
+
+
+
+

The Americans have learned to invest.
The middle classes no longer hide their money away:
everyone is putting it in bonds and investment funds
and in this way they double it.
Wow! Let's make money!

Last month alone
Wall Street doubled its shares:
from 500,000 to 1,100,000!
What more can you ask?
A whole nation with money!

Arthur Lehman is beside himself:
he watches
in the street
those busy crowds of $7.21s
destined even to become $10s
and each time he cannot help but hear
a magnificent choir
chanting at the top of their voices
"THANK YOU MR. LEHMAN!"

And there again, what is Wealth (W)
if not a mathematical formula?
Arthur has worked it out like this:
Wealth is a result that depends on
the simultaneous increase of
    Risk (X), Ambition (A), Productivity (Pr)

multiplied by a crucial parameter known as FC
or Favorable Conditions:

$$W = FC \cdot f(X,A,Pr)$$

The favorable conditions in this case
would be none other than political:
what more can a bank ask for
than such a generous government?
No control on financial groups.
Taxes on capital reduced to the minimum.
Rates of interest at almost zero.
What is this if not a free ride?

Better, of course, not to talk to Herbert about it.
He, being a Democrat, with all his wild liberal ideas, doesn't agree.
And the fact that Arthur is his brother doesn't ease the conflict:
"Despite the fact that I don't expect for one moment
to find flesh and blood in a banker,
if you and Philip had a minimum—and I say a minimum—of public
     spirit,
you would recognize that this financial anarchy cries out for revenge!"

"Why do you want to hold nature back, Herbert?
The market has always existed, and it wants freedom!"

"Freedom! Have you ever asked yourself what is the price of freedom?
Your mouths are all full of this word,
but can you possibly fail to realize
that too much freedom means the end of rights?
Is the thief free to steal? No, it's a crime.
Is the drunkard free to go 'round swearing? No, because it's uncivil.
And you, with all respect: if you see a pretty young girl,
do you think yourself free to squeeze her hips?"

"You confuse freedom with arrogance."

"Exactly: that's what it is. You financiers are arrogant."

"We apply scientific criteria."

"You apply them with no muzzles, no leashes.
Three citizens out of four live in poverty.

Five percent hold one-third of all the wealth in America!"

"And you're one of them, Herbie: what are you complaining about?"

"About the fact that it's unjust, Arthur!"

"Oh for goodness' sake! And how many other things are unjust?
Sickness is unjust: you get sick, I don't.
Hurricanes are unjust, earthquakes are unjust!
You want to try and stop those? You can't.
The law of wealth is part of human society
you can't change it, even if you don't like it."

"It's pointless talking to a banker about ethics.
I'm putting you on guard, if you want to understand:
you're creating a monstrous system
which cannot last for long.
Industry everywhere, factories all over the place:
who will they sell to if the vast majority has no money?
You pretend that America is rich
you like to say the whole world is on the road to affluence
but when will you open your eyes?
Or are you going to open them when it's too late?

Philip Lehman
for his part
has now learned to smile at these arguments.

It's not worth talking to Herbert:
it's a pointless effort
all the more since everything's under control.

Each night
Philip examines the situation
checks the problems
follows the fingers of the dwarf
concludes that
absolutely the best thing
is
to ride the wave.
Perfect.
Ride the wave.

And not just the wave: the clouds too.
For no other reason than that Lehman Brothers
has been investing now for some time
in shipping transport
but now
for some time
has launched into conquering the sky
and each time Philip hears the sound of an airplane
he is happy to look up
and think *"that's one of ours."*

This also makes Philip smile,
a smile that has never been so perfect:
Lehman controls banks everywhere
from North America to Germany
from England to Canada
and only in Russia do they keep us away
even though Mr. Leon Trotsky
has said: *"All the same, in Moscow gold is gold
and we communists haven't abolished money . . ."*

So there's plenty to smile about.

Early
each morning
like today
Philip Lehman
arrives in Wall Street
with a smile on his face.

Each morning
with a smile on his face
he buys a newspaper
from the Italian kid
who calls out at the street corner.

With a smile on his face
he drinks a coffee
served at the counter
leafing through the paper
reading the figures.
Then he wipes his lips

with his handkerchief
picks up his bag
and heads toward the entrance.

By that time
each morning
like this morning
Solomon Paprinski
is already
standing on the
taut
straight
wire.
"Good morning, Mr. Paprinski!"
"Good morning, Mr. Leh . . ."

It's as though time
had stopped still.

At that moment.

Stop.
Halt.
Still.

Solomon Paprinski
after fifty years
for the first time
has fallen
down
has fallen
to the ground.

His ankle broken:
finished, forever.

It is Thursday October 24.
Of the year 1929.

10
Ruth

Teddy
is the first stockbroker
to kill himself.
He puts a gun in his mouth at 9:17 a.m.
in the restrooms at Wall Street.
It's Thursday October 24.
Year 1929.

Teddy ran off
took to his heels
as soon as he realized
that everyone on the trading floor
all of a sudden
is selling
selling
selling
"but what the hell's going on today?"
they're selling
selling
"what's going on today?"
they're selling
selling
yet till yesterday
shares were sticking to people's hands like glue
and now
all of a sudden
they want to unload them
everyone
to be rid of them!
They want to see money, real money
not shares
not securities:
money.
Full stop.
Money.
Full stop.
Money?

Teddy isn't used to money.
You don't see money on Wall Street.
Money is tacit.
For years, now:
increase value
price goes up
this is what they've taught him:
the more it costs, the stronger it is
the more it costs, the bigger it is
the more it costs, the more to celebrate
yes, okay
agreed
but if then
all of a sudden
someone *sells?*
Teddy knows how to pay, of course
but in shares.
And if someone doesn't want other shares
but only only only wants *money?*
If he no longer feels safe
if he wants to see
if he wants money
here
in front of him
now . . .
"then what do I do?"
"then what do I do?"

Teddy ran off.
Locked himself in a bathroom.
Bullet.
Trigger.
Fire.
Bang.

Bang!
And the horses race off!
All in a line
no one pulls away yet
with number 1 Nelson
2nd Davis
3rd Sanchez
4th Tapioca

5th Vancouver
6th . . .
Bobbie Lehman's horse is number 6
his Thoroughbred, Wilson:
12 trophies
12 races
12 podiums
12 times Bobbie Lehman has sat on the terraces
white suit white tie
immaculate
with binoculars
restrained, dignified
—a man of measure—
hissing between his teeth
"That's it Wilson! Go on Wilson!"
but only between his teeth
not opening his mouth
immobile, expressionless
even when Wilson at number 6 pulls away
as he usually does
and unstoppable
unstoppable
unstoppable
crosses the finishing line
Wilson wins
Wilson wins
Wilson wins
Wilson wins
once again
the thirteenth time
that Wilson has won
that Bobbie Lehman has won.
Today too, here
at Churchill Downs, the top race.
Bobbie smiles.
Nothing more.
He smiles.
Has he won? Yes.
Has he triumphed? Yes.
But he is restrained.
A man of measure.
Bobbie Lehman says nothing.
Just a smile.
Even when he sees

a green hat with veil
and two eyes beneath the hat
peering at his mouth:
"Do you know there's some blood coming from your lip?"
"Pardon me, Miss?"
*"I said you have a drop of blood
here, on the side of your mouth."*
"I? Do I?"
"Yes, sure. As if you've bitten your lip."
"I don't bite my lip, Miss."
"Will you let me wipe it off?"
"Wipe it off, Miss?"
"With my handkerchief: it will stain your suit if it runs down . . . May I?"
"If it's necessary."
"It's urgent."
"Very well."
"There, it's done."
"That's very kind. I'm obliged to you, Miss."
"I may be kind but I'm not a Miss."
"You're married? Do I know your husband?"
"Jack Rumsey, ex-husband."
"I'm sorry."
"I'm not. Long live divorce! I'm still celebrating."
"Very frank."
"Realism, pure realism. In fact, you can offer me a drink."
"I'm expected at the prize giving."
"It's your horse that's won?"
"So it seems."
"Heavens, are you Robert Lehman?"
"Unless proved otherwise."
"Now I understand why you bite your lip."
"I really don't bite my lip."
"Oh you do, you do it a lot."
"You're mistaken."
"And the blood on your lip?"
"Pure chance."
"Let's take a bet?"
"I never bet."
"You're most amusing! Shall I come with you to the prize giving?"
"It's not permitted."
*"Are you joking? You Lehmans can do as you please
from biting your lip to whatever else."*
"I told you . . ."
"Don't repeat yourself: it's tedious. Let's go to the prize giving!"

"But if they ask me . . ."
"If they ask who I am, just say: Ruth Lamar."
"Ruth Lamar."
"Here, stop: can't you see you're biting your lip?
I've won!"

Vernon
is the second stockbroker
to kill himself.
He blows his brains out at 10:32 a.m.
at his desk
second floor at Wall Street.

Ever since everyone
on this infernal Thursday
began selling madly
Vernon hasn't stopped a moment
he hasn't lost heart:
the shares are holding for now
there's a drop, yes, but 3 percent
you just have to keep calm
to say that if all the others fall
there's a chance for big opportunities a moment later
just keep calm
yes, keep calm
—*"light another cigarette, Vernon"*—
the drop is now 5 percent
it's no big loss, 5 percent
—*"light another cigarette, Vernon"*—
he reads the numbers on the board:
Goldman Sachs has lost 30 million
—*"light another cigarette, Vernon"*—
he checks his shares:
down 15 percent in not even half an hour
he looks at the board again
Goldman Sachs loses 40 million
—*"light another cigarette, Vernon"*—
he checks his shares:
down 25 percent
"I'm not going to pick up like this"
"I'm not going to pick up like this"
Goldman Sachs loses 50 million
—*"light another cigarette, Vernon"*—

down 27 percent
down 30 percent
down 34 percent
"I'm not going to pick up like this"
"I'm not going to pick up like this"
—*"light another cigarette, Vernon"*—
he opens the drawer
down 37
bullet
down 38
"I'm not going to pick up like this"
down 40
trigger
down 44
fire!
down 47
bang
down 4 . . .

---

4 . . .
3 . . .
2 . . .
1 . . .
Hurrah!
Applause from the whole street.
Doors open:
the start of the Lehman Collection art exhibition.
Seventeenth-century Flemish masters.
Bobbie Lehman feels at home
in his element
Bobbie the connoisseur
Bobbie the expert
Bobbie who for years
has traveled the length and breadth of Europe
in search of paintings and drawings:
now it is he who inaugurates museums and galleries
at the table with the dignitaries
white suit white tie
immaculate
he has just praised the power of chiaroscuro
"which exalts the union
between realism and the ethereal transcendence of light."

Applause throughout the room.
And at the end of the speeches
a queue to congratulate Mr. Lehman
who shakes hands
greets
and kisses the hands of the ladies.
Ruth Lamar is behind him
smoking her Philip Morris—
which Lehman Brothers also finances.
"*Do you know your hands shake when you speak in public?*"
"*Let me say hello to these people:
good evening, Mrs. Thornby.*"
"*And yet it's true: your hands shake,
I've been watching you, I do it each time.*"
"*You shouldn't.*"
"*Not allowed?*"
"*I don't like it when other people see you looking at me.*"
"*As if they don't know . . .*"
"*Keep your voice down! To many, you're still a married woman.*"
"*Divorced.*"
"*They don't know that. Good evening, Mr. Guitty.*"
"*There: can't you see your hand is shaking?*"
"*Because I'm not at ease, that's all.*"
"*That's all.*"
"*I'm 37! I don't want people to think I'm playing around with . . .*"
"*With a pretty divorcée?*"
"*Keep your voice down!
Good evening, Mrs. Downs.*"
"*So marry me.*"
"*Pardon?*"
"*Let's get married, darn it!
I've already done it once, I know it's not the end of the world.*"
"*Good evening, Mrs. Meldley.*"
"*If we get married will I be able to look at you?*"
"*Oh, Professor Rumoski!*"
"*After all, it's just a swapping of rings, no more no less.*"
"*My dear Mr. Nichols!*"
"*Life isn't so different once you're married, I guarantee.*"
"*Senator Spencer!*"
"*But I tell you now, we'll get married in Canada.*"
"*General Holbert!*"
"*And then away from here, clean air:
I expect at least a trip to Europe!*"
"*You're a rather demanding woman, don't you think?*"

"I'm a practical woman, honey.
So, come on: yes or no?"

The morning
of Black Thursday
Gregory is the third stockbroker to put an end to it
with a gunshot.
Peter is fourth.
Jimmy is fifth.
Dave is sixth.
Fred is seventh.
Mitch eighth.

They got off the tram
like every day
entered the Stock Exchange
like every day
opened the lists
like every day
and there
the disaster
as if on the tram
—the one they take each morning—
the end of the line were not at the end of the route
but had leapt up
suddenly like that
"everyone out: all out, end of the line!"
End of the line?
End of the line.
Gregory, Peter, Jimmy, Dave, Fred, Mitch
one after the other
they said: *"that's it!"*
—*"end of the line!"*—
when they saw
—*"end of the line!"*—
when they realized
—*"end of the line!"*—
that the dream, here, this morning, is finished.
A rough awakening.
Reality, all of a sudden.
No more numbers
—*"end of the line!"*—
no more securities

—*"end of the line!"*—
no dealings
—*"end of the line!"*—
America today has opened its eyes.
They have closed theirs: with a pistol shot.
America has stopped running
out of breath
it has stopped at the roadside
and has realized
damnation
all of a sudden
—*"end of the line!"*—
that running
after all
wasn't worth it.
So?
I'm cashing in.
I'm selling.
I'm getting off, thanks: that's enough.
Give me my money.
What money?
There's no money.
Money is a figment.
Money is numbers.
Money is air.
You can't now, everyone, all together
all at once
want money.
They look out of the windows
of the top floors
Gregory, Peter, Jimmy, Dave, Fred, Mitch:
Wall Street is packed full of people
and more are arriving, down there
—*"end of the line!"*—
and more and more and still more
"these want their money"
—*"end of the line!"*—
and more and more and still more
"these want their money."
They run off
Gregory, Peter, Jimmy, Dave, Fred, Mitch
they run off
"these want their money"
"these want their money"

"these want their money"
bullet
trigger
Gregory fires!
Peter fires!
Jimmy fires!
Dave fires!
Fred fires!
Mitch fires!
bang
bang
bang
bang
bang
bang.

What great bangs they make
these crackers and fireworks
set off here in the street
to celebrate the newlyweds!
Bobbie Lehman and Ruth, his wife
are back from their honeymoon
in their automobile
greeted by a crowd
of photographers and onlookers
at 7 West 54th Street.

A splendid honeymoon.

Europe, across the ocean
seeing that Lehman is investing in airplanes
so that it's no problem to fly.

Ruth dressed in green.
Bobbie in white suit white tie
immaculate
they wave
from the windows of their Studebaker:
"Look at them, Bobbie: these people actually have time to waste."
"They are employees of the bank, Ruth."
"Even worse: they hate you and come to welcome you back."
"I don't believe I am hated."
"No slave loves their master."

"I have no role in Lehman Brothers."
"Okay. Correction: you're the next slave master, the future slave master."
"And the current slave master would be my father."
"Can't I say that?"
"You've already said it."
"Mine is realism, Bobbie, healthy realism."
"The world isn't always as terrible as it seems to you."
"That's right: it's much worse!"
"Look at that child with the placard. It says:
THANK YOU, MR. LEHMAN!
No slave master is ever thanked."
"But you're wrong:
it's part of the masochism of the underdogs:
they hate your father and they thank him."
"I don't think I asked your opinion about my father, Ruth."
"Every time your father is mentioned, you blink.
That must mean something."
"You're a terrible woman!"
"I'm from Illinois."

Hubert
is the ninth stockbroker
to kill himself at Wall Street
on Black Thursday.
Bill is tenth.
Peter eleventh.

They throw themselves
from the top floors of the building.
They throw themselves out
at the end of the day
when it's clear that nothing is like it was before.
Hubert, Bill, and Peter
deal
in investment trusts.
Which means that
Hubert, Bill, and Peter work miracles.
As a profession.
Extraordinary gains
promised to whoever invests:
you give me your money
I'll make a profit on it
doesn't matter how

you don't need to know how
we'll do it
we know how
you give me your money
and when it matures
you'll say *"thanks"*
for, I swear, you won't believe your eyes
and that's how capital is made
yes sir
that's how capital is made.
Hubert, Bill and Peter know how to do it:
they invest money in 100, 1,000 stocks
like a river divided into droplets
Hubert, Bill, and Peter sow money in the market field
then they harvest it
then they harvest it
then they harvest it
like at one time, down there, in the cotton plantations:
they sow and harvest
they sow and harvest
but
but what happens if the sown field
all of a sudden
catches fire?
Hubert, Bill, and Peter have invested money
for sure
Lehman Brothers investment trusts
but it wasn't their money
damnation
"when it matures what do we say?"
"when it matures what do we say?"
Here everything is burned
in flames
destroyed
ashes
ashes
"when it matures what do we say?"
"when it matures what do we say?"
Hubert runs upstairs to the top floor.
Bill reaches the fourth.
Peter opens a window
"when it matures what do we say?"
"when it matures what do we say?"

Here there's nothing.
Hubert on the cornice.
Bill on the parapet.
Peter on the ledge.
And down.
And down.
And down.

"Down how much, Bobbie?"
"I've told you not to ask me."
"Don't I have a right to know?"
"Not now."
"I'm your wife!"
"The bank isn't yours, Ruth."
"Of course: keep it to yourselves!"
"I beg you not to interfere, it's a delicate situation for my father."
"For your father! Now, watch it, you'll have to do it all for yourself."
"I don't think it's like that."
"Of course it is: everything's collapsing and when everything collapses
then generally it's the children who take over."
"The only thing you're right about is that everything's collapsing: please, a
minimum of tact."
"Everything's collapsing and I have to shut up and keep quiet?"
"You'll know everything, all in good time."
"When?"
"When everyone knows."
"You insult me!"
"It's not a game."
"But what do you take me for?"
"Just keep calm!"
"I'm worth less in here than an ornament!"
"I've never said that."
"But now I understand it!"
"Ruth . . ."
"How much have you lost?"
"A lot."
"How much?"
"Millions."
"How many?"
"I can't!"
"Okay, Bobbie, that's fine:
you and I are heading for divorce."

11
Yitzchak

Ten minutes to go
to the time arranged
for the appointment.

Philip Lehman
arrived in his office
an hour and a half early:
he wanted to write down what is to be done
in block capitals in his diary.

He is sitting
in front of the mirrored wall.
And is seen reflected
beside
the Hungarian-style marble lamp;
Philip sees his reflection
with his diary open, pen in hand:
for the first time
Philip Lehman
in his diary
doesn't know what to write.

He swallows.
He can't stop looking at himself.

Six minutes to go
to the time arranged
for the appointment.

He slowly combs his hair
stares into the mirror:
he has never seen himself so old.

"Why is today more silent than usual
here in the office?
Why does the air seem like glue
that sticks to your face?
Why does the wall clock

make an infernal noise
that I've never heard before?"

Philip Lehman knows, inside, he well knows
that today is like when the sky turns black:
there's nothing to do but wait for the storm.
Pointless to pretend it's nothing:
if the sky turns blacker than black
the storm will come.
For sure.

There, the point is this.
Precisely this.
And Philip is sure:
the Wall Street crash
hasn't been a storm.
It has only been a black sky.
The storm, the real one, is about to arrive.
How can you write it down
in a banker's diary?
How can you write down
that storms are sometimes so strong
that not even an umbrella is enough?
How can you write down . . .
that instead of a storm
maybe a hurricane will arrive?

There, the point is this.
Precisely this.
Philip is sure of it:
a hurricane is about to burst.
Three minutes to go
to the time arranged
for the appointment.
Philip Lehman combs his hair
stares at himself in the mirror
forces a smile
for at the meeting of all the banks
it was decided that the real enemy is panic.
Smile, then.
Goldman has to smile.
Lehman has to smile.
Merrill Lynch has to smile.

As much as possible:
smile.
There's a whole America quaking with fear
the fear has to be stopped:
smile.

How can you write down in a diary
that the hurricane is on its way
and you just have to smile?

Philip Lehman combs his hair
stares at himself in the mirror;
behind him
hung on the wall
the plaque on which is written
THANK YOU, MR. LEHMAN.
There's a knock at the door.
Here we are.
"Enter!"

Bobbie comes in, shuts the door
sits down in front of his father.

Philip swallows.

Bobbie coughs.

Philip crosses his legs.

Bobbie looks down.

Philip loosens the knot of his tie.

Bobbie scratches an eyebrow.

"I'm listening, Robert."

"Pardon me?"

"Tell me. And don't spare me anything."

"What exactly do I have to tell you?"

"About the bank, about the crash, about our position."

"With all respect: we could ask Arthur."

"Your cousin will of course be consulted. Later."

"Later?"

"I'm listening, Robert: it's your turn now."

The clock on the wall: deafening.
Bobbie takes a deep breath.
Philip intertwines his fingers.

"The situation—if I understand it correctly—is this:
of our subsidiaries, twelve have declared bankruptcy.
The investment funds are at zero.
We have lost eight times what was expected.
The stock market is paralyzed
J. J. Riordan shot himself last night
and the Bank of United States has declared bankruptcy.
This is what I've been told at least."

Philip stands up.

He takes two steps to the right, one to the left.

Bobbie pulls out a handkerchief.

Mops his brow.

Folds it.

Puts it back in his pocket.

Philip pours a glass of water.

The clock on the wall: deafening.

"I'm listening, Robert: your forecast."

"My forecast, Dad?"

"Your forecast."

"I don't exactly know."

"Try."

"The state—according to Herbert at least—
will blame the banks for the crisis.
Many will fail, they won't stand the blow
also because businesses are already starting to close.
If businesses close they won't give back the loans
and without money from the loans, the banks will go bust."

"Is it possible that Lehman Brothers will fail?"

"I've no idea . . . I hope not, fingers crossed."

The clock on the wall: deafening.

Philip cleans his glasses.

Bobbie bites his lip.

"Go on."
"Go on where?"
"Go on."
"Herbert says they'll let the first banks
go under without lifting a finger:
the state has to let it be seen that it's not helping us."

"May I give you some advice, Robert?"

"Some advice, Dad?"

"Which you can ignore, if you prefer.
I think it's in our interest
that some banks close.
They'll give the feeling that the chaos is at its peak
but from then on it will seem like a past memory.
This is why my advice is not to help banks in difficulty:
if they ask for loans from Lehman Brothers, you say no."

"Me, Dad?"

"The state will do the same:
and it will say they were rotten apples.
From then on, however

I believe
the state will need to have strong banks
that can stand on their own feet
for without banks there's no recovery.
So I'm convinced that
if Lehman Brothers survives the first month
they won't pull us down, and you'll come out of it stronger."

The clock on the wall: deafening.

Philip looks out of the window.

Bobbie starts coughing
feeling himself almost suffocating.

His father, however, carries on:

"The banks will no longer be free:
the state will want to control you
they'll impose rules, regulations, limits.
A few months from now the economy will come to a standstill
unemployment will grow
the system, Robert, faces paralysis.
You're ready for all this, aren't you?"

"Me, Dad? I don't think so."

"But it won't last forever.
The crisis will last three, four, maybe five years."

Philip looks out of the window.

Bobbie bites his fingernails.

The clock on the wall: deafening.

Bobbie stares at his father, standing there.

Philip looks out of the window.

Bobbie loosens his shirt.

"Dear Robert, it's up to you to save us."

The clock on the wall: deafening.

Bobbie stares at his father
and seems to see him holding a sword
with which he is about to strike him
on the sacrificial altar.

He looks hurriedly out of the window:
there is no angel hurtling down
at the crucial moment to stop the killing of a son:
the sky outside is gray,
cloudy and deserted.

The angels are all up there, if anywhere,
ready to open the floodgates.

And indeed
at this very moment
it starts to rain.

> The angel said: "Do not lay your hand on the boy. Now I know that [. . .]
> you have not withheld your son, your only son, from me."
> Genesis 22:12

12
The Universal Flood

The rain is pouring
down the sign
HUNGARIAN LAMPS
that hangs above
the bare brick frontage
in this Hungarian corner
of Manhattan
where a ten-year-old runt
with cheeks like two melons
tries selling workshop remnants
to passersby.

He knows how to get by, for sure.
Surreptitiously he takes
all that gets thrown away.
Then he writes a price on it
and
unbeknownst to his father
resells it as though it were new:
there he is, on the sidewalk.
Today he's been there for hours
with his umbrella
but no one has stopped.
No one wants to buy
when it's pouring with rain.

The rain is also pouring
down the metal sign
PELOPONNESUS
in this
slightly Greek
corner of Nebraska.

So much rain
has never been seen,
or at least in these past ten years,
ever since Georgios Petropoulos
became American
and even changed his name
so the Ku Klux Klan
would not set his place on fire.
George Peterson: sounds better.

His son Pete
doesn't cry anymore.
He's growing up.
Does his homework
sitting at the restaurant counter.
His exercise books have a slight reek of oil
but who cares
since his father
has decided to make him learn math
doing the kitchen accounts.
How much I spend.
How much I earn.

Ingredients.
Oil olives bread spices.
Takings.
Morning evening lunch dinner.
"So Pete, how are we doing with the takings?"
"I've done it, worked it out
yes sir
yesterday we earned 40 dollars
35 if we allow for electricity."
"You're sure about that, Pete?"
"Of course I'm sure
and I reckon today
we'll earn 10 dollars less
as there are usually less customers
each time it pours with rain."

That's right, it's pouring with rain.
A procession of black umbrellas
fills the street outside the courthouse
where Irving Lehman enters each morning.
Today a murder trial awaits him:
a worker has killed an industrialist,
shot him at the door of his office
after the factory had closed down for good.
Irving makes his way through the crowd
his dark overcoat drenched with rain:
"Judge Lehman!" someone shouts
"Another verdict against the starving?"

Irving doesn't stop: he's used to it,
he carries on walking
avoiding the puddles
toward the court entrance.

"Judge Lehman!" a journalist calls
"Do we have another case like that of Freddy?"

Irving shakes his head.
The case of Freddy had been a nightmare for months:
a jobless man had asked for a loan at a bank
and when it was refused he set himself alight.
Freddy's family

had sued the bank
knowing full well they had no hope.
But some cases catch public attention.
And outside, in the street,
when Irving read out his verdict
there was almost a riot:
"In the name of the American People
the finance institute is acquitted on all charges,
as it has committed no offense."

"It's no surprise your name is Lehman!" they had shouted from a
     window.
And on that day too it was pouring with rain.

There are times when the trees
even lose their leaves
under exceptional downpours:
the water sweeps them away in its fury.

Herbert Lehman is thinking precisely this
as he looks out of the window
of the party headquarters
at the gray sea that has upturned itself above their heads
and is now pouring down relentlessly.

The man sitting in front of him
however
is expecting an answer
and Herbert doesn't like to keep him waiting:
"My name is Lehman, certainly.
But this isn't why I'm here to defend the banks.
Indeed, I've always had my doubts.
But now, with great respect:
don't you think it an unprecedented move
to decree the suspension of all finance?"

The man sitting at the table cleans his glasses:
"I have in mind just a three-day halt:
we will stop the system, turn off the engines.
Then switch them back on from cold,
and see whether everything restarts."

*"The fact remains that no government in history
has ever cut the power supply to the banks,
not even for three days."*

*"In that respect, dear Herbert,
no government in history
has ever found itself in a crisis like this.
I'm of the view we have to stop,
catch our breath
and start again with entirely new regulations.
For it's clear that nothing can stay as it was.
This, after all, is what politics is about:
it gives a name to moments of transformation,
it understands what to end, what to continue, and what to begin.
What do you think?"*

Herbert nods, and returns to his seat:
"You can count on me, Mr. Roosevelt."

At One William Street

the water pours down endlessly as well
flowing like rivers
over the windows of the third floor.

Behind those panes of glass
are three rooms—practically identical—
with *Director* written on each door.

Arthur Lehman is sitting in the first on the right.

For him the universal flood has been a harsh blow:
the rainwater has drenched the banknotes
and the value of the $7.21s has visibly shrunk.

Now, driving around New York,
Arthur can no longer see joyous crowds of $7.21s
but lifeless processions of $5.16s
whose apathy is no surprise:
Arthur has had to synthesize the value Sadness (S)
through a complex formula
which depends on the sum of

Projection for the future (P_{tomor})
and Possibility for the present (P_{now}),
all conditioned by a factor WW (Wealth and Well-being):

$$S = WW \cdot (P_{tomor} + P_{now})$$

Certainly, Arthur has discovered,
it's not so true that sentiment has no place in banking:
there's an underlying arithmetical function
that connects
Enthusiasm (E) with investment (I)
and the Great Depression is the proof and the result of it.

When will this deathly dullness end?
When will we stop bumping into glum-faced ex-customers
who are so ungrateful to those who did their best for them?

There.
Ingratitude.
This is something Arthur cannot accept.
To see old Lehman fund holders
who now—if they spot him—cross to the other side of the street.
Is it acceptable? To insult a mother? .

Arthur Lehman
—as we know—
has never been a man of easy character.
But after long years of that neurotic torpor
which often afflicts mathematicians,
a disturbing impetuousness
has emerged in him with the great crisis.

Nothing new, the family felt:
after all, as a boy he had always been a devil incarnate
the one who sat himself in the front row of the Temple with his
    teddy bear,
so what's so strange,
given that all of us
sooner or later
show traces of what we used to be?

Perhaps.
But after yesterday's incident

his brother Irving has given him a severe reprimand
due in part to his position as a judge.

The fact remains
that Arthur showed no restraint
and let himself—so to speak—get carried away.

And okay, the banks are in a difficult position,
but there's always a limit.

Mr. Russell Wilkinson, in short,
had been a loyal customer until 1929:
holder of three funds and hundreds of shares,
he was the son of a certain Teddy Perfecthands
(with whom it seems, at one time, we had some dealings in cloth).

A smart guy, in other words,
if the measure of smartness can be applied to finance.
What's more
he was also a decorated war hero
having lost half a leg
in the legendary attack at Argonne.
He therefore used to wear
a wooden prosthesis
from his knee down
later upgraded to tough modern plastic
after Lehman Brothers
had financed polymethyl methacrylate.

Well.
Under an unprecedented downpour
seeing dear Russell limping along the sidewalk
and without an umbrella
Arthur
told the driver to pull up beside him
offering to take him home or wherever he preferred to go.
The rest is history.
Not only did he refuse the offer
but after years of loyal banking
he spat out the words *"I won't travel with someone who has ruined me!"*
at which
Arthur
could not contain an animal instinct:

he got out of the vehicle under the storm
and grabbed the lapel of Wilkinson's coat
shouting like a lunatic:
"*You nasty lout, filthy cripple, war hero wearing my boots,*
so it's now the bank's fault, is it?
Who gave you refrigerators, electric toasters, and irons?
Who gave you jobs in factories?
Who gave you the automobile parked outside your house
and the gasoline to drive it about?
Who gave you the radio in your sitting room? And the music?
And the telephone on the wall? And the tobacco you smoke?
And the coffee you drink?
And even the medal you wear on your chest, who do you owe that to?
To me, to the one who financed the battle! Me! Me!
Because if Lehman hadn't opened the faucet, you know what?
You wouldn't have had your lovely war!
And I tell you what: this leg is mine,
I paid for it with my money!"

And under the wall of rain
bright red
he grabbed hold of the artificial leg
pulling it clean off
and placing it under his arm
as if it were a French baguette.

Only the intervention of two policemen
brought him back to himself
and stopped things from getting any worse.

"*A pathetic scene, for you, for the bank, and for the family.*
You'll all end up in court, and don't go looking for me there."
said Irving,
now running for chief judge.

This was the climate, though.

Made no easier, as well, by the trio of directors.

For next to Arthur's room
there were now two: Harold and Allan
both promoted to directors.
Their vote counted half each

as though they were just one.
As, indeed, they were.

The move to such a high position
at a truly difficult moment
had a remarkable—and somewhat unexpected—effect
on the two young men.

As proof of the fact
that each individual reacts in their own very personal way
to the particular circumstances of the time,
Harold and Allan
were in no way inhibited
by their new appointment
but instead
had brought first of all
a burst of cheer:
America had lost its drive?
Fine: they would restore it.
America had lost its smile?
They would bring it back.

Not an easy choice.
For it just so happened that neither of them
was so marvelous at good humor,
indeed they had always distinguished themselves
for a somewhat fierce approach.

But the team spirit demanded a sudden about-face:
the wheels of hope
had to turn again
since only the hopeful will spend.
Enough then: there was no alternative
like it or not, it was time to smile.

The two Lehmans
armed with umbrellas
thus mounted a military campaign:
they had to fight to the bitter end
with the weapons of optimism.
And who cares if it wasn't the right moment:
someone had to start somewhere.
And that someone was them.

There again
with money you can achieve a lot, if not everything.
So could the two Lehman bankers be taught to laugh?

All they needed was an expert.
They were, after all, the sons of a rabbit
who had been converted into a cobra
thanks to a fitting education.
Onward.

"You, sir, have been called here
as an expert in your sector."
Harold began, most professionally,
sitting at his desk
beside his brother who was nodding:
"At a historical moment of great gloom
we are anxious to understand
how exactly
and where
you learned the technique of being so amusing."

Buster Keaton didn't answer there and then.
He merely rolled his eyes
hoping that such a gesture—so loved by children—
might ease that atmosphere of formality.
A vain hope: the two remained glacial.

All he could do then
was to attempt a brief outline of the art of comedy,
the basis of which—in his view—
was that some people were naturally funny
and therefore endowed—so he said—
with a miraculous form
of innate talent
that cannot be taught.
"Exactly the same, gentlemen, as your own talent for business . . ."
He hoped the compliment might soften the blow.
But there wasn't any need
because the message had arrived loud and clear:
that they had no chance
with those faces like sheriff's deputies:
comedy was not for them.

It went no better, the following day,
with Mr. Chaplin.

This time it was Allan who spoke,
careful at the outset to overcome
the obstacle raised by his fellow comic:
"Since you have stated
in public several times
that the art of comedy is not a gift but a craft
would you tell us what is the way
—if not to say the practice—
that makes it possible to get people to laugh?"

These words seemed to fall at first on deaf ears.
Then they saw his face turn languorous,
assuming the features of his character Charlie,
and wearing this mask
the notion was still no simpler:
to produce even the hint of a smile
he had to seem a victim, not an executioner.
Mr. Chaplin sought to explain in a roundabout way
—he hadn't the courage to say straight out—
that it was difficult
for a millionaire banker
to inspire sympathy.
All the more after the 1929 crash.

Nor did he admit that in his next film
the main characters were a factory worker and a young girl
exploited by an inhuman system.

Their last hopes were Laurel and Hardy
and here they started off more promisingly
for the simple reason
that the two had misunderstood the request
thinking that they'd been called up
to bring a minimum of gaiety
to a bank on the verge of collapse.

They therefore began, as they sat there,
to perform a couple of slapstick routines
complete with tumbles and pirouettes.
Very funny, for sure.

But would Harold and Allan ever go so far?
Transform themselves from bankers into clowns?
Go about with skittles in their pockets?
So that not only did they fail to smile
but—incredibly—they glowered.

Then the idea, set off by a bolt of anger in Harold:
"In the end we'll just have to pay to make them laugh!"

In actual fact . . .

They were diabolical, the two of them.
And this has already been said.
But is this case they were doubly so.
So they set about financing
on a continental scale
from El Paso to Seattle
a whole variety of competitions:
"THE BEST SMILE IN OHIO!"
"THE MOM WITH THE BIGGEST SMILE IN ARIZONA!"
"THE BEST JOKE IN MISSOURI!"
"THE FUNNIEST WORK COLLEAGUE IN IDAHO!"
"THE HAPPIEST CHILD IN MISSOURI!"
"THE MOST COMIC GRANDDAD ON THE MISSISSIPPI"
"CHAMPION OF CHARM IN KENTUCKY!"

As if to say:
if it was so impossible to make the two Lehmans laugh,
perhaps instead their name could bring a smile.

And at a moment such as this
with the level of poverty sky-high
America was packed everywhere
with competitors desperate for money
ready to produce the most terrifying grins
in the hope of winning a check from the bank.

The one who isn't laughing at all
however
is the third and last director.

For the last room
at the end of the corridor

—that once belonged to golden Philip—
is where his son, Bobbie, now sits.

Immobile. Glum.
Staring at the window
where the rain pours relentlessly.

He has no time to lose:
in his head, now,
there's just a cussed Ark.

> *Noach was six hundred years old
> when the floodwaters covered the earth.*
> Genesis 7:6

13
Noach

It's easy enough to say *"an Ark."*
An Ark
that floats on water
that doesn't sink
that stays up up up, on the waves.

An Ark.

Why does Noach have to build an Ark?
It's fine to save humanity
it's fine to survive the flood
but why on a boat?
Bobbie Lehman hates boats.
He much prefers airplanes.
That, yes, would certainly be fine:
to save Lehman with a fleet of airplanes.
Not boats: airplanes!
Those belonging to his friend Juan Terry Trippe;
those that cross the length and breadth of the skies;
those that Bobbie doesn't even need to see:

as soon as he hears them dart through the air
he shuts his eyes
smiles
"Pan Am: that's ours."

After all, Bobbie loves airplanes more than anything else.
He adores them.
Since an airplane gets you off the ground
an airplane takes you far away
an airplane leaves everything behind
it flies you off, up there
it lets you forget everything
—*"bye, Bobbie!"*—
it flies you off, up there
a thousand miles away
—*"bye, Bobbie!*—
it flies you off, up there
the airplane divorces you from the earth.

There, exactly.
Divorce.

For Noach, the patriarch, yes, he had to save humanity
—no small thing—
but at least he had a family.
Bobbie, no sir.
Bobbie has a battlefield at home.

Ruth is not prepared to play the patriarch's wife.
Ruth wants to play the patriarch *herself.*
Or, if that's really not allowed,
she wants to give a hand in building the Ark.
To climb on board when all is finished?
Certainly not.
To stay in the drawing room watching the rain?
You're kidding.
She's not keen on the idea of her husband having to save the world
and returning each night saying: *"the Ark's coming on nicely."*
"It's coming on nicely, sure, and I'm standing here like a statue!
I'm warning you, Bobbie, I'm getting bored!"
"You'll know everything, all in good time."
"When?"
"When everyone else knows."

"But what do you take me for, Bobbie? I'm not like your mother."
"You didn't even know my mother."
"But it's just as if I had: always at home, silent and out of the picture."
"Just calm down!"
"I'm worth less in here than an ornament!"
"Ruth . . ."
"Be careful, Bobbie, be very careful:
I'm thinking of a divorce."

A hard life, that of the modern patriarch.

It's no simple matter
to save humanity and your marriage
at the same time.

Bobbie is trying, for sure.

But it's no surprise that for several months
his fingers have been constantly trembling
"have you noticed, Bobbie?"
that he's constantly biting his lips:
"are you still doing it, Bobbie?"
that there's a constant sweat on his forehead:
"wipe your forehead, Bobbie"
that his tongue is constantly sticking to the roof of his mouth:
"aren't you feeling well, Bobbie?"
and won't come loose from the roof of his mouth
won't come loose
won't come loose
won't come loose
except to say:
"why is it me who has to play the patriarch?"

That's how it is.
It's up to you, dear Bobbie.
To you and no one else, Bobbie.
So carry on, Bobbie.
With determination, Bobbie.
One day the rains will fall, Bobbie.
And then you'll see, Bobbie: the whole of humanity will say
"Thank you, Mr. Lehman!"

There.
Exactly.
There's this too.
Humanity will say:
"Thank you, Mr. Lehman!"

But which Mr. Lehman?

That's the other problem.
For Noach, the patriarch, yes, he had to save humanity
—and that already is no small thing—
but at least he had no competition.
Bobbie, no sir.

Bobbie has a couple of cousins
called Herbert and Irving.

The first has just been elected governor of New York.
The second has just been elected chief judge of the New York Court of
    Appeals.

Much admired. Both of them.
Highly respected. Both of them.

Even Ruth has asked him, in surprise:
"Aren't you pleased, Bobbie?
You Lehmans now have a bank,
a governor, and a chief judge!"

Yes.
All called Lehman.
Maybe King George V of England is a Lehman too.
And why not, even Pope Pius IX.

While Noach Lehman is building his Ark
all the world's most powerful men
at the same time
have to call themselves like him.

Otherwise saving the world would be simple.

Now, not a day passes
without Bobbie finding at least one cousin in the papers

with headlines in block capitals:
ROOSEVELT AND I WILL SAVE AMERICA!
WE'LL BRING YOU OUT OF THE STORM!
BELIEVE IN US!
WE'RE WORKING TO GIVE YOU A FUTURE!

It's heartening to read your name each day
and each day to repeat to yourself *"it's not me."*

LEHMAN: MODEL OF JUSTICE
LEHMAN: THE PEOPLE'S HOPE
LEHMAN: UNITED WE WILL OVERCOME THE CRISIS

And all of America
from now on
in unison:
"Thank you, Mr. Lehman!"
"Thank you, Mr. Lehman!"
"Thank you, Mr. Lehman!"

No, Bobbie, it's not you.
They're not saying it to you.
Go back to putting nails in the Ark.

Meanwhile on planet Earth
it's raining raining raining
pouring
nonstop.
And though Bobbie isn't the only one to see it
there are those who are reminding him.

For the modern patriarch
also has to deal with those that slither up beside him.
Well yes: a viper in his midst,
an enemy within.

Bobbie has three of them:
Arthur, Harold, and Allan.
Surrounding him each day.

Arthur usually confines himself to starting off
always in arithmetical vein:
"We're going under, do you understand?

I reckon we have a 20 percent chance of survival.
If I were in charge, it would rise to 60 percent.
But seeing that your father wanted you here at all costs
leaving the job of first manager to you
I would like to know:
exactly
when do you intend to come up with some idea?
But a good idea, damn it, a strong idea!
Or will you just auction us off like a painting?"

Generally, to such a cordial tone,
Bobbie remains calm
answering in a whisper *"I'm working on it."*

These words prompt an artillery attack from the two brothers:
Harold: *"Thirty-six banks have gone down, Bobbie, or didn't you know*
     that?
Allan: *"Do we want to be the thirty-seventh, Bobbie?"*
Harold: *"Goldman Sachs has lost 120 million dollars, Bobbie!"*
Allan: *"You're on the right road for doing worse!"*
Harold: *"One in five Americans has been fired, Bobbie!"*
Allan: *"Do you want to follow their example and ruin us all?"*
Harold: *"You promised us an Ark, Bobbie: where is it?"*
Allan: *"Or has it already sunk?"*
Harold: *"This Ark, Bobbie, where is it?"*
Allan: *"This Ark, Bobbie, where is it?"*
Arthur: *"This Ark, Bobbie, where is it?"*
Harold: *"This Ark, Bobbie, where is it?"*
Allan: *"This Ark, Bobbie, where is it?"*
Arthur: *"This Ark, Bobbie, where is it?"*

Noach certainly had a swell life.

It's easy to be the biblical hero
when all you have to do is knock nails into an Ark
put the pieces together
one by one
cut planks from morning to evening
hammer, file, plane
then at night
with callused hands
broken back

to go back home
and enjoy the peace.

Bobbie no.

Only Herbert's lanky son
gives him a minimum of satisfaction.

Peter has grown up to be a true sporting prodigy.
He runs, jumps, plays rugby and baseball
he's a tennis ace and swims like a fish.
And this would all be very well.
The downside is that Peter Lehman
has developed, from sport,
a tendency to be rather obsessed about scoring.
As though he's looking everywhere
for the points he has to give or expects to receive.

Peter is capable of rattling off
—there and then—
the scores for every restaurant in the district.
Gold medal. Silver. Bronze.
And down through every other placing.

Peter ranks the charm of his relatives.
Gold-Silver-Bronze.
The intelligence of the family dogs.
Gold-Silver-Bronze.
The top notes of the tenors at the Metropolitan.
Gold-Silver-Bronze.
Even the comfort of beds.
Gold-Silver-Bronze.
And the honesty of politicians (his father above all).

There.
What makes Peter such a relief for Bobbie
is that the boy is constantly crowning him as winner.
"I have the deepest respect for you" he often says.
And this, for Bobbie, is much more than a gold medal.

Then, for sure, the boy is curious.
Even amusing.
Which is no less important, if you have to work all day in a boatyard.

Peter is the only one who hands you the nails.
And if you tell him about your nightmares
he manages to see something momentous in them:

"Dear Peter, I dreamed last night that I was a great ape
and as I was about to drown
I clung to the top of a rock
but the gulls started pecking at me
so as to make me fall off."

"My goodness, Uncle Bobbie: what a magnificent picture.
Seems almost like a horror film. Just think: 'The Great Ape.'
Seriously: it would make millions."

How could anyone not like him?

Otherwise, Bobbie has an uphill struggle.

He sometimes thinks that if he went back home
and said: *"I've built the Ark: it's ready! I've saved everyone!"*
Ruth would answer as usual:
"Oh yes? I'm warning you, Bobbie, I'm getting bored!"
"Ruth, I haven't been off enjoying myself!"
"And what do you imagine—excuse me—that I've been having fun all
*   day?"*
"Today I've come to an agreement with Schenley Distillers."
"Who are?"
"Distilleries. Now that drinking is legal once more . . ."
"You want to save America by getting it drunk?"
"Ruth . . ."
"I heard your cousin talking on the radio."
"Oh yes?"
"Clear ideas, right words, firm opinions."
"I'm off to bed, Ruth: I'm very tired."
"Off to sleep so soon? I feel like a woman all by herself, Bobbie."
"Switch on the radio and listen to my cousin."
"Even your father says he's smart."

Yes.
For there's this too.
Need it be said that Noach, the patriarch, had no fathers around him?
But Bobbie does.

Of liquid gold, moreover.

A golden father always there, ready, eyes open
checking on the building of the Ark
counting the nails
saying:
"Not like that, Robert! Are you sure, Robert?
    I've put my trust in you, Robert!"
and:
"I just don't agree with what you're doing.
Be careful, be careful!
You see that plaque with the words:
THANK YOU, MR. LEHMAN?
One day you will have to deserve it!
You have to think about tomorrow, Robert!
The future is coming, the future is close at hand
like your cousin Herbert says.
Be careful, I urge you: be careful!
And in this regard
your cousin Arthur has sent me some news
which I hope is not true:
you don't seriously want to spend the bank's money
on making a film about an ape?"

"It'll be a great success."

"Do you want to save America with chimpanzees?"

"It's a gorilla, Dad."

"Robert, please!
You're running a bank, not a circus,
leave the monkeys where they are!"

"It'll be a success, it's going to make millions!"

"People are losing everything:
their home, savings, work.
And you're thinking about movies?"

"If we want the crisis to end
we have to get them away from all this stuff, Dad:
movies distract people, entertain them, amuse them.
They come out of the theater and it's all different."

What Bobbie hasn't told him
is that movies distract not just people
but also help patriarchs.

Noach, for example, often goes to see them.

Incognito, of course.
Sitting in the back rows.

He has even sat at the very back
to see his latest production.
And with great enthusiasm.

But a patriarch, after all, gets tired at night
You can't pretend you're made of steel.

And so
sitting in the back row
Bobbie lifts the lapels of his coat
and allows sleep to take over.

He dozes off.

And affected for sure by the movie on the screen
in his dream, he sees another film, of quite a different kind.

14
King Kong

RKO Radio Pictures
and
David O. Selznick
present

a film by
Merian C. Cooper and Ernest B. Schoedsack

Fay Wray

Robert Armstrong
Bruce Cabot
in

KING KONG

Opening shot:
in a soft-lit New York in the 1930s
a self-important
quick-tempered
irascible
documentary director
called Arthur Lehman
is desperately roaming the workers' districts
hungry for new stars to bring to public attention
to fend off disaster.

He is talking to his agents Harold and Allan
who have him by the scruff of his neck:
"We're going under, you understand?
We reckon we have a 20 percent chance of survival.
If I were in charge, it would rise to 60 percent.
But seeing that your father wanted you here at all cost
leaving the role of director to you
we'd like to know:
exactly
when do you intend to come up with some idea?
But a strong idea, damn it, a really strong idea!
Or will you just film us in the raw as if it were a documentary?"

"I'm working on it" Arthur replies
and goes out on the street desperately searching for a goddess
when she appears, there, on the big screen:
beautiful, blond, vaguely German.
"Your name, Miss?" the director stammers.

And she: *"My first name is Bank, and my surname Lehman."*

"Miss Lehman, have you ever thought of doing a movie?"

"No, never. But if you're offering me a job, I'll say yes:
help me, I beg you, out of this crisis
I'm going to end up bankrupt."

"I'll make a star of you, Miss Bank Lehman."

Stirring music.
A battered boat is sailing on a stormy sea.
On board Arthur, the director,
is searching for a mathematical formula to prevent it from rolling.
Miss Lehman studies the film script
and asks a Hungarian sailor: *"Where are we sailing to?"*

"We're going to Skull Island, Miss Lehman:
it's not marked on any map . . .
But if you buy a table lamp from me
I'll tell you a story . . ."
"Something frightening?" she asks, looking afraid
while she pays the Hungarian 7 dollars and 21 cents.

"Oh yes: that mountain there, it seems,
is ruled by a monster like no other."

This would already be enough to frighten the girl,
but the ship's captain,
an old man with teeth all of gold,
now gets up to speak:
"I don't agree with any of this enterprise.
That monster is more like a god than a mortal being.
Careful, men: be careful."

"But we'll all die like this!" shrieks the future movie star
who is greeted
with laughter from behind:
it is the boat's cook, Herby.
"Tell that to Arthur: he won't listen to you!
The problem here goes deep down, Miss Lehman:
he would kill his own mother just to make some money.
There's nothing democratic about this thirst for movies."

"You'll all end up in court, and don't go calling for me there"
adds a cabin boy, peeling potatoes.

Dramatic music.
The ship filmed from above
approaching a reef
and dropping anchor.

The crew is gathered at the bow
around the director who is working out distances:
"We're here! It's my island! We'll make a great film, I can feel it!"

Distant sound of drums.
Miss Bank, the director, and other members of the crew
are walking in the jungle:
snakes slither between their feet
there are insects everywhere
and dense vegetation.

The sound comes ever closer.
Arthur signals to the others to crouch
behind a rock:
a group of natives in jacket and tie
are celebrating a ritual
in front of a high wall.
He wants to film them:
"Silence! No one move!
This is the famous Wall-Street tribe
bloodthirsty, cruel people
known for their human sacrifices.
Even if I have to die
they'll be in my film!"

Arthur starts filming.
When suddenly the natives catch sight of him:
"Let's get out of here! To the boat! To the boat!"

Next scene: anxious escape.

It is now night.
On board the ship, calmness seems to reign.
Miss Bank Lehman is taking some fresh air on the deck.

Sinister music.
The outline of three natives at the waterline
climbing up from a raft.
They seize the girl by her arms
hold her mouth shut
tie her with a liana
she struggles, now a prisoner.

"They've taken Miss Lehman!" a voice shouts
but now it's too late.

Rolling of drums.
Before the great wall
Miss Bank Lehman has been tied to a totem pole.
The Wall-Streeters dance in a frenzy
beating time with sticks
in rhythm with *"Up!" "Down!" "Up!" "Down!"*
Close-up of the terror-stricken eyes of the girl.

An ominous sound interrupts the dance.
Then silence.
Then a deafening roar.

Rockefeller the witch doctor strikes a gong
and a colossal figure
appears from behind the wall:
"King Bobbie! King Bobbie!" the Wall-Streeters shout
while Arthur and other armed men
jump out from the forest
all shooting at the gorilla
who rushes toward them:
"Careful, men! Be careful!" shouts the golden captain.
"That monster is a dictator" the cook yells as he shoots.
"To court! For trial!" the cabin boy murmurs before dying.

There's great chaos: bangs, shots, gong, blood
until King Bobbie gently picks up Miss Bank
and carries her away from the chaos.

"Leave my Bank alone!" Arthur shouts.
"You have no right to take her away from me, you monster!"

But his voice is lost in the wind.

Next sequence:
in the gorilla's den
where a Goya and a Canaletto can be seen on the wall.

Despite his loathsome appearance
the great ape doesn't seem so cruel.

He looks at Miss Lehman sitting on a rock.
He is intrigued by her fair complexion
and by such blond hair.
He and the girl seem so distant.
But she senses something:
"Can you understand me? My name is Bank, you Bobbie . . ."

Animal sounds in the background:
a dinosaur appears, covered with scales
blood over its teeth
and "1929" tattooed between its eyes.
It flings itself at Miss Bank, wants to devour her,
but King Bobbie seizes it by the neck,
they fight madly
until the gorilla pulls off its head:
Miss Lehman is safe once more!

Romantic music.
Bank thanks the furry Bobbie,
gives him a timid caress.
The great ape sheds a tear:
for the first time there is someone who understands him.

Sudden explosion of a grenade:
the gorilla responds in fear
"Ah, I've found you! Let go of my girl!"
Arthur yells from the top of a palm tree.

King Bobbie runs to attack him
but falls into a trap
giving out a desperate cry:
he tries to break free
but the gases have already dazed him
and the chains hold him tight.

Next scene.
New York, a month later.

King Bobbie has become a circus attraction:
on display in chains
under the banner
"The one who DIDN'T GIVE US AN ARK"
and visitors flock there in the thousands
to the joy of Harold the producer:

"This ape is big business so long as it lives."
and his brother, Allan: *"Even when it dies: we'll sell its fur."*

Children are especially delighted.
Particularly a little Hungarian boy
who goes back to the movie theater every day
since he has 30,000 dollars in his pocket.

During the usual performance
however
the press flashlights
send the gorilla into a rage:
he breaks his chains
and in the stampede
he goes out into the street bringing horror and death.

"Don't destroy my city!"
shouts the ship's cook
who meanwhile has become governor.

And King Bobbie would really like to destroy everything
except that in front of him is
Miss Bank
gorgeous and affectionate.
He closes her in the palm of his paw
and climbs up
to the top of the Empire State Building
where he is attacked
by a patrol of air force planes.

Before he collapses, fatally wounded,
King Bobbie has time for two last gestures:
first he gently puts his Bank
safely on the ledge
then, in fury,
he grabs
one of the airplanes that have attacked him.

The gorilla looks at the biplane:
it's a DH.4 fighter-bomber
inside which
behind the machine gun
is a woman soldier from Illinois
who is shouting *"If you kill me, I swear I'll make you pay for it!"*

So that King Bobbie has no doubt
and rips the plane in two as though it were paper.

After which he slumps down, and dies.

End credits.

A triumph.

15
Melancholy Song

When a bathtub is full
you pull the plug
and it empties in an instant.

This is what happened with the Universal Flood:
at a certain point *HaShem* pulled the plug
and the water drained away.

Bobbie the patriarch
—it has to be admitted—
successfully saved the business.

Okay, the Ark might not have been a transatlantic liner,
and, if only a raft, it managed to stay afloat
without letting in water.

"On board I refuse to row"
was Harold's comment
to which Allan added: *"And I refuse to fish."*
Finally Arthur:
*"Even the sharks have taken pity on us.
If I were you, Robert, I'd thank them most sincerely."*

And in that bathtub
to keep the passengers happy on the voyage
Bobbie
had even installed

a couple of televisions.
Cathode tubes.
Brand-new.
Designed and produced by Mr. Du Mont
who had assembled the first model a year ago
in his garage at home.
A radio with pictures.
A movie theater in every house.
And then who knows what else: sport, music, newsreel . . .

"Be careful, son! Be careful!"
Arthur has sent me some news
which I hope is not true:
do you really want to spend the bank's money
on financing televisions?
You want to bring Mickey Mouse into people's kitchens
at a time when they have nothing to eat?"

"Everyone wants one at home."

"Are you sure, Robert?
You want to save America with dancing girls?
Be careful not to make any false moves
I've put my trust in you, but you have to deserve it."

"There'll be a television in every home, Dad:
Ruth and I already have one."

Well yes.
Unfortunately.
It was a great mistake to give Ruth a television
since she has grown attached to it
and stays glued to it all day:
"Have you seen, Bobbie? Herbert's on TV: he's in Germany!"
"If I were him I wouldn't have gone."
"But what the heck are you saying?"
"I don't like this Hitler."
"He's not in Germany for that squirt!"
"Ah, no?"
"Herbert is carrying American greetings
to democratic Europe."
"Isn't it enough for him to run New York?
Does he want to be governor of Berlin too?"
"You're jealous, I reckon."

"I'm going to bed, Ruth, I'm tired."
"So soon?"
"Goodnight, Ruth."
"I feel like a widow, Bobbie."
"Console yourself with my cousin on television."

Then fortunately
the water level slowly dropped
and here we are again with our feet on the ground.

Strange thing to walk on land
after you have almost forgotten it.
What a shame there's nothing but mud, everywhere.

Once he is out of the boat
Noach takes stock of things:
he had climbed on board with a wife
and leaves in perfect solitude.
Not because she has drowned at sea:
while the waters were covering the earth
the patriarch
yes sir
he had to divorce too.

On board the Ark, after all,
they had a cousin who was a judge:
"It will be a long negotiation, Bobbie:
alimony, benefits, provisions.
Ruth wants a lot of money.
And I know she has written about you:
she describes you as insensitive, hostile, and heartless.
You'll end up in court, and don't go looking for me there."

In short
Noach, according to the Torah,
received at least an ounce of gratitude
for returning everyone safe and sound:
they didn't write stories against him.

There it is: divorce.
And just as they were mooring
there was a headline in *Fortune*:
GOLDEN SEPARATION
BETWEEN RUTH LAMAR

AND GOVERNOR LEHMAN'S COUSIN

What can you do?
The whole of America will read about it.
Even customers in that Greek diner
and workers in the Hungarian workshop.
Even the ushers in Irving's court
and his convicts in jail.

Is this why Bobbie can get no peace?
Around him, he can no longer bear the noise.
In the United States, now, there is too much clatter:
jazz bands play in the streets
you no longer have a chance to think
without four musicians
filling your brain with *so-re-mi-so-la-fa-do*.

How beautiful was the silence of the sea.
How splendid the splash of rain.
What peace in the Great Depression.
Today it's all music
and music is making the world reel.

All the more
since as soon as *HaShem* has emptied the bathtub
what popped out
was no longer the old planet Earth.
There was another world.
Unrecognizable.

Workers who were demanding contracts.
Women who wanted a job.
There were even Greek cooks
and Hungarian craftsmen
who sent their sons off to study economics.
In universities.

Arthur Lehman is at the point of going crazy.
He too hates songs (SG)
since they stop him from reasoning (RG):

RG < SG

How can you apply algebraic formulas
if you always have Duke Ellington (DE) pounding in your ear?
How can you calculate the life of a bank (LB)
with Ella Fitzgerald (EF) who never keeps quiet?
They're always winning:

$$(DE + EF) > LB$$

And the effect on Arthur is terrible.
He tries to concentrate, but how can you?

Especially
now that this damn Roosevelt (†)
has got it into his head to save the workers (WO).
He doesn't care about the banks
he's not bothered about finance:
he's only interested in the workers.

Herbert has made his choice: he's sticking with him.
But however strong fraternal bonds might be
there's no lack of friction.
Every day.

Exactly.
The further complication
is that directors can no longer argue in peace
without the chubby singer of the moment
taking up position between the two rivals
softening them with her melancholy love songs:

*"Herbert, do you realize you're
in danger of exploding the whole
system? You're really going too
far! Too many rights is a serious
mistake!"*

*"When slavery was abolished,
my dear Arthur, they said
exactly the same thing."*

*"Slavery was an abuse, let's
make that clear: are you
comparing negroes in chains
with workers on assembly lines?"*

*Caress me, my baby!
Break my heart, I accept it from you.
All my fears are water vapor, maybe!
Remember, my dear, that I fell in
love with you
and every blade of grass seems to
be golden!*

*Tell me nothing could ever
separate us,
hug me, my dear,
and sing me a sad song
like la-la-la-la-la
Break my heart, I accept it from you.*

"There are iron chains and
invisible chains, but they're
inhuman all the same."

"And this, coming from you?
You who wanted to confiscate
my bed when you were ten? You
and that friend of yours are
turning workers into nabobs,
it's intolerable! There's even
talk of paid vacations: are you
crazy? An employee doesn't
work and I have to pay him?
You'll bring American industry
to ruin."

"American industry is
dependent on those who work,
not on those who exploit them:
paying for more labor protection
means earning less, but it's
fairer. And that's fine by me,
even if it appalls you: that's no
matter."

"A ban on laying off, ban on low
wages, everything controlled,
everything taxed. The end for
companies, end for capital. Is
this the New Deal? The old
way was better, it cost less!
Be careful, Herbert: you're
destroying Lehmans."

"What are you trying to do?
Threaten me? Should I feel
guilty? Why, tell me. Why do I
stop those like you throwing a
sick worker onto the streets?"

"But your surname is Lehman!
Lehman! Lehman! Lehman!
Lehm . . .

Break my heart, I accept it from you.
Break my heart, I accept it from you.

I dedicate to you the whole book of
my tears,
and my window is a sea of
melancholy:
look at the moon as if it were my eyes!
Because I could not live without you:
please, hug me, my dear
and sing me a sad song
like la-la-la-la-la
Break my heart, I accept it from you.
Break my heart, I accept it from you.
Break my heart, I accept it from you.

Repeat my name, dear treasure.
I will be for you like a warm coat:
never stop to whisper your love,
because, without feeling, I could die
please, hug me, my dear
and sing me a sad song
like la-la-la-la-la
Break my heart, I accept it from you.
Break my heart, I accept it from you.
Break my heart, I accept it from you.

When I get sick, stay close to me.
Give me your hand, and I'll
keep close.
Never leave me alone, even in jest,
please, hug me, my dear
and sing me a sad song
like la-la-la-la-la
Break my heart, I accept it from you.
Break my heart, I accept it from you.
Break my heart, I accept it from you.

I repeat your name, to never forget it:
in that sweet sound I find out who
you are!
Tell me, please, you write my name
on the clouds,

At this point Arthur stops: he
opens his eyes wide and with
an ostentatious gesture like
Tito Schipa brings both hands
to his chest.

Herbert knows his brother,
knows how he loves dwelling
on his feelings of guilt:
"Thanks for having reminded
me: I sometimes forget my
surname. I think that you,
at the age of sixty, might
start reasoning, rather than
shouting. Don't you think,
Arthur? . . . Arthur . . . ? . . .
Arthur . . . !"

so the sky makes me a pillow!
And now hug me, my dear
and sing me a sad song
like la-la-la-la-la
Break my heart, I accept it from you.
Break my heart, I accept it from you.
Break my heart, I accept it from you.
Break my heart, I accept it from you.
Break my heart, I accept it from you.
Break my heart, I accept it from you.

Break my heart, I'll die happy
if my killer is you.

Oh yes.

Oh yes.

16
Einstein or the Genius

The idea of running the bank
in the sole company of Harold and Allan
has passed only briefly through Bobbie Lehman's mind,
not touching down at any airport:
it has come and gone
with a wave of good-bye.

And not because he spurns blood ties.
The point here, if anything, is the real risk
of it ending there, in blood.

And so, more out of defense than anything else,
Bobbie has opted for a drastic move.

After all, in all honesty,
aren't revolutions and coups
happening thick and fast throughout the world?
Lehman Brothers can be added to the list.

Therefore
though Dad Philip has been ranting for three days,
Bobbie has decided: a twofold strategy.

In the first place, we'll let some fresh air in.
New air, clean air.
And so
lanky Peter Lehman, son of Herbert,
arrives in the control room.
He'll take the position of director
together with Bobbie and those two hotheads.

"Peter? . . . Are you really sure, Bobbie?"

"Peter, of course. Where's the problem?"

Okay, he's barely twenty,
but the boy
has already proved himself a wonder:
King Kong has earned millions
and we wouldn't have done it without him.

What's more, an example has to be set for the new generation.
If we don't do it, who will?
Movie stars?
Mr. Humphrey Bogart has publicly complained:
they're giving him nothing but gangster movies to do.
Over the last few years he has sat more times in the electric chair
than in a dentist's chair.
And he has clocked 800 years in jail.

Our Peter, on the other hand, he'll surely be a paragon.
Sport.
Clean face.
Values and principles.

And then, let's admit it:
Bobbie hasn't forgotten
how he used to say *"I have the deepest respect for you."*
So everyone keeps quiet: Peter is promoted.

But that's not all.
His strategy goes further.

And here the problems arise . . .

Let's open the doors.

From now on we'll have a *Board of Partners*.

"You want to bring outsiders into the bank?"
"Yes, Dad."
"You want to give control to people who don't have the name Lehman?"
"Yes, Dad."
"And maybe not even Jewish?"
"Yes, Dad."
"I don't agree one inch with this lunacy."

The marvelous power of forty-year-olds:
to smile at a father who's taking you to task
making it clear to him it's a waste of time.

And then, to fly off to Japan:
now that they're taking over the whole of Asia,
it might be a good idea to bow before His Imperial Majesty.

The world is now the size of a golf ball.

And these new partners, they're well aware.
They fly up and down the planet
representing themselves and Lehman Brothers
because the partners
—quite simply—
are those
who have put
so much money in the bank
that a piece of it is theirs.
A percentage.
A slice of the cake.
Paul Mazur, John Hertz, Monroe Gutman
and a dozen others
—*"no Lehman blood"*—
shareholders
businessmen
—*"no Lehman blood"*—
called in
invited in

because a bank is a bank
and it wants capital.
Forget family!
Forget surname!
Forget exclusivity!
Are we or are we not
an international bank?

Our spirit now is modern, practical
uncompromising
we don't get excited
we follow just one principle
and it's a percentage.

Even the reforms of the Democrats
—labor protection, old age, sickness—
we have transformed these
in our own way
into a mechanism that makes millions:
you want to be sure of a safe future?
LEHMAN BROTHERS PENSION FUNDS.
You want to keep smiling whatever happens?
LEHMAN BROTHERS INSURANCE COMPANIES.
And: Health Policies
Family Cover . . .

On half of American roads
great billboards have appeared
at the top of which
are the words *Lehman Brothers*
like a protective eye
over the photo of a mother and child.
Both, of course, smiling.

The smile is everything.
Harold and Allan had already understood this
and have become obsessed about it.

This is why neither of them
has grieved in public for Uncle Arthur:
"If Lehman Brothers is betting on its smile
how can you then be seen in tears?
It's a rotten publicity strategy."

Exactly.
Publicity strategy.

The two Lehmans
have publicity in their blood.

They have even sent
their respective wives
to go canvassing
in the smartest stores in the top districts
praising
the Bank's pension funds
out loud.

Never mind that it's hardly normal
in a Manhattan jewelers
to hear two smartly dressed ladies
discussing such uninspiring matters:
"My dear, I haven't seen you looking so content for some time."

*"That's because I know that if I get incapacitated one day
my bank will pay me an allowance
and this makes me feel so happy."*

"Oh how marvelous! I bet it's Lehman Brothers!"

*"Yes, of course: my sister is insured with the Goldmans
but she would only get put in a home: I want the best."*

"I'll go tell my husband straightaway."

"Tell him that a good future is priceless."

As a first step into the age of marketing
it was a little clumsy, though not so bad.
Amateurish.

But the fact remains
the two brothers are improving by the minute.
And this is why
the new Lehman Brothers partners
sitting in black chairs
around a glass table

don't miss a word
when Harold and Allan
spell out the bank's new *Talmud*.

All are there except for Bobbie, who has gone to England.

It is Allan who starts, in cordial tone:
*"Friends, today I'd like us to consider
the meaning of the word* trust.*"*

Harold writes TRUST on the blackboard.
Allan continues:

*"Trust, my friends, means sharing something.
Sharing something important
namely our own protection.
If I trust someone
I accept that this someone is sharing my struggle
namely the battle for my well-being.
The battle for my existence.
Where every one of us is terrified of being alone."*

Harold writes SOLITUDE on the blackboard.
Allan continues:

*"If I trust someone
I believe him to be my ally
and I don't doubt for one moment that he is."*

Harold writes ALLIANCE on the blackboard.
Allan continues:

*"But above all, gentlemen,
If I trust someone
I stop doubting him
I curb an instinct that we all have,
namely suspicion."*

Harold writes SUSPICION on the blackboard.
Allan continues:

*"Because human beings have a need
—a strong need—*

for allies in whom they can have total trust.
So as not to feel completely alone."

At this point Harold puts some marks between the words:

SOLITUDE → ALLIANCE → ~~SUSPICION~~ → TRUST

Allan continues:
"If we transform trust between people
into trust for a product
we will obtain much more than new customers:
we will obtain people
who have no doubts about us."

The Lehman Brothers partners
like this argument.

And lanky Peter also likes it
and stands up to shake the hands of his cousins:
"I have the deepest respect for you both."

And all this approval
is somewhat surprising
since recently
Harold and Allan have taken to storming out,
slamming the door, right in the middle of meetings.
They never agree on anything.
They stand up in unison
as if triggered by a spring in their seats
and one of them (in turn) exclaims
"In that case, good-bye. Enjoy your disaster, gentlemen.
We're leaving the bank: we're quitting."
And they leave.

This time no.

The hymn to trust
went down so well at One William Street
that the Board gave the two brothers
a clear mandate:
we'll do whatever it takes to buy public trust.
We'll invest in publicity
let's do it immediately.

All the more since they have founded Standard & Poor's:
a whole building
full of employees
ready to tell the world
who is trustworthy
and, if so, for how much:
Standard & Poor's
like a thermometer
thrust under the arm of the economy
to tell the world
if you're Class A
if you're Class B
if you're trash
if you're in default
in other words stinking market garbage.

There was no time to lose.

Harold and Allan, meanwhile,
set to work.

Forget about wives roaming smart stores:
they had to establish tomorrow's army.

And they found their generals
—believe it or not—
in the provinces.

Valiant, armed to the teeth.
Sensational.

Mr. George Einstein and his wife, Jenny.

A seemingly likable husband and wife from Minneapolis.
In reality two armored tanks.
Mrs. Einstein a middle-aged woman
hair always neatly set
a chocolate-box smile
and an expression—let us say—very cordial.

Mr. Einstein a man with a full head of graying hair
an all-American smile
and an expression—let us say—very cordial.

Mrs. Einstein, a housewife.
Mr. Einstein, a clerk.

Morning kiss on the forehead.
Car parked in front of the garage.
"See you this evening darling."
"See you this evening honey."

Working week.
Sunday barbecue.

And all went normally, very normally,
with laundry in the machine, washing on the line,
vacations booked, mortgage to pay,
Christmas tree, a tear shed every now and then,
apple pie, turkey for Thanksgiving . . .

Until . . .
Until Mr. and Mrs. Einstein
came to realize.

They opened their eyes.
And they saw that . . .

. . . her friends:
Mrs. Phelps, Mrs. Bowles, Mrs. Tippy, Mrs. Adrian
and his colleagues
Mr. Petty, Mr. Harris, Mr. Perth
all of them
were copying them!

Whatever each of them said over dinner
they all did the following day.

Whatever each of them happened to suggest
they all immediately agreed: *"Yes, it's true! That's right!"*

So that Mr. and Mrs. Einstein
began to ask themselves:
"If we put this thing to some small advantage, my dear?

"I think we have a natural gift, Jenny: let's make use of it!"

Minneapolis was full of door-to-door salesmen
selling everything.

They just had to be taught . . .
how to persuade.

Their first pupil was Billy Malone
son of Claretta Malone the church organist.
Billy rang the doorbells of Minneapolis from morning to evening,
selling hand whisks.
Mrs. Einstein sat him down in the kitchen.
She told him to explain more or less how they worked
and having done so:
"Can I have a go?
I'd like to try selling them.
If it goes well, I'll give you the profit."

She called her friends, all those on her block.
The living room was full: she in the middle.
And . . . Billy Malone had to order
another six packs of whisks
to meet the demand.

The second pupil was Leo Bradson:
his tins of canary-yellow car paint
sold like hot cakes
after Mr. Einstein happened to mention it one Sunday morning.

When Einstein Promoters celebrated their thousandth customer
Mr. and Mrs. Einstein were happy to record their experience
as pioneers of modern publicity.

Harold and Allan
were immediately struck.
Those two had a blinding smile.

With a few well-chosen words
they would have persuaded a rabbi to buy a mosque.
"We have brought you our Handbook, Messrs. Lehman"
they said, putting a pamphlet on the table.

And here it was, their *Talmud*:

THE EINSTEIN TEN RULES OF PERSUASION

NUMBER ONE
Always use positive expressions:
don't say *"This will relieve your sufferings"*
but *"this will improve your health."*

NUMBER TWO
Behave like the person you want to persuade:
imitate the way he moves his hands, his head, the way he talks.
Be like the customer, and he will accept what you say.

NUMBER THREE
Whatever you are selling, say you have a limited number:
your listener will want to be one of the few and will pay attention.

NUMBER FOUR
Always pretend that selling is like giving:
your listener will want to give back, and will buy from you.

NUMBER FIVE
Even if the sale hasn't yet been done, smile as though it has:
your listener—nine times out of ten—will be persuaded.

NUMBER SIX
Don't pause, don't hesitate, speak clearly:
whatever you say will be more convincing.

NUMBER SEVEN
Dress well, smartly and attractively:
whatever you say will be more convincing.

NUMBER EIGHT
Look your customer in the eyes, don't look down:
whatever you say will be more convincing.

NUMBER NINE
Always be cheerful, friendly, lighthearted:
whatever you say will be more convincing.

NUMBER TEN
Never show that you want to be believed
because that's the one point that everyone will believe.

"Gold medal"
Peter Lehman mouthed, wordlessly.

As for Harold and Allan, they looked at each other in amazement:
that professor of the same name
in the newspapers
was certainly no smarter.

And they were hired.
There and then.
To fight a nuclear war.

17
Golyat

Maybe it's the success of *King Kong*,
which everyone's talking about.

But Bobbie often pictures
a horrifying monster
not attached to a skyscraper
but to the lightning conductor of One William Street,
just a few feet above his head.

Sometimes he can't avoid the temptation to lean out, to check.

He seems to hear strange noises coming from the roof.
Like a woman's cry.

And if he closes his eyes
the scene is always the same:
the monster roars in a strange language
(between Japanese and German),
while the girl is shouting distinctly:
"Save me! Only you can do it!"
Bobbie then arms himself with a slingshot
and five smooth pebbles,
aims at the monster from below

with all his strength
draws back the slingshot and lets go
but the stone drops there, not even a yard away
then he recharges the slingshot
aims from below
pulls back and lets go
but the pebble breaks into pieces
and once again
once again
still
in vain
Bobbie trembles
sweating
his tongue stuck to the roof of his mouth
he shouts, shouts, terrified
shouts for the girl to jump down
immediately, now,
for the monster is mad
and
Bobbie shouts, he shouts louder and louder
"Jump down, Ruth! Jump down, Ruth!"

Ruth.
Second wife.
Same name.
Married without letting too much time go by.
For *HaShem* saw
that Adam wanted a companion;
he created her from his rib
and said that it was good.

Ruth Owen.
Already married.
With three children.
Very good family.
Her mother an ambassador.
Her father a party member.
"All our family are Democrats, Bobbie, did you know that?
And we adore your cousin Herbert."
"Ah, that's nice."
"Am I mistaken, or do your lips sometimes tremble when you
    mention him?"

"With excitement."
"I reckon they'll make your cousin Herbert a senator."
"And why not president?"
"Maybe."
"I really hope so. I'm going to sleep, Ruth."
"Are you jealous of your cousin?"
"Goodnight, Ruth."
"I could never have a husband who doesn't admire Herbert."
"Pardon me?"
"I'd divorce him, with not a second thought. But there, look: they're
    interviewing him on television."

The TV is broadcasting too much politics.
If Bobbie had known, he wouldn't have put capital into it.

It would be better if there was dancing.
Or sport, without the slightest doubt.
There's always something to learn from sportsmen.

Jesse Owens
has won more medals than a general.

And in these last Olympics, in Berlin,
in front of the Führer,
he had the gall to beat a German.
So that, instead of awarding him his prize,
Adolf Hitler
turned heel and went home.

That's what is meant by the weight of a medal.

Maybe it's coincidence
but Peter Lehman's contribution
to the future glory of the bank
is growing day by day.

And on the Lehman Brothers podium
there's already a place for the lanky youth.

Not only does the boy avoid being distracted
by his sentimental Olympics,
where blond, brown, and red heads

are classified quite separately
and *"the important thing is not to win but to take part."*

More interesting
is that Peter the beanpole
develops intuitions worthy of a champion.
Is it perhaps the finer aeration of the brain
half a yard higher than the average?

Indeed, the athlete beats all records
even in terms of smartness.

There was proof of this
when Bobbie, his all-time sponsor,
questioned him on a vital matter:
in such a worrying time as this
when Europe is about to blow up again
what can a bank like Lehman do
to encourage people to invest?

The threat of a new world war
is like a weed killer on the lawn of finance:
those who have money keep it hidden
those who haven't, they don't go looking for it.
In short, the world holds its breath.
And if you tell it to risk
it seems you're being rash.

What's more,
chaos reigns in the American mind
and no one understands anything anymore:
now that the King of England has abdicated
to marry an American woman
not a day goes by when others
in Europe
lampoon us.

For a bank that wants to control the world
it's not a great moment
if the world is about to reignite.

"What we need, Uncle Bobbie, is a fine band of heroes.
But not normal heroes:

they're okay for ordinary times.
When everyone starts getting really scared
then we need heroes with superpowers."

Gold medal, Peter.
Perfect reasoning.

Superpowers are the only hope.

At this time when no one trusts anybody
what better than to launch a proclamation:
the gods of Olympus have come down among us
ready to fight for the human race.

A reassuring message.
A wonder drug.

Sure, a few adjustments need to be made.

Let's get rid of Olympus, let's invent a planet.
Something like—I don't know—Krypton?

And no crowns of laurel or thunderbolts of Zeus:
that's just schlock.

Bobbie read a long piece only yesterday
in the *New York Times*
about a German book.
Written by a philosopher, an eccentric.
His name, anyone's guess.
Talked about a superman
with extraordinary powers.
Isn't that just what we need?
We'll call him Superman.

And many thanks to Peter.

Excellent. Let's get going:
Operation Comic Strip.

Superman forever.
Superman for America.
Superman saves the world.

Finance for its artist
finance for its inventor
finance for its publisher:
to fill the whole of America with a new monument
and to carry this success story into every home
what better than a child's schoolbag!
Superman has to get in everywhere:
he'll be every grandma's grandson
the darling son
the passion of every woman
the model for every child.

A shot of trust in comic strip format.
A shot of optimism:
Superman keeps watch over us all
never sleeps.

Better even than Jesse Owens,
Better even than Clark Gable:
we'll take the best of both
and by blending the ingredients
we'll make our own Achilles.
Or better still: we'll make our King David
who fights Golyat
and grounds him with a slingshot.

Thanks again to Peter:
what is Golyat other than a fiendish monster,
other than the bloodthirsty Enemy?
Golyat is Nazi, Bolshevik, Japanese
Golyat marches the goose-step with clenched fist
Golyat has Adolf's mustache and the eyes of Hirohito.
And yet, however terrible he might seem,
Superman was born to defeat him.

With what?
With the biblical sling?
No sir: the sling of Krypton
for King David
mustn't face the slightest risk
of losing the fight:
a superhero is only a superhero
if he never loses to anyone in the world.

So Lehman Brothers
finances a paper superhero.
Superman is our weapon
to put American fears to rest.

Sure:
sometimes a banker is easily impressed.

It's a design flaw of the human machine.
But the banker
in addition to this
feels an age-old sense of omnipotence.

Bobbie Lehman
who grew up with ten biblical prints
hung above his head
has—let us say—identified rather too much.

First with Noach.
Now with King David.
A sort of patriarchal psychosis.

So Bobbie
having ditched the boat
has now taken up the shield of David
and in his hand a kind of sling.
To learn to kill, this is what we want.
Better than the Ark.
Especially now
especially now
when it might have stopped raining
but hailstones have begun to fall.

There's a big difference
between raindrops and hailstones.
For rain soaks
but hailstones hit, wound, kill,
hurled down from the sky like pebbles
and in an instant
they've destroyed Pearl Harbor.

That's what the radio news has said.
They've heard it in a Greek diner
and in a Hungarian workshop.

Bobbie is beside himself.
Now feeling it his mission
to save the world,
there's no difference now
　　between King David and the heir of Krypton:

END OF EPISODE

18
Technicolor

Peter Lehman, it must be said,
has always been a romantic kid.

What he lost in terms of looks
due to his disproportionate height
he gained—so to speak—in gallantry.
And it was, all in all, an acceptable compromise.
Not just for him but for the other party.

From his very first overtures
in the yard of the Jewish school
he has proved himself a real champion of courtship
worthy of the podium in many a competition:
he is showing—moreover—the first signs of a talent that is natural
unmistakable
and sometimes so clear
as to be recognized even by the boy himself
who quickly makes it his project in life
in the same way that a love of fire is translated into *"I'll be a fireman"*
a love of the sea into *"Call me admiral"*
and so forth across the whole gamut of possible occupations.

While Bobbie at the age of ten
had no doubt in saying *"I'll be a jockey"* or *"I'll be a painter,"*
Peter
would put on his most radiant smile
each time he had a chance to declare *"I'll be a fiancé."*

And let no one dare to point out
that it really wasn't a job:
he would bristle like a professional proud of his qualification
and the most he conceded was: *"Then I'll be a husband"*
to the joy of passing moralists.

The latter, moreover,
found him to be a true paragon:
he was about eleven years old
the first time he told his mother

"I'd like to present my in-laws to you."
And apart from the laughter it prompted,
the problem was that he wasn't joking:
however precocious he might have seemed,
he really was busy with plans to marry
a girl three years younger
who answered to the name of Lisette Gutman
and was—it seems—much sought after by numerous rivals.
Peter however
had competed like a true athlete,
winning the gold medal.
And therefore *mazel tov*!

He had even written
in her exercise book
the terms of the marriage bond
including the assurance of many children
(with eye and hair colors
in homage to the genetic future).

In short, a serious commitment.
Signed and sealed.

Incidentally, it seems that young Lisetta,
behind her pigtails,
concealed the impressive shrewdness
of a budding businesswoman:
and having heard Daddy Gutman making
who-knows-what remarks about her sisters' dowries,
knew full well that every marriage has its commercial aspects
and required Peter to make some kind of advance.
The exact sum was never discovered.

Then—as we know—love moves on.

And after about a month the union was dissolved.
By common consent, it seems,
according at least to what Peter announced at home
with a small terminological error: *"I'm a widow, now."*
A beginner's mistake.

But from there on
he made an impressive ascent:

like a kid who moves on from jumping fences
to real athletic contests
Peter Lehman
underwent a healthy training
to educate his mind and muscles
for the obstacle course of the fair sex.

One of the most difficult sports.
For it demands complete commitment:
control of the eyes (expression is crucial)
control of the mouth (in various circumstances)
control of the hands (mostly to restrain them)
control of the feet (since lovers take long walks)
and above all
a firm mental control
for sometimes it takes only just a word
to destroy years of labor.

The road is tough, often uphill:
no more nor less than a decathlon.
And the athlete so often becomes lost.

Despite this.

Peter, for his part,
was certainly not complaining:
results so far were encouraging
he felt he had achieved
that particular romantic touch
that is the mark of sportsmen:
a fitting blend
of physical looks and noble values.

With this approach, yes,
the medal collection was growing
but without Peter ever boasting:
his code of sentimental conduct
included a dedication to loyalty
and honest service in the ranks of the god of Love.

His case, however, was strange.

Because this coming and going of girlfriends
can be seen as appealing below the age of twenty,

after which it raises questions:
in the great season of courtship
Peter was rarely unworthy of the podium,
yes, but then?
The Olympic flame then finally went out too soon
and it was always the girls who ditched the champion
though never with hard feelings
always with a smile
always on good terms
almost as if, for one like Peter, it were impossible to think of worse.

None of them ever complained of any lack of kindness.
On the contrary.
The essential point, if anything, was the opposite:
so tall and sturdy in appearance,
Peter
turned out in the end to be too soft
so much in love with the female soul
that he could never raise the slightest resistance.
Every desire was a duty.
Every remark a written law.
Every blink of the eye interpreted as an order
to be obeyed forthwith.

It seemed in short that the boy
was caught in a strange trap:
a bold competitor in the contest between the sexes
yet as soon as he had the medal in his grasp
he transformed the adversary into a referee
and from then on
avoided all confrontation.

Well
if Peter Lehman had been a twenty-year-old
not now
but fifty years ago,
then half the girls in America would have risked anything
to win the jackpot.

Unluckily for him, however, this was the 1930s.

And since the notion of man and woman
changes over time like a flag in the wind

Peter soon had to face up to
a very real fact:
he didn't match with the ideal American man.

Or rather, to be exact:
he didn't match with the male movie star.
He realized this, as often happens,
quite suddenly: and dramatically.

His girlfriend at the time
was Helena Rosenwald.
And Peter had decidedly underestimated
the girl's enthusiasm
for these new western movies.
Then the moment came:
they found themselves in the family living-room
on a snowy December afternoon.
From the next room came the notes of a piano
played most romantically by Aunt Adele.
What better surroundings for a loving idyll?
Peter was about to give his best
with a passionate declaration in verse
when Helen looked at him perplexed:
"You're not going to pull out a poem?"
After which
having grasped straightaway that this was exactly his intention
she jumped to her feet as though stung by a tarantula
and
having pulled his arms around her waist,
she commanded in no uncertain terms:
"Oh Peter: go as if you're about to kiss me
and when you're on the point of doing so, change your mind,
push me away and go off to herd the cattle."

"But there aren't any cattle in the house, there's only Aunt Adele"
was Peter's reply
which brought an immediate end to the engagement.

And at last, everything was clear.

That evening
Peter lay awake in bed
brimming with hateful thoughts about the family bank:

it was all because of Lehman Brothers
—if not, who else?—
that the mechanism inside the American female brain
was now so badly stuck.

Couldn't they have stopped at the gorilla?
He had been no problem.

But what had followed
—if the whole truth be told—
had devastating social consequences:
by filling the big screen
with John Waynes and Clark Gables
a whole generation of potential husbands
was gassing itself.

A sad end to romantic love.
A marble tombstone for the tender man.
American women
from Anchorage down to Florida
yearned unanimously
for the brutal, scowling, aggressive man.
The man who whispers? Better if he whistles.
The man who kisses? Better if he spits.
The man who understands? Better if he snaps.
The man who embraces?
No sir
a thousand times better if he grabs you by the arm
almost ripping your dress.
Years and years of good manners
swept away by a dozen movies.

It was serious.
It was very serious.

As if no less than the American Constitution
had suddenly been thrown into the pulping mill
and people were proclaiming: *"New rules for everyone!"*
It's not so simple:
it takes time to adjust.

Yes.
With the support of Lehman Brothers money

the new romantic comedies
were destroying the whole idea of settled couples.

The man, from now on, has to be rugged
even better if he's a cowboy.

She, from now on, has to be confused
psychologically unstable
always on the brink of laughter or tears
tormented by several lovers at the same time
and unfailingly inclined to suicide.

Peter pondered the question carefully.
Hadn't they always told him
that the bank was working for the good of America?
There was a risk of a whole childless generation.

And so
leaving serious consideration of the bank's cinematographic strategies
to a future occasion,
Peter Lehman
in the meantime
drew up an emergency plan
if only to stop him winning any more medals in vain.

They wanted movies?
Then movies were what they would get.
In the end, all he had to do was follow their example,
      however much he disliked it.

What Uncle Sigmund had learned with 120 rules
Peter learned through movies:
by watching and learning
watching and repeating
trying to copy even the gestures
imitating frowns, half smiles
and why not? Even the way they spoke.

So word got 'round in New York
that a strange spectator was roaming the theaters.
In a notebook
he jotted down the actors' lines
and sometimes even repeated them out loud: almost identically.

Did he have to stoop so low?
Fine invention, radio.
Rotten idea, movies.

It didn't take more than a couple of months
to turn Peter Lehman
into a perfect mix of American movie stars.
If you watched carefully, you could catch them all
more or less without exception.

And it was in this new vein
that he decided to deal with his latest flame.

A very tough cookie.

She was Peggy Rosenbaum
a girl of undeniable charm
no doubt a disciple of the cinematographic cult
and known throughout the Temple
by no coincidence
as "the double G"
not because her father ran General Gas,
but for a striking resemblance
as chance would have it
to Greta Garbo.

Peter was madly in love with her.
And to judge at least from the language of her eyes
the diva didn't seem exactly indifferent.

So Peter took the fateful step.
First he propped himself against the Temple door
and when the service was over
lowered the brim of his hat
lit a cigarette
furrowed his brow
looking so perfectly like Clark Gable in *Dancing Lady*.

As she was leaving
in the midst of a crowd of reformed Jews
she immediately picked up the reference
drawn as if by a magnet
sidled up beside him with cinematic passion.

And then:
since movies fortunately now had sound,
from Greta Garbo she became Joan Crawford
stealing her line *"Do you find me so beautiful?"*

"Beauty can never be too much."
Peter replied plundering from the script of *Sylvia Scarlett*.

She put on a deep voice:
"Don't fool yourself: I'm a no-good woman."
(and here she copied Marlene Dietrich in *Blonde Venus*)

He smacked his lips:
*"I reckon you were made for love, and love's the only thing you should care
    about."*
(it was *She Done Him Wrong*)

She brushed a hand through her hair:
"Love's a waste of time, something I only believe in every other day."
(and in saying it she looked just like Lana Turner in *Dramatic School*)

He stubbed out his cigarette with his shoe:
"But no one can live alone, darling: it's really not worth the trouble."
(this was *Woman of the Year* with Spencer Tracy, seen the day before)

She covered her eyes, and with a husky voice
"Oh yes? Do you hate yourself so much as to love me?"
(in crying scenes she always imitated Bette Davis in *Of Human
    Bondage*)

He gave a hint of a smile:
"Honey, I've done myself much worse alone than in company."
(it was *Apache Caravan*, though out of context)

"I'm showing you my good side . . ."
she scoffed, quoting Mae West in *I'm No Angel*
and letting him complete the quote:
"If you showed me your bad side, well, maybe I'd love you more."

The partnership was working well.
To crown it all
they challenged each other to a last quick-fire exchange from movie
    love scenes:

"Dear friend, life is so short, and you're wasting time with me?"
"Girl, death lies in wait across that river, if you leave me here."
"Pardon me if I cry: life has given me nothing."
"The two of us, honey, we are two lost souls."
"How many hearts did you break before you took mine?"
"The women I've had? They all die in your eyes, seeing you dance."
"If I think about the pain I can cause in men . . ."
"No one, kid, has ever died of love."
"London would be so empty without you."
"You, baby, are a diamond that shines too brightly."
"The word love has such an effect on me . . ."
"Seeing you cry brings me a sense of terror."
"Maybe I'm a woman who's not worth all this goodness."
"I don't know if your heart's made of stone, but mine is rock."
"I couldn't bear to see you out riding with another woman."
"Have I ever shown you the road at sunset?"
"Tell me why you have chosen me."
"So much anger in these little girl eyes."
"I've nothing to offer you: I was born poor."
"There are more riches in your tears than in the whole of Fort Knox."
"Is it me you really love or because I'm an heiress?"
"I'd like to walk the path of life with you."
"Sorry, sorry, sorry! Oh God, I don't deserve you!"
"You ought to teach women the secret of your charm."
"Hold me tight, Jerry, like only you can do!"
"I'm a man worn down by life, I don't think I know how to love."
"I'm so foolish: could you ever love me?"
"What's love after all, if not a round of poker?"
"Truly, you're a horrid man, but deep down I love you."

There.
At this point
since it really was getting late
the idyll of the movie screening
was interrupted by Rabbi Nathaniel Stern
who had waited until now for the two stars to clear the doorway:
"The party's over, folks, I have to close up: it's dark."

The power of cinema.
For it was quite incredible
but Rabbi Stern was using the very same words
with which Fred Johnson shuts the bar in *Wild Hunt*.

So that Peter couldn't restrain himself,
and thinking the rabbi was a movie fan too
answered quote with quote:
he pretended to load a gun, spat on the ground, then
"Well, you old drunkard, shut this bootleg joint.
If those redskins come back tonight, give me a whistle:
I'll be here sleeping in the barn.
As for you, doll, sweet dreams:
anyone who follows you won't see the dawn."
And he went off leaving both of them
not by horse but by tram.

Now, apart from the dreadful letter
(though also fine in parts)
that Rabbi Stern wrote to all the Lehmans,
that evening
played no small part
in bringing together two kindred spirits
forever.

United by love, for sure.
And then by movies.
Which were not so far apart.

During the three years of their engagement
they were often seen dancing
like Fred Astaire and Ginger Rogers.

Or
Peter would take Peggy with him to the mountains
where she would sit by the river
combing her hair like Vivien Leigh
while he chopped wood for the fire
(not that he needed to: there was plenty of wood
but those ax strokes reminded her of Errol Flynn).

Finally
he asked her to marry him
and she replied just like in *She Wanted a Millionaire*
in other words, in the affirmative.

Under the *chuppah*
everyone found that Peggy Rosenbaum

was a Greta Garbo with traces of Katharine Hepburn.
As for Peter, wasn't there something of William Holden about him?

Even their baby girls
were perfect likenesses of Shirley Temple.

And when Peter appeared
for the first time
in air force uniform
Peggy's heart immediately leapt:
like on the big screen
clasping her children
she would watch Tyrone Power's plane take off
waving to him good-bye
filled with emotion—for sure—
but just as much with pride
since *"my husband, no, he's no deserter!*
And there are those who need him, there, in Europe.
Fly off to victory, my darling:
we're all so proud of you!"

Another perfect film.

To be shot in Technicolor
like the last *Gone with the Wind*
on which Lehman Brothers has staked millions
and color is quite something else:
the stories you see
appear to be so true.

So true that sometimes you ask yourself *"Did it happen?"*

Peter Lehman's widow, Peggy,
often thinks this:
her Tyrone Power died a hero, in his plane
in military action.

He leaves behind him many medals, including one for bravery.
He leaves a wife.
He leaves two daughters.

And an empty place in the bank.

19
Shiva

"He was a dear man, I'll miss him very much."

Laid out in a white casket
surrounded by flowers and wreaths
Mr. Lehman's face
has fortunately retained
a distant trace of happiness.

Many have come to bid farewell.
They enter one after the other
into the semidark room
set up on the first floor of the bank:
"So young, what a shame."
"At least he didn't suffer."
"America has lost a champion."
"Look at his face: just like his father."

A young boy, in the company of his mother,
approaches quietly:
he has tears in his eyes.
He strokes the dead man's hand
murmuring *"Thank you, Mr. Lehman,"*
after which
he lays a bunch of marigolds
on the silent still breast.

The rabbi came early this morning
and had some very fine words:
"He was a man of integrity."
Everybody nodded.
Someone added *"And great honesty."*
Broad agreement.
Someone else *"And great determination."*
General approval.
Someone else *"Enormous courage."*
Unanimity.
And the final unanimous conclusion: *"A rare person."*

Even the servants are speechless
closed up in the kitchen, around the table,
with tearful eyes and a lump in their throats.

As for the family, no one is missing.
Moments like this bring everyone together.

"In the face of death there are no verdicts."
comes the husky murmur of his cousin the judge
who is an expert on verdicts.
Then he sits down on a sofa
next to his wife, Sissi,
as ordinary as always
quietly predictable
whose essential contribution to the mourning has been an *"I am sad."*

Her brother-in-law has spoken more passionately:
*"This nation of ours owes him very much
the American people are more alone from now on
and I think I can say that all of New York
should devote a moment's thought to him:
we have lost a hero of our times."*
And in order to be here
he has delayed the opening of two roads.

Harold and Allan
for their part
are not overly upset:
there are fewer tears in them
than in the arid desert of Arizona.
Harold's greatest contribution
is to venture: *"He carried a great name."*
And Allan adds: *"He worked in a great bank."*
Then, end of transmission.

As for old Philip
what upsets him most of all
is not having foreseen it.
Companies don't like death
and this is why he seems truly upset:
*"Rest in peace, my poor Bobbie:
in truth you deserved much more."*

There.
On these words of his father
Bobbie
generally wakes up.

As if the dream always ended at the crucial moment
and reality were pressing to enter.

For some three years
Bobbie has been dreaming about his funeral
almost every night.
And a couple of times
on buttoning his night shirt
has said *"good death"*
to his wife instead of good night.
Understandable, after all.

And to think that around the world
there are those who are popping corks.
This morning for example
in the Peloponnesus there's celebration.
It's no small step:
from counting olives and capers
to graduating with top marks.
This is the step that Pete Peterson has taken.

He hasn't told anyone about his Greek blood.
"I was born in Sweden, near Stockholm."
For the world is moving, as we know,
and maybe the Aegean has swapped places with the Baltic.

In any event: the Swede has now pocketed his degree.
"Well done, my boy!"
Graduate of Northwestern University, Illinois.
And the Peterson family
can hardly not celebrate
with olives, anchovies, and cheese.

At the same moment
many miles away
a Hungarian family is celebrating too.
Among boxes chock-full of table lamps.

"Gratulálunk!" *
since their son
through evening classes
has also earned his bit of paper.
Well yes, the little frog has done it.
And now looks more like a toad
with a large stomach and cheeks like two melons.
So they can hardly not celebrate.
"Gratulálunk!"

There is joy, therefore, under the sun.

Yet those who do not celebrate
are the Lehman family.

For Bobbie may dream each day about a funeral
but every now and then
someone really does die.

Outside, in the street,
a banner has been fixed to the wall.
It says: THANK YOU, MR. LEHMAN!

They put it up this morning
at the start
of this rainy day
as dark and gray
as those faces that cross the doorway.

Relatives.
They alone.
No one else is admitted.
They have come from all America
For the Lehmans
are now spread through all America.

A crowd in the street.
Bank employees.
Wives, husbands.
Umbrellas up.
"Thank you, Mr. Lehman!"

---

* *"Congratulations!"*

The family is gathered in the house
all of them
it's good to see so many together:
young, old, babies.

According to ritual the closest relatives
should remain seated along the walls
should wait
greet
thank
and remain there all day.
In reality they won't.
The world has moved on.

Nor have they
let their beards grow,
the famous mourning beard
of *Shiva* and *sheloshim*
the uncut beard, as was the custom over there in Germany
a century ago
before those three brothers left
who now sit in picture frames
and who knows whether Rimpar
after the end of Hitler
is still standing
or has been razed to the ground.
According to ritual they shouldn't go out for a week.
No chance!
The economy isn't going to stop and wait.
There's half the world to get back on its feet
and it's all up to America:
Lehman Brothers, now
signs contracts over the whole earth
since the war has been big business
but reconstruction will be even bigger.
THANK YOU, MR. LEHMAN!
says the banner outside the window
but if everything goes as it must
next time
it will be written in ten languages
since America, after all, is a small patch of ground
and with Pan Am you can fly the whole world

and there's no place you can't reach
the power of airplanes
the power of financiers
the power of Lehman Brothers.

According to ritual they should prepare no food:
they should ask neighbors for it, receive it and that's all.
No chance!
As if the servants were on vacation.

And then if one thing is right
about the funeral ritual
it's the throwing of earth over your shoulder:
death to death, life to life
since, as they say in that great film
financed by Lehman:
"tomorrow is another day"
and the film has made millions,
so for the bank
it's a fine day all the same.

According to ritual they should tear a garment
rip it to pieces
on their return from the burial
at the old cemetery.
No chance!
Stuff of folklore
or rather, stuff of rabbis
stuff done by those Jews
who have just arrived in America:
those who escaped from Europe,
where for being a Jew they killed you in the camps.

You see them, recognize them, straightaway.
even from the way they sit in the Temple.
For if you're American, you have America inside you
and if you're European it's written all over your face.
Hungarians, for example.
People who, well, they still have the countryside in them
people who can wield an ax
and they don't eat: they devour.
They have great stomachs

and cheeks like two melons
then get to their feet
and do those strange European Jewish rituals.
The Hungarians!

Now that the Lehmans have American blood,
who remembers those European rituals?
Reformed Jews are keen to say it.
As if to say: *"we'll do things our way."*
And our way is not to tear clothes.

But the *Qaddish* yes.
They've repeated that
every day
morning and evening
the whole family
ever since mourning began.

The bank's office at One William Street
today
in spite of everything
stays open.

Yes, for chance would have it
that now at Lehman Brothers
everything is decided over Monday luncheon
where Harold has expressed the matter clearly:
"Closure for mourning would mean a two-million loss."
and Allan, immediately, to fend off criticism:
*"Which doesn't alter the fact that a Lehman has died
and the bank has no intention of ignoring it."*

Three minutes' silence.
For all staff.

No more, no less:
the whole world is watching us
America is a great enterprise
and Wall Street can't sleep
since the earth revolves around the sun
and the markets never fall dark.

As for Wall Street
three minutes of silence cost a fortune.
Flags, well, those yes: they'll be at half-mast.
Someone might even notice.

And for those who haven't:
Philip Lehman is dead.

20
Enemies Within

Bobbie Lehman remembers that horse so well.
It was called Atlas, a perfect Thoroughbred.
Atlas was born to win every race.
The strongest by far
quickest off the mark.
Each time he raced
Atlas set off in the pack
inconspicuously
but half a lap was enough
to shake them off
to leave them behind
to get into gear
to find himself alone
in the lead, Atlas
alone . . .
And there Atlas looked back
—the fear of being alone—
slowed his pace
became sad and small.
There's a very particular feeling
of solitude
when you're in the lead.

Bobbie Lehman remembers that horse.
And it is just the same
for America today
which his bank exactly reflects.

We have won the war.

We have killed Golyat.

At night we sleep soundly
and yet . . .

And yet it's so tough being in the lead.
Fear of heights.
Fear of falling.
And then . . .

Then being in first place on the podium is worse than being an
      outsider:
there's too much calm among winners.
It gets boring.

As a result, let's do ourselves some harm.

Sometimes it seems that human beings
really hate the idea of calm:
they need conflict
they need an enemy, always,
against whom they can fight.
Otherwise what's the point of living?

And now that Adolf Hitler is a past memory?
Now that the Japanese are nice and quiet?
Now that the world has suddenly gone silent?
Who can we take it out on?

If Superman doesn't have the monster to destroy
the comic strip makes no sense:
no one wants to know
how Superman uses his barbecue
or washes his new car.
Can the world really have no trace,
no remnant of a mad dictator?
Someone please step forward.
Threaten us.
Hate us.
Annoy us.

If not, we have a problem.

The prophet Ezekiel
wandered in a valley filled with dry bones.
And it was really boring.
But then they returned to life, and he was back in business.
When is it going to happen to us?

Well, there's always Russia.
As an enemy, it has to be said, it isn't so bad:
between two superpowers you can start up a pretty good fight
one of those that keeps you on your toes.
And the Chinese too: attractive enemies.
Not to mention the Koreans.
Though, there again, Asia's so far away . . .

To create a minimum of tension in life
we really need something to worry about at home.
A cobra in the bed.

Yes, that would make us worry like we used to!

The idea was thought up
by a senator from Wisconsin:
a brutal hunt for the *enemy within*.
In other words:
someone is playing a double game.
Find out who!
Sounds like a TV quiz show.

"You're strangling America!"
Herbert Lehman shouted
from his senator's chair:
"What will you invent, McCarthy,
in the hope of bringing traitors to light?
Let us muzzle all dogs
let us switch off the lights
let us impose silence
an evening curfew
and a ban on meetings!
Do you realize you'll transform the United States
into a gigantic kangaroo court

in which neighbors
bring charges against those who don't trim their hedges properly?
I just hope I'm exaggerating."

But he wasn't. Not in the least.
Who knows what his brother Irving would have said if
instead of having gone to discuss law up there with Solomon
he had seen judges jumping out everywhere.
And defendants, of course.
Terrified by the verdict.

Ah! At last
Good old healthy fundamentalism!

Harold and Allan immediately adapted
to the new climate of witch-hunting:
playing bulldogs suited them pretty well.
And gray-haired men enjoy a natural respect.
They consider themselves guardians of the general well-being
that vile conspirators are bent on destroying.

Not least because
it has taken them decades to learn how to smile
and the American smile can in no way be harmed.

So the two Lehmans see communists everywhere.
Even among staff in the bank.
Yes sir.
Infiltrators.

Wandering around the offices
cheerful but circumspect.
They listen.
They ask questions.
The mail—whatever it is—has to pass their desk.
In the dining room they listen in on every conversation.
Use of the restrooms is allowed, so long as it's brief.

And lastly, above all,
beware of what they say:
red words are hidden everywhere.

From time to time, therefore,
someone is called in:
"Close the door, Miss Reissner.
Please sit down.
Your manager Miss Stratford
has told us you've had a small accident."

"Oh Mr. Lehman, I'm so sorry
*I'd been feeling so incredibly ti**red***
and just fainted, there was nothing I could do.
*My doctor says it's my di**Stal in**testine*
*it gets swol**Len in** no time*
*though with this t**Russ I an**ticipate some improvement*
*I had eaten lun**Ch in a** hurry*
*I'd have been better with a snac**K or eating** less,*
*and to **cap it all***
*I was in such a dilem**Ma** over i**T** seeing that*
*then I was s**Tung** by a hornet.*
*I would have prefe**rred** to go home:*
*such misfortunes are **d**readfully hard to **pred**ict.*

"You're a marvelous typist, Miss Reissner:
the bank is most satisfied with your work.
But we need to keep an eye on you all.
Isn't that correct, Harold?"

Harold remains immobile:
he sits in the half-light, behind the beam of a lamp.
His role is to watch her emotional reactions
while his brother proceeds to script.

And indeed Allan resumes:
"Miss Reissner, the ribbon on your typewriter
is always running out of red ink
well before the black. Is this mere coincidence?"

"Well, of course, Mr. Lehman,
*I am always prepa**red** to do*
As I am told
and my colleague on the next desk
*refe**rred** me to a note—ju**St a line**—*
*all profits to be typed in **red***

I sta**red** at her and thought it was
at fir**St a** te**ase**
and yet she seemed most sincere
and I was mu**Ch in a** hurry
so I followed her instructions.
If you don't believe me, ask Miss Stratford!"

"Are you challenging the authority of your superior?"

"Oh no sir! I have not fal**Len in**to
su**Ch in**adequate ways, I assure you
in my last employment with a newspaper
owned by one of your compe**Ti**tors
ou**r edi**tor prepared a most c**red**itable reference
though our boss was none too kind
—have you seen a generalissi**Mo scowl**?—
redeveloping **red**undant p**red**atory p**red**ictions
offering no prospect of **red**emption
and the conditions were so insalubrious
I turned so pa**Le on** seeing
the we**T rot, sky** visible through the ceiling.
I had to leave before it **red**uced me to
ju**St a** tenth of my former self
sic**K or ea**sily prone to languor,
the root of all my intestinal woe.
May I go back to my work now?"

It is only at this point, generally, that Harold looks up:
"You are fired, Miss Reissner.
For conspiracy."

Fear of others.
It's spreading everywhere.
Especially in the bank,
Harold thinks, as he looks at the sign:
we have so many other people here inside
that we even carry them in our name:
LEHMAN **BR**O**THERS**.

21
Yonah

Bobbie Lehman
for his part totally disapproves.

Not just because he has plenty enough enemies
without searching for more
in the nooks and crannies of their conversations.

The point is that this atmosphere of threat
is becoming truly suffocating.

Bobbie feels so trapped
so hidden:
he and all America
are cut off
with no light
with no air
sealed up
inside the dark stomach of a great white fish.

It's no small matter
to find yourself in the stomach of a fish.

First because your voice echoes
like in a cave
and everyone hears everything.
There's the new matter of the lists:
packed together like sardines
we keep a watch on each other
so that
running a bank
has become the easiest part.
Before that
you have to avoid ending up on the lists
and hold your nose for this stink of fish.

"How ironic" Bobbie often thinks:
*"no sooner has America become great
than it has made itself small."*

And now he jostles about
shoulder to shoulder
in a tiny underwater space
swallowed up
gulped down
among fins, bones, and scales.

Crammed into this stomach
Bobbie Lehman—he who so adores airplanes—
simply cannot breathe.
They've even challenged his passport:
dubious financial dealings with the enemy.
All foreign contact suddenly stopped.

Bobbie has urged
all his family
to keep the news quiet:
if it leaked out, it would be the end of the bank.

A socialist Lehman conspirator.

"But who, Bobbie, you?" Herbert asks incredulously.

And at least
for once it can be said
his senator cousin doesn't know what to do.

The fact remains
of course
that Herbert's fans won't abandon him:
even though he's balding
he is a close equal to Elvis Presley.

Senator Lehman is always speaking on TV.
He speaks on the screens
that Bobbie Lehman has put in every home
which his wife, Ruth, keeps on at all hours:
"If you want to know, Bobbie,
your cousin comes across very well on screen."
"Sure Ruth, he'd do well in vaudeville."
"Are you being sarcastic, Bobbie?"
"Absolutely not: these days, if you want to end your career
either you have to conspire with communists

or pit yourself against Herbert Lehman."
"Your lip's bleeding and your hand is shaking."
"I'm suffering from acute Herbertitis."
"I can't follow what you're saying, Bobbie, I can't follow you:
your cousin's the only one who knows what to do!"
"Actually, he's told me he has no idea."
"He doesn't discuss serious matters with just anyone."
"That's right: he discusses them only on TV."
"He discusses them with us, his electors."
"I'm off to sleep, Ruth, I'm tired."
"I feel so taken for granted, I no longer know who I am."
"Turn up the sound on the television."
"You're playing with fire, Bobbie, be careful: I could file for divorce."

Luckily, tomorrow is Saturday.

Because television has taken on a significant weight
in the scales of American marriages:
conjugal peace is based first of all, yes,
on sharing the matrimonial bed
but more than anything else the sofa,
and there has to be
at least some point of agreement
over each other's TV favorites.

Now, the fact is that
apart from interviews with Senator Lehman
the only thing Ruth insists upon
at all cost
is the great Saturday night quiz show.

And what can a husband do
when he's already under threat of divorce?
Adapt to the ritual.

Bobbie therefore
is obliged each week
to sit down in front of the TV
to share with Ruth
(and with millions of fellow Americans)
the adrenaline of the *Game Show*:
win or lose?
Correct answer.

And woe betide anyone who falls asleep.

This is also why he's feeling stressed:
the enemy within, for him, is the enemy at home.

Isn't it strange how he's short of breath?
Bobbie just can't cope with it.
Rugs and fabrics
have been stripped from his office
in the search for some allergy.
Then they've taken out the wood.
Then disinfected.
Bobbie trembles, bites his lip, can't breathe.
And how could he breathe
in the bowels of a great white fish
in which everything is a jackpot?

Enough.

Bobbie knows, after all, what he has to do.

He knows he is the chosen one.
As always, after all.

He was Noach, then David,
now he'll be the prophet Yonah,
and when the fish spits him out onto a beach
—he and the whole nation—
then the sky will at last be clear and cloudless:
no longer this narrow hole
where we would die
sooner or later
in pain.

So onward:
all it takes is to think up some way
of getting yourself spat out from inside this fish.

Bobbie is trying.
He's doing his best.
But it's not so easy.
Willpower is important, but sometimes it's not enough.

In the meantime
it's not easy
to hold a Monday luncheon
inside the stomach of a great white fish.
And above all it's no joke
getting your tactics approved by a board of partners.

No matter.
Bobbie presses on.
It's an emergency.
Here you can't breathe.
Here you die.
Bobbie can't carry on looking for allergies.
The fish's stomach is ever tighter,
if he doesn't get out he'll go crazy:
"Gentlemen, we'll get out into the open air with electronics!
Mr. Charles Thornton, otherwise known as Tex
has shown me a revolutionary plan:
calculators, electronic brains, control units;
we should channel everything into electronics
—America is still doing it all by hand—
with electronics we could short-circuit everything
and the great white fish will spit us out!"
"We ought to calculate how much it costs and how much we'll earn."
"Good heavens!
We'll not earn anything
if we stay shut up in here!"
"With no projection of costs and receipts, we cannot take risks."
"Then let's look at transport!"
"If you tell us what you mean by transport."
"Mr. John Hertz has shown me
a finance plan for the rental of automobiles.
In other words: we give automobiles to those who cannot buy them.
Or trucks. Or motorcycles.
We'll fill the whole nation with people on the move:
the smog and noise on the streets will be such
that the fish will start coughing, and spit us out!"

"It doesn't seem to us like a sure-fire strategy."

"May I say something?" Harold asks
stroking his hand through the hair he no longer has.

"Instead of looking for strange routes,
I suggest we do the only thing that overcomes fear.
Namely: to make ourselves unbeatable.
And therefore to be feared.
And therefore safe."

"Can you repeat that, Harold?"

But Harold repeats nothing:
he looks at his brother, who gets up
and draws a missile on the blackboard.
With a nuclear symbol over it.

Bobbie protests:
"Are you both crazy? In that way, we won't get spat out
we'll all get blown up
together with the whole fish!"

Harold and Allan aren't prepared to argue:
"In that case, good-bye. Enjoy your disaster, gentlemen.
We're leaving the bank: we're quitting."
And they go.

Bobbie smiles at his partners:
this year alone, it's the tenth time
that Harold and Allan slam the door.

Everyone, as we know, has their own way of negotiating.
They'll return.

And in any event, this isn't the right way.

Maybe there's another much simpler route:
after all
don't the Scriptures say
that Yonah had to sing a psalm
to get thrown out from the beast?

Perfect.
After you have built an Ark
after you have killed Golyat
what's the problem about singing a psalm? . . .

Easily said . . .
Bobbie is not a man to waste words.

He never has been.

He says little
and, if he speaks, he bites his lip.
Bobbie doesn't use fancy words
he's not one of those who starts talking
and everyone falls silent.

Bobbie doesn't sit in the Senate.
He's just a banker
who likes to play the patriarch.

His cousin is perhaps the only person he can ask
for a few lessons: in oratory.
He's always a champion.

Herbert's reaction greatly surprises him:
"*You're asking me to teach you something? Today?*
I don't know either, cousin, not now.
I don't like this modern politics:
rather than ideas, they just talk about reactions.
All on the defensive, all in the trenches.
Did you know, I'm thinking of retiring soon?
I'll make my peace."

It's curious sometimes how life turns out.

Instead of feeling stronger
Bobbie also stammers now.
The more he tries to sing a whole psalm
the more his tongue gets tied,
nor do his lips respond.

True, it is written that Moshe stammered at first.
But what does that have to do with it?
Bobbie doesn't need Moshe, he needs Yonah.

If only this fateful psalm
could be dealt with like a quiz session!
It would be extraordinary, yes sir:

to answer a couple of questions
and as a prize
to be spat out!

There.
This in effect was Bobbie's final thought
before drifting off
in front of the television
sitting next to Ruth for the Saturday evening game show.

Since nature always
assists those in need of help,
Bobbie
had found his own way
of drifting off without closing his eyes.

And this, then, was the game show
he saw broadcast on his screen.

22
Saturday Game Show

Title sequence.

Hal March enters triumphantly into the studio
with his brilliantined hair:
"GOOD EVENING, AMERICA! AND GOOD LUCK!
LET'S WELCOME FIRST OF ALL
OUR BEAUTIFUL ASSISTANT
MRS. RUTH LEHMAN!"

Both Ruths
first and second wives
come into the studio.

"IN THIS OUR THIRTY-SECOND WEEKLY INSTALLMENT
THREE CONTESTANTS WILL BE COMPETING.
IN THE FIRST CABIN: SENATOR HERBERT LEHMAN.

LET'S GIVE HIM A WARM WELCOME!"

Cheers in the background.

"IN THE SECOND CABIN PLAYING JOINTLY
MR. HAROLD AND MR. ALLAN LEHMAN,
ARMY CHIEFS OF STAFF
AT THE NUCLEAR MISSILE DEPARTMENT!"

Applause in the background.

"AND FINALLY, COMPETING IN THE THIRD CABIN
MR. YONAH LEHMAN
ART CRITIC AND HORSE RACING EXPERT!"

Lukewarm response from the audience,
but that doesn't matter, we're used to that.

"AS ALWAYS, VIEWERS,
OUR CONTESTANTS WILL COMPETE
IN A KNOCKOUT ROUND
AND THE WINNER WILL GO FORWARD TO THE FINAL
WHERE HE'LL PLAY FOR THE JACKPOT!
SO LET'S GO, AMERICA!
I ASK THE CONTESTANTS TO PUT ON THEIR HEADPHONES
AND GO INTO THEIR CABINS.
THE QUESTIONS THIS WEEK
WILL ALL BE ON THE LEHMAN FAMILY.
SO LET THE GAME BEGIN!"

Music introducing the first round.

"FIRST QUESTION FOR OUR FRIEND HERBERT.
LEHMAN BROTHERS WAS FOUNDED
BY THE LEGENDARY HENRY LEHMAN
MORE OR LESS THAN A CENTURY AGO?
START THE CLOCK!"

1
2   Herbert approaches the microphone:
3   "THE CORRECT ANSWER IS LESS!"

Gong.

"AND IT'S WRONG! THAT REALLY IS A BAD START!"

Enter the two female assistants, enthusiastically:
"THE CONTESTANT DID NOT SAY *LESS*, BUT *AT LEAST*.
WE DISTINCTLY HEARD HIM."

Hal March talks with the judge, then:
"WELL DONE! CORRECT ANSWER!
THE SENATOR STAYS IN THE CONTEST!"

Trumpet fanfare.
Herbert is delighted. The two Ruths too.
Hal March clears his throat, then continues:
"SECOND QUESTION FOR HAROLD AND ALLAN:
EVER SINCE THE THREE LEHMAN BROTHERS
SET FOOT IN THE UNITED STATES
THE TOTAL NUMBER OF CHILDREN AND GRANDCHILDREN,
MALE AND FEMALE, UP TO NOW
IS MORE OR LESS THAN 70?
START THE CLOCK!"

1	
2	Harold and Allan consult each other,
3	then Allan writes something down
4	which Harold crosses out:
5	the two argue,
6	then reach agreement
7	and Harold speaks into the microphone:
8	"THE TOTAL NUMBER IS 92."

Gong.

"WRONG ANSWER!
THE CORRECT ANSWER IS 97 DESCENDANTS!"

Harold and Allan stand up:
"IN THAT CASE, GOOD-BYE.
ENJOY YOUR DISASTER, GENTLEMEN.
WE'RE LEAVING THE TRANSMISSION: WE'RE QUITTING."
And they leave the cabin, slamming the door.

Every lock of Hal March's brilliantined hair quivers:
"THIS IS NOT THE AMERICAN SPIRIT!

THIS IS NO EXAMPLE TO SET ON TELEVISION!
BUT LET US NOW MOVE TO YONAH LEHMAN.
HERE IS THE QUESTION:
EVER SINCE THE LEHMANS ARRIVED ON AMERICAN SOIL,
WHICH MEMBER OF THE FAMILY
DIED AT THE OLDEST AGE?
START THE CLOCK!"

1
2   Yonah is in no doubt,
3 apart from his tongue stuck to the roof of his mouth:
4 "IT WAS PHILIP LEHMAN, AT THE AGE OF 86."
5

Trumpet fanfare.

"CORRECT ANSWER! AND YOU TOO ARE IN THE FINAL!"

The two female assistants interrupt brusquely:
"THE POINT SHOULD BE AWARDED TO SENATOR LEHMAN,
   SINCE IT IS HE WHO PROMPTED THE ANSWER."

Hal March's face darkens:
"YOU SHOULD HAVE TOLD US, YONAH!
YOU HAVE NO RIGHT OF APPEAL!
THE RULES DO NOT ALLOW PROMPTING.
THE JUDGE TELLS ME
I HAVE TO ASK YOU A RESERVE QUESTION.
IN THE LAST 50 YEARS ALONE,
THE CAPITAL OF THE LEHMAN BANK
HAS REACHED MORE OR LESS THAN
TWENTY TIMES ITS INITIAL VALUE?
START THE CLOCK!"

1
2   Yonah hesitates a moment
3   begins to sweat
4   bites a nail
5   his hand trembles
6   he bites a lip
7   pulls out a handkerchief
8   stains it red:

9
10
11
12
13
14

"LET ME SEE:
I DON'T DEAL IN FINANCE.
SO I WOULD SAY . . .
THE CAPITAL HAS MULTIPLIED, YES,
84 TIMES."

Trumpet fanfare.

"CORRECT ANSWER!"

The assistants protest:
"THE POINT MUST BE AWARDED TO THE SENATOR,
SINCE YONAH IS AN ENEMY WITHIN,
HE'S DOING BUSINESS WITH THE ENEMY
AND THEY'VE EVEN SUSPENDED HIS PASSPORT."

Murmurs around the studio.
For Hal March this is a difficult week.
Now the senator joins in:
he has opened the door of his cabin
he wants to speak
but we are not in Congress here!
"PLEASE RETURN TO YOUR PLACE!
IF YONAH HAS BEEN DISQUALIFIED
THEN YOU GO STRAIGHT TO THE FINAL! . . ."

"I WISH TO MAKE MY PEACE, MR. HAL MARCH:
I OFFER MY PLACE TO MY COUSIN,
I'M RETIRING, I WON'T GO ON TO THE FINAL."
After which he removes his headphones and leaves the studio.

Gong. Then a trumpet fanfare, then another *gong.*
The assistants walk off in tears:
their lives no longer have any meaning.
The studio audience
hold up hundreds of posters: "THANK YOU, SENATOR LEHMAN."
Hal March joins the applause.

But the show has to be finished.
Half of America is tuned in.
The atmosphere is electric:

his brilliantine has even lost its shine.
"MR. YONAH LEHMAN, IN SPITE OF EVERYTHING
THE FINAL AWAITS YOU.
EVERYTHING IS IN YOUR HANDS:
ANSWER CORRECTLY
AND YOU WILL SAVE AMERICA.
AS ALWAYS, THE LAST QUESTION
IS THE MOST DIFFICULT ONE.
LEHMAN BROTHERS HAS EXISTED FOR OVER 100 YEARS,
AND IS DESCRIBED AS IMMORTAL,
BUT MY QUESTION IS:
A CENTURY FROM NOW, WILL IT STILL EXIST
OR WILL IT HAVE GONE BANKRUPT LIKE SO MANY OTHERS?
START THE CLOCK: YOU HAVE 60 SECONDS TO ANSWER."

1	This is the ultimate test.
2	There again, as we know,
3	a hero doesn't go into history for nothing.
4	Yonah examines the question coolly
5	or at least tries to:
6	if he replies that the family bank
7	will reach its second century alive and well
8	it will certainly be said *"he's someone who believes it."*
9	On the other hand
10	if he says *"No, I wouldn't bet on it."*
11	how could he show his face in the bank tomorrow?
12	
13	A fine predicament, damn it,
14	a fine predicament.
15	
16	And so?
17	
18	His tongue has stuck to the roof of his mouth, as if glued.
19	Drops of sweat line his forehead
20	like chisel marks.
21	
22	There's always the option of giving up
23	and going:

24	if the others have done so
25	why can't I?
26	
27	For the simple reason
28	that we aren't all the same, in the world:
29	there are those who slam the door and everyone says *"A great gesture!,"*
30	there are those who even get applause when they go out
31	and leave people in tears.
32	You, Bobbie, no
33	you're one of those
34	who when they give up
35	people suddenly start laughing
36	and after the laughter, like at school,
37	they put a sign around your neck
38	with the word COWARD on it.
39	
40	And so?
41	Do I say that Lehman Brothers will be immortal?
42	It's easily done, after all: I open my mouth and say it.
43	The real point is another: do I really believe it?
44	A century from now.
45	Halfway into the next millennium . . .
46	Sure, if I had asked my father
47	or maybe my granddad Emanuel:
48	they'd have had no doubts.
49	So why am I taking all this time?
50	A yes or a no is enough,
51	I can even take a chance . . .
52	And if I then get it wrong?
53	Who will then open the fish's jaws?
54	I as Yonah have to get out
55	so it is written
56	I am but an instrument of divine will.
57	And as such, what am I waiting for?
58	Go on, then, answer:
59	"IN A CENTURY THERE WILL BE NOTHING LEFT."

Gong.

The studio audience protests.
The two assistants return only to spit at the cabin.
Hal March has volcano lava instead of brilliantine:
"THE ANSWER APPEARS TO BE WRONG,
AS WELL AS OFFENSIVE, DEAR CONTESTANT.
YOU SHAME YOURSELF IN FRONT OF ALL AMERICA!"

And here.
It was at this moment
that suddenly
through a real sense of disgust
even the great white fish turned its stomach:
it moved inside as if to regurgitate,
and spat out
both Yonah
and the whole United States
several miles away.

And then we reemerged to see the stars.

And thus HaShem spoke to the fish
and the fish spat Yonah onto dry land.
Jonah 2:11

23
Migdol Bavel

The sign on the frontage
is black and white
linear
perfect
LEHMAN BROTHERS
long
stretching
from side to side
over the windows
of this new office

3,500 miles from New York
in the heart of Paris.

Bobbie is here to play host.

600 guests.
And he smiles, Bobbie smiles.
Not just because he remembers
when he was stuck
inside the stomach of the great fish.
Bobbie smiles because we're here in France
we're opening an office in Paris, *voilà*
here where Bobbie
when he was twenty
roamed auctions and galleries
buying Impressionists and Madonnas
—*Send money, Dad!*—
and now, here he is:
with the new office
he would have money on call.

600 guests.
The same who were here last year
at the art show dedicated to Robert Lehman,
here in Paris, at the Tuileries:
on that occasion
from the table of dignitaries
white suit white tie
Bobbie had praised the courage of the avant-garde
*"in which we sense liberation from tradition
and the caterpillar becomes a butterfly."*
Applause throughout the room.
And at the end of the speeches
a queue to congratulate Mr. Lehman
who shakes hands
greets
and kisses the hands of the ladies.

His wife is behind him:
smokes her Philip Morris
which is still financed by Lehman Brothers.
"Bobbie dear, in the New York office

why don't you set up a French café?"
"An excellent idea. Bonsoir, Madame Lefebvre!"
"I think the New York office is looking old, Bobbie."
"We can modernize it.
Good evening, Monsieur Guineau!"
"And after the café we ought to put in a restaurant."
"Sure, for work luncheons. My dear Rothschild!"
"A restaurant and a library."
"You deal with it all, Lee darling."

Lee Anz Lynn
is Bobbie's new wife.
Ruth filed for divorce last year.
Fortune magazine announced:
SIX-FIGURE DIVORCE
FOR SENATOR LEHMAN'S COUSIN.

But Bobbie didn't take it badly
because
after you've been in the stomach of a fish
you don't care too much about the press.

Bobbie now has other interests:
he's interested in the planet, all of it, without exception
he's interested in running
like one of his horses
but on a racetrack that goes from the Arctic to Antarctica.

Exactly:
here it is, the world, in front of him.
Assembled, all of it, at the new Paris office.
600 guests.
French
Germans
Dutch
Hungarians.

Hungarians?

Yes. Hungarians.
Seen here, like this, elegant
under these chandeliers

the Hungarians don't look like country folk
folk with axes and big stomachs.
But as we know: Paris casts a new light on everything.
And everything shines, under these chandeliers.

Only yesterday evening
Bobbie was in Arabia.

Forty-five million dollars last year alone
for the sheikhs' oil.
Bobbie looks them in the eye
talks about art and Arabian horses
invites the princes
onto his 144-foot cabin cruiser
moored in Long Island Bay.
This really is an Ark.

The day after tomorrow, however,
Bobbie will be in Peru
where they're digging more wells.

And from Peru, to Sumatra.
On his Boeing 707
Bobbie bounces
like a ball
from one place to another
for the world is as small
as a billiard table
and if he's playing golf today with Eisenhower
tomorrow he is drinking his cocktail
with who-knows-who in Singapore.

Breathing, breathing deeply.
The sun never sets
on Lehman Brothers' business.
The economy after all is movement: just this.
The economy is airports, hotels
and it's no coincidence
that Lehman Brothers
now finances luxury chains
and above all airplane upon airplane upon airplane
to move

instantly
armies of financiers
including
the sons of a Greek restaurateur
and a Hungarian lamp maker.

Time zones change
nationalities change
languages change
but we are always the same:
we are Lehman Brothers of Tokyo
we are Lehman Brothers of London
we are Lehman Brothers of Australia
we are even Lehman Brothers of Cuba
well yes
among communists
since who is it that trades in bananas
and
as well as bananas
sends arms and ammunition?

Harold and Allan came out with the idea
in front of the partners
at one of the various Monday luncheons.
On the wall they put up sheets of paper
with the words
     CULTURE, FINANCE, ARMS, CONTROL, PRODUCTS
and then organized them into a simple diagram:

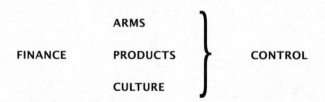

They were asked what it meant.
And they were asked politely.

But Harold and Allan thought it was already perfectly clear.
And so, as usual, they slammed the door behind them.

"They'll be back," Bobbie told the partners.

And this time he was wrong.

Because there are also times when a door really does slam shut,
above all if it seems no one understands what you're saying.

The truth is that now
Bobbie Lehman
has the world and the bank
in the palm of his hand.

Could this be why his hand is shaking?

Or could it be the dream
that Bobbie has each night?

When he falls asleep
everything at first seems real.
There's One William Street
the building where
Golyat once hung.

But this time there's no trace of monsters.
On the contrary.
A crowd of speculators
financiers
all wearing ties
and with suitcases
are queuing to enter.

Arabs
French
Japanese
Brazilians and Peruvians
all with a large sign
around their necks
with the words:
THANK YOU, MR. LEHMAN!
and this time, yes Bobbie,
incredibly it's all for you.

Ever since Herbert retired
there's no other Lehman around
to steal the limelight.

In his dream
Bobbie is in fact smiling
smiling and breathing, breathing deeply,
because he is up there
in the attic
on the top floor
where he can touch the sky
and from there he calls everyone to go up.

When they arrive up there, at the top
all wearing ties
and with overnight bags,
Bobbie raises a finger
and points everyone to the sky
meaning that if they put their cases one on top of the other
—packed full of bonds and contracts—
they can create a tower
above One William Street,
an immense tower
soaring high
and from up there, from high up,
Lehman Brothers
will dominate the Earth.

And that double-breasted army
nods in satisfaction;
each of them kneels
one after the other
and puts down their suitcase:
they form the base
then up
then up
perfectly
but when they reach the third level of the tower
there's something wrong
and
"Put the suitcase here!"
"¿Aquí dónde?"
"Über meine! S'il vous plaît."

"Pon la maleta aquì!"
"Por encima de mi!"
"ここに私のスーツケースを入れて"
"ここどこ"
"私のオーバー"
"Положи сумку сюда!"
"Сюда куда?"
"На мою!"
"把我的手提箱在这里"
"在这里呢"
"在我的"

It turns into confusion.

And each night
when the tower of suitcases tumbles down
Bobbie wakes up terrified.

He has looked everywhere for an answer:
a new—single—language must be found
for finance throughout the world.

His first attempt
was with telephones.
Millions in investment:
International Telephone & Telegraph Corporation.
Millions of miles of telephone cables
spread like rivers over planet Earth:
having filled the world with televisions
now let's fill it still more with telephones.
Communicate, *folks*!
Communicate.
And you reckon that by telephoning
we'll find a way to speak a single language?

No luck.

In Bobbie Lehman's dream
quite simply
the tower is no longer made of suitcases

but of telephones that ring
ring
constantly
and since no one
knows how to say *"get them to stop!"*
the telephones ring
ring
building up to an unbearable chorus of:
"Répondre au téléphone!"
"Выключите их!"
"Ответь на звонок!"
"Odebrać telefon!"
"彼らが停止してください"
"電話に出なさい"
"Sagutin ang telepono!"
"让他们停下来"
"接电话"

And the tower ends up tumbling down, always.

For Bobbie, another sleepless night.

So he's in a bad mood
when
at One William Street
he meets these two kids:
Ken and Harlan.
Ken aged 31.
Harlan 28.

Too young
for all the other banks.
They've asked, they've tried.
No one has believed them.
Now they try with Lehman Brothers.
Bobbie's personal office
on the third floor:
*"I don't have much time
but keep it short and I'll listen."*

"Will you say it, Harlan?"
"You start, Ken."
"I'll start, okay.

We believe in computers, Mr. Lehman.
But not the computers they're making now
those that take up the space of a whole room
and don't function unless there's cold air like in a fridge
so that those who work on them
get sick thirty times a year.
We believe in a new breed of computer.
And since we believe in it
we'd like you to finance us.
Am I going okay, Harlan?"
"Just great, Ken. But tell him about the systems."
"The systems, okay.
We believe in machines
with simplified systems,
that don't need an expert.
And since we believe in it
we'd like you to finance us.
You're with me, Harlan?"
"Perfect, Ken!"

Bobbie begins to take a liking
to these four-eyed elves.
And yet: *"I'm sorry: Lehman Brothers doesn't invest in science fiction."*

Funny how sometimes an elf
in no time at all
can turn into an ogre:
"Science fiction, Mr. Lehman? Did you hear, Harlan?"

"I heard, Ken: it's a waste of time!
Kerouac is right: death to old men!
Science fiction!
Maybe it's not clear to you, Methuselah:
we're creating a language for everyone
the language of computers
operating systems, printed circuit modules
for the whole planet Earth!
It's called 'the Future'!
And you, with those 200 years of yours,
you come to tell me it's 'science fiction'!"

And so it was that Methuselah
decided to finance

the Digital Equipment Corporation
with Lehman Brothers' money.

Not because Bobbie Lehman
wanted to spread computers across America
as he had done with TVs.
No, nothing of the kind.
Even if this was what he told the partners
over Monday luncheon
in the French restaurant
on the eighth floor of One William Street.

It wasn't quite true.

The new computer age
was opened
by Bobbie Lehman
to stop the Tower of Babel from falling down.

> *That is why it is called Babel, because there*
> *the Lord confused the language of the whole earth.*
> Genesis 11:9

24
I Have a Dream

Around the glass table
long as the whole room
in black chairs
everyone
sitting
next to each other
pen in hand
paper for notes
reading glasses
ashtrays
cigarettes cigars
liquor glasses

Bobbie at the head of the table
a full turnout
Monday luncheon
eighth floor, One William Street
all Lehman Brothers partners
sitting
in dark suits.

They don't miss a word
when the marketing director speaks
a nebulous being, with plasticized hair
whose eyes look like cellophane and his teeth of fiberglass.
But what charisma.
"Today I'd like us to consider together the verb: to buy.
To buy: what does it mean?
It means giving money in exchange for something.
This something has a value, the value is a price.
The price is the money you give me.
No more no less.
Perfect.
If you want people to buy
you have to tell them the opposite.
You have to tell them they aren't buying.
You have to tell them: 'you and I are not doing an exchange
because it's you who are winning
I'm accepting this price against my will
but nevertheless, okay, I accept it
even if—in the end—I'm losing out.'
This is what's new, gentlemen.
This is marketing.
To tell everyone that whoever buys is gaining
and whoever sells is losing.
Marketing is
to tell everyone that you're winning if you buy
if you buy you triumph
if you buy you've beaten me
if you buy you're number one.
Marketing, gentlemen
is to get folks used to the idea
that only those who buy win the war
and since we're all at war
whoever buys survives."

The Lehman Brothers partners
all sitting
in dark suits
don't miss a word
they write
nod
smile:
the Lehman Brothers partners
around the glass table,
they like this idea.

"If we can get it into the heads
of the whole world
that buying is winning
then buying will mean living.
Because human beings, gentlemen
don't live to lose.
Their instinct is to win.
Existence means winning.
If we can get it into the heads
of the whole world
that living means buying
we, gentlemen, will smash
that last old barrier which is called need.
Our objective
is a planet Earth
in which you no longer buy through need
but you buy through instinct.
Or if you prefer—to conclude—through identity.
Only then will banks
—and Lehman Brothers with them—
become immortal."

Extraordinary.
Bobbie, at the head of the table, smiles.
And when Bobbie smiles it's an event in itself.

For when his grandfather Emanuel and his brothers
founded the bank
they dreamed at most of a cotton empire
and when his father, Philip,
launched it on the stock market
he dreamed of trains and kerosene

but now
now the plan is quite something else:
here, folks, we are talking about eternal life
about giving a meaning to the world
if you know what I mean:
"I have a dream
yes
I have a dream"
and the dream is
nothing less
than immortality.

While the whole world
in these 1960s
is terrified
of some new nuclear bomb,
we Lehmans take a run-up
jump the ditch
and *voilà*
not only are we everywhere
but from now on
we will be
everlasting.

Lehman Brothers is betting on it:
"Votes in favor"
unanimous
"Votes in favor"
all sitting
"Votes in favor"
in dark suits
"Votes in favor"
around the glass table.

And onward then with the new marketing:
from now on
the watchword
is: *play-act*
yes, play-acting
pretend
that anyone can buy anything
that luxury is for everyone
that poor people don't exist

that nothing has a price
and, if it has, it's affordable
play-act
play-act
tell everyone
that every sale is a giveaway:
offers
bargains
discounts
installments
what's important is to sell
what's important is to fill the coffers
what's important is that people buy
and if Standard & Poor's
keeps the thermometer fixed under our arm
we too have a thermometer
—you bet—
and it's supermarkets.
Superstores.
Megastores.
Billboards as big as houses.
And a torrent of money that flows every day
like a sea
a gigantic
boundless
ocean
of Coca-Cola flags
red
red
red as those of Russia
red as those of China
red as the envy
that consumes
—you bet—
all of that part of the planet
under the hammer
and under the sickle
that it cannot buy
"but I have a dream
yes
I have a dream"
and it is

sooner or later
to sell to you
sell
sell
sell
to everyone
wagonloads
home delivery
without preference
without distinction
whites and blacks
no longer any difference:
we are all the same
since we all have money
sell
sell
sell
with no firsts and no lasts
with no positions
men and women
no longer any difference:
we are all the same
for we all have a bank account.
"*I have a dream*
yes
I have a dream"
and it is that all money
from henceforth
is the same
under the sun
and
more than under the sun
for NASA has asked us for money
to send a man to the moon:
"*I have a dream*
yes
I have a dream"
and it is to make money up there too.

Banker's euphoria.

What a great job to be involved in immortal matters.

Bobbie smiles:
Lehman Brothers forever.
Then he bites his lip.
Lehman Brothers forever.
Bobbie has gray hair.
Lehman Brothers forever.
But
after me
who?

25
Egel haZahav

It's true
that not a day passes
without one of our soldiers
getting killed in Vietnam
and that every day
their caskets are shown
on TV.

It's true
that John Fitzgerald Kennedy
was killed
down in Dallas
like that
all of a sudden
in front of everyone
before the eyes of the world
before the eyes of America.

And it's true
that just two weeks later
cousin Herbert
he too
died suddenly
of a heart attack.

But the fact is
that all this death around Bobbie Lehman
no longer has any effect.

Instead, it makes him smile.
More and more.

For Bobbie in the end is convinced:
now he is sure
he is quite certain
he cannot die.

The patriarchs died, yes
but at the age of 500, 600, 700
if not more
which is like saying
they too
were immortal
like the bank;
and it is right
so right
since *HaShem* cannot allow
anyone who leads a Chosen People
to die.

Is this why
Bobbie's fingers
no longer quiver?
Is this why
he no longer bites his lip?
And why his wondrous tongue
no longer sticks to the roof of his mouth?
Bobbie smiles, he smiles.

He smiles because he is 72.
What is 72 compared to 500, 600, 700?

You are young, Bobbie Lehman.
You're a kid.
And like all youngsters
you can rebel, since it's fashionable
you can do it, perhaps it's even your duty:

revolution?
Headlong!

You, Bobbie, can turn the world around
you can shake it up
tear it out of the system
snatch it
from that damned sclerotic army of old men.
Morgan Stanley is a bank of dodos.
Goldman Sachs is an open-air hospice.
Lehman Brothers no.
Lehman Brothers is a college for kids:
the youngest
is called Bobbie.

It doesn't matter if the partners
over Monday luncheon
turn up their nose:
isn't the president the boss?
So open the doors to youngsters
they'll only make us money
so
youngsters
youngsters to work
youngsters to recruit
as many youngsters as I can.

This kid
for example
who has just walked into his office
with cheeks like two melons
is barely thirty.

Those of the same age talk the same language.

He looks straight, even too straight, into the eyes:
he's an arrogant buddy,
a tough one.

After careful study, his face doesn't look so new.
But what could Bobbie have in common with a Hungarian?
And one brought up in Soho too?
Maybe . . .

But who remembers? It's so long ago.

In any event.

Big stomach
unkempt beard
the man is a lumberjack dressed as a banker:
this one beats hell out of the world
with his ax strokes.
"The surname, yes, it's Hungarian.
We're not cowards
like those who change their names.
After all, you Lehmans were German Jews, I know.
And if you were Germans
then I can be Hungarian.
Or aren't you so fond of them?
If you're not, just tell me
and I'll go.
Here in the bank you might have plenty of money
but I have plenty of ideas
and I'm not taking them to any place I don't like."
"You're a straight talker, Mr. Glucksman."
"People say you know something about horses;
so you'll know better than me
that the best horses are those that kick."
"And is this horse I have before me
looking for a stable?"
"A stable, maybe. A cage, no thanks."
"It was I who came looking for you, Mr. Glucksman
since your reputation goes before you:
it seems you're the best trader in America."
"Do you have a trading division here?"
"Not yet. But I'd like to open one
and perhaps I'd like you to run it."
"I reckon you don't know what you're talking about.
Look, those like me
they don't push a pen
they don't do gala dinners
and they don't wear cuff links."
"Then tell me exactly, so I understand:
what do you traders do?"
"We're in front of computers, Mr. Lehman
with a telephone in our ear

and another telephone in the other.
We buy and we sell shares
at the same time
on ten stock markets around the world
not just on Wall Street;
we buy where the price is right
and we sell again where there's a profit;
we move bonds and shares
several hundreds a day;
and often
we're more than willing
to arrange it so a security that's crap
garbage
looks really strong
and when it's worth double
we pass it on to whoever's fool enough.
You run a smart bank
where everything's shiny
there's a load of money and plenty of elegance:
but we do the job,
that dirty job,
where all that matters is money
and cunning.
A trading division
can earn you millions a day
but don't get any idea about putting us out on show:
we're backroom boys
and we're not into your smart ways."
"You've persuaded me, Mr. Glucksman:
when do you think we could start?"
"To build a division out of nothing
I'd need a couple of months.
I will choose the traders
all sharp guys.
And I repeat:
we can't stay here in all this plush.
Give us some other office, a place that will be our own."
"It's ready, if you wish
five minutes from here
in Water Street.
You want to see it straightaway?"

The board of partners
was not of the same view.
Not because it didn't like the Hungarian kid:
they hadn't even seen him
because on the day they were due to meet
the lumberjack had another appointment.

The fact is that the board
—all sitting around the glass table—
would prefer a rather different profile
a more respectable curriculum
someone young, by all means
but who gives us
a greater
shall we say
a greater
feeling of confidence . . .

Paul Mazur, senior partner
Bobbie's adviser
—who knew his father too—
would prefer for example
that young man from Nebraska
a certain Peterson
(apparently Swedish, though some say Greek)
who is doing well
at the highest levels:
sophisticated
reserved
well turned out
and is kept by everyone always close at hand . . .

"By everyone who?" Bobbie retorts.
"Our bank colleagues and competitors."
"In other words, a band of dodos and corpses."

Well done, Bobbie!
Morgan Stanley is a bank of dodos.
Goldman Sachs is an open-air hospice.
Lehman Brothers no.
Lehman Brothers will have a trading division
a branch in Water Street

Hungarian domain
far away from plush
far away from cuff links:
where there's quite another atmosphere
which when Paul Mazur
senior partner
steps inside
with Bobbie
old Paul almost faints to the ground:
"What's the meaning of this hellhole, Bobbie?"

But Bobbie doesn't answer, no:
Bobbie smiles.
Instead: he actually smiles.

He takes Mazur by the arm
and hauls him inside
for a guided tour inside the abyss:
rooms as large as hangars
wood and plastic tables
as long as grocery counters
and lamps lightbulbs
computer screens
next to each other
separated only by packs of donuts
the remains of Chinese takeouts
chaotic electronic whiteboards
baseball bats
boxing gloves
kids everywhere
in shirtsleeves
laughing, running
shouting loudly
waving madly
and on the ground
on the floor
bits of papers
piled up like leaves
Coca-Cola cans
ashtrays of smoldering cigarettes.

Paul Mazur
who is getting on for 80

has been talking to Bobbie nonstop:
terrified, he has been lecturing him the whole time.

And if it weren't for the fact they both have gray hair,
they might seem like a grandfather
with a naughty young boy.

Mazur carries on with the same old tune.
Bobbie nods smiling:
in fact he understands almost nothing,
for in this mad hellhole of numbers and letters
Paul's jeremiad is almost impossible to hear:

687.£.56.856.845%.37573%4975.9348.6974.58G.658326.475326745.3
7568$97.6905.4895%7647.58637.463276%765.8766590599.75i7.587
.465345.4 *"This Bedlam, Bobbie, whatever it means, I disapprove of it as
a matter of principle."* 65.56%.67.770083.2211.8039.21.9071$.8756543
4.t22.132.576.889775.643.4£32.544.456.746.584.3586.657.48.3975.
8432.65073 *"The tree of modern life doesn't necessarily produce edible
fruits, Bobbie, as you well know."* 653.7.7654.7643.8769.76543$.6532.
579.547964.76436.87%.78.90$.98 6.875.90.45%.T34.SH78.lk2t.
r47q3s2q96t5.y7fm8.3s4b.65$8.3720.9564.375.709.iy43.6583.280
.9567. *"I have always held banking practice in high esteem, not like
what you are showing me here."* 483.658.9.789.SH5$.7£.32.78956.43
.5.8712358.6$1.3892.5734.5684.73.658.3258.63.8.9563489.56894
.3658.43656.43956.895.6y8.34.6$58.93426.5.535235.45.39.35.5.
*"Can you explain the ultimate reason for this delirium, Bobbie, or do I
have to work it out for myself?"* 543.2434.876.895.835355.3.7872r.42.%7
783.3.765.9870 87g3502.175.9032.75986.328.57032.9900.65.45%.75
09 *"Your father, Philip, agreed with me about certain basic values."* 832.
65089386.3$29856.2308.95602.8635.08923.%596.98.764.66542.31.
0.8965.86598$.425.7 9650s.d236r.26590.4657.23547.65634.97290.5
7956.2395.70936.589.37209.563295.703Q286.59.82315.3096.57.90.
347908%6.7340.9.8756.7865.93 *"Lehman Brothers moreover has a
history and a name to defend."* 46 5372.6578.44.9$040.675.4%38.248
9053.2876.4783.254$3.543245.5687.98.654.21.32235.465£6y.89.895.
46.5.42. 55897.98.8753.%899.Sh%.76 *"I recall how I once read a most
enlightening letter from your grandfather in this respect."* 34.55.87."69.8.
69.89.8.4$3.5.43.1.2.544786.98'.03.7.49.82.3.£70.4.83.20957.906.
N34.57.09.3.457093.476.jo 93.47.60.93475.73.4.9.05.634 *"Bobbie, are
you listening to me?"* 8654.89.35.67.8.43.5.78.3.24532458.73.2.$69.587
.054684.59658.73.24.3651.23.562.4763.4.56.4355.76f85.49.657.32.6.
45.6.3.72153.1247.65 *"Who is running all this? Because I hope it isn't the*

mayhem it appears to be." 7845.67.8.9874.32.6.7.875.G53.&5%56
48.56.78.47.6.95.88.8.00.5.43648.32.658.30.53.8.085690328493265
46276fg.435621987490213647823 123.5987.43096.843568.6437.76%
.876$s315 *"I believe that, as a senior partner, I'm entitled to a proper
explanation."* 64832175863.4832.7095.76.19.83265.9832.418.95643
"Without taking into account: how much is this madness costing us?" 86
8834411.1753.331.1.122.68.94478.377.'3.146.8905.48.7'.06.87.'.08.540
.976.549.764.36.58.94362.5743.856.328.75.64783653465986164385
689455678 *"I want to know how all this is in keeping with some minimal
degree of public order."* 756&.54335$.45.76$.%6.76%.76$.77.34.653.5425.
890587.5678.9054.76 5.873.572.35.78.32.65.98126.3.58.94.36.8.43.
6578.32.5.14.62.56.3.45.21.4.76231587436987540976498687I346
1235987430968435686437426535218734632496809423756 87432
54351256342ks31585690328493265 46276fgmf *"If this is how you see
things, I just cannot agree, Bobbie!"* 78.23.1,8643,65329.76556.483
2175.8634.832.7095.7619.8325.64.83.21.7.58634.832.70.9576.198.
32.659.83241.895.64389hwv658943.6.5.84.65486.8753.75.7753.8765
3I77642.6530.97.849 *"I notice a feverish telephone activity, but I fear it
is entirely empty."* 50.76.9824.3657.3254.725.984632.05704.3967.09.5
.48.79065.87.o'8.6549.67348.975.46214.35623483. 658.9.789.SH5$.
7£.32.78956.43.5.8712358.6$1.3892.5734.5684.73.658.3258.63.8.9563
489.56894.3658.43656.43 956.895.6y8.34.6$58.93426.5.535235.45.39
.35.5. *"This is the first time in many years that I find myself in complete
disagreement with your view of the facts."* 543.2434.876.895.835355.3.78
72I.42.%7783.3.765.9870 87g3502.175.9032.75986.328.57032.9900.
65.45%.7509 *"We're getting old, Bobbie, and old age sometimes gives
people an exaggerated belief in the new, if you know what I mean."* 832.65
.8764,089386.3$29856.230.875.64$.8.8.95602.8635. 08923.%596.9
8.764.66542.31.0.8965.86598$.425.79650s.d236r.26590.4657.
23547.65634.97290.57956.2395.70 936.589.37209.563295.703Q286.5
9.82315.3096.57.90.347908%6.7340.9.8756687.£.56.856.845%.3757
3%4975. 9348.6974.58G.658326.475326745.37568$97.6905.4895%7
647.58637.463276%765.8766590599.75i7.587.465 345.4 *"Moreover, as
old men, we cannot place our trust in models that send future generations
astray, I'm sure you understand."* 65.56%.67.770083.22112.1432.221.80
39.21.9071$.87565434.t22.132 576.889775.643.4£32.544.6568.7483.
456.746.584.3586.657.48.3975.8432.65073 *"The world is too diverse to
have a single global market: it runs the risk of being the apotheosis of
inequality."* 65,6654.7689$.3.764.76436.87%.78.90$.98.635846385.
738657384.478365738.78346576328.95 987549.46725466.875.
90.45%.T34.SH78.lk2t.r47q3s2q96t5.y7fm8.3s4b.65$8.3720.9564.
375.709.iy43.6583.280.9567. *"It's just possible the stock market might go*

adrift, and politics too, and we cannot and must not go along with it."
483.658. 9.789.SH5$.7£.32.78956.43.5.8712358.6$1.3892.5734.5684.
73.658.3258.63.8.9563 489.56894.36.87454.487445.58. *"What
difference is there between what I see here and a lunatic asylum?"* 46
5372.6578.44.9$040.675.4%38.2489053.2876.4783.254$3.543245.
5687.98.654.21.32235.465£6y.89.895.46.5.42.55897.98.8753.%899.
Sh%.76 *"Even supposing there's money in it, I don't know whether
everything that makes money is to be automatically approved of, Bobbie."*
34.5.76580.5.87.6998'.03.7.49.82.3.£.8.69.89.8.4$3.5.43.1.2.544786.
70.4.83.20957.906.N34.57.09.3.457093.476.j093.47.60.93475.73.
4.9.05.634 *"There's an aggressive element in finance today, and I have
no intention of sinking to that level."* 8654.89.35.67.8.43.5.78.3.24532
458.73.2.$69. 587.054684.59658.73.24.3651.23.562.4763.4.56.4355.
76f85.49.657.32.6.45.6.3.72153.1247.65 *"Are the people I see graduates
or have they been picked up from the street?"* 7845.67.8.9874.3.7654.
8643.3245.76490.$6.8642.6.7.875.G53.&5%5648.56.78.47.6.95.88.
8.00.5.43648.32.658.30.53.8.08569032849326546276fg.435621987
490213647823123.5987.43096.843568.6437.76%.876$s315 *"And to
think that Wall Street has also been the glory of our country's history."*
64832175863.4832.7095.76.19.83265.9832.418.95643 *"You appear
surprisingly calm."* 868834411.1753.331.1.122.68.94478.377.'3.146.
8905.48.7'.06.87.'.08.540.976.549.764.36.58.94362.5 743.856.328.
75.647836534659865164385689455678 *"It was you yourself who taught
me that not all contemporary art is to be regarded as enlightened."* 756&.
54335$763.790.64.45.76$.%6.76%.76$.77.34.653.5425.89058 7.5678.
9054.76.3.58.94.36.8.43.6.578.32.5.14.62.56.3.45.21.4.762315874.36
987540.976498.687134.612355.873.572.35.78.32.65.981269.874309
684356864374.2653521873463.249680.942375.687432.543.512.563
42ks3158 569032849326546276f *"Squeezing the juice from a lemon,
dear Bobbie, cannot provide a job forever: the lemon finishes, and you
squeeze the rind rather than the pulp."* 78.23.15.6524.8764.6543l.4247.
42218.6532-6.483.2175.8634.832.7095.7619.8325.64.83.21.7.58634.
832.70.9576.198.32.659.83241.895.64389hwv658943.6.5.84.65486.
8753.750.97.849 *"No doubt the enthusiasm that I see is a reflection of
the world in which we live."* 50.76.9824.3657.3254.725.984632.05704.
3967.09.5.48.79065.87.0'8.6549.67348.975.46214.35623483.658.9.
789.SH5$.7£.32.78956.43.5.8712358.6$1.3892.5734.5684.7687.£.56.
856.845%.37573%4975.9348.6974.58G.658326.475326745.37568$97.
6905.4895%7647.58637.463276%765.8766590599.75i7.587.465345.
4,76 *"Have you brought me here to excite me or to shock me? I don't
understand, honestly."* 764.654 2.65.56%.67.770083.22112.1432.221.
8039.21.9071$.87565434.t22.132.576.889775.643.4£32.544.6568.

7483.456.746.584.3586.657.48.3975.8432.65073 *"I remember how I chose the job of financier because I loved the silence."* 653.7.765432.579. 547964.7.547393.75437474545.4743585.466484064-4636436.87%.78. 90$.98 6.875.90.45%.T34.SH78.lk2t.r47q3s2q96t5.y7fm8.3s4b.65 $8.3720.9564.375.709.iy43.6583.280.9567. *"This is a point of no return."* 483.658.9.789.SH5$.7£.32.78956.43.5.8712358.6$1.3892.5734 .5684.73.658.3258.63.8.9563489.56894.3658.43656.43956.895.6y8. 34.6$58.93426.5.535235.45.39.35.5.*"There is much to explain about the pleasure of an economy that remains obscure, as though it were a secret, Bobbie."* 543.2434.876.895.835355.3.78721.42.%7783.3.765.9870.7543. 98687g3502.175.9032.75986.328.57 032.9900.65.45%.7509 *"These individuals have as much to do with the nobility of the bank as I have with a rock star."* 832.65089386.3$29856.2308.95602.8635.08923.% 596.98.764.66542.31.0.8965.86598.764.76$.425.7 9650s.d236r. 26590.4657.23547.65634.97290.57956.2395.70936.589.37209.563 295.703Q286.59.82315.3096.57 .90.347908%6.7340.9.8756.7865.93 *"Have you at least asked whether a rodeo like this is entirely legal?"* 6 53 72.6578.44.9$040.675.4%38.2489053.2876.4783.254$3.543245. 5687.98.654.21.32235.465£6y.89.895.46.5.42.55897.98.8753.%899. Sh%.76 *"I won't move one step away from the fact that even today a minimal sense of moderation is required."* 34.55.87.69.8.69.89.8.4$3.5. 43.1.2.544786.98'.03.7.49.82.3.£70.4.83.20957.906.N

But all of a sudden
Paul Mazur
grips Bobbie's arm
and with a trembling voice:
"I need to know: who is that man?"

For
in fact
there's a man
standing up there
on a platform
a lumberjack with cheeks like two melons
who conducts the orchestra of the whole inferno
not with a baton
but with an ax.
Behind him
on the wall
the immense photo
of a naked negress

smeared with oil
and the words
GODDESS OF THE STOCK MARKET.

Paul Mazur
senior partner
has sworn
he will never again set foot
in Water Street
Hungarian domain
and over Monday luncheon
will express his full scorn
to his colleagues.

But after a month
the trading division
has already tripled profits.
This at least
is what Bobbie has reported,
diagrams to hand,
since the lumberjack
in fact
had no time.

The Lehman partners
like tripling profits.
Even if there
in Hungary
another goddess is worshipped.

Paul Mazur
who is getting on for 80
dies soon after.

Bobbie smiles:
it's not his problem.

> *And Aaron made an idol for the people, a golden calf.*
> Exodus 32:4

26
Twist

Bobbie Lehman is 78.
And he's dancing the twist.

He is not the only one.
The whole world is dancing the twist.
Brezhnev's Russians are dancing
and the Chinese are dancing while they play ping-pong,
the Arabs who sell us oil are dancing
and in Europe they are dancing hand in hand.
They are dancing in Japan, nonstop, on and on
they're dancing in America
where
if you're not dancing
you're out of the game.

Automobiles
trucks
motorcycles are dancing
—for if you don't have wheels on your feet how can you dance?—
houses
cottages
mansions
villas are dancing
—for everyone has to have a roof to dance!—
refrigerators
food mixers
washing machines are dancing
—for electricity provides the power to dance!—
movie theaters
televisions
aerials are dancing
—for no one dances without being seen!—
telephones
handsets are dancing
—for ringtones too can dance!—
And stocks
shares
bonds

are dancing
for the stock market—yes—the stock market is made for dancing!

Lew Glucksman is dancing
is dancing ax in hand
and it has to be said: he knows how to dance!
He's dancing with the whole trading division
set up there
in Water Street
Hungarian dominion
where those at One William Street
never set foot
indeed, if they get the chance
they'll take another street
since that stuff
no sir
that hellhole
isn't Lehman Brothers.
But what a shame that their bank
is dancing the twist
leaping on the zeros
that the Hungarian is multiplying in torrents.
So Lew Glucksman is dancing
dancing the twist and the csárdas
with red cheeks like two melons
is dancing with his computers
switched on each morning to evening
calculating
throwing out zeros zeros zeros
zeros that we
then
get to dance.

Bobbie Lehman is 80.
And he's dancing the twist.

He has spent his life shaking:
what's wrong if
the patriarch
now
has a sacred urge to dance?

After all, he's in good company
since the numbers are dancing with him
numbers from 0 to 9
combined
all together
sorted
like pictures in art shows
numbers
those numbers
which in Water Street they are handling like lunatics:
the computer keyboards are dancing
the computers are dancing
the printers are dancing
those new recruits are dancing
amazing kids
who don't dance with men or with women
but do mazurkas and polkas with numbers.

Dick Fuld is dancing
the last entry in the race
Dick Fuld is dancing
not yet 30
Dick Fuld is dancing
a skillful dancer
Dick Fuld is dancing
an expert dancer with numbers
Dick Fuld is dancing
stuck to his computer
Dick Fuld is dancing
dancing with millions
Dick Fuld is dancing
does stock market pirouettes
Dick Fuld is dancing
but only in Water Street
Dick Fuld is dancing
and dancing with Lew Glucksman
only with him
for Dick hates banks
and anyone to do with them.

Bobbie Lehman is 85.
And he's dancing the twist.

He's able to get even those
who won't dance
to dance
like the old partners
of One William Street
those who have chosen
to dance a few steps of the sirtaki
on the glass table
and in order to teach them
they've called in
Pete Peterson:
Greek
sorry
Swedish.

Pete Peterson is dancing
a banker through and through
he dances with his wife, Sally
dances with a salary of $300,000
dances with Lehman Brothers Bank
which for him is One William Street
and that alone:
he doesn't dance with Hungarians
nor with lunatics
he doesn't dance with Lew Glucksman
since he's frightened of his ax
he doesn't dance with Dick Fuld
who would look like a bear if he danced the sirtaki.
Peterson hates Glucksman
Glucksman hates Peterson
the bank hates the stock market
the stock market hates the bank
but they dance just the same
even if they hate each other
for the important thing is not to stop.

Bobbie Lehman is 90.
And he's dancing the twist.

He knows now
it's forbidden to stop
and when you dance
you have to dance

as long as your breath holds out
nonstop
without a break
ever faster
and maybe this is why
—to dance better—
Glucksman
has given his guys
baseball balls
and there between the computers
they swap
white powder
which for dancing makes sense.

Bobbie Lehman is 93
and he's dancing the twist,
in fact, he's now 100
maybe 140.
He's dancing the twist, Bobbie,
he's dancing like mad
and maybe not even he
has realized
that
while dancing the twist
the last of the Lehmans
has died.

Never since has there arisen in Israel a prophet like Moshe.
Deuteronomy 34:10

27
Squash

The sign on the office door
says: PRESIDENT.

It was once
on Bobbie Lehman's door.

Now
for at least ten years
it indicates another.

The dark office chair
never replaced
is that of Emanuel Lehman.
The mahogany desk
the bookshelf with prizes
the pictures on the walls
by a painter worth many zeros.
On the table a paperweight in the form of a globe
said to have belonged to Henry Lehman, in Alabama.
A tray with carafe
polished glasses
beside the telephone
two fountain pens.
Bunches of fresh flowers.
Air-conditioning set low.

The sofa is the same one
that Philip had.
Now it all belongs
to him
to the new head of Lehman Brothers.

And yet, in the air
there is nothing Greek or Swedish.

President Pete Peterson
is sitting at his desk.
Morning papers.
The list of meetings
arranged for the day.
The most important
however
is the first.

When they knock on the door
Peterson stands up
straightens his tie:
"Come in!"

Lew Glucksman
is never in a good mood first thing in the morning.

Today he is less than ever
for he has never liked
the offices on the upper floors
and as his pupil
Dick Fuld says:
"the higher they are, the lower I put them."

Glucksman crosses the room.
He doesn't straighten his tie
simply because he doesn't have one.
And sits down.

The Greek and the Hungarian:
face-to-face.
One from a background of olives and capers
the other from table lamps.
One is a perfect banker.
The other is a tough *trader*.
One is the president of Lehman Brothers.
The other runs the gold mine
which, as his pupil Dick Fuld
told the papers:
"Without us would be just smoke and no fire"
and Dick Fuld knows plenty about fire
when each morning
he sits down at his *computer*
with four packs
of burgers.

The Greek and the Hungarian:
face-to-face.
A silence that lasts a century.
Peterson smiles.
When he was in government with Richard Nixon
he learned to smile even at enemies
he has a perfect gift
to smile on command.

Glucksman no, not him.
He has no command over his smile

and in fact
he sits there
like a rhinoceros
that points its horn
and makes strange nasal sounds
for, as his pupil
Dick Fuld says:
"The economy is divided into suits and beasts
and since suits don't breathe
it's certainly better to be a beast."

Peterson well remembers
—he was in government with Nixon—
when the United States
opened the Chinese markets
sending a ping-pong team
to Peking.
Now he wants to do the same here.
Or isn't it a good idea?
Greek-Hungarian
ping-pong.
Ball in play.

"My dear Glucksman, what do you wish to talk about?"
"Me? Nothing."
"And yet you're here."
"You know why."
"I can guess."
"No hide-and-seek."
"As you wish."
"Talk straight."
"You talk."
"You're the president."
"I am."
"Exactly."
"Go ahead."
"Well you shouldn't be."

Ball over the line.
Hungary has responded too strongly.
Peterson smiles.
He does it brilliantly.

1-0 for Greece.
Ball back in play.

"My dear Glucksman
what do you mean?"
"Enough is enough!"
"Enough what?"
"Of playing the king."
"Me, a king?"
"You're president!"
"Perhaps you want . . ."
"I want the bank!"

Ball over the line.
Hungary is tense.
Peterson smiles.
He does it brilliantly.
2-0 for Greece.
Ball back in play.

"My dear Glucksman, aren't you going too far?"
"Not at all!"
"A bank is a bank."
"We are the ones who run it."
"You think so?"
"I have the figures."
"I would say . . ."
"Enough is enough!"

Hungary throws down the bat
takes the ball and flattens it under his heel.
End of game
for ping-pong's a dance
and
as young Dick Fuld would say:
"Squash, oh yes, that's a sport for men."

Perfect.
Glucksman now takes over the game.
And it will be squash, to the last shot
where whoever hits hardest wins.
Ball into play.

"So, Peterson, I deserve the bank."
"The whole bank in the hands of your group?"
"Always better than your dregs."
"Isn't it better to keep our roles separate?"
"Half the dish is not enough for me!"
"You want to scarf the entire bowl."
"Anything to get it away from the mice in the bank!"
"And if the bowl is not in agreement?"

Hungary loses the ball.
Advantage to Greece.
Peterson smiles.
He does it brilliantly.
The ball is back in play.

"I was saying, Glucksman, that you are not well liked."
"You mean, by the partners? I couldn't care less: they're too old."
"And if the old ones withdraw their share?"
"They won't: and if they do, I'll pay up."
"If they leave just ten of you, it will require a lot of money."
"The money's there, it won't do any harm."
"But in that case you'll find yourself down."
"I want the bank, I want your job!"
"To get rid of me will cost you millions."
"Tell me how many, you'll have the money tomorrow!"

Point in favor of Hungary.
But here
Greece interrupts the match:
takes the ball.

"I want a line of zeros and a percentage if you fail."
"Meaning? Come on, less talk."
"If you have to sell the Lehman Brothers shares
if you have to dispose of them to raise money
I will have a percentage on every sale."
"What a crazy deal!"
"Agreed?"
"Agreed!"
"Lewis Glucksman
you are the new president!"

Where ping-pong failed
squash won the day.

Where table lamps failed
olives and capers triumphed.

Because
less than a year
after that meeting
Lehman Brothers
—the immortal name—
was on offer
to the best bidder.

It is bought
for a good price
by American Express.

Epilogue

Around the table
a glass table
glass the length of the whole room
in black chairs
it seems like Monday luncheon
even if it's night,
indeed
soon
it will be dawn.

In the room, silence reigns.

A group of old men
are waiting for news.

Henry Lehman, at the head of the table.
It has always been his place.

Mayer *Bulbe*
sits beside him.

Emanuel is an arm
he wants to act:
on days like this
there's no question of sitting about.

His son, Philip,
has a diary
in front of him;
pen in hand
writes phrases in block capitals.
The last of these
a moment ago says:
"I HAD NOT PREDICTED IT."

Bobbie Lehman
is sitting beside his father:
his hand is trembling once more,
he bites his lip.
On the lapel of his white jacket
is a pin the shape of a horse.

Herbert the senator
adjusts the time on the wall clock,
though
time here
is a strange concept.
He still hasn't understood it.

His son, Peter, in military uniform,
looks at him sadly and shakes his head.

On a sofa, under the window,
Sigmund sits in lightweight suit.
Round spectacles, dark lenses:
there was much sun on the decks of the boats.

His brother Arthur taps his fingers on the table:
*"Will they have worked out
that a way out can always be found?
The situation is not desperate
according to my formulas."*

"The verdict has already been given" Irving replies,
readjusting the knot of his tie.

In the room, silence reigns.

A group of old men
are waiting for news.

Dreidel lights a cigar:
it's the fifth,
for no one has had a wink of sleep since yesterday.

Harold stares at his brother:
"Don't they say that every death is a birth?"

But Allan shakes his head:
"Ha! Babies bring a smile, but not death."

David blows his nose violently,
almost blasting it off his face:
he has never learned to control his energy.
Then he folds the cotton handkerchief back in his pocket
takes a deep breath
looks at his father, Henry:
"And what's his name?
I can never remember it."

No one answers.

"I said: who in the end
was the last one, the last president?"

Philip leafs through his diary:
"Dick Fuld."

Mayer *Bulbe* pulls a face
shrugs his shoulders:
he's a boiled potato.

Emanuel
who was and still is an arm
kicks a chair
sending it into the middle.

Bobbie sighs.

Herbert Lehman
scratches his head:
"Maybe there's still hope."

"The verdict has already been given" Irving replies.

"Maybe another bank will help us out."
Sigmund smiles, for he has completely forgotten
all of his 120 *mitzvot.*

Bobbie sighs:
"In 1929 we didn't save any bank.

Out of choice."

And silence reigns, once again, in the room.
A group of old men
waits for news.

The telephone rings.

All fourteen look at each other.

Henry moves.
Lifts the receiver.
Answers: *"Hello."*

Then listens.

Looks at the others.

Hangs up.

"It died a minute ago."

They stand up.
Around the table.
All of them.

They will grow their beards
in the coming days
as the ritual requires.
Shiva and *sheloshim*.
They will respect the Law
as it is prescribed
in every duty.

And morning and evening
they will recite the *Qaddish*.

As it used to be done over there in Germany
in Rimpar, Bavaria.

Glossary of Hebrew and Yiddish Words

ADAR—month of the Hebrew calendar, corresponding to February–March.

ASARAH BE TEVET—festivity in remembrance of the siege of Jerusalem in 588 BCE by Nebuchadnezzar II. Literally "the tenth of the month of *Tevet*," or the central day in the Hebrew month of *Tevet*.

AV—month of the Hebrew calendar, corresponding to July–August.

AVRAHAM—Abraham, prophet.

(DER) BANKIR BRUDER—(the) brother banker.

BAR MITZVAH—(literally "son of the commandment"). Expression formed by *bar* (son) and *mitzvah* (commandment). This expression refers to the coming-of-age ceremony when an adolescent reaches religious maturity. From that day, the young man is no longer dependent on his father but becomes responsible for his own actions, assuming the rights and duties of an adult and therefore, if he commits a sin, is liable to punishment. The ceremony is conducted on the first Sabbath after the boy's thirteenth birthday. His family meets at the synagogue, and during the ceremony he is invited for the first time to read the Torah.

BARUCH HASHEM—(literally "blessed the Name"). Thanks to God. HaShem ("the name") is the reverential substitution for the divine name Jhwh, which cannot be pronounced.

BAT MITZVAH—(literally "daughter of the commandment"). Ceremony in which a young Jewish girl who has reached twelve acquires the status of "woman" and assumes the obligations of religious character.

BEIN HA-METZARIM—festivity to remember the destruction of the First and Second Temple of Jerusalem (586/7 BCE and 70 CE). Literally "three weeks between days of fasting" (of the Seventeenth of Tamuz and the Ninth of Av).

(DER) BOYKHREDER—Yiddish, (the) ventriloquist.

BULBE—Yiddish, potato.

CHAMETZ—Hebrew, leaven.

CHESHVAN—month of the Hebrew calendar, corresponding with October–November.

CHUPPAH—nuptial canopy under which the wedding ceremony takes place. It is a cloth supported on four poles held by four men. Once the couple leave the canopy they are united in matrimony.

DANIYEL—Daniel, the prophet.

DREIDEL—Yiddish, spinning top. A game traditionally played during the festival of *Hanukkah*. It is a four-sided spinning top on which each side bears a letter of the Hebrew alphabet, which together represent the words "Nes Gadol Hayah Sham" ("A great miracle happened there"). These letters also form part of a mnemonic phrase that recalls the rules of the games in which the *dreidel* is used: *Nun* stands for the Yiddish word *nisht* ("nothing"), *Hei* stands for *halb* ("half"), *Gimel* for *gants* ("all"), and *Shin* for *shtel ayn* ("put in").

DUKHAN—podium of the officiant in the synagogue, placed in front of the Ark/Aron.

EGEL HAZAHAV—the Golden Calf, symbol of idolatry, made by Aaron while Moses was on Mount Sinai.

ELUL—month of the Hebrew calendar, corresponding to August–September.

GEFILTE FISH—Yiddish, fish balls.

GEMARA—(in Aramaic literally "conclusion," "fulfillment"). Part of the Talmud that collects comments and discussions on the *Mishnah* developed during the fourth to sixth centuries CE. It is also used as a synonym for the Talmud as a whole. These teachings are written in the Eastern Aramaic language, so-called Talmudic Aramaic.

GHEVER—Hebrew, man.

(A) GLAZ BIKER—(a) glass of water.

GOLEM—formless material or mass. In the later tradition it indicates a clay being animated by the name of God and created to defend and serve the Jews of the ghetto.

GOLYAT—Goliath.

HAFTARAH—(literally "separation," "parting," "taking leave"). Probably derives from the root *patar*, which means "to conclude," "to terminate." Indicates a selection from the books of the prophets or the hagiographies that follow the reading of the passage of the Torah (*parashah*) in the synagogue ritual of the Sabbath and festival days.

HALAKHA—(literally "path to follow") conduct, behavior. The written and oral prescriptive part of the Torah containing legal material that regulates conduct and daily life. The *halakha* is regarded as the revelation received by Moses on Mount Sinai and is contained in the Torah, both in writing (Pentateuch) and above all orally, later codified in the Mishnah, in the Talmud and in the *midrashim*, known as the *halakhic midrashim*.

HANUKKAH—(literally "dedication"), the Festival of Lights, commemorating the reconsecration (Dedication) of the Temple of Jerusalem in 164 CE by Judas Maccabeus. The festival begins at sunset on the twenty-fourth of the month of *Kislev* (usually in December) and lasts eight days, during which the candles of the eight-branch candelabrum are lit one by one.

HASELE—Yiddish, rabbit.

HASHEM—(literally, "the name"). Expression of reverence in substitution for the divine name Jhwh, used in the Bible and in the Hebrew tradition.

IYAR—month of the Hebrew calendar, corresponding to April–May.

(DER) KARTYOZHNIK—Yiddish, (the) card player.

KATAN—Hebrew, child.

KETUBAH—the marriage contract. The parchment containing the wording of the contract is often richly decorated with designs and symbols. It sets out the husband's financial obligations toward his wife, seeking to protect her in the event of divorce. According to Jewish custom, the husband alone can request a divorce and has to pay a large sum of money to his wife. The *ketubah* is signed by the husband and handed to the wife; the wedding blessings are then recited.

KIDDUSHIN—the rituals of the wedding ceremony.

KISLEV—month of the Hebrew calendar, corresponding to November–December.

KOSHER—complying with Jewish dietary laws.

LAG BA OMER—religious festival celebrated on the thirty-third day of Omer, the day that marked the end of the plague that killed disciples of Rabbi Akiva. The mourning and restrictions observed during the period of Omer are suspended, and the day is celebrated with outings, music, and various kinds of entertainment for children.

LIBE—Yiddish, love.

LUFTMENSCH—Yiddish, dream man, dreamer.

MAMELE/MAME—Yiddish, Mamma, mom, dear mom.

MAZEL TOV—(literally, "good star"), "good luck, congratulations." Expression used to convey congratulations and best wishes during celebrations such as *Bar Mitzvahs*.

MEZUZAH—(literally "doorpost"). The word refers to a ritual object, a parchment on which are written the passages of the Torah corresponding to the first two parts of the *Shema*, a prayer of central importance to the Jewish religion. The *mezuzah* is placed on the doorpost, to the right as one enters, at a height of about two-thirds of the door, and in any event at hand height.

MIGDOL BAVEL—Hebrew, the Tower of Babel.

MILAH—circumcision. It represents the consecration of the pact established between the people of Israel and God since the time of Abraham. It is *mitzvah* to subject the Jewish baby to *milah* on the eighth day after birth, even if that day coincides with the *Shabbat*, with holy days, and with *Yom Kippur*.

MISHNAH—from the Hebrew word that means "recite the lessons," "study and review." The *Mishnah*, which is the code of oral tradition, the body of teaching passed down by Moses, has become one of the two parts of the Talmud (the second is the *Gemara*). The final version of the *Mishnah* dates from the end of the second century CE and includes sixty-three tractates divided into six orders regarding religious regulations, social relations, civil and criminal law, marriage, etc.

MITZVOT—the commandments that God gives to every Jew. They are contained in the Torah and have the purpose of teaching man to live according to the will of God. There are 613, of which 365 negative and 248 positive. There is another classification of the *mitzvot*. There are horizontal *mitzvot*, which deal with relations with other humans, and vertical *mitzvot*, which deal with relations between man and God.

MOSHE—Moses.

NER TAMID—(literally "eternal light"), oil lamp that hangs from the ceiling of the synagogue, in front of the Aron, and is permanently lit in remembrance of the seven-branch candelabrum at the Temple of Jerusalem.

NISAN—month of the Hebrew calendar, corresponding to March–April.

NOACH—Noah, patriarch.

PESACH—Passover (literally "passage"). Festival that commemorates the Flight of the Jews into Egypt. The main festival of the year.

PURIM—(literally "lots," "fates"), festival that commemorates the freeing of the Jews from massacre by Hamam, principal minister of King Ahasuerus of Persia in the fifth century BCE, as described in the Megillah of the Book of Esther. It is celebrated on the fourteenth of Adar and is the most joyous festival of the Jewish calendar, equivalent in spirit to the Christian carnival. It is customary to wear masks.

QADDISH—(literally "sanctification"), one of the oldest and most solemn Jewish prayers recited only in the presence of a *minyan* comprising at least ten Jewish males who have reached thirteen, the age of religious majority, from which every Jew is required to observe the precepts of the Torah. The central theme is the exaltation, magnification, and sanctification of the name of God.

RAB/RAV/REB—abbreviation of rabbi (literally "great," "distinguished"), indicating the master, or rabbi, the religious leader of the Jewish community.

REB LASHON—Rabbi Language, reference to a traditional Jewish legend.

RIBOYNE SHEL OYLEM—Yiddish, Master of the Universe.

ROSH HASHANAH—religious festivity that celebrates the start of the year, Jewish New Year, celebrated on the first day of the month of *Tishri* in Israel, the first two days in the Diaspora. Festival of a penitential nature, it is characterized by the sound of the *shofar*, a ritual horn.

SCHMALTZ—Yiddish, from the German *Schmalz*, "fat," "fatty material." In the homes of Eastern European Jews, *shmaltz*, made with goose fat, replaced butter on bread.

SCHMUCK—Yiddish, idiot, mad, stupid. Literally, dick.

SCHNORRER—Yiddish, beggar, sponger, freeloader.

SHABBAT—(literally "cessation"), Sabbath, weekly day of rest. Festival that celebrated God's rest on the seventh day of the creation. Characterized by rest from work activities and by the ritual of the synagogue.

SHAMMASH—attendant, servant, sacristan of the synagogue.

SHAMMES—Yiddish version of *shammash*, sacristan of the synagogue.

SHAVUOT—(literally "weeks"), festival that commemorates the gift of the Torah to the Jewish people on Mount Sinai. It takes place seven weeks after Pesach. Known also as Pentecost, since it occurs fifty days after Passover. In ancient times it celebrated the first fruits and the harvest. During the festival, it is said, the sky opens for a very brief instant, and those who make a wish at that moment will see it answered.

SHELOSHIM—indicates the period of thirty days that follow burial (including the *shiva*). During *sheloshim* those in mourning are not permitted to marry or attend a *seudat mitzvah* ("festive religious meal"). During this time men refrain from shaving or cutting their hair, from wearing new clothes, etc. Since Judaism teaches that the deceased can still benefit from the merit of *mitzvot* done in their memory, it is customary to offer merit to the deceased by assembling groups of people who study the Torah together in their name.

SHEMA—(literally, "listening"). Prayer of central importance in Jewish ritual, is recited twice a day, in morning and evening prayer.

SHEVAT—month of the Hebrew calendar, corresponding to January–February.

SHIVA—(literally "seven"). Indicates the traditional seven-day period of mourning on the death of close relatives. During this period mourners gather in the house of one of them and receive visitors.

Going to visit those in mourning is regarded as a great *mitzvah* (commandment) of courtesy and compassion. Traditionally there is no exchange of greetings or words, and visitors wait for those in mourning to begin the conversation. Those in mourning are not obliged to make conversation and, indeed, can ignore visitors completely. Visitors often bring food and serve it to those present so that those in mourning need not cook or carry out other activities.

SHOFAR—ram horn. The sound of the *shofar* recalls the sacrifice of Abraham (called by God to immolate his son Isaac, substituted at the last moment by a ram) and will announce the arrival of the Messiah. Used in certain religious festivities (*Rosh haShanah, Yom Kippur*), it is now also used in Israel for particularly solemn secular events.

SHPAN DEM LOSHEK!—Spur the horse! Reference to a song in Yiddish tradition.

SHVARTS ZUP—Yiddish, literally "black broth."

SIVAN—month of the Hebrew calendar, corresponding to May–June.

SUKKA—hut.

SUKKOT—Hebrew, huts, plural of *sukka*. A festivity that celebrates and recalls the exodus of the Jewish people into the Sinai desert to reach the promised land of Israel. It is celebrated on the fifth day after *Yom Kippur* during which a hut is built using branches where food is eaten and prayers are offered.

SÜSSER—in Yiddish and in German, means literally "sweetness."

TALMUD—(literally "teaching," "study," "discussion"). It is the sacred, normative, and explanatory text that forms the basis of Judaism, the so-called Oral Torah. It combines *Mishnah* and *Gemara* and brings together rabbinic discussions of the period between the fourth and sixth centuries CE.

TAMUZ—month of the Hebrew calendar, corresponding to June–July.

TEFILLIN—Phylacteries, two small leather boxes that orthodox Jews tie onto their left arm and their forehead. The two boxes contain two sheets of parchment with four passages from the Torah. The *Tefillin* are worn every day during morning prayer except for the Shabbat, festivals, and the ninth day of Av.

TERBYALANT—(literally "turbulent").

TEVET—month of the Hebrew calendar, corresponding to December–January.

TISHRI—month of the Hebrew calendar, corresponding to September–October.

TORAH—(literally "teaching," "law"). It is the law given by God to Moses on Mount Sinai. The Written Torah comprises the first five books of the Bible (Pentateuch): Bereshit (Genesis); Shemot (Exodus); Vayikra (Leviticus); Bemidbar (Numbers); Devarim (Deuteronomy). The Oral Torah is the tradition of the masters collected in the works of rabbinic literature and never completed.

TSU FIL RASH!—Yiddish, literally "too much noise!"

TSVANTSINGER—coins of twenty, or small change.

TU BISHVAT—Festival also called New Year of the Trees. Literally "fifteenth of the month of *Shevat*," or the central day of the Hebrew month of *Shevat*.

TZOM GEDALYA—(literally "fast of Gedalia"). Festival that commemorates the killing of the governor Gedalia.

V'HAYA—the second part of the *Shema*, a prayer of central importance in the Hebrew liturgy.

YELED—Hebrew, boy.

YITZCHAK—Isaac.

YOM KIPPUR—(literally "day of atonement"). Indicates the solemn day of fasting and prayer for atonement and repentance, celebrated on the tenth of the month of *Tishri* (between September and October). This is the only occasion on which the high priest of the Temple pronounces the name of God inside the Holy of Holies. Currently, in the synagogue, the celebration includes a solemn confession of sins and the sound of the *shofar*.

YONAH/IONAH—Jonah, the prophet.

ZEKHARYA—Zechariah, the prophet.

A NOTE FROM THE TRANSLATOR

An Italian translation generally opens a window on some Italian landscape. Not here. There are no Italian characters. Three Jewish brothers emigrate from Germany to America in the 1840s and establish one of the great banking dynasties. The story spans 150 years and begins among the plantations of Alabama before moving to the offices of a New York bank, the mansions of wealthy Jewish families, and the pews of their synagogue.

The voices change as the novel progresses. Small-time immigrant cotton traders of the 1840s had a voice quite different from that of their wealthy children who grew up in New York to witness the Wall Street crash and their sophisticated grandchildren who knew little about their German roots. The story ends in the 1960s when the last scion is dancing the twist and the bank has taken its first steps into the computer age. Massini captures all of this with mesmerizing clarity in Italian, and my task was to translate it convincingly, finding a language appropriate to each period and place.

The novel is written in blank verse, so I also had to follow its rhythm and cadences. I had to remain faithful to the original meaning, but of paramount importance was its sound. Each line had to sound *right*, as well as being as readable and compelling as the original.

Many chapters are built like well-constructed episodes in a drama, while others revolve around a wordplay that can only be read on the page: the constraints of Prohibition are told around the word "NOT"; two lovers woo each other with spoof quotes from Hollywood movies; and when we reach the McCarthy era, references to Communism are hidden inside the surreal though otherwise innocuous conversation of a bank secretary.

These are the sorts of challenges that translators relish.

Richard Dixon

Here ends Stefano Massini's
The Lehman Trilogy.

The first edition of this book was printed and
bound at LSC Communications in
Harrisonburg, Virginia, May 2020.

A NOTE ON THE TYPE

The text of this novel was set in FF Scala, a typeface
created by Dutch typeface designer Martin Majoor in
1990. Named after the famed theater in Milan, Majoor
originally designed this old-style serif typeface for
the Vredenburg Music Centre in Utrecht. In the years
since, FF Scala's popularity has grown substantially,
and today this typeface is widely used in fine printing
and book design, due to its clarity and elegance.

HarperVia

An imprint dedicated to publishing international voices,
offering readers a chance to encounter other lives and other
points of view via the language of the imagination.